FERAL OUTBREAK

FERAL OUTBREAK
by SEAN LISCOM
Published by Creative Texts Publishers
PO Box 50
Barto, PA 19504
www.creativetexts.com

ISBN: 978-1-64738-081-6

FERAL OUTBREAK

SEAN LISCOM

DEDICATION

Living where we live, you meet some pretty interesting people. Honestly, I can't help but add a little of their personalities into each book I write. They are just about as diverse of a group as you could ever meet, and they're all cool as all get out. We're always looking out for each other. We'll drop whatever it is we're doing and help one another out. It's just the sort of thing you do when civilization is so far away.

So, here's to Lanny & Peggy, John & Tammy, Manford & Tina, and last but not least, Chris. We're a small, spread-out community, but it's reassuring to know I have such good friends. My heartfelt thanks to each and every one of you!

TABLE OF CONTENTS

PROLOGUE

There was a world of controversy regarding the events of 2020. It was a year that none of us will ever forget, that much is sure. Was the virus man made and unleashed on an unsuspecting population by people with nefarious intentions? Was it nothing more than a freak of nature? Maybe it was mother nature flexing her muscles to show humans what she was capable of. Or worse, as terrible as things were, could it have only been a near miss? I'll come back to that last one in a minute.

The pundits taking to the airwaves and social media twenty-four hours a day weren't any help, to be honest. Wear your mask! Wash your hands! Stay home! That was just one side of the rhetoric. The other side was telling you to live your best life! Go to the party! Enjoy the concert! The virus was nothing worse than the common cold, or maybe the flu. What was certain was that nobody could agree on anything and by the end of the year, I don't think anyone was even listening anymore.

We allowed 2020 to slip quietly behind the veil, hoping that 2021 would be better. In some ways it was. In other ways, not so much. We did manage to skate through without the feared resurgence of the virus though. That had to count for something, right? As we closed out 2022 without any major incidents or breakouts, many of us thought the virus had been handled. We finally put it all behind us and '23 was looking pretty good. At least it was, until seemingly overnight, it wasn't.

Alarm bells started going off the first week of July. Unfortunately, nobody was listening. We'd been so over-saturated by the media, all of us figured it was a giant nothing burger. More fear-mongering. What was worse was that nobody wanted to be the first to say this might be something far worse than what we dealt with in 2020. By mid-2023, those that didn't know better were trying to quietly sweep everything under the rug. After all, who wanted to be responsible for destroying the world's economy for a second time?

Those that did know better, and weren't above putting their careers on the line, tried shouting from the rooftops. Still, nobody was listening to their wails. In the weeks that made up the month of July, there had been a massive surge in the reported flu cases, that much was true. It was also true to say that this flu variant had a much lower mortality rate than previous flu strains. What was seemingly lost on the average citizen of the world was that it wasn't flu season.

While no one was paying attention or showing any real concern, things took a drastic and deadly turn in early August. Ten days into the month and mankind was thrust into the middle of an existential crisis the likes of which had never been seen before. There was no turning back, and there was no avoiding it....

I

CHAPTER 1

August 4ᵗʰ, 2023.

"No! I said no when you asked me an hour ago and I'm telling you no again," I continued to protest when I pushed my chair away from my desk. I glanced up at the wall clock. "It's 4 O'clock, on a Friday, and you want me to fix a problem YOU created. No!"

"Please, I'm begging you, Shane! C'mon man, you know half the shop has called out in the last few days!" my boss, Chad Walters was resorting to his weak voice and helpless hand gestures.

"Chad, I've had this vacation on the books for a year and you know that! I'm not missing out on this trip or putting it off for you or anyone else. It's not happening," I pulled my dark blue sports jacket off of the chair back when I stood.

"You're the only person here that knows the ins and outs of the shipping schedule! You're the only one who can fix this."

"I said no! I didn't screw this up and I'm not taking the heat over it! You knew that truck was supposed to leave here yesterday morning and it was you who decided it could wait 'til today. I told you that the driver would leave, and he did. It was you who decided the assembly guys could take a half-day off on Wednesday. It's your fault the load wasn't ready and it's your fault that you gotta wait 'til Monday to get another rig in here. So, I'll say it again in case you didn't understand me the first half dozen times. NO!" I slipped my arms into the jacket.

"I could fire you," Chad tried a power play.

"You could, and it still wouldn't fix your problem. Besides, I'd like to see you explain to your father how you lost the contract for the federal servers AND you fired the most senior man here all in one day," I smirked and picked up my briefcase.

"You might be the senior man, but I'm your boss! I demand….." I cut him off with a finger pointed right at his face.

"Chad, before you finish that sentence, you need to understand something. Yes, technically speaking, you are my boss. You also know the only reason for that is because I turned down the job. Your father, the founder of this company, and I negotiated my contract. The only, and I mean the ONLY, person that gets to demand anything from me is him. Now, if you'd like, I can pick up that phone and call him. I'm sure that once he has been brought up to speed, you might be the one looking for a new job," I shifted hands holding my briefcase and reached for the receiver.

1

"You wouldn't!", instead of bothering with an answer, I picked up the receiver and punched the first memory button, and switched it to the speaker. After the second ring, Chad punched the disconnect button. "Fine! You win!"

"I always do," I grinned and hung the receiver back up.

"What do I need to do? How can I fix this?" resignation heavy in his voice now. I reached over to my computer monitor and pulled a sticky note from its bottom corner. Reaching across the desk, I handed it to him.

"That's the phone number for a Hotshot driver based here in Las Vegas. I took the liberty of alerting him several hours ago that he would be getting a call from you," I smiled again and picked up the keys to my truck.

"You asshole!"

"All you had to do was ask nicely and take some responsibility for your screw-up. You should also know that his transport charges are pretty steep for last-minute things like this. Expediting the load so it gets to Texas on time is also going to be pricey. He's expecting your call. Might I suggest you call him right away if you plan on fixing this mess?" I didn't wait for him to come back with a retort. I just walked out of my office.

Chad wasn't a bad guy, I thought to myself as I strode through the double glass front doors of Walters Enterprises. He was ten years my junior and at 25, he still had a lot to learn about his leadership position within the company. He'd been thrust into the position a little over a year ago. He was fresh out of college and didn't possess any real-world management skills, or people skills for that matter. Truth was, he still didn't. His father, Richard Walters had begged me to take the job when he had retired. I wanted absolutely nothing to do with it.

I'd been the Global Logistics Manager for seven of my seventeen years with the company. I was at the point where I was writing my own ticket now. I got a new company truck every two years. I had a very good six-figure salary and a Cadillac insurance plan that was 100% paid for by the company. My 401k was on track to keep me in a six-figure income when I retired at 50. Why would I want the headaches of the position Richard offered me? I mean, that would be the only additional thing added to the list if I had taken the job.

As it was, I basically ran the company. Just because I didn't have that CEO tag on my office door didn't mean anything. Richard confided in me that his son, Chad, didn't have the stones or the wherewithal to be the big kahuna. Richard also knew that his son was nothing more than a figurehead with a fancy title. Of all 170 employees at Walters Enterprises, I was the only one on contract. Chad didn't even have one and he should have been smart enough to ask for one before he came on board.

I opened the back door of my new 2023 Dodge one-ton 4x4 and tossed my briefcase on top of the backpack containing my clothes. I closed it and stepped back to look at the rig. I'd only had it a week now and totally loved it! It was solid black except for all the chrome up front and the rear bumper. The windows had a super dark factory tint. The 6.7-liter diesel had more power than I could ever imagine using. The only drawback to it was the large white oval sticker on the front doors with the company logo. There again, I'd thought ahead and had magnetic signs made up for this rig. I pulled both of them off and tossed them in the back seat when I climbed in.

I started the truck and kicked the air conditioning over to high. When my phone connected to Bluetooth, I figured I should probably call Richard and let him know what was going on. I backed out of my parking spot and then headed out of the parking lot before I made that call.

"Hey, Shane!" Richard answered the phone on the third ring.

"Hey, boss!"

"Uh oh. If you're callin me, boss, this can't be good!"

"It's all sorted out now, but I thought you'd want to know, Chad and I butted heads before I left the office."

"Oh? Aren't you supposed to be leaving for vacation today?"

"Yeah, just pulled outta the parking lot. Anyway, I sent you an email about the shipping debacle regarding the servers for the federal offices in Texas. I took care of it and hired a Hotshot driver to pick them up at five this afternoon. I know the guy and he'll have them there by the deadline. I didn't tell Chad that. I kinda wanted him to sweat a little. I did give him the number so he could call the driver and fix his own mess though."

"If you already took care of it, why are you calling me?"

"Richard, you know how well I do with demands, right?"

"Oh, yeah. All too well," he chuckled.

"Let me just say he pissed me off. I'm over it, and I didn't bite his head off. The thing is, you might want to warn him about taking that tone with the other managers and supervisors. Lord knows you don't want me to get after him."

"Okay. He's supposed to come to the house this weekend for dinner with me and his mom. I'll talk to him about it then."

"Thanks. I know I've told ya this before, but I feel like I'm tattling every time I have to give you a call. I hate that."

"I know you do, bud. I hate that I have to have you babysit him. I've been thinking about our arrangement though."

"Gonna hire a nanny?" I joked. Richard gave me a hearty laugh.

"Maybe. I was just thinkin that when you get back next month, the three of us need to sit down and have a long discussion. Over lunch and a couple of drinks. What do you think?"

"We can do that."

"Good. You still headed up to your grandfather's place by the Oregon border?" he changed the subject.

3

"Yep. Hitting the freeway in about 30 minutes and then it's northbound for me."

"I'm on to you, Shane. I know you only go there because there isn't any cell service," he laughed again.

"You know it!" I grinned to myself. There was some spotty cell service up there. I just kept my phone off unless I needed it. Work phone calls were definitely something I didn't need.

"Next year I'm gonna send you with a satellite phone!"

"Like hell!" both of us laughed at the exchange. The laughing was interrupted when Richard went into a coughing and hacking spell.

"Damn summer colds!" he cursed when he caught his breath.

"Yeah, I heard it's goin around. Listen, I'm just about to my place so I'm gonna let you go."

"Sounds good, my friend. Have a great vacation and I'll talk to you in a month!"

"Will do, boss. Say hi to Sharon for me. Get well and I'll talk to you later," I hit the disconnect button on the screen.

My house was at the end of a cul-de-sac, so I made the turn wide and backed the big truck up to the garage door. When I put it in park and shut it off, I hit the remote for the garage door and could see it begin to lift in the rearview mirror. I retrieved my briefcase from the back seat and headed into the house. The first stop was to turn off the alarm.

I'd already loaded the packs containing all my personal stuff in the truck. I did that last night. The only thing I had left to pick up was the giant coolers full of meat, beer, water, and all the other goods I'd need to go off the grid for thirty days. They were already packed with ice, and I didn't want to keep them under the tonneau cover in the late summer heat because it would prematurely begin the ice melting. After changing out of my work clothes and into something more suited for the wilds of northwest Nevada, I set about loading everything.

Everything had its place in the bed, including the four full five-gallon cans of diesel and four more filled with gasoline. Where I was going, it was a good plan to have extra fuel. The gasoline was for the side-by-side waiting for me in the barn, and the diesel was for the backhoe parked next to the barn. With all of the gear stowed snugly like giant puzzle pieces, I pulled the tonneau cover closed. One last trip through the house to make sure I wasn't forgetting anything, and I set the alarm. Walking quickly out through the garage, I closed it behind me.

Normally I would have just cut up through central Nevada. I'm not sure if it really was faster or just more mind-numbing. Both were probably true. This time I had a slightly different agenda though. An agenda that would take me through Carson City before I cut back to the east. For the first time in the 12 years I'd

4

been going to the cabin, I was going to take a friend with me. A friend of the female persuasion.

Rayne Andersen was so far out of the normal spectrum for me. Generally, I chased after the stereotypical blond hair, blue eyes, and petite build. Rayne was none of that! She had long dark chestnut hair, and honey-colored eyes, and she stood as tall as I did at five foot eleven. She had the build of a professional volleyball player. She was also out of my spectrum because, while I found her very attractive, I found myself thinking about her as a good friend. It was weird.

We met back in January at a supply chain seminar in Reno. After mispronouncing her name, she curtly informed me that it was pronounced just like rain, as in rain showers. Properly admonished, I didn't make that mistake again. Honestly, after that first run-in, I thought she was kind of a bitch. She proved me wrong when several of us got together after the seminar for drinks and dinner.

Turned out that we weren't all that different. She was the supply chain manager for a company that built liquid oxygen pumps down in Carson City. Like me, she felt the whole seminar was nothing more than a waste of time. As the drinks began to flow freely, she became a lot nicer, and she apologized for jumping in my shit over her name. We exchanged phone numbers and kept in touch after that. I was able to hook her up with some of my shipping contacts, and she shared a few of her own.

Back in July, the subject of my upcoming vacation came up and she wistfully said something about wishing she could do something like that. Before I could think about it, my mouth jerked into gear and asked if she wanted to join me. With the long silence that followed, I was sure she probably thought I was some sort of creeper. To my surprise and her credit, she said she'd think about it. Twenty-four hours later, she called to tell me that she would join me so long as she had her own room. I told her that could absolutely be arranged.

CHAPTER 2

I didn't need it, but I stopped in Indian Springs to top off the fuel tank and grab some snacks and drinks for the road. After fueling the truck, I pulled into a parking spot right in front of the convenience store and went inside. I'd been in here more times than I could count and was always impressed with how clean and well-lit it was. They were always well stocked and even carried the iced coffee I liked. So many of the places on this route could be dark and gloomy. I grabbed an assortment of iced coffee drinks, a bag of sunflower seeds, and some gum, and stopped by the heated display of hotdogs.

"Those are kinda old," the lady behind the counter said.

"Eh, it's fine," I replied. I set my haul on the counter and picked up the tongs to retrieve a pair of dark and shriveled hot dogs. I dropped both of them in one of the to-go paper containers, grabbed two buns, then took everything to the front counter.

"Find everything you needed?" she started ringing up my items.

"Yep," I pulled my wallet from my back pocket and patiently waited.

"I'm throwing in the hotdogs for free. I was gonna throw 'em out any....." her voice seemed to catch in her throat. She put her hand over her mouth, backed away from the register, and commenced coughing. Before the fit was over, she buried her face in the crook of her arm. Finally catching her breath, she cleared her throat. "Sorry," she apologized, coming back to the register. She wasn't touching any of my stuff and there was still a plexiglass shield over the top of the counter.

I had one of those immune systems that seemingly stopped everything. I couldn't remember the last time I'd gotten a cold or anything else. During the whole Covid thing, I only wore a mask when the establishment I was visiting required it. I'm pretty sure I used the same blue paper mask throughout the entire pandemic. I wasn't concerned in the slightest now either.

She finished scanning everything and I swiped my card. She asked me if I wanted a bag, but I politely declined the offer. With everything in my arms, I pushed my way through the doors and headed back to my truck. Before the door closed, I heard her go into another coughing fit.

When I was done arranging everything on the front seat and center console, I looked back into the store just in time to see two other patrons, a man, and a woman, rushing around the counter. The woman was on her cell phone and judging by the frantic waving of her free hand, something had gone really wrong. The man that was with her stood from behind the counter shaking his head.

6

"What the hell?" I asked myself aloud. Yet again, my brain was slow to react as I threw the door open and started back into the store. That's when I saw the fine mist of blood on the plexiglass separating the customer from the cashier. Both patrons looked at me when the doorbell chimed. All three of us looked at the security guard who came running in through the short hallway that separated the store from the attached casino. In one hand he had his radio, in the other was an AED. I think it was the same automatic external defibrillator we had at work. Not knowing what else to do, I followed him behind the counter.

We found the woman unconscious on the floor. Blood was smeared all over her face and it looked like it was leaking from her eyes too. The security guy was feeling her neck for a pulse. When he didn't find one, he sprang into action. His training with the AED was definitely showing itself. Rather than cut open her shirt, he just ripped it open. The plastic buttons flew in every direction. He was placing the pads when another security guard shoved his way to where we were. Before he took a knee, he asked me to move to the other side of the counter.

For ten full minutes, the small crowd that had gathered watched as they tried the AED with no success. A Nevada state trooper was the first on the scene quickly followed by the ambulance. The EMS crew didn't hang around. They loaded the cashier on the gurney, strapped her down, and hauled ass with one of the security guys doing CPR. The second security guard and the trooper commenced to getting everyone to fill out statements about what they saw. An hour after it all started, the ordeal was finally over, and I was back on the road. The clock on the truck's display told me it was almost 7 pm.

"Hey," I greeted Rayne when she answered her phone. "I got hung up and I'm running behind. It's going to be closer to 2 O'clock before I get to your place. Is that still going to be okay?"

"It's all good. Doesn't matter if it's 1 am or 2 am. You gonna be okay for the rest of the drive though?"

"I should be fine. I got all kinds of liquid energy here in the truck," I laughed.

"You sure? You can crash on my couch if you want."

"Yeah, I'm sure. If I get too tired, I can just plug in the truck's NAV system and let you drive for a while."

"Okay. Since I've got you on the phone, do I need to pack anything other than clothes and toiletries?"

"If you've got a good pair of boots, that might be a good idea. Otherwise, I've got everything else we'll need."

"Already got 'em packed. I gotta ask, full disclosure and everything, you sure you still want me along on this trip?" she asked.

"You sure you still want to hang out with an almost complete stranger in the middle of nowhere for a month?" I chuckled when I asked.

"I could ask you the same question, Shane."

"Fair enough, I guess you could. Well, I'm sure if you are."

"Good! See you around two."

"See ya," I hit the disconnect tab on the screen and settled in for the long drive.

The drive to my grandfather's property was a nine-hour drive from my home in Vegas. That's if I went straight up through the central part of the state. It was a trek I'd made at the end of every summer for the last 12 years. The first time, back in 2009, I dreaded it. That first trip up there was right after my grandpa passed away. He'd left the 120 acres to me, but the funny part was, nobody knew anything about it! Not my sister or my parents. I think the only two people that knew of its existence were my grandpa and his lawyer. This would be the first time I took somebody else with me. I was a little nervous about it.

I can still remember the lawyer urging me to go see the place after the reading of the will. I'd asked him about selling it, but he'd been very persistent. So, I went. I was skeptical, to say the least when he handed me the hand-drawn map of how to get to the place and the keys. It was so far removed from everything that he had warned me to take extra gas with me for my car. When I finally set my eyes on the place, the skepticism was replaced with intrigue.

According to the lawyer, the original home was built sometime in the late 1800s. Probably around 1898 or so. Back then it was nothing more than a stone-walled, single-room structure. My grandfather spent his later years making huge improvements. What started as a 20x20 building was now close to four times that size. He had replaced the original roof with modern steel trusses and steel sheeting. He also added four skylights to add natural lighting to the interior.

The new section he built had large bay windows that overlooked the green meadow and creek that were less than 100 feet from the front door. He kept the original woodstove, but it was more for the ambiance. To keep the whole place warm in the winter, he added a massive wood furnace. It served double duty to keep the water hot for the added indoor plumbing. Somewhere along the line, he had found an old cooking stove that also used wood instead of gas or electricity.

Along with adding all the plumbing, he also ran wiring for the lights and whatnot. Back then, all of it was powered by a diesel generator. The solar power and battery bank were something I added two years ago. It wasn't anything fancy, but it would power a full-size fridge, microwave, and small chest freezer whenever I would visit.

The other building out back of the house was an enclosed pole barn. That's where I found his old seventy-something F-250 and the flatbed trailer he'd hauled all of the building materials in on. Since there wasn't room for it in the barn, the ancient case backhoe was parked under an awning off to the side of the barn. Every year, without fail, I could put the batteries back in them, and with a little coaxing, they would light off. My only contribution to the vehicle selection was the four-seat side-by-side that I left parked on his trailer behind the Ford.

When I told Rayne she could have her own bedroom, I wasn't kidding. The roughly 1600 square foot home boasted two bedrooms and a full bathroom now. The kitchen was of ample size and furnished with modern appliances to accent the old stove. The living room also doubled as the dining room, but it too was furnished with a big couch and a pair of overstuffed recliners. All three pieces of furniture faced the old wood stove. It was a great place to catch a nap in the afternoon.

At first, I was worried about keeping Rayne entertained for a month. That quickly passed when I told her about the side-by-side and all the surrounding country to explore. When I told her about the decent-sized reservoir that was stocked with trout, she genuinely got excited. She loved fishing but hadn't been since her father passed in early 2020 from covid complications. I think the real selling point for this vacation was the natural hot springs not more than half a mile from the house though. I know it was one of my favorite attractions during my visits.

The rest of the drive to Carson City was uneventful as long as you didn't count the close encounter with a herd of deer just outside of Tonopah. That was enough to get the ole blood pumping for a bit. Rayne lived on the north side of the capital city, but I stopped on the south side of town to fuel up again. I ran into the store long enough to grab a hot cup of something akin to coffee. It had been sitting on the heating element for far too long.

The cashier here was also sick. His eyes were sunken in, and he had a cough too. I noticed it right after going into the store and almost did an about-face right back through the door. The only thing that kept propelling me forward was the need for coffee. After swiping my card again, before I pulled away from the pump, I called Rayne to let her know I was getting close. After hanging up with her, I plugged the address into the truck's navigation and took directions from the female computer voice.

I'd never been to her house. In fact, I thought she lived in Reno until we started putting this trip together. That's also when I learned that she got the house in her divorce three years ago. It was one of those ugly deals where her ex fought every detail during the proceedings. Fortunately for her, his lawyer was just as much of a narcissist as he was. She got the house in the end and that was the only thing she wanted. There was no alimony and they never had kids. She didn't even want either of his cars. Just the house and for him to never contact her again.

CHAPTER 3

When I backed the truck into Rayne's driveway, the garage door began to open. The light behind her silhouetted her shape. She had a backpack thrown over one shoulder and a duffle bag by her feet. After I shut the truck off, she picked up the duffle and started toward the passenger side. She opened the rear door and tossed the bags on the seat and floorboard.

"I take it you're ready to get going?" I asked with a grin. I could see her matching grin in the dome lights.

"I was ready the day we started talking about this! Hang on a second and let me lock up the house," she abruptly closed the door and jogged back into the garage. I stepped out so I could stretch my legs a little. From outside of the truck, I could see her car parked in the other bay of the two-car garage. I couldn't help it. I had to go see it for myself.

What I first thought to be a white Dodge Challenger turned out to be a whole other beast, or should I say Demon? The bright white paint was set off by all the black accessories. The black windows, bumpers, rims, and grill all made it scream for attention, but it was the Demon emblem between the door and front tires that my eyes were fixated on.

"No freakin way!" I said in a hushed voice.

"You like my little grocery-getter?" Rayne asked from behind me. I was so intent on the car; I never heard her come back into the garage. I could hear the smile in her voice.

"Is that your car?"

"Yep. It was my present to myself after the divorce. Rick never let me drive his Corvette. Guess he didn't think I could handle it."

"That's a hell of a present….. I gotta know….. Is it as fast as they say?"

"Faster," came her one-word answer. Again, I could hear the smile in her voice.

"Would it be too much to ask for a ride when I bring you home?" I tore my eyes from the sleek lines of the car and looked at Rayne.

"Well, I know a nice wide-open stretch of highway. I mean, it's really the only way to, ya know, let her breathe a little fire."

"Aren't you afraid of getting a ticket?" I took a step back.

"Wouldn't be the first one. What can I say, I like to go fast. Speaking of going fast, don't ya think we should get on the road?"

"Uh, yeah. If I stand here looking at this car any longer, I'm gonna have to wash all the drool off of it," I smiled and headed back out the garage door. Rayne was right behind me.

We left her place at 2:30 and the navigation display told me we'd arrive at our destination just after seven. With the full tank of fuel, we wouldn't have to stop until we reached Denio Junction. A quick fill-up with diesel, maybe grab a few snacks, and then we could be at the cabin at 8 am.

"So, I remember you telling me that you inherited the property, right?" Rayne asked from the passenger seat once we were on the freeway again.

"Yeah. That's right."

"And you've been coming up here every year since?"

"Yep."

"You spend a whole month out there, by yourself?"

"It wasn't always a full month. Right after I got the place, I only had five days of vacation. After that trip, I started saving my PTO just for the trip. Once I got promoted, part of my contract gave me 30 days a year plus my sick time. I could come up here for three months if I cashed that in too," I explained.

"By yourself though. Surely a guy like you has brought other girls up here, right?"

"Nope. I've always come by myself. This is the first time I've ever brought anyone with me."

"Should I be honored or scared," her smile in the dim light from the truck's dash display seemed mischievous.

"Well, ya got nothin' to be scared of. I gave you the coordinates to share with someone you trust. If you decide you're bored outta your mind, I can take you home whenever you want. I hope that doesn't happen, but the option to bail out is all yours."

"Then I guess I'll just be honored to be along with you. As long as the fishing is good, the side-by-side is fast, and the sunrises are everything you said they are, I can't see myself getting bored."

"The sunsets are pretty good too."

"Nice! I do have a serious question though."

"Okay?"

"I don't know much about your politics or which way you lean. It's also safe to say that we don't know a whole lot about each other. I mean, this is only the second time we've met face-to-face, right?"

"Um, yeah?"

"Okay, are you offended by guns?" she blurted out. That was not the question I was expecting.

"Open the center console," I instructed as I reached up and turned the dome light on. She did and grinned a toothy grin when she looked inside the console. That's where my Colt 1911 and three spare magazines lived. To keep it from rattling around, I had taken a piece of foam and made the cutouts to keep everything snug. She closed the console, still smiling. "Does that answer your question?" I asked.

"Yeah," she reclined the seat just a little, unhooked her seatbelt, and lifted the front of her T-shirt just enough to produce a Springfield XD from an appendix holster. "Probably not the show and tell you were hoping for, but I thought we should just get it out of the way. I didn't want to have any awkward conversations later. You know, is that a gun in your pocket, or are you just happy to see me?" the way she said it caused me to burst out laughing.

That little exchange set the tone for the rest of the drive. It was the little icebreaker both of us needed. From then on, we talked about just about everything. She asked more detailed questions about my work, and I asked about hers. I learned that she was an only child. She was less than a year younger than me. In fact, her 35th birthday was in two weeks. Her mother still lived in Phoenix, Arizona. When we got onto the subject of past relationships, she pretty much left no stone unturned when it came to her ex-husband.

She and Rick met in college and got married right after graduation. All of the red flags were camouflaged by the initial red-carpet treatment he gave her. It didn't take long for things to go downhill though. A year after they were married, he took a job in Reno without talking to her about it. He basically just told her that they were moving, and her fledgling career didn't matter. When she did find work after the move, he would find a reason to make her quit.

Basically, he never wanted her to leave their house unless he was with her. It was all about maintaining control and a lot of gaslighting. When that wasn't enough for him, it turned into outright physical abuse, violent physical abuse. If it weren't for her father finding out what was going on, she fully admitted she'd have never had the courage to leave Rick. Her father, AKA Master Chief Dan Andersen, Retired, made the drive from Phoenix to Reno, met Rick at work, and took him to lunch.

From what Rayne said, it was more akin to taking him out behind the woodshed. After that, Dad came to the house, loaded her and her belongings into the back of his truck, and took her to an apartment he'd rented on the other side of Carson City. Other than court, that was the last time she ever saw Rick. She never looked back either. Since the divorce, she'd landed a sweet job that paid great. She'd learned to do all the things she'd always wanted to do.

Her 2018 Demon was a regular participant at the drag strip. She had learned to ride dirt bikes, and horses, and how to shoot guns. She had a concealed weapons permit, and she was enrolled in jujitsu classes. She finally had the self-confidence to do everything she was never allowed to do when she was married, things she enjoyed before she went to college.

I'm not sure why she was so open with me. At one point, she was wiping tears from her face as she recalled one particular incident with Rick. Rather than try and say anything, I just let her talk while I listened. When she finally concluded her story, she looked expectantly at me. I obliged her with my own tales of growing up on the northern Maine coast. My parents and my sister all still lived there. Being more or less the black sheep of the family, I left home right after high school.

First I went to Kentucky to try my hand at coal mining. That didn't last more than six months. I quickly learned that those guys were next-level kinda guys. After that, I got a job on a drilling platform in the Gulf of Mexico. Yet again, it was way more work than a teenage me wanted. Three months later, I found myself at a warehouse in Vegas. At the time, I had no way of knowing that was the job I'd stick with.

About the time she was getting divorced, I went and got my concealed carry permit. It wasn't something I'd really given any thought about until I had some death threats from a guy I fired. His drug-addled brain focused on me as being the root of all his problems. Fortunately, the cops found him, and he ended up back in prison over parole violations. That was actually the scariest part of the whole thing. The cops picked him up two blocks from my house with a loaded and stolen gun.

With her life story out there for me to hear, I felt confident that she wanted to hear about some of my sordid stories too. Again I obliged and told her about my dating life. I even threw in the story about dating a stripper named Wanda. It wasn't a proud moment in my life, but she got a few laughs from it.

The four-and-a-half-hour drive to Denio Junction went by faster than I ever expected. Having someone to talk to and laugh with made it seem like a quick trip to the store. When I pulled up to the gas pumps in Denio Junction, the sun was fully in the sky and the temperature was already starting to climb.

Rayne went into the store to use the restroom while I filled the truck. When I was done, I pulled up and parked the truck in a parking spot. I gathered the trash and empty cans, locked it, then headed for the door. A quick stop at the trash can for a deposit, then I was inside. Rayne was just coming out of the bathroom, and I could see her eyeing the small restaurant at the far end of the store over the top of her sunglasses.

"You hungry?" she asked when we were together again.

"Yeah, the smell of bacon is making my mouth water!"

"C'mon, my treat," she headed for the counter and stools.

CHAPTER 4

August 5th, 2023.

With bellies full of bacon, eggs, hashbrowns, and toast, Rayne picked up the tab and we headed out to the truck. I held the door open for an old guy who was on his way into the store. As he passed by me, he started coughing and hacking. I started outside but paused for a moment and looked back at the old-timer. He was still coughing into the crook of his arm.

As I pulled the keys from the pocket of my jeans, I was thinking about all the sick people I'd encountered. Yesterday afternoon, Richard said he was sick. The cashiers at Indian Springs and Carson City. Now this guy. Yesterday morning, a full third of the warehouse crew at work had called out sick. So had several of the office people. I hit the unlock button and then hit the remote start as I followed Rayne across the parking lot.

"Have you noticed a lot of sick people in the last few days?" I asked once both of us were in the truck.

"Yeah. Half of my shipping and receiving people have been out over the last couple of days," she clicked her seatbelt and slid her sunglasses over her eyes.

"I had a bunch of people out too," I pulled out of the parking spot and then pointed us west on Highway 140.

"You know that there is a nasty summer cold going around, right?"

"Yeah, that's the same thing my boss, the owner of the company told me."

"It's been all over the news since about Tuesday."

"I don't watch the news. What have they had to say about it?" I asked.

"Just that hospitalizations are up and they're working to figure out if it's a new Covid strain or something else. You don't watch the news?"

"Just the weather channel. I figure they are probably the only ones that don't make shit up. They think it's Covid making a comeback?"

"No, they didn't say that. There is a theory going around about people having weakened immune systems being extremely susceptible to this year's flu strain. Why the weather channel?"

"It helps me predict possible delays for inbound and outbound freight. It's not flu season yet though."

"Yeah, I think that's what's got everyone scratching their heads. That's pretty smart. Would that be one of your pro tips? Why the sudden concern about the flu?"

"Pro tip?" I asked.

"Yeah. Like using the Hotshot drivers for expedited loads. That kind of pro tip."

"Oh, yeah. It's saved my behind more than once."

"So, the flu?" she questioned.

"I told you I got hung up yesterday on my way to your place. It was at a convenience store in Indian Springs. The cashier was hacking and coughing and then collapsed. They tried using an AED but couldn't get her back. Then the cashier in Carson City was sick. That old guy back there," I pointed over my shoulder with my thumb toward Denio Junction.

"She died?"

"They were still doing CPR when they loaded her in the ambulance. It didn't look good."

"Man. You saw all that?"

"Yeah. That's not what's bothering me though. It's all the sick people. It just kinda seems weird," she was about to say something when my phone started ringing. The caller ID showed it as NHP. Nevada Highway Patrol. I hit the answer button.

"Shane O'Neal," I answered.

"Mr. O'Neal, Trooper Barnes. I took a report from you yesterday at Indian Springs. Remember me?"

"Yes, I do. Is everything okay?"

"Yes, sir. I'm just following up with all the witnesses. Just calling to tell you that you weren't exposed to anything other than maybe the common cold. It appears that the victim suffered a cardiac event that was totally unrelated."

"That's good news. Is she, the cashier, doing okay?"

"Unfortunately, EMS wasn't able to revive her en route and they had no success once she reached the hospital. That's the sad part, but the good news is that everyone else should be just fine," Trooper Barnes reassured me.

"I really appreciate the call, Trooper. Thank you."

"You bet. Have a great day, Mr. O'Neal," then he hung up.

"Hmmm, cardiac event," I mused out loud.

"See? Nothing strange about that. Besides, even if it was Covid making a comeback, wouldn't you rather be quarantined out here?" she smiled.

"Yeah, I guess you're right," I conceded. We spent the next 15 minutes riding down the two-lane highway in silence. She was the one to break it.

"We getting close?"

"We got about another half hour on the pavement. Then it'll be almost an hour once we're on the dirt. Maybe a little longer," I answered.

"Well, I have something of a confession to make. I probably should have done it sooner but….."

"Having second thoughts?"

"No, it's not that," she drew in a deep breath, held it for a second, and then let it out. "When you asked if I'd like to tag along, I almost said no. The only

15

reason I agreed to this is that I need some new adventures in my life. I agreed because this is something I've never done before. Dreamed of it? Yes. Done it? No. I haven't taken a vacation since I got my job three years ago. I was somehow convinced it wouldn't be there when I got back."

"You talked about taking off on the side-by-side, fishing, hot springs, fresh air, and incredible stars in the sky at night. Those are all things I need more of in my life," she paused as if contemplating her next words carefully. "What I don't need is a man in my life. I'm finally living for myself, and I don't want that to change. I'd understand if you had second thoughts about this," she pushed her sunglasses up onto her forehead and looked at me. I took mine off and set them on the dash.

"Rayne, let's get something straight right here and now. I invited you because I wanted to share. I absolutely did NOT invite you along because I want to get in your pants. Truthfully, I'm a guy and of course, it crossed my mind. That said, it's not why you're here. I want to share this adventure with a friend. I wanted someone to fish with, ride around in the Razor all day and come blowing back in with nothing but fumes in the tank and dust billowing behind us. I wanted a friend along so that we could sit in the hot pond, staring at the stars and solving the problems of the world over a cold beer."

"You and I aren't that different. I have a lot of acquaintances, but my circle of friends can be counted on one hand, and it seems to be getting smaller every year. I really, really hope I can count you in that circle too. Now, if I've been anything other than a gentleman, please say so and I'll adjust accordingly. This trip is all about having fun, eating too much home cooking, and maybe drinking a little too much. It's about letting the regimen of our work and all the associated stress go for a while. That's it, that's all. No more, no less," I took my eyes from the road long enough to see the expression on her face.

She held my gaze for a moment before looking out the windshield again. Before she looked away, I caught a glimmer of understanding in her honey-brown eyes. After another minute, she picked up her cell phone and powered it off. She opened the glove box, dropped it in, and then closed it again. She slid her sunglasses off of her forehead and onto the bridge of her nose.

"You sure?" she finally asked.

"Positive," I replied.

"You gonna let me show you how to drive the Razor like it was meant to be driven?" a smile was playing at the corner of her mouth.

"Keys are in the safe and they're yours to use whenever you want," I picked up my cell and shut it off. I then dropped it in the center console.

"Cool," was her one-word reply. Her smile was still holding firm.

"As long as you let me teach you how to fish."

"Oh, hell no!" she started laughing. "I've been fishing since I was old enough to walk!"

"So? I grew up on the coast of Maine!" I retorted with a chuckle.

Once the light-hearted banter took over, the serious concerns that were on her mind seemed to vanish. The stories of her fishing with her dad seemed to bring out all the good memories. Some of them had me laughing so hard my side hurt. She got to laughing so hard, she snorted a couple of times. That only intensified the howling laughter from both of us.

As we talked, I couldn't help but think of why I asked her to come along. It was true to say that I wanted to share what I had. The solitude, the being alone was like an elixir. Nothing else in the world mattered. Except, well, it was lonely when you had no one to share the experience with.

Then there was the other thing. I was also very truthful when I told her I didn't bring her along because I was expecting something to happen between us. I was just looking for a friend and I thought she could fit the bill. Yes, she was very attractive, and yes, I'd wondered if there might be a spark there. That was just the guy part of my brain. I knew that there was no way anything long-term could work. She wouldn't leave her job and I wasn't about to leave mine. I was just happy to have someone to enjoy this adventure with.

I wasn't lying either when I told her my circle of friends was getting smaller. After T.J. was killed in a car accident last year, there was only one left. Ann and I had dated in high school and somehow managed to remain friends all these years. Good friends.

She still lived in Maine with her husband and their three kids, but we still talked once a month or so. I would even chat with her husband, Mark. She and her family would still go hunting and fishing with my family. As the saying went, she, and even Mark to some extent, was one of those friends who would help you hide a body. I needed more friends like that. Hell, I just needed friends. Period.

When we reached our turnoff, I had to stop the truck so I could unlock the gate that was across the road. When we got past it, she got out, closed it, and re-locked it, then climbed back in her seat. We were in the home stretch now with only 18 miles left, but these were the worst miles of the whole trip. The dirt road we were on had some deep ruts left over from the previous winter. It was rocky and rough. The suspension of my one-ton made it even worse. By the time we reached the BLM access road, I thought I might have knocked a couple of fillings loose.

The BLM Road wasn't too bad. It was just very washboard. Anything under 30 miles per hour and it was tough keeping it between the ditches. Anything over 40 and it was the same problem. The next turnoff brought us to the gate of my property. Rayne got out to repeat what we did at the first gate. As I was waiting for her to climb back in, I could see that the two-track road had undisturbed cheatgrass growing on it. That could only mean that nobody had been down the road.

At the halfway point, we had to cross through a dry wash. It had severely eroded since my last visit. This one required four-wheel drive and some serious navigation to keep from denting my new truck. After that, it was smooth sailing all the way to the house. When we pulled up alongside the front deck, Rayne just stared out the passenger window at the front of the house.

"Whatcha think?" I shut the truck down.

"It's beautiful!"

"Did you see the meadow?" she looked wide-eyed at me, and I pointed out my window at the small herd of antelope that was grazing there.

"Wow!"

CHAPTER 5

August 5th, 2023.

"Okay, just some ground rules and words of caution," I stopped her before she could get out of the truck. She looked back at me and placed her hands on her lap. "Ya gotta watch for snakes. I don't care about the bull snakes, but the rattlers don't get a free pass. If you come across one, let me know. There are also scorpions, bees, and wasps. They won't do much more than piss you off unless you're allergic. You're not allergic, are you?" she answered with a shake of her head.

"There are badgers, but I've only seen one in all the years I've been coming up here. They're fast and they are mean as hell. If one should come after you, shoot it. Then, shoot it again. That brings me to my second point. Stay armed whenever you are outside of the house. I don't care if you're sitting on the porch swing enjoying your coffee. Have a gun within reach. It's not people I worry about, but some of the wildlife out here will try and eat you. We should try and avoid that."

"There are some chores that have to be taken care of before we can relax. The well pump needs to be turned on and run for a half hour or so to clean out any sediment. The house breakers will need to be turned on so the fridge and freezer can cool down. All of the furniture is covered with drop cloths and those will need to be gathered up. As you can see, there are storm shutters on the windows, and they will have to be opened up. The wood furnace needs to be lit so we can have hot water. It's basically just housekeeping items that need to be taken care of to bring the place out of hibernation."

"That's just what has to be done today. Tomorrow, we can put the batteries back in the side-by-side, work truck, and backhoe. Then I'm gonna have to take the backhoe down to fix that nasty spot in the driveway. I'm gonna have to run the weed-whacker to clean up all the dried grass around the house and probably the chainsaw to take off some of the low branches on the trees. After all that is done, then we can relax," I finished. She looked at me thoughtfully for a moment.

"Then I guess we should probably get after it."

"Okay then," I pulled the keys from the ignition, found the front door key, and handed them to her.

While she went up to open the door, I opened the tonneau cover and dropped the tailgate. She came back to help me carry the coolers into the kitchen and then we hauled our bags inside. When she looked at me, obviously questioning which bedroom her stuff went in, I pointed her in the right direction.

19

With the truck unloaded, I got to the task of turning the water and power on. I was just gonna do it by myself, but she insisted on following along. I was surprised when she started asking questions about how everything worked. Not just that, but she wanted me to show her what switches to flip and valves to turn. She was absorbing it all like a sponge. At her insistence, I allowed her to fill and light the wood furnace. There again, I simply instructed while she did the actual work.

"How long does it take the fridge and freezer to cool down?" she asked.

"A couple of hours and they should be good."

"So, what do we do now?"

"We get to get out of the heat and go inside. We still need to gather all the dust covers."

"Gotcha, she answered as we climbed the steps to the porch.

By four that afternoon, all the chores were taken care of, and the BBQ on the back porch was just about ready for some steak to be tossed on it. Rayne had already emptied the coolers, keeping out a huge porterhouse for dinner tonight. She seemed tickled when she came across all the fixins for loaded baked potatoes and fresh bundles of asparagus. In no time, she took over the kitchen.

We sat in the recliners and cleaned our plates of the delicious meal she prepared and cooked. I had to hand it to her, the girl could cook! By 6 pm, all the dishes had been washed and both of us were ready to be done for the day. She took a shower, while I dozed in my recliner. When she was finished, I ran under the hot water. That was enough to do me in. Both of us were in bed by seven that night. It had been a very long day that had started at 5 am the previous day.

August 8th, 2023.

For the first time since I'd been coming to the cabin, I awoke to the fragrance of coffee wafting into my room. The sun wasn't quite up yet but the grey sky outside of my window told me it would be soon. I'd slept in an old pair of sweats and a baggy, threadbare t-shirt. It had stayed warm enough in the house overnight, that I never did slip under the blankets of my bed.

After a long stretch and a yawn that came from somewhere really deep within, I sat on the edge of the bed. I slid my bare feet into my slippers and wandered out of my room. A quick look toward Rayne's room and I saw her door standing open too. In the kitchen was a freshly brewed pot of coffee with about a cup missing from the decanter. When I pulled my cup from the cabinet, I saw her through the kitchen window. She was sitting on the porch swing. I filled my cup and then went out the open front door. The squeaking of the screen door seemed to startle her a little.

"Morning," I announced with a mock toast.

"I didn't wake you up, did I?"

"No, not a chance. What time is it? 5:30 or so?" I put my butt against the railing so I could face her.

"About that. I don't think my body has figured out it can sleep in for a few days," she smiled.

"It takes about a week. The hardest part is getting back into the swing of things when you have to go back to work," I returned the smile and sipped my coffee.

"Eh, I've always been an early bird. Anymore, it seems like I work best on four or five hours of sleep."

"You can only do that for so long," I cautioned. "It's not good for ya. Leads to some nasty health issues. Did you sleep okay last night?"

"Honestly? Not really."

"What happened? Too much on your mind or something?"

"No, nothing like that. This is going to sound strange, but it was too quiet!"

"That doesn't sound strange at all. We don't realize how noisy and loud our lives are. We're like the pot of water and the frog. All that sound just creeps up on us and it permeates everything. When it's suddenly gone, that's when we realize it."

"When I went to bed last night, I closed the blinds and drapes, I closed my door too. It was pitch black in there, and that's when I realized how quiet it was. It was like some sort of sensory deprivation thing going on."

"Try leaving the blinds and curtains open. It helps. You can also turn on the clock radio. Not gonna get any stations, but the static helps with the quiet."

"More pro tips?"

"Yeah," I laughed. "You gonna be good for helping me around here today? If you need more rest, we can make that happen."

"Nah, I'm good. Once I'm up, I'm up," she shotgunned the last swig of coffee. "You want some breakfast? I make a killer omelet!"

"All right, I think we need to get something else on the table," I looked at her seriously.

"What?" concern flashed across her soft features.

"I told you yesterday that I don't expect anything from you. That includes you doin all the cooking!"

"Oh," she chuckled.

Rayne did indeed make a killer omelet. I also found out that she was pretty good with a set of wrenches. Somehow, the carburetor on the old Ford had gotten gummed up over the last year. She had the carb off and on the workbench in the time it took me to get the backhoe fired up. She assured me that she would take care of it, and she urged me to leave it in her hands. I did and took the backhoe down to fix the driveway.

An hour later, she rolled up with that old truck purring like a happy kitten. Dare I say it, the thing sounded better than it had for the last couple of years. Since I was just finishing the dirt work, I took the offered bottle of water and we drove both vehicles back to the house. Not only had she fixed the truck, but she'd also gotten the Razor running and pulled off the trailer. Between her willingness to learn new things and her varied skillset, I knew it was the right thing to bring her along.

August 18th, 2023.

"You wanna run into Denio Junction with me? Maybe grab a burger and some fries?" I asked from my side of the porch swing. We were sipping on some iced tea after our trip to the fishing hole earlier that morning.

"Getting tired of my cooking already?" her half-grin told me she was just ribbing me.

"Nope! We just need to get some gas for the Razor. Usually, 20 gallons will last the whole trip, but we've been driving the hell out of it."

"Burgers and fries it is!" she jumped off the swing. "Let me get washed up and do something with this mop on my head," she strode into the house without waiting for an answer. I downed the last of my tea and went to the barn to grab the gas cans. Just as I closed the tailgate, she came out of the house. Her hair was freshly brushed, pulled back into a ponytail, and hanging out the back of her baseball cap. She pitched my truck keys to me and locked the house door before trotting down to the truck. Before I could even get to my door, she was already in and buckled.

"Getting tired of looking at my mug?" I joked as I got behind the wheel.

"Huh?"

"You seem awfully anxious to head into civilization."

"No!" she laughed. "You mentioned burgers and the thought of a bacon cheeseburger with all the fixins just sorta lit a fire under my ass!"

"Oh, ranch for the fries too!" I dropped the truck in gear and pulled away from the house.

An hour and a half later we pulled into the gas pumps at Denio Junction. Before I could shut the truck off, Rayne announced that she'd go order food while I got gas for the Razor and filled the truck. Since there was nobody else at the pumps, I started filling the truck with one pump, and the gas cans at another. Five minutes after she headed into the store, Rayne was walking back. The bottom of her shirt was tucked behind the grip of her Springfield, and she kept checking behind her.

"That was quick," I quipped. Judging by the unusual look on her face, something wasn't right. "Everything okay?" I asked.

"No. something's wrong," her voice was low.

"What?"

"Store's front doors are unlocked, but the sign in the window says closed. Some of the stuff by the register has been knocked on the floor. The lights are all on but there ain't nobody in there and Shane, there's a pool of blood on the floor!" I stared at her for a second but didn't answer. Instead, I threw open the passenger door and grabbed my Colt out of the center console. When I spotted my phone, I powered it up and handed it to Rayne.

"Call 911!" was all I said before heading for the front door.

CHAPTER 6

August 18th, 2023.

I stopped at the front door and looked cautiously through the glass. The rack of postcards that had been on the counter was now strewn across the floor along with the broken candy jar and all of its contents. I spotted the phone receiver dangling from its coiled cord. In the middle of the tile floor, I could see the pool of dark, dried blood Rayne had told me about.

I slowly, gently pushed the door open and stepped inside. I was hanging onto the grip of my Colt like it was a child's security blanket. It was still pointed at the ground, but the safety was off. Scanning the store, I saw no one. Stepping to the end of the counter where the register sat, I looked behind it. There were several packs of cigarettes scattered across the floor, but no people.

From there, I worked my way toward the restaurant and bar area. There was nothing of note to be found here either. No clues, nothing. Against my better judgment, I stepped into the kitchen area to find nothing amiss. It was like the staff had just left after cleaning up for the day. Backing out the same way I came in, I changed direction and headed to the storeroom at the back of the store. That door was locked. Wanting to leave nothing unchecked, I even stepped into the bathrooms. They were empty too.

"What the hell," I whispered to myself and made my way out the front entrance. Rayne was stomping her way toward me.

"I just got off the phone with the Humboldt County Sheriff's office! Do you know what they told me?" she didn't wait for me to answer. "They said they are aware of the situation and that we just needed to go home! I could hardly understand a word that good ole boy was trying to spit out! The dude must've been on his third pack of smokes cuz he was hacking so damn bad," she said as she animatedly waved her hands in the air.

"He was coughing?" a distant klaxon suddenly started going off in my head.

"It sounded like he was hacking up a damn lung! What did you find in there?" she pointed at the store.

"Where's my phone?"

"It's on the front seat. Passenger side," she turned and followed as I quickly walked to the truck. I set the Colt on the seat and picked up the phone. Looking at the screen, I could see that I had 62 new voicemails.

"What the....." I opened my voicemail and played the oldest message first. It was dated August 9th.

"Shane, Chad here. I need you back in the office as soon as you can get here. My dad passed away last night so yeah; this is an emergency. Call me back as soon as you get this," I could feel the blood draining from my face at the news of Richard's death. I started the next message which was also dated the same day.

"Shane, it's mom. I need you to call me back as soon as you get this," resisting the urge to call her immediately, I went to the next message which was dated August 10th.

"Mr. O'Neal? My name is Trish Walters. We've never met but you work for my husband, Chad. He's extremely ill and he asked me to call you to let you know he needs you here to take over while he's sick. Please call me back as soon as you can. Thank you," I pulled the phone from my ear and stared at the screen.

"What's wrong?" Rayne asked from behind me.

"Check your phone," I reached in and pulled it from the glove box. As soon as she had it powered up, I saw her expression change.

"Thirty-three voicemails? Over three hundred new text messages? What the fuck?" she blurted out. I realized I hadn't even looked to see how many text messages I had. The answer to that question was 432 unread messages.

All of that could wait for a few minutes. I dialed my mother's number, but it just rang. I couldn't leave a voicemail because the box was full. The next call I made was to my father's cell. Same thing. With shaking hands and a building sense of dread, I tried my sister. It was her husband who answered the phone.

"Hello?"

"Jesus, Scott! What the hell's going on? I can't get ahold of Mom or Dad. Is Lynn okay? The kids?"

"Shane?" Scott asked and then started coughing.

"Yeah, it's Shane! What's going on? Let me talk to Lynn!"

"They're….." more coughing. "They're dead."

"Who? WHO'S DEAD?" I shouted into the receiver.

"Everyone. Everyone's dead….." There was more coughing, a loud thud, and what sounded like the phone clattering across the hardwood floor of my sister's house. That was followed by a sudden silence.

"SCOTT!" I shouted. There was no reply, only deafening silence. I shouted for him three more times before I disconnected the call. I tried my parents again but got nothing. I tried my sister's number again but got no answer this time. I pulled up my old friend Ann and called her. I was about to give up when she finally answered.

"ANN!"

"Shane?"

"Yeah, Ann! It's me. What the hell is happening? Have you talked to my parents or Lynn?"

"Oh, Shane….. Did nobody tell you?" her voice was soft, apologetic.

"What? What did nobody tell me?" I could feel my knees getting weak and shaky. I grabbed onto the door with my free hand. Somehow I knew what she was going to tell me. She wouldn't lie to me.

"I'm so sorry, Shane. It's this new virus. It's killing everyone….. They're all….. They're gone….."

"No, no, no….." I felt myself slipping down the side of the truck until I landed on my butt. "No, this can't be right! This has to be some sort of mistake! Some sick, twisted fucking mistake!"

"I'm sorry, Shane. I'm so very sorry," my longtime friend tried to console me. "Are you still in Vegas? If you are, you need to get out of there."

"No, I'm up at the cabin," I wiped the tears from my face.

"Are you sick?"

"No. Neither of us is."

"You have someone with you?" Ann questioned over the miles.

"Yeah. A friend of mine came with me," I looked around for Rayne but didn't see her.

"Have either of you been exposed to someone with flu-like symptoms?"

"Uh, yeah. I think I was," I pushed myself off the ground, trying to find my resolve.

"How long ago?"

"I don't know. Ten days ago I guess," I walked to the front of the truck and found Rayne sitting on the ground, her face in her hands.

"Okay. If you haven't gotten it by now, you're probably immune like me and Lilly. Has your friend been exposed?"

"She's been with me the whole time, but she said a bunch of people at her work were sick," I knelt in front of Rayne causing her to look up at me. Her eyes were red and swollen. Tears had obviously been streaming down the sides of her face. I put the phone on speaker so I could set it down. Not knowing what else to do, I gently put my hand on Rayne's shoulder.

"She's probably fine too. Listen to me though. You two just need to stay where you are. It's not safe to go anywhere."

"What do you mean?"

"Shane, this virus has about a 90% mortality rate. For some of those that get infected, some of the ones who survive, something happens to them. It's like they go insane. They are extremely violent."

"What?"

"It's like they become rabid. It has something to do with swelling around their brains. It happened to Mark, and I had to….. Well, it happened to Mark."

"What did you have to do, Ann?"

"I shot him," her voice sounded hollow.

"Jesus….."

"Me and Lilly are safe now. That's all that matters. We're up at your parent's hunting camp. We brought plenty of food for the two of us. We're going to be okay."

"What about Jayden and Summer?"

"They're buried in the backyard of our house alongside their father."

"Oh my God, Ann!"

"All of us are dealing with loss right now. Me, you, and probably your friend. All we can do is try to survive this. Promise me that you will stay put and stay safe. Please promise me that."

"Yeah, you do the same. Give little Lilly my love."

"I will," she said and disconnected the call.

"Your family?" Rayne asked quietly. I couldn't force the words past my lips, so I just shook my head. She started crying again. "Mine too," she took my hand from her shoulder and held it between hers.

We sat in that empty parking lot for well over an hour. Sometimes we talked, sometimes we sat in hopeless silence. Sometimes we just took turns crying on each other's shoulders. When both of us finally exhausted our tears, I walked her to the truck and helped her in. After I finished filling the gas cans and the truck, I slouched into the driver's seat. We sat there for another hour going through voicemails and messages.

The majority of mine were work-related save for one from my dad, three from my mother, and three from my sister. Everything else was people calling in sick to work. Chad begging for me to come back, two from his wife letting me know he was dead, and she was sick. From the look on Rayne's face, her messages played out about the same. She finally tossed her phone up on the dash.

"What are we going to do?" her voice was just above a whisper.

"I don't know. I don't even know where to start. I think I'm still in denial about all of it."

"I can't believe….." her soft voice trailed off.

"I know," I put the keys in the ignition and started the truck. I pulled away from the pump but jammed on the brakes after 30 feet or so. Rayne's eyes instantly looked around to see why I'd stopped. I reached over and turned on the stereo. I had the full satellite package. A male voice immediately emanated from the speakers.

"….. CDC is requesting all citizens remain indoors under self-quarantine. Every state is deploying its National Guard to maintain order in the streets and to prevent any further instances of violence. If you or a loved one need medical attention, you can reach the national hotline at *75 from any landline telephone or cellphone. Local medical personnel will be directed to your location as quickly as possible. Please be patient and remain where you are. Be advised, response times may vary due to the high volume of calls. Together we can get through this new pandemic. With your continued cooperation, we can shorten the timespan required for isolation protocols. Thank you," there was a short pause and the message started again.

"Hello. This is Director Lionel Simmons of the Centers for Disease Control. During this unprecedented resurgence of the virus known as Covid, we must take drastic measures. With the full backing of the President, the entire country will be locked down today, August 14th, 2023, at 5 pm. Air travel, rail lines, and all forms of sea travel will be halted. All interstate travel will be suspended. All businesses will be closed, and the CDC is requesting all citizens remain….." with the message now repeating itself, I shuffled through all my preset stations. Every single one had the message playing.

"Oh my God," Rayne locked eyes with me and whispered.

"Yeah, that message was from four days ago," I muttered under my breath. I turned the stereo off again. I picked my phone up and handed it to her. "Go through and call every person in my contacts. See if there's anybody left out there," I instructed. Then I pulled out of the parking lot and headed back to the cabin.

CHAPTER 7

Less than a minute after I gave her my phone, she returned it to the top of the center console and grabbed hers off the dash. As her thumbs tapped rapidly on the screen, she explained that instead of calling, she was sending out a single text to all of the people on our contact lists. It was far more efficient than trying each and every number. Smart, I thought. She had just climbed back in the truck after securing the first gate when her phone chimed. Instead of driving down the road, I put it in park and waited for her to check the text message. This was the last really good spot for cell service.

"It's my boss," she typed furiously on the tiny keyboard. "He's alive. He said he got sick but recovered. Says everyone else he knows is sick or has died already."

"Where's he at?" I asked.

"That's what I just asked," her phone chimed again. "He's at his vacation home up on the south shore of Tahoe. He wants me to come up there….." She was tapping buttons again.

"You wanna go?"

"Hell no! I'm fine right here and that's what I told him!"

"It's your call," I reminded her. She checked the new message.

"Hang on….." more rapid typing as she scowled at the screen. "What the hell?"

"Everything okay?"

"No. Something's way wrong here. Somebody else must have his phone….."

"What makes you say that?"

"He said I'd be fired if I didn't come up there. Lots of typos too. That's not like him at all….." another chime from the phone and she looked at the screen again. "I don't think so, asshole!" her voice was suddenly filled with venom.

"What's the matter?"

"He just went off on a tirade about all the things he wants to do to me!"

"Ann said some people became violent after getting whatever this is," I told her.

"It's that or it's not him!" I watched her block the number. "I ain't puttin up with that!"

"Yeah. Don't blame you!" I shook my head and put the truck back in gear.

"Ann, do you trust her on this? Rayne asked as we bounced down the road.

"I trust her. Especially on things like this. She's an epidemiologist for the state of Maine. That and I've known her for a lot of years."

29

"That's good enough for me," she reached into the back seat and found her bottle of water. After taking a sip, she began again. "What are we going to do, Shane? I don't know about you, but there is no way we can go back with all this happening. We're safer out here, right?'

"Yeah, we're safe out here. I'm not worried about people just showing up. We've got enough food to eat for a couple more weeks. I'm inclined to just do what Ann said and stay put," she seemed to accept that answer.

"I guess the bigger question is what do we do in a couple of weeks when the food starts to run low?"

"I don't have an answer for that, Rayne. All I know is that right now, my mind is just running on instinct. I'm distracted thinking about my family. I can't help but wonder if someone took care of them when they passed. Honestly, I still can't believe they're gone….." The ringing of my cell phone through the truck's sound system jolted me out of my thoughts. Looking at the display, it was one of my co-workers, Lucas Williams. I tapped the answer tab.

"Lucas?" I answered.

"Man, am I glad to hear a friendly voice! This is some crazy shit, right?"

"I've only got bits and pieces. What's going on around there?" I asked.

"Me and the new kid you hired, Kevin, we're layin' low right now. This whole city has come off the hook, dude! We need a safe place to go cuz this place is a friggin dumpster fire!"

"Listen to me, Lucas. I have it on good authority, you need to get out of the city. Get some supplies and get the hell out of there!"

"No shit, man! I figured you were already dead, but since you ain't, how about me and Kevin head up your way? We got wheels, we just need to know where you are."

"That's no good, Lucas. We're too far away. Find somewhere outside of the city and just keep your head down. I talked to a friend of mine who works for the CDC. That was her advice, and that's exactly what we're plannin on doing."

"Who's we? You already got someone with you at that little hideout of yours?" his voice seemed accusatory.

"Yeah, I've got a friend here. We came up together and I'll tell you what, we don't need anyone else here. We've only got enough food for two, no more."

"Who is it? Is it that little blonde from accounting?" the more he talked, the more he sounded like he'd been drinking. "I bet it is! You fuckin dog!"

"Shut up Lucas! It's none of your business who's here with me!"

"Easy bro! No need to get all hostile! Can't say as I'd blame you one bit! In fact, I'm kind of envious! I'm stuck here with Kevin and you're bangin' the bitch from accounting! Maybe me and Kevin could come up and….."

"Hey, Lucas?" I cut him off.

"Yeah, bro?"

"I ain't your bro, and you can go fuck yourself!" I reached over and disconnected the call. "Any chance you could block that number?" I asked Rayne.

"Sure thing, bro," smiling, she picked up my phone and blocked the number.

"Was it me or did he sound drunk?"

"It sure sounded like it. Is he normally an asshole?"

"No, he's not. The guy goes to church with his family every Sunday and he's probably the most strait-laced person I know. I've never even heard him cuss or tell a dirty joke."

"Think he was infected?"

"That, or out of his mind drunk. Find Ann's number and call it for me, please," I requested, and she did it. Ann picked up after the first ring.

"Shane?"

"Yeah, Ann, it's me. I have a question for you," I slowed the truck to a stop right in the middle of the BLM road. I didn't want to lose the connection.

"Okay?"

"Earlier, you said some of those who survive get violent, right?"

"Yes."

"I just got off the phone with a coworker and he sounded like he'd been drinking. He was making, well, lewd comments. This was coming from a guy who never cusses. Before that, Rayne was getting lewd comments from her boss via text message. Is that part of their behavior or were they just being shitheads?"

"That's part of the behavior, Shane. It's the beginning stages. It starts with inappropriate comments and escalates from there. With all of the swelling going on in their brains, they lose all inhibitions and fear. They can't feel pain, at least not like we do. As it progresses, their adrenal gland goes into overdrive. They don't sleep or eat but they gain almost superhuman strength. They can actually break their own bones and not feel it. In time, their body just burns itself up."

"Jesus....."

"That's not the worst of it though. One of the last reports I saw claimed that a few can maintain enough control to keep from burning up. They maintain control over eating and sleeping. Even though they can't feel pain, they are more reserved than others. They are better at blending in. Make no mistake though, they only have one mission and that is to rip you to pieces."

"That's why you said it wasn't safe to be anywhere other than the cabin, right?"

"Yes. From what you've told me, it's in the middle of nowhere and that's the perfect place to be right now. That's why me and Lilly escaped to the hunting camp."

"Ann, I'm Rayne. Do you know how long this is going to last?" she asked from the passenger seat.

31

"I don't have an answer for that, Rayne. Sorry. It's one of those deals where if you're immune, you're good. If you're not, then it's only a matter of time before you contract it. I've urged anyone and everyone to find a hole and pull the dirt in behind them."

"What are the odds of this thing mutating? Will that affect our immunity?" Rayne followed up.

"Great question. I haven't seen any documentation since the 14th, so this is strictly an educated guess. This strain is extremely virulent and extremely deadly. I hypothesize that those that survive it are already working off of a mutated version. Possibly two different versions. One causes total madness with eventual self-destruction. The other causes madness, but it's less pronounced. That's why they can maintain control over their basic functions. Does that make any sense? As for our immunity, I don't know," Ann said.

"Yes, it does. Another question if I may."

"Sure."

"When someone first starts to show signs, how long before they, you know."

"Let me back you up a few steps. Everyone starts with flu-like symptoms. The average time from onset of symptoms to death is in the neighborhood of 72 hours. If it hasn't killed them by the fourth day, it's probably not going to. Out of ten survivors, seven will more than likely go on to recover. That recovery is likely long and painful."

"Of the remaining three, it will look like they are recovering. That is until they aren't. At this point, they are about five days post-onset of initial symptoms. Those that go into self-destruct mode last about a week before they burn in. As far as the other type, I have zero data to work with. They could last until they are found out and put down."

"Is there any hope of recovery for them?" Rayne asked.

"No, and my advice is going to sound harsh. Put them down. Don't try to reason with them and DO NOT turn your back."

"At the risk of sounding stupid, are they like zombies?" I could see Rayne flinch a little when she used the word.

"Yes and no. Once they've got a mind to, they will stop at nothing to rip you to shreds. If you shoot them, they will go down and die. Word of warning though. If you're faced with one, just empty the damn magazine into 'em. You should also know that they tend to band together."

"What?" Rayne and I said in unison.

"Yeah. I've seen evidence pointing to the fact that they tend to run in packs. I saw a lot of anecdotal evidence of this behavior when I was still in Augusta. At first, I thought it was 15 or 20 people trying to start a riot. That's not what it was at all."

"They don't try to eat you, do they?" I asked.

"Oh, they'll bite, scratch, kick, punch, and generally try everything to do bodily harm. You can't get infected that way, but it won't matter. If a pack catches you, you're as good as dead. They'll just rip you limb from limb."

"Great," I muttered.

"Shane, Rayne, just stay away from any place with a population of more than you two."

"That's our plan, Ann. We're almost back there now. Do you know, was anybody able to take care of my family when they died?" I felt a lump in my throat when I asked.

"I took care of your mom and dad. I had to go there to get the keys to the cabin and the gate. I buried them out by your mom's rose garden. I hope that was okay."

"What about Lynn and her family?"

"I never made it over there, sorry."

"Okay. Thank you, Ann."

"Of course. I need to let you guys go now. I've got a lot of stuff to do before full dark sets in. I'm keeping my phone charged, but I have to leave it in the car to do that. If you call back and don't reach me, that's probably why."

"Okay, thanks again, I said.

"Yes, thank you, Ann," Rayne added before I disconnected the call.

CHAPTER 8

August 18th, 2023.

"I need a drink," Rayne said flatly as she opened the door to get out of the truck. "Scratch that, I need to go get fucked up. You in?"

"Lead the way," I replied as I slid out of the truck too. I followed her up the steps and into the house. She went straight for the pantry, and I pulled two shot glasses from the cabinet. When she returned, she cracked the seal on a brand-new bottle of 100-proof Jack Daniels triple mash whiskey. She then poured about two fingers worth into each glass. With the bottle still in her left hand, she slammed back the shot with the other.

That's how the rest of the day went. We'd gotten home just after 5 pm and didn't stop drinking until sometime around midnight. Of course, we'd slowed down after the first couple of shots, but we still managed to wipe out 2/3rds of the bottle. There wasn't a lot of conversation mixed with our drinking. Both of us were still too shell-shocked and raw from the news we'd received about our families. I can't remember who drug out the blankets but both of us covered up and passed out in the recliners.

August 19th, 2023.

As soon as I opened my eyes, I knew it was going to be a rough morning. My eyelids felt like they had been filled with sand. My mouth felt like I'd been chewing on cotton balls and toilet paper. The pounding between my ears started the second I turned my head to look for Rayne. I had to ask myself if I'd gotten in a fight last night and lost. Every inch of my body was rejecting the notion that I needed to get up and go to the bathroom.

While I was in the bathroom, I took some ibuprofen for the worsening headache and body aches. It had been a decade and a half since I'd been this hungover and I'd forgotten that it could actually hurt to brush your teeth. The sound of the bristles grinding over my teeth sounded like a busted chainsaw in the cavern my brain used to inhabit. I'm pretty sure it was shriveled up and convulsing from the loss of brain cells last night. After a splash of cold water on my face, I made my way to the kitchen.

I filled my mug from the half-full coffee pot and then went out to the porch. Rayne was sitting cross-legged on the swing. She must have been feeling it too. Her sunglasses were shading her eyes along with her baseball cap pulled down low. She sipped her coffee with both hands wrapped around the mug. Without a word, I sat next to her. She set her mug down and reached over to take mine from me. I didn't have the pain tolerance left to argue. She then reached down by the foot of the swing and came back up with the bottle of Jack we'd been working on last night. She dumped about half a shot into my coffee and handed it back.

"Fixed it for you," she tried to smile but failed.

"Hair of the dog?" I asked.

"Yeah."

"Does it work?"

"Sure," she half-heartedly shrugged her shoulders. I sipped from the mug and then rested my head against the back of the seat. For a minute, I thought about retrieving my sunglasses from the truck. Instead, I settled for just closing my eyes. She and I sat there in complete silence for 20 minutes drinking the spiked coffee. When both our cups were empty, she took them into the kitchen to refill them. When she returned, she didn't spike either one.

"You gonna be okay?" I asked.

"Before you came out here this morning, I was doing some math in my head," she didn't answer the question.

"Okay?"

"Based on the numbers your friend Ann was tossing out yesterday, there are, or soon will be, close to 300 million dead people in the United States alone. That's roughly 33 million survivors. Of that 33 million, about 15 million of us will have natural immunity. That leaves somewhere around 18 million who are either too sick or worse, lost their ever-loving minds. Statistically speaking, it's probably a fifty-fifty split," she slowly sipped her coffee. "Do you want the worldwide numbers I came up with?"

"You came up with all that sitting here this morning?"

"I did."

"I've been sitting here trying to figure out how much longer before my head implodes and you're doing math?"

"I'm pretty good with numbers. That and I just rounded everything to make it easier," her smile was weak. "I've got some other numbers you might want to hear."

"Well, talk slow."

"Okay. It's obvious we can't go home. Are we in agreement there?"

"There's nothing at my house that I need."

"I'd like to get my car, but other than that, there's nothing I need there either. We can keep eating like we are and still have enough food for another 16 days. You were spot on when you did your shopping. I guess the question facing us is what do we do then? We could cut back and probably make up another week. Again, what then?"

"We can fish more to help stretch that even further," I offered.

"We can, and we will. We can't live off of fish alone though. Neither of us has a hunting rifle unless you're holding out on me," she allowed a soft smile. "There's a lot of things we'll need if we're just going to hide out here. Not just the food, but other things."

"Like?"

"Weapons for hunting and self-defense. Hygiene products for you and me. Fuel for the chainsaw and Razor. Fuel for the old Ford and the backhoe. We're gonna need more firewood if we're gonna stay warm in the winter months. It probably wouldn't hurt to have some first aid supplies too. The list is endless," she finished. I had to admit, she was right on all accounts. I'm not sure how her mind went there so quickly and efficiently. Mine was still a jumbled mess of cobwebs.

"You're right, Rayne. Since you've been giving this some thought, where do we start?"

"The gas pumps still had electricity yesterday. I think we need to start there. We take our cans, and we go into the store and grab every single one they had on the shelf. I know they sell them; I saw them. We should take both trucks too."

"What if nobody is there?"

"Huh?" she looked confused.

"We can't just take the gas cans. What if nobody's there to ring us up?"

"We hope nobody is there, Shane. We go in there and we take everything we need to survive. We load both trucks until we can't possibly fit another thing on them!"

"You mean….. Steal?"

"I know, and I can't believe I'm condoning outright theft! Last night, I was on the road to an existential crisis of epic proportions. This morning, I realized that I plan on surviving this thing. For me, there's no other option. My family is gone. There's nothing I can do about that. I can sit here and have a pity party, or I can survive, and that's what I intend on doing! I really hope you're along for the ride too, Shane. I need your answer now though. If we're going to act, we have to do it now," she looked at me over the top of her sunglasses.

When I was 10 years old, I stole a package of baseball cards from a local comic book store. I can remember how thrilling it was to do something I'd been told to never do. For as long as I could remember, my parents taught me to be honest and to do the right thing. Thieving those cards hadn't been my idea, but I had gone along with it.

When my father found out what I'd done, he walked me into that store, made me return the cards, and apologize to the store owner. After that, we walked the mile home in silence. I could feel his disappointment at what I had done. When we got home, he made me sit at the dining room table and contemplate just where I'd gone wrong.

FERAL OUTBREAK

After an hour, he sat opposite of me and asked me why I'd felt the need to steal. As soon as I tried blaming it on my friends who'd encouraged me, he got up and left the table. An hour later, he returned, and we started the conversation all over. It took four hours for me to realize that I alone was responsible for my actions. Sure, I'd been encouraged to do it, but ultimately, I was the one who carried out the act. After I owned up to it, he let me decide what my punishment should be.

I told him I would mow the front and back yards every Saturday for the rest of the summer. I was surprised when he easily agreed. My ten-year-old brain didn't realize I was dealing with a clever and cunning man. Friday after he got off work, he picked me up and we went to the hardware store, and he started looking at new lawnmowers.

He went through all of them. He'd read the specification sheets and try to decide how much horsepower would do the job. We were in that aisle for an hour. He finally decided on a mower that would be suited to my penance. It was an old-style push mower that was powered by me. It had two wheels, seven spiral blades, and a long handle for me to push it with. To say that I'd grown up to have strong feelings against theft was probably an enormous understatement!

"Well?" Rayne prodded.

"Meet me halfway?"

"Huh?"

"If there's still power and the credit card machine works, can we ring it all up so I can pay for it?" I asked. I thought she would laugh, but she didn't.

"Yeah, I suppose we could do that," came her quick concession.

-

It took another hour before either of us felt well enough to get moving. In that time, she grabbed a pad of paper and a pen. We brainstormed some of the things we'd need to be on the lookout for. Everything from toothpaste to flashlights. After that, when I was feeling a little more human, I dumped all the diesel from the cans into the backhoe. It took all of it with room for a little more. All of the gasoline went into the F250. By noon we were making the trek into Denio Junction.

The conversation with Rayne this morning, as surreal as it was, was a nice distraction from the tragedy unfolding in our lives and all around us. Part of me still couldn't comprehend that any of it was real. As a reality check, I turned the radio in the truck on. The recorded message we'd heard yesterday was still on an endless loop. Even after listening to it for half an hour, I was still in denial. This had to be a nightmare I couldn't wake up from.

37

If that weren't bad enough, here I was leading a two-truck convoy to go rob a gas station. I had every intention of paying for everything we took. It might take my company credit card and both of my personal cards, but damn it, I was going to make it right. The thought of it made me crack a smile and chuckle to myself. The world was falling apart, our survival paramount in our minds, and I wanted to pay for things that would keep us alive. I mean, even if we took everything that wasn't nailed down, who was I going to pay? I might be able to swipe my cards, but would any of it matter? I guess I still had a little emotional damage from spending an entire summer mowing three acres of grass by hand!

CHAPTER 9

August 19th, 2023.

The Denio Junction market was one of those places you stopped at when you were headed out to the middle of nowhere. It was your last chance to get fuel or a burger. There were Boonie hats for the would-be prospectors heading out to any number of opal mines. They had cigarettes, beef jerky, gas cans, postcards, and even refrigerator magnets. If you needed it before heading out on your adventure, they probably had it. We were here to take it.

Rayne pulled up on one side of the pumps and I pulled up on the other side. I was relieved to see the digital displays were still lit. She swiped her credit card and began filling the Ford. I did the same thing on my side. While her truck was filling, she ran inside to retrieve the gas cans we'd seen on one of the shelves. She returned with four of the plastic five-gallon cans and then ran back for more.

All in all, she brought out eight of the red cans for gasoline and eight for diesel. Added to the four of each we already had, that would get us 60 gallons of each type of fuel. She left me to fill those, and she backed the Ford up to the front door when she was done filling its tank. I ended up swiping my card a total of four times at the pump before I too backed up to the door.

"Can your solar system handle another freezer?" she asked when she came out with a handbasket full of canned foods.

"Easily. Why?"

"There's a giant chest freezer in there that's plum full. We could take it with us....." she dumped the basket into the bed of her truck and then started back inside. I followed behind her to see what she had in mind. The freezer in question was an industrial-sized unit that was just over six feet long. The manufacturer's tag on the end said it was a 30-cubic-foot model.

"What's in it?" I asked as I opened one of the two lids. I answered my own question. Right on top were two dozen packages of bacon. Under that were another two dozen 1-pound packages of hamburger meat. That was just what I could see, and I didn't bother opening the other door.

"That would be a good haul!" she winked.

"We should have brought the trailer," I mused.

"Go look out back," she grinned as she filled another basket with more canned food.

"What?"

"There's one of those enclosed trailers parked by the back door. If you want to go hook it up to your truck and haul it around the front, I can empty the freezer so we can move it,"

"I guess if we're committing felonies, we might as well see how many we can tack on, right?" I smiled stiffly.

"Might as well," she headed out with her full basket again. I went to the back of the store and found the previously locked storeroom door standing open. The doorframe was splintered. I stopped and peered into the dark room. Reaching for my Colt, I had the sudden realization that I had left it in the center console of my truck.

I heard Rayne come through the front door and turned to ask her if she was the one who kicked in the door. I'd no sooner turned my head when a deep primal scream came from the storeroom. I had just enough time to catch a glimpse of the man racing toward me. Just before he collided with me, I could see the snarl curling his lips and his outstretched arms reaching for me.

He hit me with a force I had never felt before. His hands were immediately around my throat stifling anything from getting past his grip. Together, we flew backward. I managed to keep my feet under me for two steps, but his weight and momentum drove me down into the display of potato chips. He was straddling me as the back of my head slammed into the concrete floor and his grip was doubled with his body weight being added to the chokehold.

I tried clawing his hands away, but they wouldn't budge at all. I tried bucking my hips and anything else I could think of. All of it was no match for his strength. My vision was beginning to go dark around the edges when I heard a loud, metallic CLANG! His grasp lessened if only slightly and I was able to suck in just a little air before he clamped down again. There was another CLANG followed very closely by another one.

I felt one of his hands release my throat, Just as I sucked in another breath, I tasted copper in my mouth. This was followed by a scream that I could only assume came from Rayne. There was another CLANG followed by the loud report of two gunshots. The mass of the man collapsed on top of me, and his fingers loosened from my windpipe. All I could do was lay there gasping and gagging. Rayne pushed the man off of me and knelt next to me.

"Shane!" she was frantically wiping blood from my face.

"I….. I'm….. Okay," I managed to force the words out in a hoarse, cracking voice. She helped me sit up. That's when I saw the source of the CLANG I'd heard. There was a 10-inch cast iron pan laying on the floor next to me. It was covered in blood and bits of hair and flesh. Once she was sure I wasn't going to fall over, she ran to the cooler. She brought back a large bottle of cold water and a roll of paper towels.

"Let me clean you up!" she was pouring some of the water into a handful of paper towels. Then she proceeded to wipe the man's blood from my face. She gave me the bottle so I could wash my mouth out.

"Thanks," was all I could croak out.

"Shhhh," she put a finger to her mouth and looked toward the front door. "Someone's coming!" she whispered. She picked up her Springfield that was by her knee. "Move," she was pushing me out of the line of sight of the front door.

"HELLO!" a man's voice boomed into the store. "C'mon! I know there's somebody in here! Come on out! I ain't gonna hurt ya!" Rayne peeked around what was left of the chip display, immediately ducking back.

"Shit," she whispered.

"I saw you, little lady! Why don't you make things easy for both of us and come on out!" Rayne motioned for me to stay down and then she stood to face the man. "Damn! You a pretty little thing!" he howled.

"Why don't you just get whatever it is you came in here for and move along? No need for any trouble," her voice was dead level. From the way she was half hidden by the display stand, her gun hand was well concealed.

"Won't be any trouble, missy. Why don't you just come on over here and give me what I came in for?" he laughed.

"You take another step and I'll end you!"

"You and what army, bitch?"

"I said stop!" Rayne barked. I could see her trigger finger slip onto the trigger.

"Come on baby….." his menacing voice was replaced by three quick shots from the 9mm handgun. The third expended shell hadn't even hit the floor yet when she fired until the slide locked back. Hot brass casings rained down and clattered on the floor.

"FUCK!" Rayne screamed. She dropped the empty handgun in my lap, grabbed the cast iron pan, and went to work. I looked around the corner just in time to see the heavy pan crash down on the still-writhing man's skull with a CLANG. Three more hits and he was finally still. "FUCK!" she screamed again.

I struggled to my feet and then scrambled around the corner to where she was. She was on her knees with her feet tucked under her butt. The deadly cast iron pan was next to her. As I approached, I could see she was shaking uncontrollably. Her breathing was ragged and filled with gasping sobs. Both of her hands held her face. When I put a hand on her shoulder to comfort her, she lashed out with an elbow and a scream. She spun to land on her butt and started kicking with her feet.

"Whoa. Whoa. It's me, easy!" I tried to calm her. Her face was twisted with sheer terror. "Rayne, It's okay!" I knelt in front of her.

"I….. I….. I….." she stammered as her face changed to recognition. With no warning, she lunged toward me like she was on springs. I caught her but ended up on my backside. Her arms were wrapped tightly around me, and her blood-splattered face was buried into my chest. She was squeezing handfuls of flesh on my back so tightly; I thought I might cry out in pain.

"It's okay. You're okay," I soothed with a broken voice while rubbing her trembling back. We stayed like that for ten minutes before I felt her hold begin to falter. When she finally pushed away from me, she wouldn't look at me.

"I'm sorry," she mumbled with downcast eyes. Before I could answer, she pulled completely away and stood shakily. She walked past the body in the middle of the floor and went straight to the counter where the cash register was. She bent down, out of my sight, and came back up with a carton of cigarettes. She tore it open and removed one pack. Packing it against her hand for a few seconds, she tore the pack open and removed one of the smokes. Placing it between her lips, she dug around until she found a pink disposable lighter. She lit the smoke and took a long pull from it. She held her breath and then finally released it.

Her hands were shaking as she savored each long drag. She still wouldn't make eye contact with me. With all of the trauma that had just occurred, I was willing to let it go. If a smoke helped her settle down, that was fine with me. I looked down at the man she'd beaten to death with a frying pan. My breath caught when I realized he was wearing a uniform with a cop's duty belt around his waist.

I moved to the body and rolled him onto his back. There were 12 bullet holes in the front of his uniform shirt. The body armor he wore underneath stopped all 12 rounds. The holster on the right side of his belt was empty but there were still four magazines for his pistol in their pouches.

"It went under the shelf," Rayne pointed toward the shelving unit next to the body. "He drew it and pointed it at me."

I bent down and spotted the Glock. I retrieved it and tucked it in the back of my pants. I thought about just taking the full magazines but took the whole belt and all of its accessories. I set it aside and then took a good look at the patch on his shoulder. This guy was from Burns, Oregon. Rayne came up beside me. She took one more long drag, dropped the butt on the floor, and ground it out with her foot.

"I shot him eight times, Shane. All eight were center mass. Just like I was trained. This wasn't his first rodeo. There are 12 holes in his shirt." her voice was lifeless. She knelt next to the body. "You picked the wrong bitch to fuck with, asshole!"

42

CHAPTER 10

August 19th, 2023.

"You okay?" I looked up at Rayne when I asked.

"Leave it alone, Shane. I'm not in a good place right now. I'll talk about it, but not now," she tore her gaze from the dead officer and retrieved her Springfield from the floor.

"When you're ready," I shouldered the duty belt and stood. When she walked past me, headed for the front door, she stopped long enough to pick up the frying pan.

"Let me reload and then we can finish loading up."

"You sure? We can just call it a day, try again tomorrow."

"We finish this today. I don't want to come back here," she headed toward the Ford. The frying pan clattered into the bed, then she collected a spare magazine from the front seat. After exchanging the full one for the empty one, she slid the compact pistol into its holster behind her belt.

I watched as she then stripped off her blood-splattered T-shirt to reveal a black sports bra underneath. She tossed the T-shirt on the ground and grabbed a roll of paper towels from the bed of the truck. Using a bottle of water, she soaked the towels and wiped the blood from her face. That was followed by wiping the blood from her torso that had soaked through her T-shirt.

Once all the blood had been wiped clean, she tossed the pink and red paper towels on the ground. She took a moment to remove her baseball cap and undo her long ponytail. She ran her fingers through her hair and then wound it up into a bun. After adjusting the size of the cap, she put it back on her head so that her hair was underneath. Checking herself in the side mirror, she sighed, stood straight, and turned to face me. She just stood there in her hiking boots, blood-splattered blue jeans, black sports bra, and black baseball cap.

"I thought you said you weren't a creeper," she joked but her voice sounded as dead as the two men on the floor of the convenience store.

"I, um, I just wanted to make sure you were okay," I said feebly.

"I'm fine," there was that lifeless, distant tone again. "We need to make sure we don't have any more surprises," she grabbed her pan and headed back into the store.

We spent half an hour combing the store and a couple of buildings around it. There was a small motel that turned up two bodies on the bed in one of the rooms. Both had been dead for some time. We just pulled that door closed and moved on. The August heat hadn't been kind.

Once we were sure our immediate surroundings were clear, we got the trailer hitched to my truck and pulled it around the front. We took turns removing items from the stuffed freezer. One of us would unload, while the other kept a watch. When it was empty, we slid it to the front door and then muscled it into the back of the enclosed trailer.

Before anything could defrost, we packed all the frozen foods, meat, and even ice cream back into it. We'd have to at least run an extension cord to it tonight, but it should be fine. From there, we took turns loading anything of use. With the addition of the trailer, we even loaded soda and beer by the case. All of the bottled water went in first, but we had the space for the other stuff, so why not? Rayne had stayed nearly silent through the whole process. Whenever I could get a glimpse of her eyes, I could tell she was working something out in her head.

"Where'd the cop come from?" she asked when we closed the door of the trailer.

"The patch on his shoulder….." I started.

"Not what I'm asking. How'd he get here? Did he drive? Walk?"

"I hadn't thought about it," I admitted. "What's it matter?"

"If he drove his cruiser, we might find some useful stuff in it. Stuff we need."

"You want to go check the RV park behind the motel?"

"Let's drive through on our way out. Follow me," she just walked away and headed for the Ford. I watched her toss the cast iron pan onto the seat and then climb in. At first, I didn't think she was going to wait for me, but she stopped just short of the turn-in for the RV park. She must have had the old truck down in first gear because I was having to ride the brakes to keep from running into the back of her.

At the far back corner of the park, we found his cruiser nosed into a deep ditch. Rayne pulled slightly past it and then climbed out of her truck. She had her Springfield leveled on the car. When I got out, I used my Colt to cover her backside. While she intently moved toward the car, I was watching the pair of RVs parked about a hundred feet down the road.

"Clear!" she said just loud enough for me to hear. She was leaning into the open driver's side door when I glanced in her direction. Between watching her and watching the surrounding area, my already sore neck was feeling worse by the minute. That's when I decided to just walk around looking straight ahead. It was easier on my neck.

The next time I looked in her direction, she was waist-deep into the trunk. She Came out with a tactical vest and a short, black, rifle case. When she brought them to the truck, she set them on the ground next to my rig. Not saying anything, she went back to the cruiser to continue her rummaging around. Next to be dropped off was a small black duffle bag, a hand-held radio, and another case of water. All of that came out of the trunk. Her next trip back to the car resulted in a shotgun being dropped off to be loaded into my truck. She picked up the hand-held radio and turned it on.

"Hello? Is there anybody out there?" she asked into the microphone. There was no response. She tried it twice more but finally gave up.

"What's in the black case?" I asked while she threw stuff onto my backseat.

"That's an AR-15 rifle. The duffle has eight magazines for it, four more for that Glock, and a whole bunch of ammunition. We can sort it all out when we get home. She closed my door and started walking toward the Ford.

"I guess we're ready to go," I muttered under my breath.

The hour-and-a-half trip to the cabin took a little longer because the trailer slowed me down. Rayne was leading the entire way and I could swear I saw puffs of smoke coming out of her rolled-down window. I didn't care if she smoked. I did want to know what made her feel the need though. Ever since the attack, she'd been cold, distant, and preoccupied. The fact that she wouldn't even look at me bothered me more than anything. The look on her face when I first tried to comfort her still haunted me.

It was almost dark when we parked in front of the cabin. My neck hurt. My head hurt. I was hungry, and I was starting to get a little irritated because of all of it. I shut the truck off and watched Rayne stomp into the house. Never once did she look in my direction. That was enough. It was time to get to the bottom of this. There was no way she was going to treat me like this in my own house. I strode through the front door in time to see her go into her room and close the door behind her.

"Rayne," I said, knocking on the door.

"In a minute," came the terse reply. From my side of the door, I could hear dresser drawers slamming shut. Was that crying?

"Rayne! We need to talk, now!" when the door flew open, she had her backpack on her shoulder. She was dragging her duffle.

"I knew this was going to happen, Shane! I knew it!" the whites of her eyes were red from crying. Tears were trying to break free from the corners of her eyes.

"Whoa. What are you talking about?" I lowered my voice slightly.

"Get out of my way," she tried to force her way past me. I refused to yield.

"Talk to me, Rayne. I'm not moving until you do!"

"Please move," her voice was cracking, and the tears were starting to roll down her face.

"Not until you tell me what the hell is going on," I argued. She dropped her bags and put her hands to her face. That's when the sobbing began. The cold façade she had put up collapsed to the floor as quickly as she did. The sobbing was growing violent. I knelt in front of her.

"Leave me alone!"

"No. Talk to me, Rayne."

She drew in a sharp, stuttering breath and looked up at me. The tears were flowing freely. This was the first time I'd been able to hold her gaze for more than a few seconds. She sniffled a few times and she took a few more of the catching breaths. All the while those honey-colored eyes were locked with mine. We stayed like that, just staring at each other, for at least five minutes.

"You're a nice guy, Shane. One of the few decent guys I know. Well, knew. Save yourself the trouble and let me leave," her voice was barely above a whisper.

"I'm not moving, and you're not leaving."

"Shane….. I killed two men today. I beat them and I shot them….."

"You….." she held up a hand to silence me.

"I told you about my ex-husband. What I didn't tell you, what I didn't go into detail about, was the beatings I would suffer at his hands. I was beaten because dinner wasn't to his satisfaction. I was beaten if the house wasn't clean enough. I was beaten until I gave in to his every whim. Sometimes he would beat me unconscious and take what he wanted from me….. All the while, he got away with it. He knew people. He had high-profile friends. He told me more than once that he could kill me and get away with it."

"My father caught wind that something was wrong. He didn't know what, but he was damn sure going to find out. He climbed in his old Ford pick-up truck, almost the exact same as the one that's sitting out front right now, and he drove all the way to Reno. Rick thought he was a tough guy. My father showed him what tough really was. A 66-year-old, retired Navy Chief, beat Rick to within an inch of his life. He also told Rick that if he told anyone that his injuries were anything other than an accident, he'd kill him. Rick wisely believed him."

"After the divorce and long after my father had returned home, Rick showed up on my doorstep late one night. He smashed his way in, obviously drunk off of his ass," she paused, took a deep breath, and dried her eyes. When she looked at me again, she started to speak very slowly and deliberately. "I swore to my father on his deathbed, that I would never let another man hurt me….. Shane, they will never find Rick's body or his fucking Corvette. I upheld my word to my father and refused to be cowed again."

"You mean to tell me, you….."

"Yep. One blow to the back of his head with a cast iron skillet was all it took."

CHAPTER 11

I stared at her, and she stared at me. I could tell she was waiting for a reaction of some sort or another. I knew, without a doubt, there had been some trauma in her life. Was I expecting this? Was I expecting her to admit to murdering a man? The answer was simple. No. I couldn't blame her for doing what she had to do. Her ex-husband was a piece of shit who thrived on beating, abusing, and destroying women. I didn't feel one iota of sorrow for him being un-alived. I did feel horrible because she was forced to take such drastic actions.

"Rayne....." I began slowly, still holding her gaze.

"Just let me leave, Shane. I know you don't want me here anymore," she started to push herself off of the floor. I gently put a hand on her knee to stop her.

"Rayne. You saved my life today. The guy that jumped me, would have killed me had you not intervened. You defended both of us against the cop. You saved my life twice in the span of about three minutes. You pulled something from deep inside you, you did something I couldn't do."

"This morning, you sat in the porch swing and talked me into stealing stuff to keep us alive. You did that because, and I quote, you intend to survive this thing. Your mind went there because you spent seven years of your life trying to survive. I don't have those experiences in my arsenal. I don't have that mindset, and I don't have the same defense mechanisms you have."

"You think I want you to leave because of your past? Well, you're wrong. Two things; Your past is why I'm still breathing, and your past is just that, the past. This may be hard for you to believe, but I could give two shits about what happened to Rick. At the risk of sounding redundant, your past and his past collided the night you killed him. He got dead and you're still here. That's all that matters."

"Shane....."

"You're a survivor, Rayne. All of the traumas that got you here define who you are today. You could have just found another abusive relationship, but you didn't. You could have just given up on all of it, but you didn't. Instead, you've risen above and thrived through all of it. You're a better person because you wanted to be better. You survived because the will to do so was inside you the whole time. It still is! Let me tell you something else; we're going to survive this because of you and the way you think."

"You're the first person who's ever said that," she spoke quietly.

"Which part?"

"The part about my past defining me. I've always been told that it's not a defining factor."

"Think about it, Rayne. Would you be such a badass if you hadn't gone through all that shit with Rick?"

"Probably not," she admitted.

"That's right. Now, you just need to own it. You've done things you had to do to survive. No more, no less."

"You don't want me to leave?" she asked hesitantly.

"No, I don't. If you still want to leave, that's on you, but I'd prefer you didn't. If it helps, I can't think of anyone else I'd rather be stuck here with," I tried a smile. I could see the corners of her mouth curl upward slightly.

We sat there, on the floor in the doorway to her bedroom for another hour. In the end, she agreed to stay at the cabin with me. She spent a few minutes putting her hastily packed belongings away and then joined me in the driveway. Out there, I had run an extension cord from the house to the back of the enclosed trailer for the freezer. We brought some of the other stuff in the house and agreed that we'd unload and store the rest of our loot the following day.

The cop's gear was amongst the stuff we hauled inside. With everything else settled for the evening, Rayne walked me through the weapons we'd taken from the abandoned cruiser. The rifle was an AR-15 with an optic of some sort mounted on top of it. There were a total of 12 30-round magazines for it and each one was loaded to capacity.

The pistol I'd taken from the cop was a Glock 19 9-millimeter. Between the magazines on the gun belt and the extras in the small black duffel, there were eight of the 15-round mags. The shotgun was a Remington 870. Its tube magazine held seven rounds plus one in the chamber. In the ammo duffle, we found four boxes of double ought buck. Each box had 20 shells in it.

The black tactical vest had pouches for three of the AR-15 mags and three that would hold the Glock mags. It had a small first aid kit, a pouch for the radio, and a holster that fit the Glock. The inside of the vest held large ceramic plates for front and back protection. There were smaller plates on each side.

Both of us were glad that we sought out the cop car. The weapons and ammo were a fantastic find, but we were really glad we had gotten to them before someone else could. They were a big boost for our defensive capabilities.

While I set about cooking dinner, Rayne excused herself to go take a shower. As soon as she was done, she took over the kitchen while I showered. The hot water went a long way toward making me feel better. Just getting the dried blood off of me was huge. By the time I was done, so was dinner. It wasn't anything fancy tonight. Both of us were too tired from the stress of the day.

With full stomachs and clean bodies, both of us retired to our beds at about the same time the sun dropped behind the hills to the west. If I thought I'd felt like hell this morning when I woke up hungover, going to bed was worse. My back was bruised from Rayne grabbing handfuls of flesh and the collision with the potato chip display. I still had a rather nasty knot on the back of my head and my neck felt like it had been wrung by a giant.

August 20th, 2023.

I'd been staring into the darkness of my room for over an hour. At least that's what the glaring red numbers on the clock radio accused me of. Having gone to bed so early, it was no surprise I was wide awake at 3:30 in the morning. I couldn't help but wonder if Rayne was going to be okay. The girl had been through so much shit since she got out of college.

There were so many questions I wanted to ask her about the night she killed her ex-husband. Things like; why didn't she just call the cops? Why bother to hide the body? What did she do with him? His car? There was so much to unpack with her admission. Those would have to wait, maybe forever though. Now was not the time to go there, and I wasn't sure the time would ever be right.

I spent a lot of time thinking about my parents and younger sister. What happened to my nephew? Was there anyone left alive in my hometown of Bucksport? What about all the people I worked with? Of the 396 contacts on my phone, I'd only heard back from two. Ann and Lucas. Ann was safely hidden away at my mom and dad's cabin deep in the Maine forest. With any luck, Lucas, and Kevin would never be heard from again.

Then I had to wonder how this whole thing had happened without me seeing any of the signs. If this had happened during the height of Covid, back in 2020, the red flags would have been flying. As it was, I couldn't remember hearing anything about it from anyone. I stayed as far as I could from any of the social media platforms, I didn't watch the news or even listen to the radio. I had a music playlist on my phone, and I got the news I needed from the weather channel. Yeah, I had internet service. I couldn't remember for the life of me when the last time was that I used it though.

Had I so removed myself from all forms of media that I just missed it all? What about all the people who'd called in sick the day I left? Why didn't I see that clue? Maybe I'd just become desensitized to it. I mean, the wall-to-wall coverage of Covid was why I decided to isolate myself from the news in the first place. I never really bought into it or the vaccine they offered. I never got it, and I didn't know anyone who'd died from it. I just got tired of listening to the talking heads ramble on about it.

I also had to ask myself what I'd have done if I'd seen the red flags going up. I wasn't a survivalist, prepper, or whatever they called themselves nowadays. I owned exactly one gun. I went grocery shopping every week because I didn't think it was necessary to do anything else. Even during the great toilet paper scare of 2020, I didn't buy into all the panic buying. If I needed ass wipe, I'd grab a roll from the supply closet at work. I know I wasn't the only one and there was always toilet paper there.

Before I knew it, my thoughts were going back to the events of yesterday. I could still see the face of the man who tried to choke me out. The whites of his eyes were red from all of the broken blood vessels in them. I could see that at one point, he'd been bleeding from his eyes, ears, and nose. That bleeding had started anew with the effort of trying to kill me.

The guy was fairly small in stature, maybe five foot six inches tall. He had a slight build too. There were no bulging muscles to explain his unnatural strength. I did know that if Rayne hadn't intervened when she did, he'd have more than likely done irreparable damage to my throat. It was still swollen and difficult to swallow anything. I could only imagine what the bruises would look like today.

That brought up another thing. Rayne said she'd hit Rick in the head once with a cast iron skillet. I had no reason to discount her recollection of the event, but how many blows did my attacker sustain before she had to shoot him? Was it three? Four? The dude should have at the very least, been out cold after the first hit. Then there was the cop. She had to pulverize his skull to get him to stop thrashing around. That guy had taken 12 bullets to the chest. Yeah, his vest stopped the rounds, but what about internal organ damage? There had to be some, right?

From the conversation Rayne and I had about the weapons she'd scavenged from his patrol car; it seemed as though she knew her way around guns. Later on, in that same discussion, she told me that her father was a big gun guy and apparently had quite the arsenal at home. From a young age, he made sure she knew how to shoot and maintain guns. The guns we had now looked cool as hell, but I admittedly didn't know jack shit about them.

I was going to have to change that. It wasn't like when I had a guy making death threats against me. Now, it really was a matter of life or death. Nobody was coming to save us. We were on our own. Initially, I was slow to get on board, but after yesterday, I was all in now. I needed to change my whole mindset. I needed to be able to defend myself and I needed to be able to defend Rayne. Like it or not, we were a team now and she couldn't be the one to bring all the fight to the table. I had to step up my game or it could kill both of us. Like her, I too wanted to survive this.

CHAPTER 12

At 5:30 on the button, I heard Rayne come out of her room and caught a glimpse of her passing in front of my open door. A moment later, I heard her getting the coffee pot going. After that, she made her way back to the bathroom. I decided then that it was a good time to get out of bed. I was sore, but just laying around was making things worse. I should have just got up when I first woke up. I might have been better off.

Still wearing my baggy sweats and t-shirt, I slipped my feet into my slippers and stood. The lingering effects of having my head smashed into the concrete the day before caused me to feel a bit wobbly on my feet. Fortunately, it passed rather quickly. When I walked out of my room, I almost ran into Rayne coming out of the bathroom.

"Morning," my voice was hoarse and scratchy in my throat.

"Does that hurt? You sound like hell," she stopped and looked at me.

"A little," I croaked.

"I have just the thing to help with that," she grinned and stepped past me, and headed for the front door. Not knowing what she was up to, I went and poured two cups of coffee. When she came back through the door, she was carrying two pints of ice cream from the freezer we'd taken yesterday.

"Ice cream for breakfast?" I asked.

"Believe me, it'll help with the swelling..... Why not?" she dug two spoons out of the drawer and headed for the recliners.

"Can I ask you a question?" I asked after the first half of the pint was gone. She was right. It did help.

"Sure."

"Do you know how to work the guns we got yesterday? The rifle and the shotgun?"

"Yes."

"Could you teach me what you know?"

"You grew up in Maine and don't know how to shoot?" she cocked her head when she asked the question.

"My dad was the big hunter of the family. I hated it. Besides, I learned to shoot with a bolt action, neither of those are bolt actions," I pointed my spoon at the weapons that were still on the coffee table.

"I see. I can teach you what I know, but I'd be hesitant to actually put rounds down range. It's not like we've got a lot to work with in the first place."

51

"Is it the same concept when it comes to pulling the trigger? I'm a decent shot if it's the same. I guess I just need to know how they work. How to load them and all that."

"Yeah, I guess as long as you know how to use the sights, it's pretty much the same. Loading them and maintaining them is a little more detailed than an old bolt gun, but it's easy enough to learn," she set her ice cream down, finished the last swig of coffee, and took both of our cups to the kitchen. With refilled cups in hand, she came back and sat down again.

"Is that something we could do today?" I asked.

"Sure. We should probably get everything unloaded from the trucks first though. We should probably do some sort of basic inventory too. It would be good to know where our weak spots are after yesterday's supply run."

"Absolutely!" I agreed.

As the day wore on, the insides of my throat started to feel better. We even managed to work out some of the sore muscles. The bruises were tender, and they probably would be for a while. The black and blue marks around my neck picked up tinges of purple and yellow that were hard to miss.

The vast majority of the items we'd stolen, taken, I corrected myself, were of the non-perishable sort. Boxes of cereal, crackers, oatmeal, and even pancake mix. The canned goods accounted for tuna, chili, tomato paste, and various soups, with some canned meat thrown in. There was white and brown rice, spaghetti, mac-n-cheese, and elbow noodles. Some of the items came by the case and were taken from the storeroom.

The stuff that filled the freezer was mainly for the small diner. Various types of meat, frozen vegetables, and frozen hash brown patties made up the lion's share of its contents. The ice cream was just an added bonus as far as we were concerned. There were cases of alcohol that supplied the small bar and there were cases of cigarettes. With boxes and stacks of cans lining the walls of the living room and kitchen, we hadn't even gotten to the cases of soda and water yet.

When we stopped for lunch, Rayne had me put a bag of frozen peas on my neck to help with the swelling. She heated up a couple of cans of soup, and then we were right back to work when we were done eating. With the trailer empty, we refilled it with the full cases of water, soda, alcohol, cigarettes, and anything else that was still in an unopened case. After filling it to the point that we almost couldn't close the door, I backed it into the barn.

"Man, I can't believe how much stuff we hauled home," I commented as we were walking from the barn to the house.

"Yeah, I'm definitely going to have my work cut out for me for the next couple of days."

"How so?"

"Well, now that we have everything inventoried, I need to figure out how many decent meals we have at our disposal."

"Sorry, I kinda forgot that that's what you do for a living. Not with food, but parts and whatnot."

"Yeah, it's what I did," her smile was rueful.

"Sorry."

"It's fine, Shane. I still find it just a little difficult to wrap my head around everything. I mean, two weeks ago, I couldn't wait to get off work to go home and pack for this trip. I was looking forward to it so much!" she was silent as we climbed the stairs of the porch.

"Now I realize that if I'd told you no, I wasn't coming with you, I might very well be dead. At the very least, I'd be surrounded by dead and dying people. One simple choice probably saved my life. It all hinged on a yes or no answer," she continued once we were standing in the kitchen.

"Ya know, the day I pulled out of Vegas, I was faced with a choice too. Just like yours, it was a yes or no choice. I could have stayed and helped my boss, but I chose not to. I picked no, you picked yes, and here we are trying to ride out the end of the world together," I said, washing my hands under the kitchen faucet.

"Fate sure has an odd way of working doesn't she?" she was washing her hands as I dried mine.

"She sure does. I spent the better part of last night wondering why I was spared, what's so special about a guy like me? Why am I here when everyone I gave a shit about is gone. Well, almost everyone," I handed her the dish towel. She grinned when she took it from me.

"You still got a little bit of a thing for Ann, don't ya?"

"I wasn't thinking of Ann."

"Who then?"

"You. I give a shit about you, Rayne," I watched her eyes go wide with surprise.

"Shane, I already told you….."

"I know what you said," I cut her off. "I heard you loud and clear. It's not like that though. The biggest reason I asked you to come along on this trip is because I was hoping to find a friend in you. Before all this happened, I had decided that I needed friends. Ann was it. She was the only one of my friends still living. I had a lot of acquaintances, but nearly no friends. I'm pretty sure I found the friendship with you that I was looking for," I confessed.

"Why me?"

"Permission to be completely honest?"

"Don't hold back," her expression was curious and serious all at once.

"When I first met you back in January,"

"When you called me Ray-Nee?" she smiled.

"Yeah. Up until dinner that last night, I thought you were kind of a bitch. Once the conference was over and all of us were chilling at the bar, I realized that I was wrong. I had misjudged you. When you smiled at people, when you interacted with them, I could see the real you. So damn many of those people wore fake, tight-lipped smiles. They would talk shit behind their peers' backs. I never once saw that from you. I gave you my business card in the hopes that I'd hear from you and be able to get to know you."

"Here I thought it was for professional reasons."

"It was!" I protested. "In the beginning, it was completely professional! As little pieces of you came out over the phone, I thought I'd like to know more about you. You seemed like a person I could hang out with. When I told you that I'd be on vacation for the entire month of August, you asked me if I had anything good planned. Remember that?"

"Yeah, I remember," she admitted.

"When you said you wished you could do something like this, I didn't even think about it. My mouth was moving faster than my brain when I asked you to come along."

"Did you regret it?"

"At first? I did, but only because I was worried you'd think I was some sort of creep or serial killer or some shit."

"What are the odds of two killers staying at the same cabin in the middle of nowhere?" her blank expression was impossible to get a read on.

"I….. I….." I stammered.

"Relax, Shane! I'm fucking with you!" she burst out laughing. "Or am I?" she was suddenly serious again. Fortunately for me, she couldn't hold a straight face for more than a few seconds. When she started laughing again, it was infectious.

"I do have a question or two for you," she said after the laughter died down.

"Don't hold back," I used her line.

"Do you have any regrets about bringing me along? Knowing what you know now?"

"No, I don't." I was already shaking my head before she finished the question.

"Okay. Why the friend zone? Why not something more, you know, intimate?"

"This is gonna sound weird, Rayne," I leaned against the counter. "You want the long or the short of it?"

"Let's hear the whole thing."

"I've already told you that I needed friends. Real friends. That's what I came into this looking for and hopefully found. You are very, very attractive and I'm not just talking about your body and looks. You can turn wrenches, fish, hike, cook, and drive the Razor like no one else. You're intelligent. I'm not talking book smarts, although you've got that going for you too. The problem is a romantic relationship between us would never work. Especially knowing what I know now."

"I don't understand."

"Rayne, first of all, I'm not about to leave my job and there is no way in hell I'd ask you to leave yours. I'm not about to give up my life in Vegas and again, I could never ask you to give up yours in Carson City….." Her head was cocked to one side and her eyebrows were both raised. "What?" I asked.

"Ummm. I can and do really appreciate all of that, but you seem to be forgetting one tiny little detail….." her voice trailed off.

"What am I forgetting?"

"I don't think either one of us has jobs to worry about anymore," her statement was like someone flipping on the light switch in a dark room.

"Oh," I whispered. She closed the distance between us and put a hand gently on the side of my face.

"I'm not saying yes, but I'm not saying no to anything other than being friends. You've already got my friendship and that's the basis of everything. It's something I desperately needed too. You've given me something I never thought I'd have again, and you gave it with no strings attached. You gave it freely. Thank you," she leaned in and gave me a light kiss on the cheek.

When she pulled her face away, she locked eyes with me and kept her hand on the side of my face. I didn't know what to say, so I just kept my mouth shut. After a few more seconds, she removed her hand and stepped back. She was about to say something but stopped short. She turned her head like she was listening intently for something. The features on her face began to subtly change.

"You hear that?" she asked.

"I don't….." I started to say but then heard the sound of distant thunder. Rayne hastily turned and strode out of the front door and down to the driveway. The entire time she was scanning the skies. I followed and we quickly located the source of the sound.

"Military?" she asked, pointing at the white, twin-engine jet streaking across the sky from west to east. It was leaving a trail of heavy smoke from one engine, and it was losing altitude.

"I don't think so, but whoever he is, he's in trouble!"

CHAPTER 13

August 20th, 2023.

"He's not gonna make it to an airport. Is he?" Rayne asked.

"No. he's headed in the wrong direction. I imagine he could set it down on a road though. Highway 140 has some decent long stretches that would make a good runway."

"You think he'll try and set it down?"

"I think he's gonna end up on the ground one way or another. Run and grab my truck keys. I'll get the trailer unhooked," I started for the barn, and Rayne ran back into the house.

By the time I was done unhooking the trailer, Rayne ran into the barn. She had the tactical vest on, but not fastened. She also had the AR-15 hanging on her shoulder by the sling, the shotgun in one hand and she tossed me the keys with her other hand. She stopped at the passenger door long enough to slide the AR and the shotgun onto the front seat, then she ran to the door of the trailer. A moment later, she was climbing onto her seat and tossing one of the first aid kits from the store onto the backseat.

As I drove, she resized the vest to fit her figure. Once she was happy with it, she slid the Glock into its holster, checked the AR, and then clipped it to sling points on the vest. The entire time she kept the barrel pointed at the floor. She then turned her attention to the shotgun.

"Ever been bird hunting?" she asked.

"Yeah, but I used my dad's double barrel 12 gauge."

"You've never shot a pump?"

"No."

"It's easy. This is your safety," she pointed to the small button. "Red is hot, black is not. There's one in the pipe, so all you gotta do is press the safe button, aim, and pull the trigger. Once you release the trigger, pull the slide all the way back to eject the spent shell, jam it all the way forward again and the next round is ready to go. Think you can handle that?" she demonstrated the general motions.

"Yeah, I can do that."

I drove the BLM road a little faster than I was comfortable with, but it got us back to Highway 140 in 45 minutes. That was the first time we'd seen the thick black column of smoke rising to the east. On the pavement, I pushed the big diesel to 90 and held it there. She had more to give, I just didn't feel the need to go any faster. The plane was already on fire and there wasn't much we could accomplish by getting there maybe five minutes faster.

FERAL OUTBREAK

We found the crash site roughly eight miles southwest of Denio Junction. It was located on one of those long, flat straightaways. I was sure no one could have survived what we saw when I pulled the truck to a stop. The main fuselage was broken into three distinct sections. The cockpit was the farthest away, the main cabin was about a hundred feet closer, and the tail section containing both engines had been flung out into the sagebrush. It was the tail section that was fully engulfed in flames.

"I'm stopping here. I'm not driving through all that debris," I told Rayne.

"That's fine," she threw her door open, "Follow me with the shotgun and keep your eyes peeled!" she slid off of the seat, brought the AR to her shoulder, and started to cover the hundred-plus yards to the main wreckage. I grabbed the shotgun and mimicked her actions once both of my feet were on the ground.

She slowly and steadily made her way forward with me following roughly 20 feet behind and to her left. I don't know what she was looking for, but I found the wreckage fascinating. From the very beginning of the debris field, I hadn't seen any evidence that the plane had landed on its wheels. There were deep gouges in the asphalt and then small pieces of the plane everywhere.

There was a piece of luggage, a briefcase, and the keyboard from a laptop. A drink cart was sitting on its wheels right in the middle of it all. It was dented, smashed, and scraped, but sitting upright. There was a seat lying face down on the shoulder and it took me a second to realize there was a body strapped into it. All I could see was one foot that was missing its shoe. Whoever had been in the seat was obviously dead.

Continuing to follow Rayne, I inadvertently kicked a hand laying in the middle of the road. It was just a hand, probably a woman's, from the wrist to the fingertips. The nail polish on the nails was scraped. The nail beds were highlighted with crimson red. Rayne must have heard me cuss under my breath because she paused for a second to look in my direction. Sure that I wasn't hurt, she continued to move forward.

Everything that I'd seen up to this point should have had some impact on me, but it didn't. Honestly, I think I was just so damn scared that fear and adrenaline were ruling over everything. I'm also sure that there was no defense mechanism for what I saw next. I stepped around a large piece of the wing and found the bloody mess sprawled out in front of me.

At one time, not long ago, it had been a human being. Now, it stretched over seven feet from the top of its head to its toes. The legs were twisted together. I mean, literally twisted like a wire bread bag tie. The pelvic region was facing the ground, while the rest of the torso was on its back. The arms were bent in several places where there were no joints. The left arm was hanging by tendrils of flesh at the shoulder. The head was missing the lower jaw and one of the eyeballs was hanging to the side. The other was missing altogether.

The entire body was burned and devoid of any clothing except a bloody tennis shoe on one foot. As gruesome as the sight was, it was the smell that caused me to choke back the vomit fighting its way up from my stomach. I turned away and covered my mouth and nose in the crook of my arm. When I stepped on and squished the missing eyeball, there was no holding back any longer. I doubled over at the waist and explosively emptied everything from my stomach. That was followed by some of the hardest dry heaves I'd ever experienced in my life.

"C'mon, keep moving," Rayne grabbed my arm and forced me forward. I did catch the look on her face when she glanced over at the body.

"Help!" we heard the weak distress call coming from where the main cabin was resting on its side. Rayne pulled me along as she headed that way. Before we got there, I was able to suck in a couple of deep breaths and choke down anything else trying to come up my throat.

As we closed the distance, we could hear the call for help clearly. The cockpit had sheared from the main fuselage where the side door had once been. The tail section had broken off just behind where the wings used to be. Both entrances into the main cabin were blocked by twisted metal and hundreds of electrical wires. Rayne let her rifle hang by its sling as she started pulling stuff out of the way where the tail section used to be connected.

"Help!" came the man's voice again.

"We're comin! Just hang in there!" she shouted into the cabin as she continued to throw stuff. She finally had a hole wide enough for her to shimmy through. "Stay here and watch our backs," she ordered before stripping off the tactical vest and AR. She handed them to me and then disappeared through the hole. From my spot outside, all I could hear now were the soft murmurs of the man and Rayne talking. She was in there for a full 10 minutes before she finally came out again. Her hands and forearms were covered in bright red blood. It was all over her dark blue tank top and jeans too.

"God! Are you okay?" I rushed closer to her. She held up a hand to signal that she was fine.

"It's not mine," was her flat statement.

"His?" I pointed past her into the cabin.

"Yeah. He'd been holding pressure on an arterial bleed in his leg. There's nothing we could have done for him," she was looking around for something.

"What are you looking for?"

"Something to wipe this damn blood off!"

"Oh," I began looking for a rag or something, anything to help. Everything I found smelled like fuel or hydraulic oil from the plane.

"We need to account for all the bodies. Three flight crew and four passengers. He thought there might have been another survivor," for the second time I watched her strip her tank top off and use it as a rag to clean blood from her hands. She was wearing the black sports bra underneath again.

"Two in the cockpit?" I asked.

"Should be. Run up there and check. Just be careful," she warned. I acknowledged her with a nod.

The cockpit was lying on its side, and I had to make my way through the curtain of electrical wires to gain access. Inside I found the pilot and co-pilot still strapped into their seats. Standing on God knows what, I reached around until I could feel for pulses in their necks. Both were dead. I withdrew my hand, resisting the urge to wipe it on my pants. I gave a cursory look around the destroyed cockpit. I found a black, soft-sided briefcase and took it when I climbed out of the wreckage. A cursory glance at its contents told me that it contained some ID and a Logbook. I took the bag with me when I went back to where Rayne was.

"Two crew in the cockpit," I reported.

"What's that?" she pointed to the bag.

"Pilot stuff. Logbook, ID. Not sure what else."

"Ah," she tossed the blood-soaked tank top on the ground and put the tactical vest on over her sports bra.

"I heard you talking to that guy in there, what did he have to say? What happened?" I asked and pointed toward the main cabin.

"A lot. Now's not the time though. I'll fill you in once we're gone from here," her reply was unusually curt. "So, we've got three bodies between here and the cockpit, right?"

"Yeah."

"How many back that way?" she pointed back toward the truck.

"Two. There's one still strapped into a seat back that way. We'll need to go see if that body has both hands still."

"Huh?"

"I found a hand too. It didn't belong to the human pretzel. That one still had both hands. Well, what was left of 'em anyway," I tried to avoid letting my mind replay that scene again.

"Okay. Go check the one in the seat. Let me try and get a little more of this blood off and I'll help you look. Keep your head on a swivel!"

"Okay," I turned and jogged back to where the body had been pinned under the seat. As much as I didn't want to, I flipped the seat onto its back to expose the body still strapped into it. I wasn't positive, but it was probably a safe assumption that this one had been a man. Everything from the center of his chest on up had been turned into hamburger from sliding across the pavement and then the dirt. He still had both of his hands too. I turned to head back toward Rayne, but she was walking toward me. She was carrying a messenger bag in one hand.

"This puts us at five bodies plus a hand with no owner," I told her.

"If the owner of the hand is still alive, they couldn't have gone far. That's a pretty significant injury. Show me where the hand is."

"Yeah," I pointed to the general direction where I'd found it and started walking that way. "You think someone survived this? Besides the guy in the cabin?" I asked.

"I'm not thinkin anything, but he was sure there was another survivor. We really need to account for everyone before we leave. I'd hate to leave someone out here that's injured,' she remarked.

We searched the crash site for an hour and never found the owner of the hand. After that, we spent another hour gathering the bodies and covering them with anything we could find. We ended up leaving the pilot and co-pilot strapped into their seats. The damage was so great that both men were held in place by the twisted metal. By the time we were walking back to the truck, the sun was beginning to set. Rayne picked up the suitcase and briefcase I'd seen earlier.

I thought about asking her why but decided to just let it go. I was curious about the messenger bag too but didn't bring it up. I kinda figured she was in scavenging mode. She tossed all three into the backseat. Both of us were worn out from the long day and kinda just sagged into our seats. I started the truck and made a three-point turn to get us headed in the right direction.

"Pretty gnarly thing back there, huh?" I said to break the silence in the cab.

"Yeah. More nightmare fuel I guess."

"No kidding. Was the guy in the cabin able to tell you what happened? Why they crashed?"

"Yes, and a bunch of other things too."

"Like what?" I prodded. Instead of answering, she opened the center console. Apparently not finding what she was looking for, she closed it again. "What are you looking for?"

"You got your phone on you?"

"No. It's on the kitchen counter. Why?"

"We need to talk to Ann. She's probably the only one who can make any sense out of what that guy told me."

"What are you talking about?"

"Shane, that plane was chartered by the CDC. The four passengers were scientists. They were flying out of San Francisco, headed to Atlanta. You know what's in Atlanta, right?"

"That's where the CDC headquarters is."

"Correct. Anyway, they were being shot at when they took off and one of the engines was damaged. He said they barely made it over the Sierras when the engine let go. That's not why they crashed though," she took in a deep breath before starting again.

"One of the passengers, a woman, went berserk and attacked the third member of the flight crew. Another of the scientists rushed to help the crew member and in the tussle that ensued, the mad woman had the scientist pinned against the door. She opened it! The man was instantly sucked out and he went straight into the good engine."

"The plane was already at a low altitude so there wasn't any explosive decompression. She was in the process of killing the crew member when the plane crashed. He said it was like watching a rabid dog tear a rabbit to pieces."

"Jesus….. That means….."

"That means that the sole survivor of the crash is possibly a one-handed woman suffering from a psychotic break. Cool, huh?"

"Thanks, Rayne. I don't think I'm ever going to sleep again….."

"But wait! There's more….." She did her best impersonation of a late-night TV pitchman.

CHAPTER 14

August 20ᵗʰ, 2023.

"Where does Ann fit into all this?" I asked.

"That messenger bag I grabbed, it's got a bunch of statistics and stuff the scientists had been working on before they were forced to flee San Francisco."

"How's she supposed to help with that? It's not like she can just run into the office."

"No, I know. He said….. Shane, he said the woman who went mad was perfectly fine until she wasn't. He also said something about their initial casualty estimates being very wrong. Now, I don't rightly know what all that means, but he also said that we need to get that information to the CDC. Ann is the closest thing we have to someone who can understand the information and possibly get it into the right hands."

"Yeah, you're right. She might be able to make a phone call or something."

"I think we should wait till morning before we go find a spot with good cell reception. It kinda bothers me being out here after dark," she offered.

"I like the way you think."

"Afraid of the dark?" I could see the smirk on her face in the light coming from the dash.

"I didn't use to be….."

We parked in front of the dark house and went inside. Rayne was the first through the door, so she flipped on the front room lights. She stripped off the tactical vest, dropping it in her recliner. The AR was put on the coffee table right next to where I put the shotgun. She excused herself to go clean up. I went into the kitchen, located my phone, and plugged it into the wall charger. I was probably going to need a full battery for the call to Ann tomorrow.

"You still hungry?" Rayne asked as she came back into the kitchen. She had put a black T-shirt on and was drying her face with the hand towel from the bathroom.

"Starving!" since I was standing next to the fridge, I opened it and pulled out the plate that the chicken breasts were defrosting on. I set it on the counter and reached back in for two cold beers. I popped the caps off and handed her one.

"Thanks," she took the offered beverage. "Can you run out back and start the barbeque?" I answered with a mock toast after a long hard drink that drained half the bottle.

When I came back into the kitchen after lighting the barbeque, I saw the front door standing open, but I didn't see Rayne. That's when I remembered the stuff she'd thrown in the backseat of the truck. I was about to go to the front door when

I heard the truck door shut. That just confirmed what I was thinking, and I altered my course for the fridge. After everything I'd seen today, another beer sounded good. Maybe it would help me sleep a little.

After popping the top, I set it on the counter and pulled the cutting board down from the cabinet. It went on the counter with my beer. I then opened the silverware drawer and pulled out a knife for the potatoes I was about to dice up for dinner. I retrieved those and an onion from the pantry and started washing them off. I heard the screen door open and then close but didn't bother looking up.

"Did ya forget the bags?" I asked, still washing potatoes. There was no answer, but I heard her shuffling feet behind me. I froze when a familiar smell hit my nostrils. Jet fuel and hydraulic oil.....

I spun around and what I saw was straight out of a horror movie. The woman was wearing a bloody and soot-covered lab coat. Half of her once blond hair was burned away leaving half of her head and face covered with burns. Blood and other fluids were leaking from the cracks in the charred flesh. Her legs were also burned with pieces of charred and discolored clothing hanging from the edges of the worst burns. A rag that was dripping with blood covered the stub of her arm where her hand used to be.

"Fuck me!" I said it under my breath, but it was all it took to kick things off. She lunged for me with her one hand outstretched. I hurled the potato I had in my hand at the same time I jumped to the right. The potato bounced off of her head as she continued her advance. I deftly snatched the knife off the counter as I flew past it. For someone who was burned to a crisp and was bleeding all over the place, she was still quick and nimble.

She was coming at me much faster than I could back away. With the distance between us diminishing rapidly and finding myself backed against the wall, I stabbed straight toward her with the knife. With her forward momentum, the knife buried itself deep in the right side of her chest. She didn't even slow down. With her remaining hand, she grabbed a handful of my shirt and effortlessly flung me across the kitchen.

I landed on my side and quickly rolled into the living room. Before I could get to my feet again, she was charging at me. As I made it to my knees, we collided. Even though she couldn't have weighed much more than a hundred pounds, it felt like getting hit by a speeding car. Rather than trying to push her away, I rolled with her one more time. This put me in the position of being on top.

I was sitting straddle her waist; she was lashing out with her hand and stub. I was able to deliver two savage blows to her face, but they didn't seem to faze her at all. She got her fingers wrapped around my throat, but her hand was too small to gain any real purchase. Using both hands, I wrenched it free and twisted it as hard as I could. This got me a guttural, primal scream as the bones in her forearm snapped like dry twigs. She was still trying to club me with the stub. Every time she hit me with it, I could hear the squishing of the rag covering the wound.

Fighting through the flailing limbs, I landed another solid hit to her face. The devastating blow broke her jaw and cocked it to one side. She continued to flail and try and buck me off. It dawned on me that trying to beat her to death was going to quickly wear me out, so I changed tactics. Grabbing the handle of the knife that was still embedded in her chest, I twisted it and then pulled it free.

Through the frenzy of flailing arms and screams, I stabbed her in the chest until she stopped fighting. I don't even know how many more times I stabbed her after she went limp. Leaving the knife sticking out of her chest right where the heart should have been, I rolled off and just laid on my back trying to catch my breath.

"Rayne!" I yelled as the thought of her suddenly burst into my head. I got to my feet and ran outside. As soon as I hit the top of the stairs, I could see her sprawled out, face down, next to the truck. "RAYNE!" I yelled again, clearing the six steps in two long strides. I went to my knees beside her and rolled her onto her back. My hand shot to her neck to feel for a pulse.

"Thank God!" I said as I put one arm under her knees and the other under her back. I scooped her up and took her into the house. I was headed for the couch, but in the light of the kitchen, I could see the cut and lump above her left eye. I laid her gently on the couch and quickly checked her for any other injuries. I guess I remembered more of the basic first aid I'd gotten at work than I thought I had.

Not finding anything obvious, I went and got a clean wet rag from the kitchen. I used it to clean the blood and dirt from her face. The laceration above her eye was close to two inches long and still bleeding. I was trying to hold pressure on it and hold the wound closed at the same time. I knew head and face lacerations could bleed a lot, but this kinda had me worried.

It took nearly 30 minutes before I got the bleeding to stop, for the most part anyway. Rayne never moved but her breathing was consistent as was her pulse. I went back to the kitchen to retrieve a dry cloth and some frozen vegetables. On the way back I nearly tripped over the body of our assailant. After placing the clean cloth and makeshift icepack on her forehead, I went back to the body.

I pulled the knife from her chest and dropped it into the sink. Thank God my grandpa had installed stone tile in the kitchen. This was going to be a mess to clean up. I thought about going to the barn to get a tarp but didn't want to leave Rayne alone. There was already blood everywhere, so I just grabbed the body by its feet and drug it out the front door and down the stairs. The head made a clunking noise as it bounced down the stairs.

I then went back in and checked on Rayne again. After that, I got the mop and bucket from the hall closet. As I cleaned up the mess, I'd check on Rayne every few minutes. If things were normal, I'd have called an ambulance a long time ago, but things were far from normal. I didn't know what else to do for her, so I was just trying to keep myself busy. I was about halfway through cleaning up when it came to me that I should have at least made sure there were no more crazies outside. Or in the house for that matter. The sudden realization freaked me out a little.

I went and got the Glock out of Rayne's tactical vest and grabbed a flashlight out of the junk drawer in the kitchen. The first order of business was to clear the house. Room by room, closet by closet, I made sure there was nobody but the two of us in the house. I'm sure it was a sloppy attempt, but at least I was trying. I was about to lock the back door when I remembered that I'd lit the barbeque nearly an hour earlier. I stepped out long enough to put the lid on it and close all the vents.

Working my way back through the house, I stopped to check on Rayne again. There was no change, so I went out the front door. The crazy lady was still on the ground and still dead. Using the flashlight to light the way, I searched around the trucks, even looking inside them. That's when I discovered the tailgate of my truck was down. There was blood in the bed and a small hole in the tonneau cover where the lady had ripped a hole in it so she could reach the handle on the outside. She must have climbed in when we were busy searching the crash site for her.

Even though I was now fairly confident that nobody else was here, I made a quick search of the barn and the pumphouse. Every location was thoroughly cleared before I went back into the house. Upon entering, I pulled the screen door closed and locked it. I repeated the move with the front door. I then went from room to room again closing and locking all the windows and drawing the blinds closed. When I returned to the living room, Rayne let out a soft whimper from the couch.

"Hey," I said softly, sitting on the edge of the couch next to her. Her eyes fluttered open. I could see confusion and fear at first. When they locked with mine, she began to calm down a little. "You're okay. You're safe."

"What the hell....." she started but stopped short. She sat bolt upright. "Outside! She jumped me!" she was gripping my arm now, panic in her voice.

"It's okay! I got her," I said in the most soothing tone I could muster. "She's dead."

CHAPTER 15

"She jumped me. The bitch jumped me! She slammed my head into the side of the truck. I didn't know she was there until it was….. Until she had ahold of me. It happened so fast!" Rayne was trying to recall the attack. Her sudden movements had caused the head wound to start bleeding again. She was holding the rag and the ice pack in place to try and stem the flow of blood.

"She almost had me too. I thought it was you coming in from outside. You're not gonna believe what my first weapon of choice was."

"Let me guess, you're charming smile?" she shot me a half grin.

"You're close. I threw a potato at her!"

"You what?"

"I threw a potato at her. Nailed her right in the head," I said rather proudly.

"You….. I….. What do I even say to that?" she laid back and rested her head on the armrest.

"Let me look at that," I scooted up a little so I could see the gash above her eyebrow a little better. The low level of lighting in the living room wasn't much help, so I grabbed the flashlight off of the coffee table. While I was looking at the wound, I checked her pupils.

"Am I gonna live, doc?"

"Your pupils are equal, so that's good. That cut is pretty nasty though. If you were in an emergency room, they'd be putting some stitches in it," I reported.

"Well?"

"Well, what?"

"If it needs stitches, you're gonna have to do it."

"I don't have a suture kit and I ain't no doctor! I don't have anything to numb it with either!" I almost laughed until I realized she was dead serious.

"Get a barbless fishing hook and the lightest, smallest fishing line you got. It'll work. Won't be pretty, but it'll work. There are some needle nose pliers on the workbench in the barn. Gonna need those too. Scissors, don't forget the scissors."

"Rayne! No!"

"You'll defend yourself with a fucking potato, but you get squeamish about sewing up my forehead? C'mon, Shane," she stared at me with her open right eye.

"I can't hurt you like that! I can pull the wound closed with Band-Aids!"

"I'm no stranger to pain, Shane. Go round everything up and sterilize it with some of that cheap vodka we brought home. I'll have this numb by the time you're done doing that," the way she said it, I knew there was no talking her out of it. She removed the rag and put the bag of frozen corn directly on her skin.

With no further argument, I went and got all of the supplies she said I'd need. The hook, fishing line, scissors, and pliers were all thoroughly washed with soap and hot water and then dropped into a bowl of vodka. I set the bowl on the coffee table and then retrieved two clean towels from the hall closet. One was laid out on the table and the tools were laid on top of it. The second towel covered the arm of the couch to soak up any blood.

I washed my hands a second time and then rinsed them with some of the vodka from the plastic jug. I let them air dry until she was ready for me to sew up her forehead. In the meantime, she talked me through how to tie the fishing line to the hook, how to hold the impromptu needle with the pliers, how to tie each knot and the proper effective spacing.

"You ready?" she asked.

"Are you?"

"It's as numb as it's going to get. You'll have to be fairly quick because it won't stay numb for long. Pick up your tools and get ready to go to work. Use one hand to douse it with alcohol and then get after it. Okay?"

"Not okay, but I guess since we're here," I nodded. She removed the bag of frozen corn, and I did everything just as she'd instructed. When I got down to the last three stitches, I could see her gritting her teeth and controlling her breathing to get through the pain.

"Done!" I snipped the line for the last time. Vodka-infused blood had run down the side of her face and into her hair when I rinsed the freshly stitched wound clean. She let out a long, measured breath.

"You got anything for a headache?" at least she smiled when she asked.

"Yeah, I got you," I went into the bathroom and brought back some painkillers. She dry swallowed them and then chased them with a hearty drink from the jug of vodka.

"You did good, Shane. Thank you."

"So, let me get this straight. The mild-mannered, supply chain manager from Carson City knows how to do stitches in an emergency. Please, please, please tell me this has nothing to do with that sack of shit ex-husband of yours. If it does, I'm gonna bring him back from the dead so I can kill him again!"

"Believe it or not, it has nothing to do with him. When I was about 15, my dad took me on a fishing trip to this really remote fishing hole. The fishing was awesome, and he was cleaning one of our catches for dinner. The knife slipped and he cut the shit outta the palm of his hand. We were three hours from anywhere, so he had me sew it up for him. He never did go to the doctor. Just kept it clean and then snipped the stitches out himself when the time came," she smiled at the memory.

"Well, you did say that he was tough! He's probably the reason you're such a tough chick," I grinned and winked at her. She just smiled.

August 21ˢᵗ, 2023.

Before getting comfortable on the couch with Rayne, I finished cleaning up the mess on the kitchen floor. With that task done, I made a quick trip through the shower to get all the blood off of me. This was becoming a habit, it seemed. All clean, again, I slipped into my sweats and T-shirt. I was still hungry, and I knew Rayne was too. Instead of barbeque chicken, I built a fire and cooked the chicken in the oven. After we ate, both of us fell asleep on the couch.

When I awoke this morning, my neck had a monster kink in it from sleeping sitting up. Sometime during the night, Rayne had stretched out and now her legs were lying across my lap. She had pulled the blanket off of the back of the couch to keep herself warm. As much as I wanted to get up and make coffee, I didn't have the heart to disturb her. So, I sat there and tried to rub out the stiffness in my neck until she finally stirred.

"Morning," I said when she opened her eyes. She pulled her arm from under the blanket and touched the bandage on her forehead. She winced from the touch and then looked at me.

"I had the absolute worst dream I've ever had in my life. Except, I guess it wasn't a dream. You stayed out here all night?"

"If me staying out here was the worst dream you've ever had….." I let my voice trail off with a grin.

"No, not that!"

"Oh! Here I was thinking you were trying to offend me," my immediate retort caused her to smile.

"No, the whole psychotic scientist chick. That really happened, right? It wasn't a nightmare?"

"Yeah, that really happened," I scooted out from under her legs and padded barefoot into the kitchen. I couldn't resist the urge to make sure the dead body was still outside. It was.

"Thank you," Rayne called from the couch. She was sitting up now.

"For what?" I started preparing the coffee maker.

"For everything you did last night. Everything. You were so gentle with me!"

"What?" I spun to see her looking over the back of the couch at me. The impish smile on her face was from ear to ear.

"Gotcha!" she stood and used the armrest to steady herself for a moment. "Although, I guess we can't say we've never slept together now!" her grin was bordering on devilish.

68

"Well, I won't tell if you don't," I laughed and hit the button on the coffee maker. She was trying to walk to the bathroom but was having a hard time maneuvering. I came out of the kitchen and got ahold of her arm. I steadied her and helped her get down the hallway. When we got to the bathroom, she used the counter to get to the toilet. I pulled the door closed and waited in the hallway.

"Shane?" she called after the toilet flushed.

"Yeah?" I called back.

"You can open the door. I'm decent."

"Yeah?" I asked again, opening the door slowly.

"I'm going to ask you a question, but I need you to know just how embarrassing this is for me," she was using the countertop to keep herself upright. The pants she'd been wearing were piled on the floor across from the toilet. I quickly averted my eyes so as not to see anything I wasn't supposed to. I'd seen her in her bathing suit at the hot springs, but this was different.

"Okay?"

"I….. Um…... I need to take a shower, but I'm not….. I'm having trouble keeping my balance….."

"You need help?"

"I'm sorry. Yes," her face flushed with embarrassment.

"Rayne, we're friends, right?"

"Yeah."

"If you were shithouse drunk, I'd hold your hair while you puked. You took a helluva blow to the noggin last night and you need me to help hold you up so you can shower. That's all this is. No need to be embarrassed," I stepped past her and turned the hot water on, and pulled the shower curtain all the way open.

Even though I'd told her not to worry about being embarrassed, I had a hard time heeding my own advice. It was definitely awkward. After she stripped down, I helped her into the shower and pulled the curtain as far closed as I could. I had to keep one hand gripped on her upper arm to keep her steady while she washed. When she was done and had turned the water off, I handed her the towel so she could cover herself while I helped her out.

When she was more or less dry, she wrapped the towel around her body, and I helped her to her room and the edge of her bed. At her direction, I retrieved clothes from the different dresser drawers. It took a few minutes, but we finally managed to get her dressed in some sweats.

"I can't believe this shit," she groaned as I helped her into the recliner she'd laid claim to.

"It's all good," I reassured her and went to get two cups of hot coffee.

"Can I ask one more favor?"

"Name it," she took her cup from me, and I started to sit in the other recliner.

"I need the messenger bag out of the truck….."

"No problem," I set my cup on the table and picked up the shotgun. I checked the safety and then went and got the bag. In the daylight, I could see where Rayne's head met the side of the truck. There was a dent in the sheet metal between the doorframe and the back of the cab. She really did get her bell rung hard. "Damn," I ran my fingers over the dent.

After returning to the house, I relocked the front doors and delivered the bag to Rayne. She sipped her coffee and read through the documents. I got pancakes started for breakfast. Whatever she was reading, it must have been interesting. It was holding her attention so well; she allowed her cup of coffee to get cold.

CHAPTER 16

August 21ˢᵗ, 2023.

Rayne nibbled on her breakfast while I took the shotgun and went outside. She was so engrossed in the papers from the messenger bag that she hardly acknowledged my presence. I figured that would be a good time to bury the dead woman in my driveway. After retrieving the wheelbarrow and shovel from the barn, I loaded her into the wheelbarrow and took her down by the meadow.

I started to dig the hole by hand but only made it about six inches before the dirt became too hard for the shovel. That's when I went back to the barn and brought the backhoe down. Within 30 minutes, I had the hole dug, the body placed, and all filled back in. I put the backhoe, shovel, and wheelbarrow away, but didn't feel right about leaving the grave unmarked.

After rambling around the shop area of the barn for another half hour, I fashioned a cross out of pieces of a 2x4. I had no idea what to put on it. The woman had no identification, so I just put the date of death and the manner as a plane crash. Sure, she'd tried mercilessly to kill me, but she'd been someone's sister, daughter, wife, maybe even mother. She deserved a little dignity in her death. She was sick, not evil.

After planting the cross, I toted the shotgun back into the house and washed up in the kitchen. Rayne was still reading intently. So intently, she only looked up once to make sure it was me coming into the house. When I was done cleaning up, I made two tuna sandwiches and took one to her.

"Thanks," she said, still not looking up.

"After lunch, we need to change that bandage on your forehead. Ya got a little blood soaking through the dressing," I pointed at the bandage and then sat in my recliner.

"Uh-huh," she grunted.

"Interesting reading?"

"Huh? What?" she looked over at me.

"Interesting reading?" I repeated the question.

"This is fascinating. Er, terrifying," she closed the thick white three-ring binder and set it on the coffee table.

"Wanna give me the cliff notes version?"

"Yeah, sure. So, the scientists on that plane were all infectious disease types. One of them, the woman, was Army and worked out of Fort Detrick in Maryland. They were all in San Francisco trying to figure out how this thing is spread. That was their main focus, but they were looking at mortality rates and whatnot too. Basically, using the numbers they and other teams like theirs had gathered, they figured that the natural immunity rate is closer to 25%. That's much higher than was originally thought. That's not a bad thing," she stopped long enough to take a bite of her sandwich. After swallowing, she continued.

"Another number that was way off the mark initially was the mortality rate. Ann said it was around 90%. In actuality, it's closer to 70%. Again, that's not a bad thing. The problem is that the number of infected who go mad is much higher than those original estimates."

"The math gets pretty inconsistent and fuzzy when it comes to factoring those poor bastards into the equation. What Ann had right was that it always starts with flu-like symptoms. The time from first symptoms to death is still in the three-day range. Those that die are mainly older and anyone immunocompromised. The hotly debated subject was if this was targeting people who were less than healthy. They were hypothesizing that people like us are immune because we don't have any underlying illnesses."

"Anyway, what these scientists observed in those that got sick and survived was that within five days over half of them developed encephalitis symptoms ranging from mild to severe. Those with severe symptoms are the ones who Ann said went into self-destruct mode. Probably like the one you just buried. Those on the other end of the spectrum are probably more like the cop we encountered."

"The latter is the most dangerous because they can maintain some sort of control. They can drive, carry on a conversation, and act pretty much normal. They lose a lot of their inhibitions and impulse control, saying and doing things that, well, you know. The bad news is that many can, and often do, progress to more severe symptoms. Meaning that if we didn't take that cop out when we did, he'd have eventually turned into what you killed last night. With me so far?" she took another bite.

"What's encephalitis? I've heard of it but I'm not really sure what it is," I asked.

"It's swelling of the brain. So, to put it in the easiest terms to understand, you can think of these people as being rabid. They are in a progressively bad mood as the swelling continues. In a lot of ways, they're like that rabid raccoon. Unlike the trash panda, they can do many of the things they used to do. Once the swelling becomes too great, that's when you get the psychotic scientist chick. At that point, they've lost all control and have nothing but murderous intentions."

"The other un-nerving thing is that there is now empirical evidence where those infected band together into a pack. Some of these packs have been seen numbering close to 100 individuals. From personal experience, one is a handful. Could you imagine having a pack of them coming at you?"

"How's that even possible? If they're losing their minds and attacking everyone, what would cause them to band together?

"They don't know. Plain and simple. What they did see was that the mild cases would run with other mild cases and severe with severe. There were lots of guesses as to why that is, but nothing they could find that would hold water. The other thing they were just beginning to notice was that there was an emerging hierarchy between the two groups. They weren't able to flesh any of that out further because things were getting too hot, and they had to leave in a big hurry."

"What do you mean by hierarchy?"

"Initial signs were pointing to a leadership kind of role for the less severely infected. It's like they were using those more severely infected like foot soldiers."

"How in the hell is that even possible?"

"I don't know any more than what I just told you. They were just beginning to see that sort of behavior before they had to leave," she shrugged her shoulders.

"They still have some intelligence, right? They'd have to, considering all the things they can still do. I heard that part correctly, right?"

"Yeah, you heard that right."

"So, when they form a pack, does that mean they hunt as a pack?"

"Um, they didn't really get into that, but the evidence suggests that they are opportunity hunters….."

"That doesn't fit with what happened yesterday and last night," I said flatly, shaking my head.

"What do you mean?"

"That chick I killed last night, she could have attacked us when we were out searching for her, but she didn't. Why?"

"I don't have an answer for that."

"Maybe it's because we were armed, and we were hunting her. She hid in the back of my truck so she could wait until the odds were in her favor."

"That's crazy talk, Shane!" she almost started to laugh.

"Is it? There was only one female scientist and you said she was Army. The tactics she displayed last night tell me that she was stalking us after we got home. She took you in a surprise attack, an ambush. Why didn't she just snap your neck and be done with it?"

"I'm listening," she took the last bite of her sandwich.

"You were neutralized and no longer a threat. Had she killed me, she probably would have returned to finish you off. I'm tellin' ya, Rayne, she may have been losing her mind, but she remembered enough to keep her attack swift and silent. Now go back to what I first asked you. Do they hunt in packs?"

"I guess it's a real possibility."

"I'd put it out there that, yes, they will take a target of opportunity, but I'd also suggest that they will stalk their prey. Think about it, Rayne. That plane, those people were forced to flee San Francisco under fire. Was it a coordinated attack or was it sheer numbers that forced them to flee? Was it infected people that made them bugout, or was it something else?"

"You bring up some good points," she conceded.

"I'm just asking the questions. We've encountered three of the infected so far and all three displayed some of the same characteristics. The first guy that jumped me did so with an ambush. The cop tried the direct approach, but his intentions were clear. The scientist was, well, you know how that turned out."

"Yeah. Are we still going to call Ann today?" she changed the subject.

"I think we need to wait until tomorrow. Give you a chance to steady up a bit. If not tomorrow, then the next day for sure."

"We really need to get this stuff to her. She might know what to do with it," she pointed to the binder.

"Here's the thing, Rayne. You dented the side of my truck with your head last night. I stitched up your forehead with shit from a tackle box. Both of us slept on the damn couch last night because we were too freaked out to sleep in our own rooms, alone. This morning, I got to see you buck-ass naked because you were too wobbly to take a shower on your own. I buried the body of a woman I killed in my house. Would you be willing to say that it's been a hell of a day?"

"When you put it like that, yeah. I've had about all the vacation I can stand!" she laughed.

"You and me both. Listen, Ann can wait until tomorrow. Whatever is in that binder you got there can wait one more day. Now, if it held the cure or something like that, we'd be on the road right now, but it doesn't."

Rayne spent the afternoon reading more of the CDC binder, even taking notes this time. The wound on her head looked angry, but not in an infected sort of way. Even so, I caked on antibiotic ointment under the clean bandage. I knew it had to hurt, but she never let on to how much pain she was really in. Throughout the day, I still had to assist her down the hallway and into the bathroom. Each time she had a little less difficulty.

Dinner wasn't anything spectacular, just my rendition of spaghetti. We sat in our recliners to eat with a couple of scented candles on the coffee table. Instead of the bottle of wine I'd originally planned on, we settled for soda over ice in a wine glass. All in all, it was a successful mission to make Rayne smile and let her just enjoy the evening. It was a bit weird though. Both of us knew the world we left two weeks ago was gone. We still weren't positive about what replaced it, but we knew it couldn't be anything good. For a few hours though, nothing outside of my cabin existed. It was perfect.

It rapidly became obvious that neither of us wanted to retire to our separate rooms for the night, again. A lot of that was attributed to nothing more than fear. After being attacked in my own home, it was far from an irrational fear. Rayne slept on the couch, and I slept in the recliner closest to her head. The Glock was tucked into the side pouch of the recliner along with the flashlight. Several times through the night I was woken up by the popping sounds of the house cooling, but my mind was positive it was something else entirely.

I felt like I'd stepped up my game today. I never went anywhere outside unarmed. I was paying much closer attention to my surroundings. Doors were getting locked and so were windows. While I hadn't had the opportunity to fire the shotgun yet, Rayne made me empty the tube magazine and do some dry fire practice. She made me unload and reload it dozens of times to build my confidence. She was a good teacher, a patient teacher.

CHAPTER 17

August 22nd, 2023.

I was up long before the sun, or Rayne. Instead of making the mistake of just lying around again, I got up and went into the kitchen to start the coffee pot, The light from the kitchen was bright, but the couch she was sleeping on was in a shadow and it didn't seem to bother her in the least. I saw my phone and picked it up. It was still powered up and plugged in. That's when I had an idea.

I grabbed the binder Rayne had been reading and put it on the counter. Opening it to the very first page, I used the phone's camera to take a picture of it. After 20 or so pages, the coffee was ready, and I poured myself a cup. When I got to page 198, I was notified that my camera roll was full. After a few whispered choice words, I deleted over 100 photos of mostly work-related stuff. I wouldn't need those anymore; I mused as I hit delete.

When I was done photographing the pages, I had to start a new pot of coffee. I scrolled through each photo to make sure the page was clear enough to read. That took another hour. Satisfied that they were all readable, I moved them to one file and then attached that file to a draft email. I reasoned that Ann would want to see the book for herself and this was the best way to make that possible. I also reasoned that if cell phones were still working, her email would be too.

I was thinking about a plan to get to good cell coverage today if Rayne was up to the task. If she was still unsteady on her feet, it would be a non-starter. There was no way I was going to take her anywhere if she couldn't stay on her feet. I was also considering how much fuel my truck had used going to the site of the plane crash and back.

I could have filled it using the diesel we brought home, but that would leave us nothing in reserve. I felt that was a piss poor plan at best, and disastrous at worst. We needed more fuel here at the cabin. There were no two ways about it. What to do about it though? We'd taken all of the fuel cans from Denio Junction. Should we try to go all the way into the town of Denio on a quest to find more? Would the fuel pumps still have power? At some point, the power would fail, right?

The sun was up now, if only barely. I checked on Rayne and she was still sleeping soundly. I slipped my bare feet into my tennis shoes, picked up the Glock and a full cup of coffee then went out the front door. I quietly latched it behind me and then proceeded down the stairs. I stood in the driveway for a few minutes just kinda surveying everything.

Figuring the barn was probably the best place to start my quest, I headed that way. My grandpa was a bit of a packrat. Not in the hoarder sense, but the "I can use this for......" kind of packrat. At the time of his death, he undoubtedly had dozens of projects he was working on, and all the stuff he needed was stored in the barn. I never really dug into any of it, I had always just kind of worked around it.

I wasn't sure what I was looking for. I knew we needed a way to haul more fuel. I also knew we'd need a way to extract that fuel from an underground tank if we had to. I needed to come up with something that could extract fuel from vehicles too. With that in mind, I headed straight to the workbench and the array of toolboxes and parts bins. There were various sizes of hose and copper tubing in neat rolls hanging against the wall above the bench.

It was a roll of copper tubing that drew my attention. I pulled it from the wall and laid it on the bench for further inspection. It had a diameter of about three-quarters of an inch. I sipped my coffee and just stared at the roll before me. It took about five minutes for a plan to begin to take form. I removed a hacksaw from the top of the toolbox and cut off a foot of the material. I cut it at a steep angle on purpose.

I replaced the roll on the wall and went to work on the foot-long section. Using a file, I sharpened the end that I had cut. I tested it several times against an empty plastic oil container. When I had it sharp enough to pass through the container with little force, I placed it on the bench and began phase two of my project.

I needed a pump that would be suitable for diesel fuel, and I remembered seeing one of those old hand crank deals out by the fuel tank that was used to supply the diesel generator. I'd already decided that the 200-gallon tank could fit in the back of my truck, I just needed a way to fill it. I found the hand pump and took it back into the barn. Much to my disappointment, it had gotten water in it at some point. The crank handle was frozen in place with a thick coating of rust.

That had to have been my fault and I was kicking my own ass over it. I was the last one to use it after all. I was about to give up on the thought of using it when I remembered seeing a second one. I knew it was in a cabinet here in the barn or was it on a shelf..... I couldn't remember exactly, so I just started searching everywhere. It took half an hour, but I finally found it tucked away in a steel cabinet.

It wasn't the only thing in there. Right next to it, still in its box and brand new by the looks of it, was a 12-volt diesel transfer pump. Absolutely elated with my find, I took it to the bench and opened it up. Sure enough, it had never been out of the box! I laid everything out on the bench then I headed back to the house to refill my coffee cup. I had a plan in my head, now I just needed to put it all together on the workbench.

"Whatcha got goin on out there?" Rayne asked from the couch. She must have just woken up because her mug was still on the counter.

"I'm working on a fuel transfer system," I filled both mugs and took her one.

"For?"

"I was going over it this morning and we're going to need more fuel. We used quite a bit making the run to the crash site and we don't have much in the way of reserves," I sat in my recliner.

"Good thinking. Are we still going to try and get ahold of Ann today?"

"If you're up to it. I had some ideas there too."

"Do tell," she sat up slowly.

"I took pictures of every page in that binder of yours and then I attached them to an email to send to her. You just know she's gonna want to see it for herself."

"Boy, you're on the ball this morning," she chuckled.

"I think it's all just starting to really hit me. Reality is setting in," I said seriously.

"What?"

"The whole end of the world thing. Even if this isn't it, it's made me realize that we're on our own out here. All the things we've seen and done over the past couple of days..... Nobody is coming to help," I looked over at her and she was looking back at me over the top of her coffee mug. It looked as if she'd paused mid-sip. I decided to continue.

"The run to the store in Denio Junction was a good step. It gave us some food security. Eventually, we're going to need more. We've got some decent firepower, but we're going to need more. We've got gasoline and diesel, again, we're going to need more. As much as I'd like to just hunker down here for the duration, we can't. We're gonna have to poke our heads out to make supply runs if we plan on surviving this thing. We have to take steps to ensure we can ride it out for as long as we need to. No matter how long that is," I finished. She seemed to contemplate that for a few moments.

"You're right," she finally spoke. I nodded.

"We still need to get that email sent to Ann, but I don't want to just willy-nilly drive somewhere to send it. We need to combine that with a supply run. We did a good job of cleaning out the store, but we need to strip the entire place clean. The motel, the RV park, and we need to see if my fuel transfer system will work. Depending on how well we do in Denio Junction, we need to consider a run to Denio itself. I think that the more supplies we can lay in now, the better off we'll be."

"Long-term stuff, that's what you're thinking, right?"

"Exactly. We also need to figure out how to communicate with the outside world. Even if cell phones are still working, how long will that last? We're going to need more firewood if we're going to stay warm this winter. There are just so many things we need to think about, and it all came at me like a runaway freight train this morning."

"One bite at a time, Shane," she set her mug down and picked up the pen and paper from the coffee table.

"What?"

"It's how you eat an elephant. One bite at a time," her grin was nice to see. "Since you have projects you're working on already, and since I'm not going to be of much help out there, why don't I start writing down all the things you're talking about? That way, when we go back to civilization, we can have a plan."

"Sounds good. You're the organizer between the two of us," I rose from the comfortable recliner and picked up her mug. I refilled both of them, returned hers, and then went back to the barn.

By noon, I had the fuel tank loaded into the bed of my truck and strapped down. Working smarter and not harder, I used the backhoe to lift it and set it down in the bed. I probably could have manhandled it, but why? When Rayne and I ate lunch, she went over the list she was compiling with some additions of her own. Stuff I didn't even think of like winter coats and long johns. Battery chargers for the house solar system and a backup generator to run them on cloudy days. It was that stuff that could make all the difference.

After lunch, I attacked the pump project with renewed energy. It took a few hours, but what I finally came up with should do the trick right nicely. The copper tubing that I'd sharpened to a point on one end was fitted inside a 20-foot-long piece of rubber hose. The other end was affixed to the new pump. In the same cabinet where I'd found the pump was a new nozzle that fit on the discharge side of the pump. It was about 10 feet long. I cut up an old extension cord to use for the power leads and I left those about 20 feet long. With alligator clips on the end going to the battery, it was quick and easy to get power to the pump.

To test it, I stuck the intake hose into a five-gallon can and pumped the fuel into my truck. It worked flawlessly. I'd never been accused of being the handiest person around, but I was pretty impressed with my work. All of that was put in the bed of the truck for our supply run. I also emptied as many of the diesel cans as I could. The backhoe was full and so was my truck.

CHAPTER 18

August 23rd, 2023.

Pulling up to the pumps at Denio Junction, I knew right away we were gonna have to work for the fuel we needed. All of the screens on the pumps had gone dark sometime since our last visit four days ago. Rayne stayed in the running truck while I located the cover for the underground tank filler neck. Once it was located, I moved the truck right next to it.

Rayne was feeling better today. The episodes of vertigo seemed to have passed. That was the single deciding factor for making this run today. She kept watch with her AR-15, while I hooked everything up. There was a padlock on the filler neck, but I'd anticipated that and brought the big pair of bolt cutters for just such a problem. I dropped the copper probe and the suction line down the hole until I could feel it touch the bottom of the tank.

The discharge handle was stuck in the filler neck of the tank in the back of my truck with the handle locked open. I had brought the battery out of the Ford because I didn't want to risk draining the ones in my truck. As soon as I connected the leads, the pump kicked on and I heard the pitch of the motor change when it started pulling fuel up the line.

"Nice!" Rayne said with a wink.

"Yeah. Not bad if I say so myself," I grinned and winked back. I dropped the tailgate and climbed into the bed. After I'd unscrewed the tops for the eight five-gallon cans, I used the nozzle to fill them. It would take a few minutes to fill the two-hundred-gallon tank and I wanted the smaller cans full first. Just in case we were forced to make a hasty departure.

"What else is left in the store?" I asked sitting on the bed rail.

"There's not much left in there. I think it's stuff like baseball caps, T-shirts, and some junk jewelry. We cleaned 'em out pretty hard," her eyes were scanning our surroundings.

"Start with the RV park?"

"Yeah, after we make the call to Ann."

It took a total of 25 minutes to fill the tank and another five to stow everything safely. The last thing I needed was the battery shorting out on something and lighting my truck on fire. We pulled away from the building into a wide-open parking area, probably for semi-trucks that came down this way. I left my phone hooked up to the Bluetooth in the truck so that both of us could talk to and hear Ann.

"Ann," she answered after the second attempt. The first had gone to a full voicemail box.

"Ann. It's me and Rayne. Are you doing okay? You sound kinda tired?" I asked.

"It's good to hear from you!" she didn't answer my question.

"Ann, Rayne here. Listen, we've had some developments here and I think you might be able to help us. You got a few minutes to talk?" she got right down to business.

"What kind of developments?"

"A couple of days ago, a plane crash-landed on a highway not too far from the cabin. It was a CDC charter coming out of San Francisco, headed to Atlanta. The short version is that we have a messenger bag with a binder that someone needs to see," Rayne explained quickly.

"Ann, I just sent you an email with photos of everything," I interjected as I tapped the send button on my draft email. "It's gonna take a minute to send, it's a damn big file."

"Guys, I wish I were in a position to help, but things went to hell here yesterday. Lilly and I are in the car trying to get farther into the woods."

"Can you get to Baxter State Park?" I asked suddenly alarmed for my friend's safety.

"That's where we're headed. You thinking of the abandoned campground?"

"That's exactly what I was thinking. You won't have any cell service up there though!"

"I know, but hopefully it's remote enough that we won't be found again. Okay, I got your email. I'm going to forward it to a colleague in Atlanta."

"Thanks! We didn't know who else to send it to," Rayne said from her seat.

"Okay, it's sent," she said after a brief pause. "I attached your email and phone number in case he has any questions."

"Okay."

"Shane, Rayne, this thing is a whole lot worse than I originally thought."

"We know," Rayne answered for the both of us.

"I'm gonna lose service any second now. You guys stay safe."

"You too, Ann!" I answered.

"Rayne, you still there?" she asked.

"Yes, Ann."

"I don't know you, but if Shane trust's you, that's good enough for me. Take care of him, please. Shane?"

"Yeah?"

"From everything I've heard about her over the past couple of months, it sounds like you finally found a good one, buddy. Take care of....." the phone cut out.

"A lot of history there?" Rayne asked after a few seconds of silence.

"A lot."

"She sounds like a cool chick. You'll have to tell me about her sometime."

"Yeah," I put the truck in gear and headed for the RV park behind the store.

"Mmmm hmmm," Rayne smiled a genuine smile. "Take us all the way to the back where the cop car is. That way we're pointed in the right direction in case we gotta book outta here."

When we got to the cop car, both of us realized that things had changed since the last time we were there. Rayne had closed the doors and trunk of the cruiser, but now they were all wide open with stuff laying on the ground all around it. Someone else had been here. I slowed the truck to about 5 miles per hour and I heard Rayne slip the safety off on the AR-15.

"There were two travel trailers down there the other day," I pointed to the lone truck and trailer remaining.

"Yeah. Pull up in front of the truck. I want to check it out."

"Okay," I turned the wheel of the truck and we idled to a stop right in front of where the newer F350 was still hooked to the 5th-wheel trailer.

I left the truck running but made sure the key fob was in my pocket. It would stop the truck from leaving without us once I was outside of it. I always thought it was a cool security feature, but now it was downright handy. Both of us got out of the truck at the same time. I had my shotgun; Rayne had her AR pointed in the direction she was traveling.

At the door to the RV, she reached out, pounded on it with her fist, and backed a few feet away. She repeated this twice more with no response coming from the inside. On her next approach to the door, she reached up and tried the door handle. At first, I thought it was locked, but she jiggled the handle and it finally swung open. Her startled scream and sudden movement caused my shotgun to rise in the direction of trouble.

She jumped backward and backpedaled a few more steps. Both of us nearly shot the very dead corpse that fell down the stairs, landing in a heap on the ground. I was far enough back that I didn't get the full effects of the body being closed up in an RV in the late August heat. Rayne took the brunt of that. She took a few more steps away from the corpse and the cloud of flies that had emerged from the doorway. I could see her gagging at the smell.

"Damnit!" she choked. "Fuck that! There ain't nothing in there worth that!" she was still gagging and backing away. As awful as the whole scene was, I was fighting the urge to laugh.

"There might be something worth the trip inside....." I moved back to the crew-cab 4x4 truck hooked to the trailer. The doors were unlocked, and I leaned in looking for the keys.

"What are you doing?"

"I'm looking for the keys. They're not here," I closed the door of the truck and looked at the open door of the trailer.

"You don't want to….." she started but I was already moving. I huffed and puffed a few times before drawing in the deepest breath I could. I ran up the stairs into the cloud of flies. I quickly scanned the countertops but didn't see the keys. When my breath was running out, I turned and saw them hanging on a hook next to the door. Snatching them off the hook, I ran back down the stairs. When I drew in a deep breath, I quickly realized I wasn't far enough from the body. The smell of decomposing flesh filled my lungs, and I was the one coughing and gagging.

"Serves ya right!" Rayne laughed. I couldn't answer but I held up the keys to signal my victory.

To our surprise, the big Ford diesel lit right off. There was no telling how long it had been sitting there, but it acted like it had been started that morning. We were also happy to find the fuel needle solidly past the full mark. It wasn't hard to figure out how to unhook it from the trailer and within five minutes we had it pulled up next to my rig.

"Happy birthday," I said to Rayne as I opened the door and got out. She shot me a skeptical look. "Best I could do," I grinned and motioned her toward the open door.

"Thank you. I'm surprised you remembered," she smiled and climbed in.

"Where to now? Denio?"

"I'm thinking that we should clear the motel and give the store a once over just to make sure we didn't miss anything."

"Works for me," I pushed her door shut and got in my truck.

The motel wasn't that big. Ten rooms plus the office and laundry room. When we made our search, one of us would stay in the doorway while the other entered the room. It was a safety thing. Rayne loaded the backseat of her new truck with heavy blankets, sheets, pillows, and pillowcases from the laundry room. We had a washer and dryer at the cabin, but it was one of those stacked apartment kinds. It could take forever to wash and dry anything other than light loads of clothes. The heavy blankets would be needed come winter because I had none. She also took all of the detergent, small bars of soap, and small bottles of shampoo. Those were brought out by the case and put in the bed of her rig.

Thinking ahead this morning, she had packed us a lunch of leftover spaghetti from last night, and a couple of sodas. We'd been drinking plenty of water, so a cold soda wouldn't hurt either of us. We were both sitting in the cab of my truck eating when my phone rang. The now foreign sound caused both of us to jump.

"Shane O'Neal," I answered and flipped it over to the speaker.

"Mr. O'Neal, we share a common friend. She forwarded me an email from you this morning. Do you know what I'm talking about?" the man's voice burst from the speakers.

"Yeah, I do. Who is this?"

"Tell me, who is our mutual friend?"

"Ann. Who the hell is this?"

"My apologies Mr. O'Neal. I had to make sure I had the right person. My name is Roger McDonald, I'm with the CDC in Atlanta. Ann put your information in the email she sent me, and I can't get ahold of her, so I thought I might call you."

"Okay?"

"If I have this right, am I to understand you are in possession of critical documents that were on their way to us here in Atlanta?"

"Yeah. I photographed everything and attached it to the email."

"There was nothing else in the bag?"

"No, it was just the binder," I glanced at Rayne to see her looking at the phone with a scowl.

"I see. Would you mind telling me how you came to be in possession of these documents? I'm sure you already know this, but the plane that was carrying the documents and my coworkers is very overdue," I wasn't sure if I liked the insinuation he was making. Rayne reached over and tapped the mute button for the microphone.

"This isn't right," she said.

"What?"

"Not one question about his coworkers, the plane, or anything else. He's trying to find out where we are. You can't tell him!" I stared at her trying to figure out her angle when Roger spoke again.

"Mr. O'Neal? Why don't you tell me where you are so I can send some people to gather the original documents?" she looked at me with her right eyebrow raised. I tapped the screen to unmute the call.

"I'm not comfortable giving out that information, Mr. McDonald. You have pictures of all the information I had. That should be all you need."

"Come now, Shane. I just need to know where you are. Are you with Ann? I doubt that because your phone number has a 702 prefix. If I remember right, that's a Southern Nevada number. Just tell me where you are."

"As I said, Roger, I'm not going to tell you that. I did my part and passed on the information. You have everything I have."

"Have you been sick, Mr. O'Neal?" his voice had a subtle change as he tried a different tactic.

"Nope. I'm fine."

"All the more reason to give me your location. We are actively looking for survivors to bring to safety."

"Like I said, dude. I'm fine and don't need help. Unless you have a real question for me, I'm gonna hang up."

84

"Listen here, punk! Tell me where the fuck you are!" Roger blurted out, shocking both of us.

"Why don't you ask your mom, fucker!" as I reached to end the call, I could hear him screaming profanities into the phone. I looked at Rayne. "How'd you know?"

"That he was infected?"

"Yeah!"

"Paranoia is a big giveaway and one of the first signs."

"Why so much concern about where we are?"

"He was probably hoping you were close by."

"Why?"

"He was hunting. He was trying to lure you in."

"You can't be sure of that."

"You heard his outburst at the end."

"Yeah, but still."

"He was hunting, Shane."

CHAPTER 19

After the phone call, we finished our lunch and made one last pass through the store. We just wanted to make sure we got everything of use before we left. Neither of us wanted to go in the store though. There were two dead bodies in there that had to be pretty ripe by now. They'd been there for four days, and God only knew how long the power had been off. With no air conditioner keeping the place at a well-regulated temperature, we were sure to be greeted with something like what was in the trailer.

After deciding that I'd be the one to go in while Rayne watched the trucks, both of us peered through the glass of the front doors. Both bodies were in the same places where we'd left them. The only difference was that the cop's body was now lying face down. We'd left him lying on his back. His right pant leg was pulled up to reveal an empty ankle holster and his grossly engorged calf.

"I didn't even think to check if he had a backup piece….." Rayne muttered and looked around.

"Me neither."

"I guess there was a lot going on at the time. Just make a quick check and then get your ass back out here. Okay?"

"Trust me, I won't be loitering," I pushed the safety of the shotgun off. I filled my lungs with as much air as they could hold and moved through the door.

Before the door had even begun to swing shut behind me, the shotgun was up and pointing everywhere I was looking. I gave the large puddle around the cop a wide berth and moved deeper into the store like I had a purpose. By the time I reached the diner, I needed a breath. Using my free hand, I bunched up a handful of my T-shirt, pulled it over my mouth and nose, and exhaled the spent breath. I was worried about what smells would come when I drew in that first deep breath, so I held off as long as I could.

The wadded-up T-shirt fabric helped, but barely. It took everything I had to keep from gagging. The shock of that first breath was the worst. Once I was past that and in full control, I took a few more panting breaths and then continued my search. Arriving at the bar, I found more evidence that someone had been there since we had been.

On the bar was a pile of bloody rags that used to be Denio Junction T-shirts. One of the half-empty bottles of whisky we'd left behind was now empty and lying on the bar. The smell wasn't as bad back here, or maybe I was just getting used to it, so I repeated the same process I'd used in the diner. Lungs full again, I moved through the closed door into the dark storeroom.

I pulled the flashlight out of my back pocket and let its beam guide me. There was yet more evidence back here. In between a short set of shelving units was an unrolled, bloody sleeping bag on the concrete along with another empty whisky bottle. Back here, fairly removed from the carnage of the main store, I should have been able to take in a decent lung full of air. The smell back here proved to be the worst yet. The deep inhalation I was planning on caught in my throat and ended up being more of a gasp and gag combined.

I didn't have a free hand to cover my face with, so I had to force the rank air into my lungs. I spun and headed for the door into the store but stopped in my tracks. My flashlight beam fell on the wall separating this room from the other and it was covered in blood. Most of it was nearly black but the pools on the floor were still holding their crimson color. In a state of near panic, I shone the beam around the section I hadn't been able to see before now.

That's when the choking and gagging became uncontrollable. There were three men tied to the shelving units with their own entrails. Their severed heads stared blankly at me with empty eyes from the shelves next to their eviscerated bodies. They had been stripped naked and I don't think there was anywhere that their flesh hadn't been touched by a knife. The blood at the feet of the closest one was still bright red. I saw it still dripping into the pool below the body. That's when I saw the pair of bloody footprints leading out the back door. One set was bare feet, the second wore tennis shoes. I did the only sensible thing. I ran!

I burst through the door of the storeroom and nearly tripped over the bloated body of the guy who tried to choke me out. I stayed on my feet and jumped completely over the body of the cop. When I hit the front door, I saw Rayne standing about halfway across the parking lot, maybe 50 feet from me. She had her rifle pointed at a man who was covered in blood and holding an equally bloody machete.

"STOP RIGHT THERE!" I heard her yell through the fog of my thoughts. I didn't stop running once I was out of the store. In a scant few seconds, I covered the ground between me and her. She yelled her warning at the advancing man again as I came alongside her. She took her eyes off the target for a millisecond to look at me. That's when he let out the howl of a banshee, raised his machete, and broke into a run.

Before Rayne could reacquire the target, I let loose with a round from the shotgun. The hit from the double-aught buck staggered him, but he didn't go down. Rayne fired twice with the AR before he went to his knees, dropping the weapon in his hand. With another shell racked into place, I started walking toward the still-howling man. Rayne followed me. I could hear her saying something but couldn't make it out through the ringing in my ears. With the end of my barrel less than five feet from his face, I pulled the trigger. The explosion of pink mist, bone fragments, and brains sprayed across the parking lot.

"WHAT THE FUCK WAS THAT?" she screamed and grabbed my shoulder and spun me to face her.

My eyes didn't settle on her though. I caught the blur of movement coming around the corner at the far side of the store. I brought the shotgun to bear and shoved Rayne out of the way, hard. As she hit the ground, I let the big gun buck again. Racking the fourth round, I leveled it and fired. That one caught the woman who was running at us from behind in the legs and sent her tumbling into the dirt. I racked the fifth round, closed to within ten feet of the shrieking woman, and pulled the trigger again. Half of her head vanished.

I half turned to look at Rayne. She was just starting to get to her feet. I cleared the spent shell from the chamber and racked in number seven as I walked toward her. I couldn't tell if she was pissed or what, but I apologized for basically throwing her out of the way.

"Sorry," my voice sounded more like it was in my head instead of coming out of my mouth. The six booms of the shotgun and two loud pops of the AR had seriously impaired my sense of hearing.

"Don't be," she dusted off her jeans. I bent down and picked up her ball cap and sunglasses. "How'd you know there were two of them?" she asked. I told her about what I'd found in the storeroom and her eyes went wide.

"I don't know about you, but I think I've had enough of the big city for today," I tried to smile when I said it. I felt like it came off pretty weak. My hands were shaking now and so were my knees.

"I think I agree," she reached over and took my trembling hand in hers. "You did good, Shane. Take a few minutes to sit down and drink some water. This will pass," she squeezed my hand and led me toward my truck. Once I was seated on the tailgate and had downed half a bottle of water, she spoke again.

"I guess if there was ever any doubt, there isn't anymore."

"Doubt about what?" I asked.

"They do hunt, and they are capable of coordinating that hunt with others."

"Yeah."

"If I didn't already say it, thank you," she picked up my shotgun and began reloading it from a box of shells she'd gotten out of the backseat of my truck.

"It wasn't quite as cool as you jumping in with a frying pan and cleaning their clocks, but I didn't do too bad if I say so myself," I grinned. The massive levels of adrenaline had left my system in torrents and my hands were no longer shaking. Now, I was just tired.

"You did well my friend. You did good," she patted my knee and laid the reloaded shotgun on the tailgate.

After a short, serious discussion, we decided that there was nothing left to find in Denio Junction. It was getting on in the day and a trip anywhere other than home was out of the question. We'd found another truck, some linens, and some toiletries. We'd been able to gather enough fuel to stave off any diesel fuel issues for a while. Now, both of us were just ready to be done and head back to the cabin.

I led the way with Rayne following closely behind. I knew she was busy watching behind us for any signs that we might have been followed. I was busy scanning the road ahead of us for signs of trouble. We did have to slow down and take the shoulder of the road when we passed the site of the plane crash, but everything else was smooth sailing. Well, it was until we reached the turnoff with the first gate.

I'd pulled the nose of the Dodge close to the gate so Rayne would have enough room behind me to get off of the two-lane highway. I kinda laughed at myself because I was still thinking about the possibility of her causing a traffic jam. In the middle of nowhere. In the friggin apocalypse. She had parked on the shoulder and was waiting for me to open the gate. I was about to climb out and do just that when the phone rang.

"Shane! Thank God you answered! I've been trying to get ahold of you all morning!" Ann sounded distant and slightly garbled through the cell connection.

"What's going on? Everything okay?"

"I got a shitty connection, so if I lose you, sit still and I'll try calling back! I've got some new information you need to be aware of!"

"What is it?" I asked as Rayne walked up to my window. I motioned her to get in on the passenger side.

"I've been able to get in touch with a couple of my colleagues at the CDC. They are telling me they've started to figure out what's happening with these people. Apparently, in the most severe cases, their bodies are losing all of the vital nutrients keeping a normal human being….." her voice got really garbled for a moment. "Combined with the brain swelling….." the speaker went silent.

"Ann! I lost you! Can you repeat that?" I looked at the display and could see that we were still connected.

"…..Swelling. It's causing them to ….. damaged or destroyed amygdala….."

"ANN!" I glanced over at Rayne and could see the frustration on her face too.

"Is this any better?" Ann asked.

"Slightly, I lost you after something about swelling."

"All of the infected are losing the nutrients needed to keep their bodies running normally. In most cases, or the first tier, they succumb after just a handful of days….." She started breaking up again. "…..most violent and most prone to eating anything with red meat….. including….. think it might be an attempt to recover the loss of essential….." the line went dead again. This time it completely disconnected.

Glancing at the display, I could see that I didn't have any service bars on my phone. I backed away from the gate and pointed us back to where I knew I could get reception. It was only a half mile of backtracking before the phone started ringing again. Rayne connected the call as I pulled to the shoulder.

"Can you hear me?" Ann's voice crackled.

"We got you. We're pulled over at a decent spot, so hopefully that doesn't happen again. It's still not a great connection though," I answered.

"Okay. Anyway, it's the second and third tiers you need to be concerned with. Those in the second tier exhibit the most violent tendencies. Fortunately, it also seems as though they also have the shortest lifespan. There's a long story behind that, but we don't have time for it now….." she started breaking up again.

"I'm losing you. Ann!"

"….. Third tier. Trust me when I say it's bad! They retain enough control to be able to do anything you and I can do….. Lifespans are much longer and there hasn't been enough time to determine just how long that might be. As long….. Maintain their food intake….. Cats, dogs, cows, and even….. Generally going after the vital organs after they beat it to death."

"You're still cutting out, Ann."

"….. Elevated adrenal….. is off the charts in some cases….. actually breaking their own bones due to over-exertion….. like a case of tetanus, but that's not what this is. Like I said, tier two is bad, but it's even worse in tier th….." the line went dead again.

"Damnit!" I hit the redial button. It rang once and went to an automated message.

"We're sorry. All lines are currently unavailable. Please try your call again at a later time," as we sat on the side of the road, I tried to call Ann four more times only to get the automated message.

"What now?" Rayne asked.

"Let's give her a few minutes to call back," I suggested. Thirty-three minutes later the phone rang. Rayne beat me to the connect tab on the screen.

"Shane?" Ann began again.

"Yeah, we're here."

"I don't know how much longer the cell signals are gonna hold out, so I'll try and keep this short….." she started breaking up again. "Medical diagnosis has been all over the place. As bad as the tier twos are, it's the tier threes you….. about. They pos….. symptoms of t….. and the ability to reason. They….. think and bargain like you and I c….. stuff in the binder you….. kinda like a guide….. obsolete now…... away from population centers and stay…..."

"I know there's not a lot of time, Ann. I gotta know though; is this natural or manmade?" Rayne asked from the passenger seat.

"….. initiator virus appears naturally occurring. It's something in the….. acting with. Nobody….. predicted this….. perfect storm scenario….. enough test….. otherwise."

"I didn't get all of that," Rayne leaned closer to the display as if that would help reception. There was no response from Ann.

"Ann?" I called and looked at the screen. Where the bars for cell reception should have been, there was only a red X. "We lost her again."

We spent another hour driving up and down the road trying to find a cell signal. Our efforts were all fruitless. After a lot of debate back and forth, Rayne and I decided to continue on with our day. Neither of us could piece together the warning Ann was trying to relay to us. We knew there was a warning in that garbled mess called cell calls, we just couldn't put together how dire it might have been.

I drove us back to the gate and put the truck in park. Rayne climbed out and walked back to her new truck. I also got out and I went to put the key into the lock on the chain holding the gate closed. Both were lying on the ground next to the post. The chain had been cut.

I stepped to the side so Rayne could see me and waved for her to come back over. Looking at the tracks in the dirt on the other side of the gate, I figured that at least two vehicles had passed through. One of them had rear dual street tires. Rayne joined me looking concerned. The concern grew when I pointed to the cut chain and then the tire tracks.

"We're not expecting any company, are we?" she asked and scanned our surroundings for trouble.

"No, we're not. This doesn't mean we're gonna have visitors though. A lot of folks around these parts know this is a shortcut over to the BLM road. That could be where these folks were headed," I tried to reason. For some reason, I doubted my own words even as I said them. Judging by the look she gave me; she wasn't convinced either.

I picked up the lock and chain. I unlocked the lock and handed both over. There was still enough chain to relock the gate after we passed through. When we started moving again, it was slow going. Being in the lead, I was the one tracking the vehicles that had made their way down this road. I felt my heart sink just a little when I saw that they had turned in the same direction we were going.

It was hard to keep an eye on the tracks as we traveled the BLM road. It was hardpacked and washboard as hell. When we rounded the last corner and the gate to my property came into view, I planted my foot on the brakes and slid to a stop. The full tank of diesel in the back made me slide just a little farther. The gate to my property was wide open and the tracks we'd been following led down the road to my home.

CHAPTER 20

August 23rd, 2023.

"What do we do?" Rayne asked. Both of us were standing by the open gate looking at the tracks.

"C'mon. We're gonna take the trucks up to the pond and walk in. I don't want to drive right into the middle of whatever the hell this is," I motioned her back to her truck and I climbed into mine. When I dropped it into gear and stepped on the gas, I did it a little harder than I'd intended, causing the rear wheels to spin a little. I was pissed about this new development!

Whoever this was seemed to know exactly where they were going, and I think that's the part that bothered me the most. I was racking my brain trying to figure out who this could be. My grandpa's lawyer passed away like five years ago. Nobody that I worked with knew the location of the cabin. Hell, even my own family didn't know. They could never be bothered to come to see the place.

The pond wasn't really a pond. It was a small lake that the county called a reservoir. Still, all the locals who knew of its existence called it a pond. The boat ramp with its small parking lot was where I chose to leave the trucks. They were pretty well hidden by the small grove of aspen trees separating the BLM road and the parking lot. This was also the same place Rayne and I had done all of our fishing.

While you couldn't see the cabin from the pond, it was an easy hour's walk to get there. When we left the trucks, I had my Colt tucked into the back of my pants and the shotgun. Rayne had her vest on with the Glock and the AR. We jogged the hardly visible trail until we reached the last hill before the cabin would become visible.

There was a lot of cover-up here with the large rock outcroppings and pinyon-juniper trees. We got off the trail and moved slowly until we had a decent vantage point. From where we were crouching behind some jagged rocks, it was close to 800 yards to the cabin. My breath caught in my throat and anger boiled inside of me at the sight of the large RV and small SUV parked in my driveway. While I couldn't make out many details, I could see four figures moving about.

"Looks like two men and two women," Rayne said looking through the optic of her rifle.

"What are they doing?"

"Eh, it looks like they're unloading stuff from the vehicles."

"What? If they think they're moving in, they got another thing coming!" I growled.

"It definitely looks like they're moving in. They're taking suitcases and stuff inside."

"Do you see any weapons?"

"Ummm," she paused for a few seconds. "It looks like one of the guys has a deer rifle slung on his shoulder. It's too far to make anything else out. You locked up before we left, right?"

"Yeah, I did. Makes me wonder how they got in the house seeing as how they cut the gate locks," I grumbled.

"So, what are we going to do?"

"It's just about dark. I think we should move up around the back side of the house and go down there after the sun sets. Find out just who the hell these people think they are."

Over the course of the next hour, we slinked our way into a position much closer to the backside of the cabin. We'd managed to cut the distance in half, but we'd also lost sight of the vehicles and people who were going in and out of the front door. Neither of us could see the blinds or curtains on the backside of the house move and nobody had come out the backdoor.

With no signs of movement, we took our time inching our way closer. When the sun was finally below the horizon, we got close enough that we could hear voices from inside the house. We couldn't make out what they were saying, but we could hear two men and two women. The kitchen window on the south side of the house was open and I could smell meat cooking. Bacon to be exact.

Rayne and I were staged on either side of the steps leading up to the back porch once it was fully dark. I passed my flashlight to her since she could operate the AR with one hand and hold it with the other. It was one of those advantages over the shotgun I was carrying. I led the way up the stairs with the door key in hand. She moved to the knob side of the door, and I was opposite of her.

Holding all of the loose keys in the palm of my hand, I slipped the door key in and twisted it slowly. Feeling the lock disengage, I turned it back and removed it from the lock. Not wanting them to jingle and give us away, I silently slipped them into my pocket. Rayne held up three fingers and started the countdown. When the last finger fell, I reached across the door and twisted the knob.

Gently pushing it open, Rayne moved inside. We could hear the voices much clearer now. With Rayne on one side of the hall and me on the other, we moved in unison toward the front room. She hadn't turned the flashlight on and wouldn't unless it became needed. I could hear her straining to listen to the four voices emanating from the kitchen. At least we knew they were all in one place. Arriving at the end of the hallway, we still didn't have a visual of our unwanted guests.

"Cheers everybody! We made it!" a man's voice boomed from the kitchen and either glasses or bottles clanked. Probably bottles I thought. Rayne picked that particular moment to step into the clear. Her AR was leveled at the intruders, finger hovering over the trigger. I stepped out and stood next to her with the huge bore of the shotgun pointed toward the kitchen. Pretty close to 15 seconds passed before our presence was announced by one of the women screaming and dropping her beer.

"NOBODY MOVE!" I shouted.

"WHOA!" both men said in unison and shot their hands into the air. The pair of terrified women assumed the same posture.

"Who the fuck are you people?" I questioned.

"Janice?" I heard Rayne say from next to me, her rifle barrel dropped slightly.

"Rayne? Is it really you?" the woman who'd dropped her beer asked in a shocked tone. She started to step forward.

"NOBODY MOVE!" I shouted again. "Rayne? Would you care to explain this?" I glanced over at her. Her face was a mask of disbelief.

"Who are they?" Rayne ignored my question and asked Janice one of her own.

"This is Chase, my boyfriend. That's his brother, Kyle, and his girlfriend, Angie," Janice answered with her hands still in the air and her voice shaky.

"I've known Janice since I was eight," Rayne's voice was much lower, and I was struggling to hear her. "She's been my best friend for just about ever. She's the one I gave the coordinates to."

"What coordinates? Oh….." It didn't take me but a second to catch up. When Rayne and I were planning this trip, I'd given her the GPS coordinates of the cabin as a safety thing for her. I told her to share them with a trusted friend. Apparently, she'd done just that.

"Um, can I move the pan of bacon off the heat?" Chase asked.

"Nice and slow," I answered. After he slid the pan over he raised both hands again. "Well, Rayne, what are we doing here?" I looked at her again. She lowered her rifle a little more before she spoke.

"Jan, come with me. We need to talk in private," Rayne motioned her forward. The pair then went down the hallway. I could hear murmurs of their conversation.

"Any of you been sick?" I asked the remaining trio. All three shook their heads and answered with no's.

"Full disclosure, man," Chase started. "When we left Portland, there were eight of us. One by one, the other four got sick. Carla, Monte, and Brian all died within three days. Bruce got sick, and we thought he was going to be okay. Kyle had to put him down after he flipped out and went after the girls," he nodded at his brother.

"When did this happen?"

"Like ten days ago, man. The rest of us have been fine."

"So, you thought you could just waltz in here, cut the locks on the gates and eat my food?" I could feel the anger rising again.

"It wasn't like that, man. We were trying to find someplace secluded. You know, away from all the crazy shit happening in the cities. Janice remembered this place, so we came here. Didn't really have any other options."

"There's a lot of....." I started but Rayne and Janice came back into the room.

"Can we talk?" Rayne whispered in my ear. "In private?" I looked at her and back to the four people standing in my kitchen.

"Just stand there. Don't even pick your noses," I growled and followed Rayne down the hall.

"I'm sorry, Shane. I just gave her the coordinates because she's been my friend forever."

"I'm not even pissed about that! I'm pissed because they just showed up here! They're in there cooking my food, drinking my beer, and acting like they own the damn place! I'll also tell you that if they think they're sleeping under my roof, well, it ain't gonna happen!"

"You're right. They have the RV, and they can stay in....."

"Who in the hell said they were staying?" I barked. "Rayne, I'm not trying to be an asshole, but it's a fucking numbers game. We have provisions to last the two of us for a decent amount of time. If we add four mouths to that, we're fucked. I seem to recall that you've been with me each time we've made a supply run to a one-horse town and it's ended in a shitshow each time."

"They have their own provisions," she put her hand on my arm to try and diffuse the situation a little.

"Just how long is that going to last? How long until we have to make a run into a bigger city just to find enough to make it a few more days?" I lowered my voice a little. "Besides, how do we know we can trust them? Sure, you've known Janice a long time, but the other three?" I asked. She let out a long, even breath before she spoke.

"Shane, I understand that it's your house and it's your rules. That is and will remain the number one thing with me. If you say they have to go, I will respect your wishes and ask them to move along. I ask only that you consider what's at stake before you make your final decision. Okay?" she asked. I held my tongue but nodded for her to continue.

"Kyle and Chase are both avid hunters. They bagged an antelope yesterday and have a fridge full of its meat. Those two have been responsible for keeping the others fed when the food they had ran out. When I say they are avid hunters, they make a living from guided hunts all over the US and Alaska. That's how they made their living."

"Angie is an experienced paramedic with ten years riding an ambulance. An ambulance she cleaned out before they left Portland. You and I can do stitches in a pinch, but she has the tools, medications, and training to do it proficiently. Her skills are something we could really use around here."

"What about Janice? Any special skills we can use?" I asked. She took another pensive breath and let it out.

"When I say that she's been my best, most loyal friend, that doesn't even come close to describing what she's done for me, Shane. I told you what I did to Rick, right?"

"Yeah."

"There's only one other person on the planet that knew that secret. She's the one who helped me dispose of him and his car. That's the kind of friend she is."

CHAPTER 21

August 23rd, 2023.

"Rayne….." I stared at my feet. I didn't even know where to go with this. With my free hand, I rubbed the temple on the left side of my head. Every time I thought I was done with all the heavy mental processing; she had a way of hitting me with something else out of the blue.

"Please, Shane. They won't be a burden on our resources, and we can use the help. You said it yourself. Eventually, we're gonna have to make supply runs into more populated places. We've tapped everything from Denio Junction except the fuel, and even that's going to run out sooner or later. With extra sets of eyeballs, we can do it with a better margin for safety and we can leave someone behind to keep an eye on the cabin," her voice was low, and her hand was on my arm again.

"You have to believe me; I had no idea Janice would come here. You're the one who told me to give the coordinates to someone I trusted. I did, but not because I didn't trust you. I realize that things were normal back then, none of us saw the end of the world happening. She came here because of what I told her about you."

"What?" I looked up and met her gaze. "Did you think I was some creep that was planning something bad?"

"No!" her reply was instant. "Quite the opposite in fact. Now, I know a lot has changed in the last couple of weeks. The fact that you're a good guy hasn't, and I don't ever see that changing. She came here because I told her that I felt safe with you. They didn't have a safe place to go."

"Can you vouch for the other three?"

"Janice trusts them."

"That's good enough for you?"

"Shane, she knows things about me, she's been a party to some things that would land her, both of us in prison for a very long time. She's kept those secrets."

"You're not taking her side because of that, are you? Maybe some sense that you owe her one?"

"Not at all. Especially not now. She's good people. She wouldn't have brought the others if she didn't trust them the way she trusts me. The way I trust you."

"Fine," I said after a very long pause and a lot of time searching her eyes. "They stay in the RV though. If I get any sense that games are being played, they're gone. Do I make myself clear?" I conceded.

"Thank you," she leaned in and gave me a peck on the cheek. All I could do was shake my head and let out a sigh.

-

We returned to the front room and the four newcomers were still standing in the kitchen. Their hands were down, but I'm pretty sure they hadn't moved from their spots. They looked first at Rayne and then at me. I was sure they had overheard at least portions of our conversation and they were awaiting a verdict from me.

"Here's the deal," I began. "Rayne has talked me into letting you stay. The terms of your stay are conditional though. If I suspect anyone of you is trying to pull a fast one, all of you are gone. Our supplies are finite, if you become a burden on them, all of you are down the road. You'll pull your weight when it comes time to make supply runs and you'll protect this cabin as if it were your own. If you don't, if you think this is nothing more than a crash pad, you're out."

"There's a lot of work that has to be done both here and when we go somewhere. You pitch in and work your asses off. It's that or you can just climb back in your rigs and leave now. This is NOT a democracy! It's my place and my rules. Don't like it? There's the door," I pointed at the front door for emphasis.

"Let's also be clear about something else. I trust Rayne. Rayne trusts Janice. Janice trusts you three. I don't know any of you and if we're being honest, I don't trust you. Rayne has earned my trust. You'll have to earn it too. If that sounds harsh, I'm sorry you feel that way. Don't like it? There's the door. Have I made myself clear enough?" the foursome shared glances and nods before Chase answered for the group.

"Your terms are acceptable, sir. I think there's something we need to clear up too if I may?"

"Go on."

"Coming here wasn't our first choice. In fact, Janice didn't even suggest it until five or six days ago. Finding the gates locked, actually gave us some hope. I didn't want to cut the chains, but hopefully, you saw that I cut them in a way that they could still be used. When we got here and found the house empty, we thought that either you'd left or something bad had happened."

"Speaking for all of us, we're glad you're here. We, all of us, have no issues with pulling our weight. Kyle and I can hunt or chop firewood or whatever it is you need. The girls can pitch in with whatever you need. That stupid RV has become our home and we have no problem staying in it. It's actually pretty comfortable."

"You've been very clear with what you need from us, we can appreciate that. Clear, concise communication among all of us will help ease any tensions that may arise. You said that you don't trust us, and frankly, we get that, but until we get to know you, it's gonna be hard for us to trust you. Does that make sense?"

"Yeah, I get it," I admitted.

"I think I can also speak for everyone else when I say that I'm glad you didn't shoot first and ask questions later," he smiled a broad, white smile. The comment got a couple of the others to smile too. He stepped forward and extended his hand. "Since we haven't officially met, I'm Chase."

"Shane," I took the offered hand. After that, there was a round of handshakes and official greetings.

With the greetings out of the way, the tension in the room seemed to drop quickly. I also learned that it wasn't my bacon they were cooking or my beer they had been drinking. It was stuff they had brought with them. Janice cleaned up the broken beer bottle and offered me one from the 12-pack they had brought in from the RV. I accepted. After about 10 minutes, Rayne pulled me aside.

"We need to go get the trucks," she said.

"I know."

"Here," she handed me her keys from her pocket. "I'll keep an eye on things here. Take Janice and get the rigs."

"But....."

"I know what you're about to say. Wait here," she did an about-face and walked to her friend. There was a short exchange of words in which Janice looked at me several times. She finally reached into the back of her waistband and handed Rayne the handgun she'd had hidden. A few more words were exchanged before Janice walked up to me.

"Rayne says you need help bringing your trucks home?" she asked.

"Did she tell you that we'll have to walk about an hour from here to get them?"

"She did. That's fine. I need to stretch my legs anyway."

"Follow me then," I picked the flashlight up off the counter and headed out the front door. Janice didn't hesitate to follow.

"So, you two have known each other for a long time?" I asked trying to make polite conversation during our trek.

"You could say that. We were eight when we met at school. So, 26, no, 27 years ago. Been best friends ever since."

"Even through college?"

"After high school, I went and got my CDL and did long-haul driving for a while. I sure wish I'd gone off to college with her," I could hear something in her voice, a wistfulness.

"Regret being a truck driver?"

"No. Not at all. I made decent money and got to see a lot of the country. Places I'd have never seen otherwise," that tone was still there, and I think I knew what she was thinking.

"Rick?"

"Yeah. That pile of shit. If I'd been there, I might have been able to change things."

"You know what they say about hindsight, right?"

"Yeah, I know. I just feel bad about everything she went through. Before she got married to that douchebag, she was so fun and full of life. She's gotten better since the divorce, but I don't think she'll ever be like she was."

"That kind of abuse changes a person. Ya know?"

"She told you about it?"

"She's told me enough. I didn't ask for all the details of their marriage, but I got the gist of it. I'm pretty sure that if I'd known her then and found out what was going on, her father would have had some help beating the hell out of him."

"Did she..... Um..... What do you know about Rick?" she asked hesitantly. I stopped on the trail and looked directly at her.

"I know that he can't hurt her or anyone else ever again," I said flatly.

"She told you?"

"Yeah. She told me," I started walking again.

"And?" Janice was alongside me again.

"And what?"

"It doesn't bother you?"

"Not even slightly."

"Really?"

"Does that surprise you?"

"From what Rayne told me about you, I guess it shouldn't."

"Do I even want to know?" I chuckled.

"Let me just preface this by saying that Rayne's my ride-or-die chick and vice-versa. You might know a lot about what happened in her marriage, but I know it all. Every last sick and twisted fucking detail. I know what happened the night Rick had his accident," I could see her make air quotes in the moonlight. "There are no secrets between the two of us."

"I tell you this so that what I tell you next means something, okay?" she looked at me and I answered with a nod. "She called me back in January, right after you two met. She told me everything she knew about you, which wasn't much. I took it upon myself to do a little freelance research on the subject of Shane Andrew O'Neal. Admittedly, I was a bit shocked to find out that you were just some boring corporate dude."

"Hey now," I started to protest but she waved me silent.

100

"When she told me about this trip to your cabin in the middle of nowhere, the red flags started flying. I dove back into my research to scour the dark recesses of the internet for any dirt on you. I couldn't find so much as a damn speeding ticket in the last nine years. I even went so far as to look up the ownership records of this cabin of yours. Again, there was nothing to find but what you'd told her. That's my girl and I was doing everything I could to keep her safe, I hope you understand that."

"I can understand that. She's lucky to have a friend who'd go to such lengths."

"Thank you. Here's the thing though; she likes you, Shane. She REALLY likes you. She's not good at showing her feelings anymore. Sometimes she says or does the wrong thing, but she really likes you. You also gotta understand that when it comes down to brass tacks, she hardly knows you. Sure, y'all have been hanging out for a couple of weeks, but it takes longer than that to really know someone. Phone conversations can only cover so much. Do you understand where I'm coming from?"

"Yeah, I get it."

"As her friend, I'm going to ask you a favor."

"Okay?"

"Go slow with her. You're her rebound guy, Shane. Don't break her heart. She's still pretty fragile and won't recover from that. She's got a strong poker face, but she can't survive that again."

CHAPTER 22

August 23rd, 2023.

"We're not like that, Janice!" I protested as we reached the trucks.

"Maybe not. Not yet anyway. I'm just going off of what she told me the day you guys left to come up here. We were on the phone for three hours and there was something there. Something in her voice. Did she tell you that you're the first man she's seen since Rick?"

"No."

"Well, you are. That was a huge leap for her. Don't blow it buster, or you'll have to answer to me," she smiled when she said it, but there was an undertone in the way she said it. "If it makes any difference, this is the first time you and I have ever met, and so far, I like you too."

"Thank you, I think," I fished both sets of keys out of my pocket and handed over Rayne's.

"I'll follow you," she turned and went to Rayne's truck. I climbed in mine, and we pulled out of the parking lot after giving the rigs a minute to warm up.

Well, I wanted clear lines of communication between me, and these new people and it looked like I was gonna get it. Janice was hardly what you'd call discreet. Without a doubt, I was very curious about what all Rayne had said to her best friend in those phone conversations.

I liked Rayne. There was no doubt about that in my mind. Was now the time for a romantic relationship? I didn't have an answer for that, but I was leaning toward no. If none of this happened, and things had just progressed naturally during our stay at the cabin? Maybe. Probably not, but maybe. I thought about what Rayne had said, I'm not saying no, but I'm not saying yes either. That made me grin a little as we pulled into the driveway at the cabin.

The RV and the little SUV had been moved over by the barn and out of the driveway. It was getting late, and I didn't want to deal with the fuel or other things we'd brought home. I'd just deal with it in the morning I decided as I got out of my truck. Janice was waiting to hand over the keys.

"Thanks for your help getting these rigs home," I told her as she handed me the keys.

"Glad I could help," she started to turn and head toward the RV.

"Janice?" I called after her.

"Yeah?"

"Rayne's my friend too. That's all she'll be unless she wants more. That ball is solidly in her court. Okay?"

"Fair enough," she said and then walked away.

I walked into the house and locked the doors behind me. I set the keys on the counter and then made the rounds to make sure all of the doors and windows were closed and locked. As I walked by the slightly ajar bathroom door, I could hear the shower running. I glanced through the crack and saw Rayne's clothes piled on the counter. I pulled the door all the way closed and continued to lock the place down for the night.

The smell of bacon was still heavy in the house causing my stomach to grumble. There wasn't any left of course. Even cold bacon would have hit the spot right about now. It did please me to see that they had taken care of the dishes, even making sure the cast iron pan was clean and ready to go again. In the fridge, I found the very last of the spaghetti. There was enough for two people. I was about to go ask Rayne if she wanted some too when I heard the bathroom door open.

"You eat yet?" I asked as I turned to look at her. She was still toweling her hair dry.

"I'm starving!" came her reply. I dumped all of it into separate bowls. I heated it in the microwave and grabbed some silverware. When it was done heating, I took everything over to the couch. Rayne wrapped her hair in the towel and plopped down next to me. "Thank you."

"I figured you'd have eaten already."

"Not for that. Thank you for letting them stay here. It means the world to me that you can trust my judgment like that. So, thank you."

"That Janice is a bit of a pistol," I remarked just before stuffing a forkful of food into my mouth. That got a chuckle from her.

"She's always been like….." her face froze with fear as she looked at me. "What did she say?"

"She said a lot," I chuckled but that just solidified the fear in her eyes.

"I'm serious, Shane. What did you two talk about?"

"Ya know, we talked about your ex a lot," I tried to avoid the real question. "Shane….."

"Relax, Rayne. Yes, she and I talked about you. Well, she did most of the talking and I did most of the listening. She's worried about you and about where the two of us are going. She's doing her part as a best friend."

"What did you tell her? Wait, what did she tell you?"

"We're fine, Rayne. The conversation Janice and I had about you changes nothing between us. Now, it's late, I'm exhausted, and I'm hungry. We've got a lot to do tomorrow, especially when it comes to getting our guests settled in," I shoveled more food into my mouth. After I swallowed, I continued.

"I know that there are no secrets between you two. If you want the play-by-play of the conversation, talk to her. Everything is fine though, okay?" I finished.

She eyed me suspiciously for a moment before she silently dug into her food. When both of us were done, I put a new bandage on her forehead and tucked her in on the couch. I kicked my shoes off and retired to the recliner.

"What do you think Ann was trying to tell us?" she asked just as I closed my eyes.

"I get the feeling she was just trying to tell us again how dangerous the infected can be. I mean, what else could it have been?"

"I dunno. I feel like we missed a lot of that conversation. Important pieces of it anyway."

"Yeah. I know," I conceded. In the long silence that followed, I finally slipped into a deep, exhausted slumber.

August 24th, 2023.

Not used to hearing noises outside, I was jarred awake by a car door closing. The sun was up, but it hadn't been for long. I was reaching for the Glock in the side pocket of the recliner when I remembered Rayne and I weren't alone anymore. I sighed, tossed my blanket aside, and gently let the foot of the chair down. With a yawn and stretch, I pushed myself out of the chair.

The first stop was the kitchen to fire up the coffee pot. I looked out the window as the decanter filled with water. Chase was leaning against the passenger side of the little SUV, a Toyota RAV4 by the looks of it. He was sipping his coffee and cleaning his deer rifle using the hood as a workbench. With the coffee pot starting its gurgling and hissing, I made a trip to the restroom.

After taking care of business, I brushed my teeth and washed my face. Damn, how long had it been since I'd shaved? I tried to remember but couldn't quite put my finger on the day. It wasn't going to be today either. At least the dark stubble was hiding most of the bruising on my neck. Done in the bathroom, I went back to my recliner and pushed my feet into my shoes. By the time I was done tying them, the coffee maker was done. I filled a mug and then went outside.

"Morning," Chase said when he looked up from his work.

"Good morning," I returned the greeting. "Going hunting?" I motioned toward the stripped-down rifle with my mug.

"Nah, me and Kyle were just gonna go do some scouting this morning. If it's okay with you. I mean, it is your property."

"That's fine. What are you scouting for?"

"Whatever's tasty and got four legs," he smiled. "Antelope for sure and I'd like to know what the deer population looks like around these parts."

"I heard you got an antelope the other day?" I sipped from my mug.

"Yeah. He wasn't much to brag about, but he filled the little freezer in the RV. Ever had antelope?"

"Once. A guy I worked with had me over for a barbeque. If I'm being honest, it didn't really taste that great."

"That's a shame. Sounds like he didn't do much in the way of prep work. Was it pretty strong?"

"Yeah."

"Well, don't take nothing out for dinner. Me and Kyle will take care of it. Let ya taste something that's been prepared and grilled right!" he slid the bolt that he'd been cleaning back into the receiver and worked it a few times.

"Looking forward to it!" I remarked then took another sip of coffee. "Mind if I ask you a serious question?"

"Anything, man," he laid the rifle across the hood and started cleaning up his supplies.

"What's it like out there? Rayne and I haven't been much of anywhere."

"It's ugly, bro. I don't even know how to describe it," he put his supplies back in their bag and picked up his cup. "You ever watch them TV shows with the zombies?

"No. I don't watch TV."

"Well, there's like sick people everywhere. Before we left Portland, there were dead people everywhere too. Dead behind the steering wheels of cars. Dead stacked like firewood outside of apartment buildings..... The fucking stench, it was bad. The hospital we took Monte to..... It was horrible. They weren't even taking the dead to the morgue anymore because it was overflowing. The wails of the sick, no doctors or nurses anywhere. Fuck, man. It was bad," he just stared at the hills across from us.

"That wasn't the worst part though. We saw our first rager at the hospital. It was like the dude was out of his mind on drugs or something. He wouldn't stop screaming, he was smashing skulls with a wooded chair leg....." he looked at the ground for a few seconds. "It took six of us to bring the dude down."

"Rager?"

"Yeah, man. That's what we call 'em anyway."

"Your friend, Bruce? He turned into one of these ragers after getting sick?"

"Yeah. We really thought he was getting better. He'd been on the cranky side all day, but hell, all of us were. We were camped by this little stream, eating dinner, and he just snapped like a dry twig, bro. Angie said something and boom! Before any of us could figure out what the fuck was going on, he had his hands around her neck, throwing her around like a rag doll."

"All of us jumped on him, but he was throwing us off like we weren't nothing. I kicked him in the side of the head but all that did was piss him off even more. He was slamming Angie against the ground. Her face was turning blue and shit. That's when Kyle grabbed his rifle, this rifle," he pointed to the one on the hood. "Stuck the barrel right in his ear and pulled the trigger."

"Damn."

"You seen any ragers?"

"Yeah. Rayne took out two four or five days back. I took out one in my kitchen, and I got two more yesterday."

"No shit? Here?" he pointed at the house and then started nervously looking around.

He seemed to relax a little once I explained the whole story about the crazy scientist chick and how she got here. When I told him about Rayne taking two out with a frying pan, he let out a low whistle and made a joke about not letting her in the kitchen if she was in a pissy mood. It was probably safe to assume he knew nothing about Rayne's past exploits with a 10-inch cast iron pan.

CHAPTER 23

It was shortly after that when Kyle came out of the RV. Both dug small backpacks from the back of the Rav4. Chase pulled out a second rifle and they both donned their gear. They headed to the west across the stream and meadow. It was obvious Chase was the talker while Kyle was the quiet one. Even during the few minutes I'd had to get acquainted with them last night, he didn't have a lot to say. Of the two, if I had to guess, Chase was the eldest.

I was headed back to the house for more coffee when Angie and Janice appeared from the door of the RV. Janice was holding two cups and Angie had several Ziploc bags in her arms. Once they managed to get the door closed behind them, they joined me on the porch. I was holding the door open for them.

"Ladies," I greeted them. Both smiled and cheerfully returned the greeting. I found Rayne standing in the kitchen nursing her own cup of hot brew. If I hadn't been looking for it, I would have missed it entirely. There was the briefest moment where she and Janice shared eye contact. They must have had a full conversation in the second and a half their eyes were locked. The shorter Janice didn't appear to yield one bit.

Sensing that there was a conversation they needed to have out loud, I refilled my mug, grabbed the keys for the trucks, and excused myself. I'd rather go step on a rusty nail than stand there and listen to them talk about me. There was no way I was going to be drawn into that conversation! Heading back outside, I felt like I might have just dodged a bullet.

My first stop was to start my truck and let it warm up a minute. While it was doing that, I went and started the backhoe. I planned on using it to lift the full fuel tank out of the back of my truck. I wanted to put it right back by the diesel generator my grandpa had used. The thing hadn't been run in years, even before I hooked all the solar stuff up. Hopefully, that project would take me into the early afternoon.

I'd managed to avoid going into the cabin until about two in the afternoon. I was just about to head that way because I was getting hungry. I had just finished cleaning all the grease and diesel fuel off of my hands when I spotted Rayne headed my way. She had a tall glass of iced tea and some sort of sandwich on a plate.

"How's it goin?" she asked and set everything on the tailgate of my truck.

"She's fighting pretty hard," I motioned to the stubborn generator. "The fuel system had to be flushed and I had to clean the filters the best I could. It's not like I can run down to the auto parts store to get new ones. That for me?" I pointed at the food.

"Yep. Last of the bread, so enjoy it," she twisted and sat on the tailgate. Something was on her mind, and I think I was about to hear it.

"You and Janice get a chance to catch up?" the tea tasted good when it hit the back of my throat.

"We did. I know I said it already, but I'll say it again; thanks for letting them stay."

"Well, we're less than a day into this new arrangement and it seems to be working," I smiled and took a bite of the peanut butter and jelly sandwich.

"I'm glad you think so….." she paused. "I'm a little embarrassed, Shane."

"What for?"

"Janice told me everything about your talk last night. I just don't want you getting the wrong impression of me, or her," her smile was tight-lipped.

"It's like I told you last night. Nothing between the two of us had changed. It just goes right back to what you said the other night, or day, or whatever it was. I'm not saying yes, but I'm not saying no."

"You sure you're fine with that?"

"I was then, and I am now."

"Okay," her smile loosened up a little. "Need a hand with the generator?"

"You know diesel engines too?"

"Eh," she shrugged her shoulders. "What I don't know, I can make up!"

Between the two of us, we got the old generator to spit and sputter. We were still coming up short on getting it running. Both of us were getting tired of looking at the thing, so we called it a day when Chase and Kyle returned from their scouting trip. They stowed their rifles in the back of the SUV and then went into the RV. Rayne and I went into the cabin to wash up. I was drying my hands when the brothers came in. They were carrying onions, potatoes, tomatoes, cucumbers, carrots, and a 12-pack of beer. All of it was deposited onto the counter."

"Wow! Where'd you find all that?" Rayne exclaimed.

"This? We found all this in a garden over in Lakeview three or four days ago. We've still got quite a bit and we'd be more than happy to share," Chase answered.

While Rayne fawned over the fresh vegetables, I got to thinking about where they had found them. There had to be some gardens over in Denio. We still had some fresh stuff in our stores, but like everything else, we were going to run out. What about seeds for a garden in the spring? Was it too late to grow a garden this year? I realized I had no idea; I'd never planted a garden before. What was one more thing on an already long list of things to do and learn to try and stay alive?

"Ever do much hunting around here?" Chase broke me from my thoughts. He was removing the steaks from the plastic bags in which they'd been marinading.

"Uh, no. Never was big into the hunting scene," I answered.

"From what me and Kyle saw today, it shouldn't be any trouble keeping meat on the menu. You got some decent-sized herds of deer and antelope in the neighborhood. We saw a few and they looked healthy as could be! Never had the time?"

"To hunt? No. I used to go with my dad when I was a kid. Hated every minute of it."

"That's fair. If ya want a beer, help yourself," he motioned at the 12-pack on the counter with the tongs. He took them, and the platter of raw steaks then headed out the back door for the barbeque. Kyle was right behind him with two beer bottles.

"You found all those vegetables in a garden?" I asked, looking at Janice and Angie.

"Yeah. We stopped at this little farmhouse outside of Lakeview looking for gasoline. If there was anyone there, we were going to see if we could trade for the gas," Angie answered.

"There was nobody there though. Wasn't any gas either. Plenty of diesel, but no gas. We got to looking around and found this garden out back of the house. So, we took what was ripe and left the rest on the vine. Angie left a note on the front door in case anyone ever came back," Janice finished the story.

"Have either of you ever grown a garden?" both nodded in the affirmative. "Is it too late to start one here?"

"Well, it's almost September, and I know your weather will probably turn cold before anything comes up. Do you have seeds you want to plant?" this was Angie.

"No, I don't. I was mainly curious. Do you know where I could find seeds?" I leaned against the counter and twisted the top off of a beer bottle.

"This time of year? Some of the big chain stores might still have some in stock. Most places carry them as a seasonal item."

"I see....."

"Long-term goals?" Janice asked.

"Yeah. Seeing those fresh vegetables and seeing our dwindling supply got me thinking. We've made a couple of trips to Denio Junction, but the thought of raiding a garden never entered my mind," I admitted. "What about bread? Any of you ever made your own bread?" Janice shook her head in answer to the question. Angie was nodding.

"I have. I had one of those fancy bread machines and would always make fresh bread around the holidays," she said.

"Are the ingredients hard to find? What about a bread maker?"

"You can buy the stuff just about anywhere. Even the bread maker," she offered.

"More stuff for the supply list?" Rayne asked.

"You mean the list that just gets longer and longer?" I grinned.

"You thinking about making a run somewhere? Janice asked. Rayne took the answer.

"It was a thought. Ya know, the longer this goes on, the more stuff we're gonna need to hold out for the duration."

"Mind if we look at the list?" Janice hadn't even finished her sentence when Rayne was sliding the notebook across the counter to her.

I watched as the three women scoured through the list for half an hour. While they talked, they were busy slicing up the vegetables. Chase was in and out several times to retrieve various seasonings and some onion slices. I wasn't really sure what he was cooking up on the grill, but it smelled heavenly every time the breeze would waft the smell through the cabin.

By the time he brought in the platter of six thick steaks, the ladies had finished their work with the vegetables and their revised list of items we'd need to make it through the coming winter months. Just about everyone grabbed a fresh beer and a plateful of food. All of us went out on the front porch to eat.

As we ate, the conversation quickly turned to the supply list and where we could find those supplies. Both Chase and Kyle looked at the list but didn't have anything to offer on that front. Kyle suggested going up to Burns, Oregon in a bid to find what we needed. Chase threw out Klamath Falls. Both were just as quickly shot down as being too far. I wasn't familiar with either city, so I didn't have any input either way. It was Janice who threw Winnemucca, Nevada into the mix.

During her career as a long-haul truck driver, she'd made many deliveries and pick-ups there. Most of what she was hauling at the time looked a lot like our supply list. The only real concern would be the population. How many ragers would we find? How many immune? None of us had the foggiest idea how many people lived there, but we all knew it was more than enough to give us a shot at seeing both ragers and immunes.

In the time it took us to eat dinner, we'd collectively planned a run to the city of Winnemucca for the day after tomorrow. Kyle and Angie would stay behind to keep an eye on the cabin while the rest of us went to the big city. Rayne would drive her truck with Chase riding shotgun and Janice would ride with me. I couldn't wait to see what conversations would be had with our pairing.

Tomorrow would be spent hooking up my grandpa's trailer to my truck and the enclosed trailer would go behind Rayne's after we emptied it out of course. The fifth-wheel hitch would also be removed to allow for more cargo capacity in the bed. I'd be taking along my fuel transfer pump to allow us to fill both rigs before heading home.

"Well?" Chase asked, looking at my empty plate?"

"That was probably one of the best steaks I've ever eaten," I confessed.

"It's all in the prep work and how ya cook it," he grinned and took my plate from me. "Now you can say you've had good antelope!"

CHAPTER 24

Our day started a little after 7 am even though all of us were up by six. Last night was the first time since the mad scientist invaded my home that Rayne and I slept in our own rooms. I had to admit, it felt good to stretch out in my bed rather than being confined in the recliner. It was comfortable, but it was never meant to be slept in for extended periods of time.

The first order of the day was to get the enclosed trailer empty. With the help of the brothers and the backhoe, the massive chest freezer was deposited on the back deck. We didn't even have to empty it out to move it this time. Simply lifted it with the boom and set it where I wanted it.

Once we had the flatbed trailer out of the barn, we unloaded all of the full cases and covered them with a large tarp. The barn did a good job of keeping most of the weather out, but not all of it. I put the battery back in the old Ford and we took one of the heavy-duty deep-cycle batteries out of the RV. Not that it would make my pump setup pump any faster, it would just last longer than the standard battery.

Just before lunch, Chase brought me a retention holster for my Colt. I had one just like it, at my home in Las Vegas. He also traded me shotguns. He had the same exact weapon only his had a sling that would hold extra shells and a flashlight affixed to the front of the barrel. It was only a temporary exchange, but one I welcomed.

Over lunch, we discussed how things would work tomorrow. Janice and I would take the lead all the way into town. Janice would direct us first to the huge ranch and feed store. There, Chase would act as our lookout with his scoped rifle while the rest of us loaded Rayne's truck and her trailer.

Once hers was full, mine would be next. With the list as a guide, we figured we could get a great deal of what we needed there. Angie had added a lot of medical supplies to the list but all of us balked at the idea of going to a hospital. Her suggestion was to look for smaller clinics, dentist offices, fire trucks, and ambulances. We told her we would do what we could but made no promises.

The rest of the afternoon was spent loading up various supplies we'd need for the outing. Each rig was equipped with a small first aid kit, shovels, bolt cutters, a small tool kit, and drinking water. Extra ammunition for each weapon in the group was also loaded up. Nobody knew what to expect tomorrow. Hopefully, everything would go nice and easy. The problem was, Rayne and I didn't exactly have a stellar track record for nice and easy.

FERAL OUTBREAK

Everyone was up at 5 am and ready to pull out of the driveway by 5:30. It was going to take us close to three hours to make the drive to Winnemucca. To my surprise, Janice was all business this morning. She had a road atlas sitting on the dash, a .30-.30 rifle on the back seat, and a thermos full of coffee that kept our cups full once we hit the highway. From behind the mirror finish of her aviator sunglasses, she was watching the road and the mirror on her side. I had to remind myself that she and her group had spent a lot of time on the roads already.

Our first stumbling block came only five miles from the outskirts of the small city. The trailer Rayne was pulling had a blowout on the right rear axle of the tandem axle unit. She started frantically flashing her headlights to signal me to pull over. I did and she guided her rig in behind me. Before I'd even brought the truck to a full stop, Janice had grabbed her rifle and was out the door.

I thought she was going to go help change the tire, but she moved out ahead of my truck. She was watching the area like a hawk. I left my truck running, grabbed my shotgun, and went back to see what I could do to help. I found Rayne surveying the damage. Chase was behind the trailer watching our backs.

"We don't have a spare," Rayne said as she kicked the ruined tire. Chase must have heard her because he stepped closer.

"Get it jacked up and get that tire off. Once you got it off, get one of those ratchet straps from your truck and tie the axle up. We're close enough to town that we can limp it the rest of the way in," he instructed and moved back to his lookout position.

It only took us a few minutes to get the tire off, but I had no clue how to do what Chase had told me to do. He must have recognized the frustration on my face when he intervened. He had me move to cover our backside while he slid under the trailer with the heavy-duty strap. Five minutes later, he rolled out and let the jack down. The hub of the axle stayed about eight inches off of the ground.

"Mount up!" he ordered and then we were underway again.

I'd been through Winnemucca every year for the last 12 years on my way to and from the cabin. I'd even had to drive to the city on several occasions to get electrical or plumbing stuff for the cabin. The first year I went through, I did all of my grocery shopping there. That said, I wasn't even close to familiar with the place, but it was easy to see that everything was wrong.

In my mind, I'd built up this apocalyptic image of the city being on fire with wrecked cars and dead bodies littering the streets. I thought it would look like a warzone from some massive-budget Hollywood blockbuster. What I got was much milder than all of that. There were a couple of traffic collisions involving someone hitting a parked car or light pole. I did spot a body or two either trapped inside a car or on the front porch of a house.

The farther we got into the city, the eerier it became. There was obviously no power because none of the stoplights were working. There was some litter blowing on the breeze, but not much. I think it was the quiet that was getting to me. It felt like we were the only living beings in the entire city. That was proved wrong when I spotted the pack of dogs running down a side street. Two or three of them were fighting over something as they drug it down the street. I couldn't help but gasp in disbelief when I realized it was a human leg they were fighting over.

"Janice?" I was still watching the animals with a morbid fascination.

"Yeah?"

"This virus, or whatever it is, does it affect animals too?"

"Not that I know of. Dogs are a big danger though. Most of them have already gone feral. Try to pet Fido and you won't get your hand back."

"Noted."

"The ranch store is up another block, your side of the street," she pointed. As the parking lot came into view, she gave me further instructions to park directly in front of the store with the nose of the truck pointed at the exit. That was easy enough to accomplish because there were only three other cars in the parking area. "Keep it running until me and Chase come back. No matter what you hear, do NOT come in after us. Got it?"

"Okay."

She grabbed her rifle and stepped out of the rig. She waved Rayne in to park next to me. After leaning in the driver's window and giving her further instructions, she and Chase headed for the front door of the store. I watched in my side mirror as they tried the door and found it locked. With Janice keeping watch, Chase pulled something that looked like a leather wallet from his back pocket. He knelt in front of the lock and went to work.

It didn't take me but a second to realize that's how they got into the cabin when they first arrived. Chase must have been pretty good at picking locks because he made quick work of the one keeping us out of the store. He stood, put the pick set back in his back pocket, and held the door open for Janice. She led the way inside with her rifle against her shoulder.

"It was weird to see in Denio Junction but it's downright eerie here," Rayne startled me from my thoughts. She was standing next to my open passenger-side window.

"Did you see the dogs?"

"Yeah. Chase said to stay away from 'em. Said they're pretty wild now," she shifted on her feet so that she could change her view of the street in front of us.

"It's not what I expected," I said.

"The city?"

"Yeah. It's like we're the only people left alive. It's like….. It's like everyone just vanished."

"I laid awake most of the night trying to prepare myself for piles of bodies and burned-down buildings. You know, rubble and trash everywhere with bullet-riddled cars. This?" she waved her hand around. "This is almost peaceful in a really weird, bizarre sort of way."

"A peaceful apocalypse?" I grinned. Of course, that was a short-lived thought when two gunshots rang out in rapid succession from inside the store. They were followed a second later by a third. I was watching the storefront in my mirror when Janice and Chase both came out. Chase was rolling a tire next to him.

"You okay?" Rayne asked as they approached.

"We're fine. The store is secure, and all of the back doors have been blocked. The only access now is past us. Let's get this tire changed and then we can start loading up. I grabbed my shotgun and joined Chase at the trailer with the missing tire.

"You found that in there?" I asked him. Rayne and Janice were both acting as lookouts.

"Yeah."

"They sell tires too?"

"It's a ranch store. Of course they do," he sounded a little irritated as he jacked the axle up.

"Sorry. I've never been in one of those places," I said sheepishly. "Was there a rager in there?" I tried to change the subject.

"Yep. Ain't gotta worry about that one anymore," was all he had to say about the subject. I hadn't known the sandy-haired man for very long, but it was easy to see that his normal, easy-going personality had changed. It made me wonder what had really happened inside the store.

I guess I was about to find out. As soon as he dropped the tire on the ground and removed the jack, he climbed on top of the trailer so he would have an unobstructed view of everything around us. Janice ushered us through the front door. She grabbed one of the flatbed-style shopping carts and Rayne and I did the same thing.

"We need to start with the full case stuff in the back of the store. There was a rager back here and we took care of her, but you need to prepare yourselves," was all the warning we got when she led us through the double doors into the back room of the store. The smell of death was thick, as was the coppery smell of blood. It was dark back here and as soon as we flipped on our flashlights, Rayne and I both took in a sharp breath.

The body of a nude woman was laying in the middle of the floor. She had two neat bullet holes in her chest and another in her forehead. The blood puddle around her was still expanding. Believe it or not, that wasn't the worst part. The entire front of her body was covered in cuts. Some looked like cat scratches, others looked like they had been inflicted with surgical precision. These weren't random either. The bloody and festering wounds were carved into words on her flesh. Words like pain, die, kill, and hate. The word murder was carved on her abdomen. They were on her limbs and torso, over and over again.

"What the fuck….." Rayne said exactly what I was thinking.

CHAPTER 25

"Yeah, that's one we haven't seen before," Janice commented as her flashlight beam played across the body. "We all know what we need to get, so we better get to it."

For the next two hours, we took anything and everything we thought might be useful. There were heavy winter coats, gloves, stocking caps, jeans, t-shirts, and just about every other type of apparel you could think of. I loaded three heavy-duty generators, and three 2-inch high-pressure water pumps along with hoses and nozzles. It was Kyle who added them to the list for fire suppression and irrigation needs.

Brand new guns with extra magazines were stacked in the back seat of both rigs, floor to ceiling. Many of the accessories were put into the enclosed trailer. Thousands of rounds of ammunition were dumped from their boxes into plastic ammo cans and then hauled to the trailer. We cleaned out all of the veterinary supplies. Everything from antibiotics to wound wrap went into the trailer. There was fishing gear, cast iron cookware, and power tools. Six big chainsaws with extra chains, cases of 2-cycle oil, engine oil, dozens of car batteries, and even a dozen spare tires for the trailers rounded out the load for the enclosed trailer.

We took a short break before we began loading the trailer behind my truck. Chase gave Janice the scoped rifle and he came to help with this load. There were four 100-gallon in-bed transfer tanks for transporting fuel. All four fit perfectly in the bed of my truck. A dozen plastic 5-gallon gasoline cans were strapped into the flatbed along with 10 more of the yellow ones for diesel. Inside the back of the store, we found a rack containing 16 of the 7.5-gallon propane tanks and all of them were full. We even took the half-full one from the small forklift.

Hand tools were bundled together and put inside bed toolboxes. Those were then strapped to the flatbed. Shovels, axes, rakes, hoes, Pulaskis, and splitting mauls were all taken. Tool kits, fuel stabilizers, wheelbarrows, fuel transfer pumps with everything to make them work..... There wasn't anything we couldn't load up and strap down. We even cleaned out all of the straps because we needed them.

It was sometime around two in the afternoon when we finally had to put an end to the pilfering. We just didn't have any more room. While we ate the lunch we'd brought with us, Janice crossed items off of the list. When she was done, she presented it to the rest of us.

"Well, the good news is, we got about half of what was on there. The bad news is, we got about half of what was on there," she stated. "We scored some stuff that was just too good to pass up and I don't think any of us wanted to leave it behind. The guns and ammo being one of those items."

"So, we make another trip tomorrow?" Rayne asked, handing the list back to her.

"I don't want to make this trip again tomorrow. Period. I have an idea though," she answered with a coy grin.

"Aw shit," Chase muttered under his breath.

"Hear me out before you start with that. There's one of those moving van rental places just up the road. I think we should go procure a couple of them. It's that or we come back tomorrow," she shrugged her shoulders.

"Don't they usually have their own fuel pumps too?" I asked.

"Most of 'em do."

"Then I vote that we go there. It'll give us the extra rigs to do this in one trip and we can fuel everything up while we're there," I patted one of the tanks in the bed of my truck as I said it.

"Rayne?" Janice looked at her friend.

"Might as well," she answered.

"Chase?" she asked her boyfriend.

"You know me, Jan. Lead the way," he said with a toothy grin.

We finished our lunch of tuna and crackers while we made the short drive down to the truck rental place. The front gates were locked but the bolt cutters made quick work of the chain. Fortunately, the parking area gave us enough room to turn and pull up on either side of the filling port for the underground tank. I got to work setting up the transfer pump I'd made. Both trucks were first to be filled and then I moved on to filling the tanks in the back of my truck.

I didn't rightly know how much diesel fuel weighed, but I knew that with 400 gallons back there, I was probably going to be pretty close to the weight limit of the truck. The trailer was already weighing me down pretty good, and I'd be adding to that weight when I filled the plastic fuel cans.

Janice was my lookout while Chase and Rayne went to find the keys to a pair of box vans. A quick discussion before they left had them looking for keys to the biggest vans they could find. We figured it would be a good thing to have too much room over not enough, again. That conversation led to them bringing two 26-foot moving trucks around the front 15 minutes later.

After they parked them, Rayne picked up the slack on lookout duty and Chase went to assemble another of the transfer pumps. We had everything we needed, and he kept it handy when they went on the trailer. It took him about 20 minutes to assemble it, then he dropped the pickup hose down the same hole I was using. With the additional pump, everything was topped off 30 minutes later.

FERAL OUTBREAK

Before leaving the rental place, Janice unboxed four FRS radios and gave all of us one. She also gave us extra batteries just in case. When we pulled out, she was leading the way in one of the box vans, I was right behind her, Rayne was behind me, and Chase was bringing up the rear with the second van. Our destination was one of the big chain grocery stores. It was only a 10-minute drive and instead of pulling up out front, she led us around back.

"Chase, back up to the loading dock right next to me," her voice was loud and clear through the small speaker.

"Copy," Chase replied and pulled past me and Rayne.

"Shane, Rayne, stay by the curb out there and give us plenty of room to pull away in case we gotta leave in a hurry. Chase and I will handle loading these two rigs. You guys watch our backs."

"We copy," I answered for both of us. After both vans were backed up to the loading docks, I watched Chase pick the lock of the door leading to the receiving office. They were through the door in under a minute. I grabbed my shotgun and stood with Rayne about halfway between where we'd parked and the two vans.

"She's a bit of a take-charge kind of gal, isn't she?" I said to Rayne.

"Don't you mean bossy?" she chuckled when she said it.

"She's focused."

"You can say it, Shane. Yes, she can be bossy. She's been that way for as long as I've known her."

"It's not a bad thing. Hell, she's someone I'd hire to be a manager or supervisor. She's not afraid to get her hands dirty. That's a good quality to have in a leadership position."

"So, you like her?"

"You said it, she's good people. I can admit when I'm wrong, Rayne. I was wrong about not wanting them around. All of them seem like really good people to have on our side," she nodded her head at my admission. As we stood there chatting and watching our surroundings, we could hear electric pallet jacks going in and out of both box vans. Whatever those two were loading up, it sounded like there was a lot of it.

There was a wooded field behind the grocery store that was separated from the parking lot by a six-foot-high chain link fence. It was overgrown with brush and thick with trees. We were more concerned about watching either end of the parking lot where there was no fence. It was when a large flock of birds took flight from the tree canopy that both of us began to pay more attention.

"Someone's out there," she pointed to the field.

"That's what I'm afraid of," I put the radio to my mouth and spoke. "Janice, Chase, we might have company coming through the field out back."

"You know what to do about it!" Janice answered immediately. "Give us another 15 minutes and we'll be ready to de-ass this place."

119

"Copy," I answered. Whatever had startled the birds hadn't shown itself yet. Both of us could hear tree limbs breaking but it was hard to get a good bearing on where the sound was coming from.

"That sounded closer," she remarked after the last cracking sound. Both of us were intently looking for the source. It should have been visible by now but was still eluding us. We were so intent, I nearly jumped out of my skin when Janice's voice came from the radio clipped on my belt. I turned to my left and reached for the radio, but my hand never made it that far.

"Rayne!" I said at the same time I raised my shotgun. Not even 50 feet away, eight very ragged and haggard men had snuck up on us. We'd been looking in the wrong direction for the threat.

"Behind us!" Rayne barked and opened fire with her AR. None of the men in front of me fell but they broke into a sprint straight for me.

Somewhere in the back of my mind, I could hear the sharp report of Rayne's weapon. Still, none of the men charging at me went down. I jerked back on the trigger of the scattergun. The lead man, who was less than 30 feet away now, spun with the impact to his left shoulder. He staggered for a couple of steps, but I'd just unleashed the second round. This one knocked him to the ground.

I racked the third round and let it fly before he face-planted. That one went low and took another man's knees. He went down just as the shotgun bucked for the fourth time. They were so close that there wasn't even any need to aim anymore. One man's arm was removed from his body by the double-aught buck. The fifth round hit one center mass and threw him off of his feet.

Round six turned another's head into a chunky spray. The seventh round was another center mass shot. The eighth round was so hurried it caught the man who was reaching for me in the groin. The force of the impact spun him around and threw him to the ground. Running on pure, unrestrained adrenaline, I pumped the shotgun again, but it didn't fire. I realized it was empty. The last man hit me like a ton of bricks.

As we fell, he wrapped me up in a bear hug, and I tried to deflect the force of the impact by spinning to the right. I lost my grip on the shotgun when we hit the ground. The now useless weapon clattered across the pavement. I'd succeeded in tempering his blow and the subsequent impact with the ground. It was a combination of my spinning and his momentum that caused him to lose his grip when we impacted the ground. I kicked away from him and pulled my Colt from its holster. Before I could raise it, he pounced on me again.

He raised up to smash my face in with his fist when the Colt barked once, and then twice. He looked almost surprised as I shoved the gun into his chest and proceeded to empty the magazine. With my free hand and a buck of my hips, I shoved him off of me. Looking at where Rayne had been, I was horrified to see her on the ground with a screaming woman wearing green hospital scrubs sitting straddle her. The woman's bloody hands were wrapped around her throat. Rayne wasn't fighting back.....

CHAPTER 26

August 26th, 2023.

Rayne's lifeless body was being slammed repeatedly into the concrete when I scrambled most of the way to my feet. Hunched over, I half ran and half staggard to cover the 20 feet separating us, never fully gaining my balance. I smashed into the blonde woman, driving her from atop Rayne. We hit the ground in a roll. Flailing arms and legs were swinging and grabbing wildly as we tried to gain purchase on each other.

After the third or fourth roll, I ended up on top with my hands around her throat. No matter how hard I squeezed, she was still thrashing around and trying to get to my throat or eyes. I could feel her windpipe collapse, but she continued to fight. The only thing that got me was that it made her quit screaming. She was bleeding from every orifice on her head and her bloody eyes were wide with rage. I squeezed with everything I had as she scratched my arms.

The barrel of a rifle appeared before my eyes. The tip of the barrel was forced into the woman's eye, causing it to dislodge from the socket. There was a muffled boom and her head disintegrated. Brains and blood sprayed everything, including me. I looked up to see Chase standing over us. He withdrew his rifle and worked the bolt to chamber a fresh round.

"HELP ME GODDAMNIT! SHE'S NOT BREATHING!" both of us turned when Janice yelled. She was feeling for a pulse.

"GO!" Chase ordered. "I got the rest of these pricks," he leveled his rifle and popped one of the wounded men that had attacked us.

"No pulse! I'll breathe, you do compressions!" Janice said as I dropped to my knees next to her and Rayne. I unbuckled the tactical vest she was wearing, and Janice helped me get it off. Remembering my training from the CPR class I had to take at work, I found the proper placement for my hands on her chest. Janice tried once to give her a breath but was unsuccessful. She cranked her head back a little farther and got one in

Janice was counting my compressions out loud, and she'd try to force a breath in as often as she could. It took her a few seconds to get the timing just right. She was also having to keep a lot of tension on her neck to keep the breaths going in. At the moment, time meant nothing to me, and neither did the cracks from Chase's rifle in the background. As soon as I made that first full compression, I felt things crack under the force I was using.

"You fuckin BITCH! Come on Rayne!" Janice panted. Sweat was rolling from under her brunette bangs. Right after she gave her a breath, she made me stop CPR and felt for a pulse. "Give her a breath!" she demanded and moved into a position to do compressions.

"Here!" Chase dropped down next to us carrying a red canvas bag stenciled AED. Janice stopped compressions and ripped her tank top open right down the middle. Chase turned on the AED unit and plugged in the pads.

"Knife!" Janice looked at Chase when she said it. With his free hand, he pulled a black knife from the back of his belt. Deftly flipping it so Janice could grab the handle. She snatched it up and pulled Rayne's sports bra up, then cut it right down the middle exposing her chest. She took the pads from Chase and placed them on her bare skin. The whole time this was going on, I was still breathing for her.

"CLEAR!" Chase said loudly. All three of us put some space between us and Rayne's body. After her whole body tensed for a second, Chase spoke again. "Check for a pulse!"

Janice and I both did but found nothing. She resumed CPR and I started giving her breaths again. Before he shocked her a second time, Chase had to grab his rifle and drop another rager coming toward us. He then shocked her a second time with the same results as the first. After the third shock, we felt a thready pulse in Rayne's neck, but she still wasn't breathing on her own. For another tense few minutes, I continued to breathe for her. All of us collectively let out a huge sigh of relief when she took that first gasping breath on her own.

"We need to move!" Chase said, raising his rifle to drop another rager.

"Go lock the vans up and grab the keys," Janice said after his rifle barked again. The bark of the muzzle caused Rayne to jerk slightly. Janice gathered up the AED and ran it to my truck. She threw it on the passenger floorboard and returned a moment later. "Can you carry her?"

"Yeah, I got her," I shoved one arm under her shoulders and the other under her legs. Once I was on my feet, Janice herded us toward the passenger side of my truck. She held the door open while I deposited Rayne as close to the middle as I could. Chase was on his way back when Janice slid behind the wheel of my rig. Chase jogged towards Rayne's truck.

I didn't even have the door closed when Janice dropped the Dodge into gear and pressed down on the throttle hard. She made one glance in the side mirror to make sure Chase was right behind us. Both heavily loaded trucks and trailers barreled around the corner of the building. I was looking at Rayne's unconscious form when I felt Janice let off the throttle.

"What?" I said as I looked up to see her staring out the front window. She started stepping on the brakes just as I spotted all of the shiny dots on the ground ahead of us. There was a man throwing out handfuls of nails from a five-gallon bucket. He stopped what he was doing and grinned at us.

"Fuck!" Janice growled and cranked the wheel hard. She grabbed her radio from the dash and put it to her lips. "Chase?"

"Yes dear?" his voice was clear and calm.

"They're trying to trap us! Nails on the road, we're going out the other way!" as we passed Chase, I could see him leaning out the window with his rifle. There was a single shot as we accelerated past him.

"Copy that, babe. I nailed that prick," even though I couldn't see him, I heard the grin in his voice. "Right behind you again," Janice checked her mirror to make sure. She put the radio to her mouth again.

"Gimme some room in case we gotta back out. This driveway is too narrow to flip a bitch like that again."

"No worries," he replied, and she checked her mirror again. She eased off the throttle as we approached the alley that we'd come in on. She was leaning forward in the seat trying to see around the blind corner. As soon as its full length was visible, she jabbed the brakes hard. Between the building and the concrete K-rail that separated the pavement from the open field were two cars sitting side by side. They were effectively blocking the only other exit.

I thought she was going to try and back away, but she didn't. Instead, she brought the truck to a full stop, threw it in park, and opened her door. She opened the back door and grabbed Rayne's rifle. She reached back in and pulled a full magazine from Rayne's vest. She slammed it home and slapped the bolt release.

Laying it across the hood of my truck, she started letting rounds fly. Windshields shattered and headlights exploded. When one man tried to get free of his sedan, she fed him three or four rounds. When the bolt locked back again, fluids and steam poured from under the hoods of both vehicles. One of them was starting to burn.

"Reload that!" she shoved the AR toward me when she climbed back in. "Hey beautiful," she looked down at Rayne, whose head was resting in my lap. Her butt was in the middle where the console was folded up into a seat, and her legs and feet were occupying the center of the floor. Her eyes were open, and she was frantically looking around. Her breathing was loud and ragged. One of her hands went to her chest and the other went to her neck.

"You want to sit up?" I asked as I reached over the seat and fished another magazine from her vest. She shook her head slightly and winced in pain.

"What now, lover?" Chase's voice came through the speaker of the radio. I could see Janice looking for a new escape path. Her eyes settled on the four-foot-tall chain link fence directly ahead of us and the open field beyond it.

"Follow me," she looked over at me with an apologetic look on her face. "You're auto insurance paid up?"

"Huh?"

"Sorry about your paint job....." She stepped on the throttle.

124

"Oh shit!" I grabbed ahold of Rayne and leaned over the top of her. Janice ducked at the last moment. I heard the sturdy fencing hit the front of the truck with a loud screech and then I heard it grind its way underneath the truck. She never let off the throttle.

When I could no longer hear the grinding and grating noises, I sat back up. When I went to look out the side mirror on my side of the truck, it wasn't there. There were wires and pieces of broken plastic hanging where it used to be. Janice was still on the throttle and pointing us back in the direction of the nearest street. She checked her side mirror to see if Chase was still behind us.

"Ballsy move, babe. Ask Shane if he wants me to stop and pick up his grill. It's kinda mangled but I can go back and get it."

"Leave it. We're getting the hell outta town so stick to my ass like ya love me," she said and then put the radio back on the dash. "Sorry about your truck," her apology was sincere.

"What….." Rayne tried to croak from my lap.

"Easy," I tried to comfort her as I stroked strands of hair from her face.

"Hurt….." She touched her chest and then her throat.

"It's okay, Rayne. Once we get the hell outta here, we'll make ya a little more comfortable. Okay?" Janice said and patted her on the thigh.

"Okay?" I could see the question in her bloodshot eyes. I could also see that she was in a lot of pain.

"You're gonna be fine, babe. We got you and we're headed home," I said quietly as I stroked her hair. I could feel another set of eyeballs on me. I looked over at Janice.

"Babe?" she mouthed the word accusingly.

We didn't slow down until we were about 30 miles out of Winnemucca. Janice found a wide spot on the side of the road and pulled in. Chase pulled up right next to us. When Janice got out, she walked around the front of my truck. The grimace on her face told me what I was wondering. When she pulled my door open, the edge of the door and the fender bound up. To her credit, she tried to be gentle with it at first. Finally, she just gave it a good yank.

"Why don't you help Chase transfer some of the shit out of the backseat into Rayne's truck. I'll stay with her," by the tone she used, I could tell it wasn't a request. Rather than argue, I gently slid out from under Rayne. Before I stepped past Janice, I leaned close and whispered in her ear.

"We will talk about it later. The two of us need to come to an understanding regarding OUR friend. Got it?"

"Yeah," she grumbled.

CHAPTER 27

August 26th, 2023.

It took us about 20 minutes to move enough out of my backseat and into Rayne's truck to make room for her. Before we moved Rayne to the backseat of my truck, Janice pulled the rags that had been her tank top and sports bra off. She helped her into a ranch store t-shirt that was about three sizes too big. I couldn't tell if Rayne's short, sharp breaths were from the damage inflicted on her chest from CPR or being strangled. Probably both. Between the three of us, we got her into the back seat and laid down.

When we were finally ready to pull out and make the long drive back to the cabin, Janice yielded the driver's seat to me. We spent nearly an hour in silence, me watching the road and her watching Rayne. I was trying to figure out two things; why did I call Rayne babe, and why did Janice seem to take such offense to it? I craned my neck around so I could see Rayne in the backseat. Her eyes were closed again.

"Sleeping?" I asked Janice quietly. She replied with a nod.

"Her breathing is still pretty shallow. Pulse is getting stronger though," she withdrew her hand from Rayne's wrist. She turned and faced forward in the seat.

"You gonna give me the silent treatment all the way home?" I could see her jaw muscles flex, but she didn't answer. "Listen, Janice. You were….."

"No! You listen, buster!" her voice was low but heated. "My best friend almost died, no, she did die today, and you were supposed to be watching her back! You wanna know why I'm pissed? There ya go!" she glanced over the seat again to make sure her outburst hadn't woken Rayne.

"We were overrun, Janice! They were coming at us from every damn direction!" I snarled.

"You should have been on the radio calling for backup! Had we had even a few seconds' warning, we could have stepped in! This ain't the first rodeo Chase and I have been to, ya know?"

"There wasn't time! It was either get both hands on my gun or fiddle fuck with the radio. You'd think that all the gunshots would have clued you in!"

"Well, if you'd have been paying attention, you'd have known Rayne was in trouble with a jammed rifle! You were obviously too busy to take care of her!" she crossed her arms across her chest and looked straight ahead.

"This may not have been your first rodeo, Janice, but it was ours. We were outnumbered by who knows how many. It went down faster than you might believe. Yeah, we made some mistakes. Some big ones. Mistakes neither of us is gonna make again. There were some hard lessons learned and thank God, both

126

of us are still here to learn those lessons. Everybody's going home today and that's something! We're a little beat up, but we're all still here!"

She didn't have an immediate reply. Instead, she turned her head to look out the side window for a few miles. Her arms were still crossed, and I could see her fingers gripping her upper arm tightly.

"Janice?" I softened my tone.

"What?" she growled, still looking out the side window.

"Today was, without a doubt, the scariest day of my life. It wasn't the ragers that scared me either. They were simply a problem that needed to be dealt with. You wanna know what scared the shit outta me?" I glanced in her direction, but still only saw the back of her head.

"I'll bite. What?" came the terse reply.

"Right after I killed the last guy on my side, I rolled over and saw Rayne lying there, lifeless. The woman who had her by the neck was slamming her into the concrete like a rag doll and there was no fight coming from her….. I flew into a rage of my own. Even if Chase hadn't intervened, I'd have killed her and felt nothing over it."

"When I heard you scream that Rayne wasn't breathing and didn't have a pulse, every thought process in my brain stopped except one. When I was doing compressions, when I was breathing for her, when we were shocking her with the AED, it was all the same thought. Do you have any idea what was going through my head?"

"No clue. It was impossible to read your face. You looked like a damn statue," she turned her head to face me.

"I may have looked that way, but that was hardly what I was thinking."

"You gonna tell me, or make me play guessing games?"

"I was scared because of the rage I felt toward the woman who hurt Rayne, I was scared because the only thing I could think when I felt her windpipe collapse was that she'd just die already. I was scared because when we were trying to get Rayne back, the only thing I could think of is how much I cared about her!" we locked eyes momentarily and all I could see was skepticism.

"I called her babe because I was trying to keep her calm. I was trying to keep myself calm. Yes, it's a term of endearment commonly used among couples. That's not why I said it. I said it because I wanted her to know that she was safe, that she was safe with me. I used a simple term she could understand through her pain and confusion."

"So, you called her babe just to comfort her? How noble," the sarcasm in her icy tone was loud and clear.

"I also said it because I care about her and for her. If we hadn't gotten her back, you and Chase would have been driving back to the cabin without me."

"What's that supposed to mean?"

"It means that I'd have taken every weapon I could carry, and I'd have single-handedly waged war against the ragers. Had she died, so would they....." I paused and looked at her again. She stared right back.

"They would have killed you."

"I'm sure they would have. What you don't understand, Janice is that Rayne is all I have left in this fucked up mess. Yeah, I used to be that boring corporate dude. Not anymore. I haven't been in a committed relationship in years. I was married to my work. I didn't need other people in my life. Now? Now, I'd kill for that woman in the backseat. If need be, I'd die for her....."

"You don't even know her, Shane. Seriously. How long have you two been playing house? That's all this is!"

"Excuse me?" I almost chuckled.

"Rayne is a complex woman! You've played house with her for what? Three weeks? You don't know shit about....."

"It sounds to me like you're the one who doesn't know her all that well!" I retorted sharply. "It seems to me that you're still trying to find the Rayne that existed before she got married. I hate to tell you this, but THAT Rayne is long gone. I didn't know her, but she sounded like a kick in the ass. Let me tell you something about the Rayne laying back there! She's intelligent, witty, beautiful, and as tough as they come. She's survived, no! She's thrived after going through shit that would destroy most people!"

"That's the Rayne I met back in January! That's the Rayne I've gotten to know! You and I are friends with a woman named Rayne. That's where the common ground ends. You knew the old Rayne and that's who you're trying to protect. I know the new and improved version. That woman back there," I motioned over the seat with my thumb. "She doesn't need protecting, not like you're thinking. She needs space to continue to grow. She needs space to not be pressured."

After saying what I said, Janice fell silent again. The anger and accusation in her eyes were gone. A few minutes into that silence, she turned in her seat again. She put the center console down so she could reach into the back seat easier. I half turned and could see her holding Rayne's hand. I must have hit a nerve or something because I caught her wiping a single tear from her eye.

Our progress was greatly slowed once we'd left the pavement of the two-lane highway. Everything we were driving, or towing was overloaded, and we didn't want to risk breaking anything. There was an urgency to get Rayne home so Angie could check her out. Being the only person in our group with medical training, we were relying heavily on her prognosis before feeling any real relief.

As soon as we pulled into the driveway, Kyle, and Angie both came out onto the deck. Before I could even get the truck in park, Janice shoved the door open with a loud creak and pop as the body panels bound up. She was waving and calling for Angie as soon as her feet hit the ground. She escorted her to the door behind mine, talking rapid fire.

"Grab my bag out of the car," Angie ordered Janice as soon as the door was opened. She began her assessment immediately, even before I could get out of the truck.

"Here!" Janice ran back up with a large medical bag.

"I need the cervical collars too," Angie glanced down at the bag by her feet. "Shane?"

"Yeah? What can I do?" I asked.

"The pocket right by my foot, there's a BP cuff and stethoscope. Grab them for me," she instructed. I started to hand it to her, but she asked me to wait as Janice ran back up with the C-collars. She found the one she wanted and gently wrapped it around Rayne's neck. Then she started barking orders in rapid succession.

"Shane, squeeze in here between me and the door. Kyle, over here on the right side. Janice, climb in on the other side and support her legs," it only took a few seconds before everyone was in position. "Okay, I'm going to support her head and neck. On the count of three, we're going to slightly lift her and slide her out. We'll stop when her waist gets to the edge of the seat so you two can reposition and support her weight," she looked at me and Kyle. When she received nods of understanding, she began counting to three.

As a team, we moved Rayne from the backseat to the ground next to the truck. She traded places with Kyle, letting him keep her spine stable. She cut off the brand-new shirt we'd given her and began listening to her lungs. Every time she'd ask Rayne to take a deep breath, we could see the grimace on her face as she tried to comply. Angie hung the stethoscope around her neck and then began feeling her ribs and chest. Some touches brought more pain than others. Getting her blood pressure was probably the least painful part of the ordeal.

"We need to get her in the house and into bed. I'm sure she's got some busted ribs and torn cartilage in her chest, but that's normal. Her neck has got me concerned though. I don't feel any deformations in her spine, but it's hard to tell because of all the swelling. We need to be really careful moving her."

It took all of us to transport her up the deck, through the front door, and into her room. While we had her sitting on the edge of the bed, Angie used some elastic sports wrap around her chest. The idea was to stabilize the fractured ribs and torn cartilage. The area over her sternum, between her breasts, was already black and blue.

With Angie once again stabilizing her neck and head, we got her laid down. Once we had her as comfortable as we could get her, Angie sent Kyle out to bring in the medical bag. She sent Chase to the SUV to bring in what she called her drug box. Kyle was the first one back and she immediately retrieved the scissors she used to cut the remnants of her shirt off.

She told Janice to get Rayne's shoes and socks off as she set to work cutting her jeans off. With Rayne stripped down to her skimpy underwear, Angie gave her legs, pelvis, and lower abdomen a more thorough examination. Rayne kept trying to pull the sheet over herself. Realizing the embarrassment she must have been feeling, I asked Chase and Kyle to step outside. After that, she stopped trying to cover herself.

The next thing Angie did was start asking Rayne questions about her medical history. Instead of answering with her voice, she was instructed to hold up her right thumb for a yes answer, and her left thumb for a no. She went through a litany of questions before she started prepping her arm for an IV.

"I need a nail on the wall, right there," she stated and looked at me. Without question, I bolted from the room and ran to the barn. I hadn't been gone for two minutes and when I came back in the room, she was holding an IV bag in the air. She was obviously waiting on me. With the nail hammered into place, she hung the bag up. She pulled the sheet up to Rayne's chest and then nodded for Janice and me to leave the room. Neither of us wanted to go, but we did. After five or so minutes of waiting, Angie finally joined us.

"We gotta talk….." Angie said quietly.

CHAPTER 28

August 26ᵗʰ, 2023.

"Her neck injury is the most concerning thing right now," she began once all of us were herded into the kitchen. "Without an x-ray, I have no way of knowing if anything is fractured or not. Someone will have to be in there with her 24 / 7 for the foreseeable future. She is NOT to try and get out of that bed by herself. Understood?"

"What about the broken ribs and stuff?" Janice asked.

"That's par for the course on someone who's had CPR performed on them. It happens more often than not. Now, the other concern is her airway. There has obviously been a lot of trauma in that area. When she gets hungry, nothing solid until the swelling goes down. Whoever takes the first shift with her needs to take paper and a pen. She's going to have a really hard time trying to talk. Get her to write it down and let her vocal cords rest."

"Her prognosis, based on what I know, is pretty good. Even if there are fractures in her C-spine, as long as we keep her down, should heal. It's just going to take time. That's the good news. The bad news is that I just put the last of my painkillers into her IV. It's on a slow drip, so it should get her through the night. That was also my last IV bag. Please, please, please tell me you were able to get medical supplies today."

"We never got that far. We had to leave a....." Janice began.

"We'll go tomorrow!" I cut her off and got to the point. "Gimme a list of what you need. I don't care about the other supply list; I'm talking about making a strictly medical run. I know that nobody is excited about the prospect of going into a hospital. If you don't want to go, fine. I'll go by myself. I just need a list of what I'm looking for."

"Ain't nobody goin solo, man," Chase said from behind me. He looked at Kyle. "Come on, bro. We gotta couple of rigs to refuel and unload," Kyle nodded his answer and followed Chase out the front door.

"I'll have that list for you, Shane. Thank you for making this a priority. I'm gonna go check on our patient," she excused herself leaving me and Janice standing in awkward silence. Janice suddenly felt the need to start a fresh pot of coffee.

"You got any more?" she asked as she emptied the can into the filter.

"Yeah," I reached into the pantry and pulled down another full can. I slid it down the counter to her. The silence continued as she opened the can. When she hit the power button and the small appliance started gurgling, she put her elbows on the counter and her face in her hands. I didn't know what the hell to do or say.

"Janice? You okay?" I asked. She let out a big sigh before she spoke.

"Do you love her?" she asked without turning to face me. Her bluntness surprised me.

"Honestly, Janice, I don't even know how to answer that."

"It's a yes or no question."

"Then yes. I care for her more than I've cared about anyone in a very, very long time. Is it love? I don't know. I can't say that I've ever loved anyone but my family and this is something different. I've cared about other women in the past, but again, this is something different. How do you want me to answer the question?"

"You just did," her shoulders sagged a little.

"Janice," I put my hand on her shoulder. "You have been acting like a protective father and mother. You're the wiser sister looking out for her little sister. You're her best friend and the one she tells everything to. Hell, you're the priest she can confess anything to with no judgment. I understand that. What's more, I'm not here to replace you or take her from you!" she slowly turned to face me.

"I told you when I first met you that she was lucky to have a friend like you and nothing has changed my mind about that. I also told you that I wouldn't try to push a romantic relationship on Rayne. That's not what she needs. If she seeks it out, well, that's different. Right now though, she needs the two of us to do this thing tomorrow. You and I can't go out there if we're not on the same page. That page is all about Rayne's best interests and doing whatever we can to help her. Are you with me?"

"Yeah," she slowly nodded.

"You might think I'm blowing smoke up your ass, but I need you too."

"What?" she looked up at me.

"You're her best friend. I'm going to be hitting you up for advice if she ever decides to pursue something more," I grinned when I said it. That caused her to smile slightly.

August 27th, 2023.

I pulled the midnight to 4 am shift keeping an eye on Rayne. She slept the whole time. I did not. When Janice pulled the 8 pm to midnight shift, she'd brought a couple of candles in and placed them on the nightstand. Their low light was enough to keep watch over Rayne, but not bright enough to keep her awake. The medications in her IV probably helped with that too. The chair next to her bed was far too comfortable so I found myself pacing her room in my socks.

Even in the candlelight, I could see the bruising around the C-collar. The dark splotches were ugly against her tanned skin. There were bruises showing themselves on her face now too. Her knuckles were black and blue from doing battle with bare fists when her weapon malfunctioned. I was just about to be relieved by Angie when a thought came flooding into my mind.

I was finally able to pinpoint one of the frantic thoughts that scared the hell out of me yesterday. Knowing the horrendous abuses Rayne suffered at the hands of her ex-husband. Knowing the path that led her down when he drunkenly showed up at her house after the divorce. Knowing what sort of survival instinct she had. Then seeing her lifeless on the ground..... That visual triggered something inside of me. Some primal sense of vengeance was awakened when I went after her attacker.

Not just vengeance though. There was more. There was another instinct that awakened at the same time. The need to protect her. I tried to convince myself that if it had been anyone else on the ground yesterday that I'd have reacted the same way. Except, I wasn't sure that would have been the case. I know I would have defended them and fought to save them, but would I have had the same primal response? I wasn't totally convinced that I would have.

"How is she?" Angie quietly asked from the open door.

"She's slept the entire time I've been here," I replied and moved closer to Angie.

"Here's the list you asked for."

"Thanks. Is a hospital the only place to get what we need?" I opened the folded sheet of paper.

"Try ambulances first. Vet clinics and dentist offices, any doctor's office really. Fire stations would also be a good second choice. Many of the engines had medics onboard. The ranch store you raided yesterday should have had some of that stuff."

"It probably did. It's probably buried in the enclosed trailer. Janice could probably tell you for sure."

"Okay, I'll ask her when she comes over for breakfast. Kyle and Chase are going to be looking for you too. Those boys were up late putting a little something together for you," she smiled. I was about to ask her what they were cooking up when Rayne groaned from the bed. Her eyes were open and frantically searching the room. Her hands went straight to her neck.

"Shhhh, it's okay, Rayne," Angie soothed as she moved to the closest side of the bed. I went to the opposite side. Her eyes stopped searching when they locked with mine. The whites surrounding the brown were even redder than they were yesterday. Her hand grabbed mine and squeezed tightly.

"Pee," her voice was a hoarse, coarse, grunt of a whisper followed by a cough and gasp of pain.

The brothers came through the front door 15 minutes before Janice. Kyle had a tactical vest hooked on a finger hanging over his shoulder. It looked a lot like the one Rayne had, but it didn't seem to have the armor in it. Chase had a rifle

I'd only seen in the movies. I recognized it as an AK-47, but only because of its iconic shape. The curved magazine was easy to remember. This one was all black with an optic and light mounted on it.

"Figured you might need something with a little more punch," Chase handed me the rifle.

"If a man's gonna have a new rifle, he might as well have something to haul around a few other things too," Kyle shoved the vest toward me.

"I don't know what to say....."

"Don't say nothin'. Call it spoils of war," Chase answered.

"I've never shot an AK."

"We have a few minutes before breakfast. I'll walk you through it. The nice thing about the Kalashnikov platform is that it's super simple. Even with the optic, it doesn't have a fantastic range, but she'll pack a wallop on anything close. Don't rely on the optic too much either. I had to use a bore laser to get the glass at least in the neighborhood. On your vest, there are three 30-round mags for the AK and three more eight-round mags for your Colt. I gave you the pick of the litter with the Kershaw fixed blade. The pouch on the side there is your IFAK....."

"Whoa! Slow down, man! Bore laser? Glass? IFAC? What language is that?" I had to hold my hand up to get him to slow down.

Chase and Kyle motioned for me to bring my new gear and go outside with them. As we walked. Chase explained what all the terms I'd asked about were. The glass he was referring to was an EOTech red dot sight. The IFAK was the pouch on the left side of the belt that was attached to the vest. It was an Individual First Aid Kit. He didn't delve into it any further than to say that there was an Israeli bandage, a tourniquet, and some smaller bandages.

The two walked me through every facet of operating the AK from loading and unloading it, to how the safety worked. It was noticeably heavier than the AR Rayne used. They showed me the different settings on the optic and most importantly, how to turn it off. With a dead battery, it was nothing more than a fancy decoration. It was the same for the flashlight. They also spent a few minutes teaching me what to do in the event of a jam or other issue.

When we were done with the crash course, they went back into the cabin. I met Janice at my truck. She was stowing her new rifle and tactical vest on the passenger seat. She didn't say anything and neither did I. I was more or less trying to get a read on her mental state this morning. When she had everything where she wanted it, she closed the door and walked to the front of the truck. I joined her there a moment later.

"We cool?" I asked her.

"Yeah, we're cool," she looked at her feet. "I guess I'm just worried about sharing custody of our girl," she managed a smile.

FERAL OUTBREAK

"I know I've told you this once, but I'll tell you again; she's lucky to have a friend like you."

CHAPTER 29

August 27th, 2023.

We passed the place where we'd had the flat yesterday just after eight in the morning. We'd checked our radios before leaving the cabin, but we did it again anyway. All four of us had the little radios hooked on our vests and earbuds stuck in our ears. Rather than slow our approach as we entered the city, we just blew through the deserted streets. It didn't look like anything had changed since we'd left in such a hurry yesterday.

We didn't slow down until we passed under the highway. Yesterday, we made a right at that first intersection. Today, we'd be going straight. The surface streets were a little more cluttered causing us to slow even further. Not having the trailers today would be a big advantage when it came to maneuverability, an advantage we were already using.

"It's been a few years, but if I remember right, the hospital sits on a fairly large campus just a couple more blocks up ahead," Janice said from the passenger seat.

"You've been to the hospital, here?"

"Yeah. Got my hand smashed between a powered pallet jack and the wall of my trailer. Don't know how I didn't break anything, but it hurt like hell."

"Ah. Where do you want me to pull up when we get there?" I asked as I navigated around a small silver car sitting in the middle of the road. There was a body laying across the front seat.

"Probably the emergency room. We haven't seen any ambulances and I'm hoping that's where they are. Besides, we should be able to find just about everything on that list in the ER department. If it's still intact that is. Make a left at the next intersection," she instructed.

"If it's intact?"

"When we were at the hospital in Portland when things were really falling apart, there were druggies stealing stuff left and right. Anything they could get their hands on to get their next fix, ya know?"

"I hadn't even thought of that....." my voice trailed off as we passed through the last intersection. The hospital parking lot was now visible on my side of the truck. It didn't look good.

"Shit," Janice muttered. The parking area was packed with cars, trucks, and SUVs. The first entrance we passed was blocked by two burned-out police cars. "Go all the way around back. Follow the signs," she pointed to a sign that gave directions to the Emergency Room.

Each entrance onto the hospital campus looked pretty much the same. One was the scene of a three-car accident. The next was blocked by solid lines of abandoned cars trying to get into the parking area. Arriving at the ER entrance, we found it blocked by a single police cruiser. We stopped and took a good look at where we wanted to go, the covered ambulance bay.

"Kyle, come up here and help me get this car out of the way," she said into the radio. "Don't leave without me," she smiled and opened her door. Using the sling for her rifle, she pushed it to her back as Kyle joined her. They moved in unison to the cop car. Surprisingly, the keys were still in it. Janice tried to start it, but it was totally dead. She pulled the gear selector into neutral and the two of them pushed it to one side.

Before she closed the driver's door, she pulled out the keys and tossed them to Kyle. He understood what she wanted and opened the trunk. As soon as he turned the key, the trunk lid popped open. Kyle jumped back covering his face with his arm. All I could see from my vantage point was the uniformed arm that flopped out. He kicked the arm back in and slammed the trunk shut. Even from where I sat, he looked like he'd turned three different shades of green.

Janice unslung her rifle, bringing it to her shoulder. Kyle, still regaining his composure, did the same. With one hand, Janice squeezed her radio and instructed us to follow them. The two-lane drive up to the ambulance bay was devoid of any vehicles. Janice and Kyle had put a few feet of distance between themselves and slowly walked the drive. As the ambulance bay came into view, it looked like it had been the scene of utter chaos.

Of the seven ambulances, four were backed under the awning, two had collided head-on in the middle of the parking area, and the seventh was halfway into the building where the large sliding glass doors had once stood. Janice held up a hand instructing me to stop. She and Kyle made quick, cursory inspections of the rigs to make sure they weren't occupied. None of them were. When she waved us forward, I swung wide and backed my truck up under the awning. Chase did the same with the other truck.

With Kyle and Janice watching our backs, Chase and I began to rummage through the ambulances. We didn't even bother opening individual bags. We just began tossing anything that wasn't nailed down into the back of the trucks. When I was emptying the farthest rig, I loaded everything onto the gurney. It made it easy to make one trip back to my truck. Rather than unload it and discard the gurney, it also went in. Anything that was loose in the cabinets was thrown onto a sheet, tied up, and taken. I never knew that an ambulance had things like sheets and pillowcases, but I was glad they did. Everything was taken in less than 30 minutes.

"We going inside? Chase asked Janice quietly.

"We need to. Angie had some pretty specific stuff on her list."

"We might have gotten it with everything we just loaded up," I could hear the optimism in his voice.

"We also might not have," I said and stepped past the pair. I peered into the dark emergency room but couldn't see anything moving. I raised my rifle and flipped on the flashlight. The place was a disaster.

"Shane, Chase is right. We probably got what we needed. We can go look elsewhere," the fear in her voice was palpable. I glanced over my shoulder at the three of them.

"Post up here. If I run into trouble, I'll call on the radio," I turned and stepped tentatively through the shattered glass window that had once framed the doors. I stopped by the driver's door of the ambulance and reached through the open window. Finding the headlight switch, I pulled it. The reward was instant. The whole front of the ER department was illuminated in the bright headlights.

"Shane!" Janice persisted.

"If I'm not back in 20 minutes, take what you got and get it back to the cabin," I answered over my shoulder then moved away from the opening.

To be completely honest, each forward step brought a wave of fear with it. The silence that hung in the air was heavy. There was also more than a hint of death clinging to that same still air. There were no bodies, but the evidence that there had been, was overwhelming. Several of the beds had blood-stained sheets and pillows. There were overturned surgical trays, broken computer monitors, and smashed equipment everywhere.

"You ain't goin alone," Kyle said as he put his hand on my shoulder. Not gonna lie, I almost shit my pants and passed out at the same time.

"Jesus, man!" I whispered loudly.

"Supply room," he pointed the rifle-mounted flashlight at the single door near the end of the small emergency room. I nodded and then began to move in that direction. The beam of his flashlight worked one side of the room, while mine worked the other. Our pace was slow but deliberate. When we arrived at the door, he let his rifle hang and drew his handgun. It also had a compact flashlight mounted to it. He held the gun in his right hand and twisted the knob with his left. It didn't budge.

"Watch my back," he whispered and knelt in front of the door. He removed a lockpick set from his back pocket. Selecting his tools from the kit, he got to work on the lock. It wasn't even 30 seconds before I heard the lock disengage. He put his tools away then he stood again. He repeated the process of holding the gun up and twisting the handle. This time the door opened smoothly. I watched from the open doorway as he quickly swept the room for any threats. When he didn't find any, he motioned me into the room. I pushed the door closed behind me and locked it.

138

He and I spent 10 minutes shoving things into pillowcases from the linen closet. There were IV bags, IV kits, suture kits, bandages, and dressings all went into the makeshift bags. There were airway kits, and something he called Ambu Bags. I'd seen them used in the movies when artificial respirations were being given. Like giving mouth-to-mouth but using a bag instead. Surgical tools were also tossed into the bags. By the time we were done, we had 10 pillowcases full of stuff.

"Jan, we're coming out of the supply room. All clear out there?" he spoke quietly into his radio.

"You're clear. Come on out," she replied. He grabbed one bag and opened the door. Even though she'd said it was clear, he still swept our surroundings with the handgun.

"Stay here," he said. I almost protested but thought better of it. He took about 10 steps to the nearest hospital bed. He unlocked the brakes and pushed it back to where I was. We proceeded to load our loot onto it. With all ten bags quickly loaded, he pulled, and I pushed it to the shattered door. Janice and Chase were waiting to unload it. We didn't wait for them.

Leaving the hospital bed behind, we worked our way out of the emergency room and the light offered by the wrecked ambulance. He had switched back to his rifle now and was shining the light on signs in the short hallway. His light momentarily paused on the sign indicating which way to the pharmacy.

I was watching Kyle as well as our surroundings as we moved. His actions and body language were telling me a lot about who he might have been. His footfalls were mostly silent. He moved with a slight bend to his knees and his weapon moved with his eyes. Everything he did was efficient and fluid. There were no wasted movements. I was sure that at one point in time, he had been either military or law enforcement. Either way, he was very skilled and proficient.

When we reached the next four-way intersection, he held up a clenched fist and then motioned for me to move against the wall. Letting his rifle lead, he quickly peeked around the corners. With his practiced proficiency, I could swear he'd done it hundreds of times. Sure that it was clear, he pulled a can of red spray paint from a pouch on the side of his vest. On the far wall, he painted a large arrow and the word EXIT. After he replaced the can of paint, we went around the corner.

I shone my light behind us, and I could clearly tell which way was out. Smart, was all I could think. Right in the middle of the long corridor, he stopped and looked at the sign next to a heavy steel door. On the other side of the door was a window that looked a lot like that of a bank teller. It even had a drawer where you would either place or pick up your items. The sign announced that we had arrived at the pharmacy. He removed his lockpick set again. First, he took care of the deadbolt, then he took care of the keyed lock in the handle. With both locks now unlocked, he replaced the kit in his back pocket.

Still kneeling, he reached up and tapped my thigh. When I looked down at him, I could see the dark red blood that had seeped from under the door in his flashlight beam. It had been there a while. I nodded my acknowledgment. He gently pushed me to one side of the door as he stood on the door handle side. He spoke quietly into his radio again.

"Jan?"

"Yeah, Kyle?" I could hear her answer in my earbud.

"We're at the pharmacy, about to make entry. I don't know what we're gonna find but we might be leaving here in a hurry."

"Understood."

CHAPTER 30

August 27th, 2023.

Before turning the handle, he took another look up and down the hallway. With a curt nod toward me, he gently opened the door. It only moved about six inches but the smell coming from the dark room was absolutely horrendous. He pulled the door shut again and fished around in the pouch on the upper chest of his vest. He pulled out a small tube, removed the cap, and put some of the gel on his fingertip. As he was smearing it on his upper lip, he handed it to me.

The sharp smell of menthol filled my nostrils when I rubbed it under my nose. The lingering smell of death was replaced by the near eye-watering medical minty smell. I gave back the tube and he replaced it in his pouch. With another nod, he opened the door again. Again, it stopped at about six inches, and he had to lean into it to get it open the rest of the way.

Looking into the room past him, I could see the legs of the body that was blocking the door. As he pushed, they slid out of the way, and he had it open wide enough for us to get through. Just like with the supply room, he went in first to make sure it was clear while I watched the hallway. When he was done, he waved me inside.

In the flashlight beam of my rifle, I could see that the pharmacy had been ransacked. The contents of nearly every shelf were scattered on the floor. A couple of the shelving units had even been knocked over. I could also see that there wasn't one body, but two. The one behind the door, a man, had been nearly decapitated by a massive wound to the neck. The second, a woman, looked like she'd been used as a pincushion for hypodermic needles. They were stuck in her arms, legs, feet, and even her neck. Every one of them had the plunger pushed all the way down.

"Here," Kyle tossed me another pillowcase. He then secured the door from the inside. "You know what you're looking for?" he asked.

"Yeah. I memorized the list of meds Angie gave me," I answered and started digging through the pill bottles on the floor.

"Don't bother with the fridge. I think our friend there used all the liquid stuff on herself," he shook his head and played his light across the human pincushion. He then moved off to the other side of the room and began doing the same thing I was doing.

We were looking for anything in the pain management and antibiotic families. As long as we had the bottles identifying them, Angie could sort out what was useful and what wasn't. It took us 30 minutes of rummaging around to fill half of one of the pillowcases. It wasn't a great haul, but it was more than we had before. Hopefully, it would be enough, and hopefully, it would be what we needed.

"Jan?" he spoke into the radio.

"Go, Kyle," her reply was instant.

"We're done in here. Getting ready to head out."

"Copy that."

"Tie that bag shut so we don't lose anything," he instructed and moved to the door. He was about to reach for the door handle when he froze. "Kill the light!" he hissed.

"There's someone in there!" I heard a woman say on the other side of the door. Kyle silently backed away from the door and stayed under the line of sight from the window. He and I both hid directly below the security glass so that anyone looking in wouldn't be able to see us. Three different flashlight beams played over our heads and danced around the room.

"Bullshit!" a gruff male voice answered. It must have been him trying the door handle. "Locked."

"I got it," a younger man answered.

"NO!" came the sharp reply. "What are you trying to do? You want every one of them fuckers to come down here and see what all the noise is?"

"Just let me blow the lock off, Dad! Sarah used to work here so she can run in and grab what we need. We'll be gone before they get here."

"I know exactly what we need and where it is Dad. It won't take me but a few seconds," the female argued. That must be Sarah, I thought to myself.

"Fuck….." I heard Kyle whisper under his breath.

"Fine," Dad finally conceded. "Blow the lock, Donnie."

"I wouldn't do that!" Kyle spoke rather loudly from his hiding spot. There was a sudden silence coming from the hallway. "What is it you're looking for? Maybe we can help each other out of this little pickle."

"Um, we need diabetic medications," Sarah answered.

"There's not much left in here as far as refrigerated stuff, but you're more than welcome to whatever there is. The problem is that you're on that side of the door and we're on this side. Now, I'll unlock the door, but I need y'all to back up a spell so that we might safely exit the room. Ya think we could work that out?" he asked.

"Yeah. We're backing up now," the gruff voice answered.

"Okay. Just so there's no confusion, we're armed, and we understand that you're more than likely armed too. There's no need for anyone to raise a weapon. That's how really bad things happen. Are we on the same page here?"

"I read you loud and clear, buddy," the voice was farther down the hall now.

"Good. We're coming out so everyone just be cool," Kyle reached over and unlocked the door. He gave it a few seconds before he twisted the knob. "Let's be cool now," he stood and opened the door the rest of the way.

Kyle took a quick peek into the hallway before stepping out. He still had his handgun in his right hand, but it was lowered. He held his left hand up with the palm facing the other group. I was carrying the half-full pillowcase in my left hand and had my Colt in my right. I slipped through the opening and into the hallway. He had taken a half step forward to allow me out behind him. That's when I got my first look at the trio standing not even 30 feet away. They were all standing much the same way Kyle and I were.

The older man, the father if I had to guess, was armed with a magazine-fed rifle. He was wearing black body armor that had a badge pinned to it on the left side of the chest. The younger man, Donnie, was packing a pistol grip, short-barreled shotgun. The red-headed Sarah was holding a pistol tightly in her right hand and a flashlight in the left.

"Exactly what is it you folks were here for?" Dad nodded toward me and the pillowcase.

"We've got an injured teammate and she needed something more than Motrin and hydration. Fresh socks weren't even gonna cut it," Kyle let a half-grin play at the corner of his mouth. Dad let a smile crack his surly demeanor too.

"Army?"

"Something like that, sir. You?" Kyle asked. Donnie, Sarah, and I were all looking between the two men trying to figure out what the hell was going on.

"Yep, and don't "sir" me. My ass worked for a livin."

"Me too. You need us to cover your six while you go shopping?"

"How about us boys stand the post while my daughter runs in? That cool with you?" Dad asked.

"That sounds just fine," Kyle replied. Dad motioned Sarah ahead of him. As she walked timidly forward, she shrugged her shoulders out of the small backpack she had on her back. Both of us could see the sour look on her face as she got a whiff of the dead bodies inside the pharmacy. With his free hand, Kyle removed the tube of menthol from his pouch and handed it to her. "It'll help with the smell," he offered when she hesitated.

"Take it, girl. The man says it'll help, it will," Dad said from behind her.

"Just a dab under your nose," Kyle added as she holstered her weapon and took it from him. She unscrewed the cap, put a small dot on her finger, and rubbed it on her upper lip. When she tried to hand it back, Kyle told her to keep it. She shoved it in her pocket, took a deep breath, and entered the pharmacy. Donnie and Dad moved a little closer.

"If you know that trick, you must've been right in the thick of it. Staff Sargent Cody Wilson," Dad introduced himself with an outstretched hand. "That's my daughter, Sarah, and this is my oldest boy, Donnie."

"Staff Sargent Kyle Coleman. A pleasure to meet you," Kyle took the offered hand. "This is my friend, Shane….." he looked oddly at me for a moment when I realized he didn't know my last name.

"Shane O'Neal," I offered and stuck my hand out.

The four of us were standing guard while Sarah rummaged around the wrecked pharmacy. She was in there for less than five minutes when she reappeared in the doorway. She was shrugging her backpack on again. Her face was a portrait of frustrated anger.

"Did you find what we needed?" Cody asked.

"There was one bottle of insulin that wasn't broken,"

"You got someone in diabetic trouble?" I asked.

"My little brother," she answered.

"Have you tried some of the smaller clinics or pharmacies in town?"

"We passed a pharmacy on our walk over here. The place looked like it was ground zero for a terrorist attack," Cody took the answer.

"You walked?"

"SHHHH!" Kyle hissed and cocked his head trying to hear better. He shone his flashlight down the hallway. The beam just dissipated into the dark without landing on anything. "We need to go!" he whispered sharply.

"C'mon," I motioned the trio down the hall that had led Kyle and me here. Just as we started to move, I heard the faint whistling. It wasn't a tune that I recognized, but it was definitely being made by a person. Kyle and Cody were walking backward so they could keep their lights and weapons trained behind us. We picked up the pace when a couple more whistlers joined the first.

"Janice?" I called quietly into the radio.

"Go, Shane."

"There's five of us coming out. It sounds like we've got trouble right behind us," as the words left my mouth, several more whistles joined in.

"Copy. You're plus three. We'll cover as soon as we….."

"CONTACT REAR!" Kyle shouted and unleashed several rounds from his AK-47 in the confines of the hallway. Cody's rifle joined the fight. Both men were still moving backward as they threw rounds in the direction of the enemy. Trying to hear anything Janice was saying in the earbud was totally useless.

We were moving faster now, and I spotted the road sign Kyle had spray-painted on the wall. I started to make the left turn to take us back to the emergency department but caught movement coming down the hallway to the right. I stopped in the four-way intersection and brought my rifle to my shoulder. As soon as the light landed on the bloody scrubs of the woman charging us, I squeezed the trigger. Four rounds left the barrel before she hit the floor.

She was still trying to crawl toward us, so I centered the lighted reticle on the center of her face and fired the fifth round. Her head exploded with chunks of hair, blood, and bone coating the wall next to her. I pushed Sarah and Donnie past me, keeping my light shining brightly down the hall where the woman had come from. Cody and Kyle sprinted past me with Kyle slapping my shoulder on his way by.

I took that as my queue to start moving again. Still facing backward as we moved away from the intersection, I was now in the position to cover our escape. A glance over my shoulder at the rapidly retreating forms of our group and I could see where the headlights of the ambulance were illuminating the wall. We were close now.

I heard something in my earbud and realized that it was Kyle letting Janice and Chase know to hold their fire. I took another glance behind us but didn't see any signs of pursuit. I started running to catch up to the group. Every fourth or fifth footfall and I'd look behind me again. I didn't see the man himself. He was just a dark blur in a dark hallway. What I did see was the glint of my flashlight off of his badge. I was running for everything I was worth, and he was gaining on me at an alarming rate.

Knowing I couldn't outrun him, I slid to a stop and spun all at once. I put the shiny badge in the center of the reticle and pulled the trigger as fast as I could. Even over the loud, snapping of the rounds exploding from the barrel, I could hear the impacts on my target. I knew I was hitting him, but he wasn't even slowing down. Somewhere in the fog of my brain, it registered. This rager was wearing body armor.

I recentered the reticle right between his bloody eyes and pulled the trigger. The boom had an immediate echo from both sides of me. That's when I realized that Cody and Kyle had returned to help me end this guy. It worked, and his headless body slid across the floor, almost reaching our feet. Kyle shoved me toward the emergency department. He and Cody were sprinting right behind me. When we broke into the light, Cody threw himself to the floor. Kyle tackled me, and both of us went down. Just as we went flat, a pair of rifles opened up by the ambulance.

For a few seconds, the noise inside the room was deafening. When Chase and Janice stopped firing, Cody scrambled to his feet. Kyle grabbed me by the shoulder strap of my vest, dragging me to my feet. He pushed me toward the exit. A quick look behind me and I could see three more ragers dead on the floor.

I was never so glad to be leaving an ER. The morning breeze and sunlight felt amazing. The ordeal wasn't over though. Janice and Chase were reloading and backing away from the shattered glass entryway when Kyle and Cody unleashed their rifles. They weren't firing into the ER though. Both were shooting at a small group coming around the far end of the building.

"LET'S MOVE!" I yelled throwing my rifle onto the front seat of my truck. I had it started before my ass had fully settled into the seat. I heard Rayne's truck fire up too. Chase was behind the wheel. As I dropped it in gear, Janice, Donnie, and Sarah all threw themselves into the bed and Janice slapped the back of the cab. I punched the throttle, launching us out from under the awning and down the driveway. Chase had the other two men in the bed of his truck when he pulled in behind me.

CHAPTER 31

August 27ᵗʰ, 2023.

When we passed the cop car at the ambulance entrance, I cranked the wheel to take us out the way we came in and put my foot to the firewall. The diesel was quick to respond to my demands and the rear end got a little sideways. I spotted a woman running from the parking lot on my right. She was waving a pistol at us and screaming. She cleared the four-foot-high fence between the parking lot and the sidewalk in a single bound.

"Don't do it!" I said to myself. I was watching her run into the middle of the street directly ahead of me. She stopped with one foot on either side of the white centerline. She leveled the handgun and I saw the first flash from the muzzle. My windshield spiderwebbed from a hole in the top left corner of the glass. "GET DOWN!" I yelled, hoping the people in the bed of the truck could hear me.

Just as another hole appeared in the top center, I crouched down, leaning slightly toward the middle. I never altered my course, and I never let off the throttle. I heard a couple more rounds hit the sheet metal and there were two more holes in my windshield before I felt the impact. As I was sitting back up, I glanced at the speedometer. It was showing 72 miles per hour. I glanced in my side mirror just in time to see her tumbling body go under the front bumper of Rayne's truck.

I let off the throttle and glanced over my shoulder into the bed of the truck. The entire rear window was shattered and lying in the backseat. Janice, Donnie, and Sarah were all looking back at me wide-eyed. In the scant seconds I had to look at them, it didn't look like anyone had been hit by the gunfire. Looking forward again, I could see the intersection approaching fast, so I gave her a little brake pedal.

Rounding the corner, I was on the throttle again, hard. The response wasn't what I was expecting though. We were gaining speed again, but it felt lackluster. Glancing down at the gauges, I could see the check engine light flashing and the temperature gauge was rising at an alarming rate. It was about then that I could smell the engine coolant. In my side mirror, I could see a white cloud forming in my wake.

"Shane? You okay up there?" Chase's voice came through my earbud.

"I think we're fine, but my truck is done for. I'm losing power and starting to overheat," I reported.

"Gotcha, man. Take her as far as she'll go and then we can throw everything in this rig."

"Copy," I muttered giving her a little more throttle in an effort to put the hospital as far behind us as quickly as possible.

All told we were only able to put another mile behind us before my rig shut down with almost every warning light in the instrument cluster on or flashing. I coasted to a stop right in the middle of the road with a column of steam pouring from under the hood. With no prompting, Chase pulled alongside only leaving about 12 inches between the rigs. Everyone understood what needed to happen and by the time I'd retrieved everything from inside the cab, they were almost done piling everything into the back of Rayne's truck. Even the empty fuel tank was manhandled out of my rig and onto the tailgate of the other truck. It was secured in place with three ratchet straps.

"Too bad about your rig," Janice offered from the middle of the backseat as we pulled away. Cody was on one side of her with Sarah on the other. Donnie was sitting between me and Chase. Kyle had nestled himself into all the gear in the bed.

"Yeah, I liked that truck," was all I could say.

"Is there any chance you guys could take us back to our house?" Cody asked.

"Where's that?" I shook off the thoughts about losing my rig.

"Believe it or not, it's about a quarter mile up the road. Trailer Park on the left side."

"We can drop you off, but I gotta ask; did you guys find what you were looking for at the hospital?" I half turned in my seat.

"A little bit. It'll keep my brother going for a couple more days," Sarah answered before her father could. "Might give us enough time to find more."

"You worked in the pharmacy?"

"Yeah."

"Would any of the medical bags we have in the back have what you were looking for?"

"They might. Why?"

"We don't need the stuff for diabetic emergencies, and you do. It only makes sense to just give it to you," I offered.

"You'd do that?"

"Yeah, why wouldn't we?"

"What do you want in return?" Cody's voice was tinged with skepticism.

"Nothing. We don't need it and you do. That's all there is to it."

"What was it you were looking for in the pharmacy?" Cody asked.

"Antibiotics and pain management stuff. One of our teammates got pretty roughed up yesterday and she's in a world of hurt."

"Teammate? Were all of you military?" he asked.

"No, sir. I guess the term just kinda stuck since all this hit the fan."

"Gotcha. Make the next left," Cody instructed from behind Chase.

"What about you? Were you a cop?" I asked and looked at the body armor Cody was wearing.

"No. I was when I was in the Army, but not now. I got this out of an abandoned police cruiser," he explained. The look Janice shot me gave me the same realization she'd just had. We were going to check out fire trucks and ambulances, but we'd never given any thought to police cars.

"This driveway?" Chase asked as he slowed the truck.

"Yeah. You can just stop here on the street. We've got the main drive blocked about a hundred feet in."

"I see that. Looks like a really good kill zone," I looked in the direction he was looking. Two cars were parked hood to hood blocking the road. More cars were parked bumper to bumper on either side of the street. There definitely wasn't enough room to turn this long ass truck around in the confined space. Six-foot high no-climb chain link fence appeared to surround the small trailer park and anyone trying to get in would have to come through this kill zone, as Chase had called it.

"It is and so far it's done what it's designed to do," Cody opened his door as the truck came to a stop. Sarah was quickly out the other door. As I slid out with Donnie right behind me, Janice leaned forward and said something quietly to Chase. His answer was nothing more than a nod. He also made no attempt to get out of the truck.

We spent 20 minutes in the middle of the street going through all of the medical gear we'd stolen. We had enough so I decided to just give them one of the fully equipped trauma bags. In return for our generosity, Sarah spent a few of those minutes going through the drugs we'd picked up in the pharmacy. She seemed impressed by our seemingly knowledgeable selection, and that's when I let the cat out of the bag about having a paramedic on our team.

Much to my surprise, as the trio was getting ready to depart, Janice handed them a two-pack of FRS radios and a package of batteries. I knew we'd brought extra in case something happened to ours. She told them what channel we were operating on and that we'd try and touch base with them anytime we were in town. I think it surprised Cody too.

"An hour ago, one wrong move and we'd have probably ended up killing each other, or gettin torn to pieces by the maniacs," Cody began. "Now, you've given us enough medical supplies to keep my youngest alive for a decent spell and asked for nothing in return. Ya tell me that we don't owe you squat but let me tell you this; If'n you get in a jam, and we're close enough to help, you can bet yer asses we'll come a runnin."

"That goes both ways, Cody," I extended my hand toward the man. He shook it and held it tightly for a moment.

"This virus thing seems to have turned everything black and white. There ain't no more blurred lines between the good folks and the bad. It sorta seems they got us outnumbered, but if'n we can help each other out, we might just be the last ones standing," he released my hand and shouldered the medical bag we'd given them.

"Thank you for all of this, Shane," Sarah said and held up the small bag of diabetic supplies. Instead of a handshake, she opted for a quick hug.

"Yeah, man. We really appreciate it," Donnie added after giving his older sister an annoyed look. Luckily, he went with the handshake.

We stayed on the street and watched until the small group had retreated behind the blockade. Sure they were as safe as they could be, Chase finally put the truck in gear, and we headed down the road. Kyle and Janice were riding in the backseat with me and Chase sharing the front seat.

"Where to, boss?" Chase looked over at me.

"Pull into that gas station," I pointed to the mini-market / gas station at the next intersection. "Go ahead and fill the truck and the empty tank. I'm gonna run inside for a minute. I've got an idea."

"Need a candy bar and a soda? Getting hangry?" he grinned.

"You ain't going in alone, "Janice said seriously from her seat.

"No," I smiled back at him. "I wasn't figuring on going in alone," I reassured Janice.

Chase parked the truck right in the middle of the empty parking lot and right next to the underground tank access port. I grabbed my rifle and climbed out of the truck and headed for the smashed front door. Janice was right next to me as we entered the store. My first thought was that a tornado had blown through the place. It didn't take but a few seconds to understand what I was looking at.

The stuff we were stepping over was nothing more than refuse and overturned displays. Every bit of anything resembling food was gone. All of the water was gone as were the energy drinks. The beer and alcohol had been heavily raided but there was still some left in the open coolers.

"What are we looking for?" Janice asked from beside me.

"A map."

"Planning a road trip?"

"Not that kind of map. I'm looking for a local map," I said.

"Do they still sell those or even make them anymore?"

"To be honest, I don't know," she moved behind the counter and began looking for one. I looked through all of the overturned magazine racks but came up empty-handed. She didn't have any luck either.

"There were probably maps in the ambulances....." her voice trailed off when she rejoined me at the front of the store.

"You wanna go back there?" I grinned.

"Oh hell no!"

"Angie said fire trucks or fire stations might have the medical supplies, you think they'd have maps too?"

"If my money were worth anything, I'd bet all of it that they do!" she chuckled.

"Okay. One more stop and then we'll see if we can find a firehouse," I stepped out of the store and headed to where the brothers were refueling.

"One more stop?" Janice asked.

"Yeah, I need a new truck."

CHAPTER 32

August 27th, 2023.

We didn't hang around in the parking lot for long once the tanks were full. I told Chase I wanted another Dodge truck, preferably like the one I'd just lost, and he took us to the local dealership. We'd passed by it when we were in town yesterday, so it was easy to find. What wasn't going to be easy to find was an exact replacement for my rig. I knew what the price tag on that rig looked like and it wasn't going to be easy to find its replica.

Many dealerships will take a stock vehicle, directly from the factory, and have some modifications made. I was never sure why they did such things, but I was glad they did. The truck I picked out was a 2022 model, but it had the same engine as mine and it had the same body style. In our current circumstances, the crew-cab long bed was almost mandatory. Like my last truck, this one was also a one-ton 4x4 with single rear tires.

Besides the nearly identical interior, the similarities ended there. This one had a suspension lift and oversize off-road tires. It had a massive front bumper and grill guard that held a winch and off-road lights. Where mine had the chrome grill and trim, this one was all blacked out. According to the window sticker, it also sold for close to 110,000 dollars. I grinned thinking about the conversation I'd had with Rayne about committing felonies. I guess I was well past that stage now. All of my reservations had been neatly tucked away in the file called Survival.

Leaving Chase and Kyle with Rayne's truck, Janice and I went inside to try and find some keys for the lock box on the window of the truck. We had to rifle through and break into several offices before we finally found what we were looking for in the manager's office.

We returned to the lot triumphantly with the master key for the lock box and got my new ride opened up. I gave it a quick once over and then fired it up. The only thing I could find wrong was the fuel gauge barely registered any fuel in the tank. While it warmed up, Chase pulled alongside and filled it with the fuel we'd just taken from the corner store.

"Do you want to try and find a firehouse now?" Janice asked while we waited for the fuel transfer to be complete.

"I think we need to keep our eyes open for one, but don't forget, we also need to get the moving vans we had to leave behind yesterday."

"They aren't more than six or eight blocks from here and the boys brought the keys. You wanna go grab them first and then do some sightseeing?"

"Yeah. That sounds like a good plan. Were they fully loaded, or did you need to finish up?"

"No, they were full. It's just a matter of pulling away and closing the back doors."

"Yeah, let's do that then. Just do me a favor, Janice."

"What?"

"I've already had one bad encounter with a stowaway, make sure there ain't nobody hiding in the back. None of us need surprises like that," I smiled.

Before leaving the dealership, we transferred about half of the medical gear into the back of my rig. Chase relinquished the driver's seat of Rayne's truck to Janice and Kyle climbed in with me for the short trip to where we'd left the vans. Knowing that both paved entrances were blocked with destroyed cars or littered with nails, Janice led us to the field where she'd plowed through the fence.

Kyle checked out the area with his scoped rifle while Chase cut the destroyed fence with a small pair of bolt cutters. The moving trucks were much lower to the ground than the 4x4's and we didn't want them snagging on the downed chain link. It's actually kinda surprising that neither of the trailers had gotten caught up on it in our haste to flee the area the day before.

"You guys seeing this?" Chase asked into his radio as he dragged the last section of fencing out of the way.

"No bodies," I answered.

"Yep, looks like they're all gone. Watch our backs, moving for the vans," he announced. I watched as he and his brother sprinted across the open expanse. Chase unlocked and jumped into the first van while Kyle covered him. Sure there weren't any stowaways, he closed the roll-up door. Kyle then pulled the second van away from the dock while Chase covered him.

"Moving," Chase said and both rigs turned and headed toward us.

"Copy. Follow me. Janice, bring up the rear," I said into the little radio and pulled ahead of everyone. As I was scanning our surroundings and waiting for the two vans to fall in line, my eyes settled on the big dash display. "You idiot!" I scolded myself when my eyes settled on the navigation icon. I reached over and tapped it. The screen immediately brought up a street map of our current location. It didn't take me any time at all to find that the closest fire station was only three blocks farther south and right on the main road.

"Dumbass," I muttered with a shake of my head. I led our small convoy through the field and five minutes later, we were rolling to a stop in front of the fire station. I left the truck running and opened the door. I reached back in and grabbed my rifle before heading for the front door. I didn't have to say anything over the radio because I saw Kyle jogging to join me.

I arrived at the door first and gave the knob a try. Judging by the electronic keypad, I had a feeling it wouldn't open, and I was right. Kyle took a knee, pulled out his pick set, and got to work. This one took him a few seconds longer, but he prevailed in the end. I was the first to enter with my rifle at my shoulder. He paused long enough to block the door open behind us.

Right there, on the wall of the main office was a huge map of Winnemucca. There was a lot of information that had been marked on it, but I wasn't about to take the time to inspect it. It had all of the streets and that's what I was after. It was held in place by a dozen or so push pins and we had it down and rolled up in seconds. I left it laying on the desk by the front door so that we could grab it on the way out.

Next, we moved silently into the dimly lit engine bay. It was the far bay where we found the rig we were looking for. It had a fully stocked medical bag, several oxygen bottles, and all of the paraphernalia that went with them. There was an AED and a drug box a lot like the ones we'd taken from the ambulances. Between the two of us, we were able to grab all of it and head for the door we'd come in. I still had a free hand, so I grabbed the map. All of it was hastily deposited in the backseat of my truck.

"Okay, we've gotten what we came to town for, can you guys think of anything else we need to get before we head out?" I asked, sliding behind the wheel again.

"There's still a lot we need to get, Shane," I heard Janice in my ear. "I think we should probably head home though."

"I think you're right. Follow me."

Yesterday, it was the trailers slowing us down on the rough roads. Today, it was the low-slung moving vans. By the way they were riding, it was easy to see that they were overloaded with barely any give to the rear suspension, and that's when we were still on the pavement. Off-road, I was worried they would blow out one of the rear tires. Yeah, they had dual tires, but one tire wouldn't last long under that much weight.

So, we went slow. Painfully slow. It was four in the afternoon when we finally pulled into the driveway in front of the cabin. Not recognizing my new truck or the moving vans, Angie greeted us with an AR-15. Once she realized who it was, I could see relief flood the features of her face.

"How's Rayne?" I asked, walking up the front stairs to the porch.

"As good as we can expect. She's hurting pretty bad. Did you guys have any luck finding what I needed?" she was hopeful.

"Got a bag of goodies for ya," her boyfriend, Kyle answered as he came up behind me. He reached past me to hand her the half-full pillowcase. "We got a whole bunch of other stuff in the trucks too."

"Any IV supplies?" she asked.

"Right here," Janice had that pillowcase slung over her shoulder. Angie ushered all of us into the kitchen. She quickly spread everything out on the counter.

"Is it okay if I go see her?" I asked.

"Yeah," she replied absently. Out of the corner of my eye, I caught Janice starting to follow me, but she stopped short. She glanced at me, pursed her lips, and then turned back to help Angie sort through the supplies we'd brought in. The brothers were busy hauling everything else into the house.

I peeked through the crack of the barely open door before I barged in. Rayne was propped up slightly with the aid of extra pillows and her eyes were closed. Easing through the doorway, I left it cracked as I had found it. As I approached, I could see that we'd made it back just in time. Her IV couldn't have had more than an ounce or two of fluid left in it.

The black and blue marks on her face were worse than when I'd seen them this morning. Her right eye probably wouldn't be able to open because of all the swelling. Angie had applied some ointment to her cracked and swollen lips. Even though she still had the C-collar on and the chest wrap, the black and blue splotches on her flesh were plainly visible.

I stood next to the bed and started to reach for her hand. Her scraped knuckles had been coated with the same stuff that had been put on her lips. I settled for gently brushing the hair from the edges of her face. After about five minutes, her left eye fluttered open.

"Hey," I whispered and smiled.

"Hey," her voice was just as gravelly as the last time I'd heard it.

"We were able to get just about everything Angie needed while we were in town. She'll probably be in shortly to get you some more pain meds," I tried a smile.

"Thank you," she forced the words out. I could hear Angie coming toward the door.

"You'd have done it for me. It's what friends do," I gently stroked her cheek with the back of my hand. She closed her eye again and I could tell that the slight smile was painful, but it was good to see. "Somebody else is here to see you," I said when I saw Janice come through the door right behind Angie.

Janice had been kind enough to allow me a few minutes alone with Rayne and now it was my turn to reciprocate the gesture. I took a step back from the bed and motioned for Janice to take my place.

CHAPTER 33

August 27th, 2023.

I stayed in the room while Angie changed the IV bag and then added some painkillers to the drip. It only took a couple of minutes before Rayne was fast asleep again. Angie and I excused ourselves to give Janice a few minutes with her friend, our friend.

"Is she gonna be okay?" I asked Angie once we were back in the kitchen.

"As I said, it's gonna take time. She got the hell beat outta her and the bruises are just making things look worse. I'm still concerned about a neck fracture, but we're taking every precaution we can until we know otherwise. It's just a waiting game," she offered, telling me everything I already knew.

"Okay," I said with resignation.

"I mean, the good news is that it looks like you brought back enough stuff to start up our own emergency room. At least a well-stocked ambulance or four," she waved her hand toward everything that had been piled into the living room. "I just hope we don't have to use it beyond the here and now."

"I think we can all agree on that," I tried a smile. "If I haven't said it already, thank you."

"Just doing what I can."

"Well, it's appreciated. If there's anything else you need us to go get, please say so and we'll be gone like a shot."

"I think you've brought home enough. That is unless you've got a trauma Doctor tied up in your backseat," it was her turn to smile.

Angie spent the rest of that afternoon basically turning Rayne's room into a hospital room with Janice helping her. All of the supplies we'd brought home were moved in there except for two bags that she stripped down and restocked. She was making two fully stocked medical bags for each truck that included oxygen and C-collars. The second bag that went in was the AED bag. It meant basically losing the legroom for one of the backseats, but it was well worth it.

Chase and Kyle had made themselves busy rearranging the loads in the back of the moving vans. Full, shrink-wrapped pallets had been loaded without full knowledge as to what was really on them. Chase and Janice knew it was mostly canned food, but not much more than that. By the time I joined them, they had one of the trucks unloaded and the pallets broken down in the driveway.

"Are we planning on using these rigs again?" Chase asked, tossing me a 3-pound bag of beef Jerky.

"Do we need to?" I tore the bag open and offered him and Kyle some.

156

"Yes and no. Kyle made the suggestion that if for whatever reason, we had to bug out of here in a hurry, we've got enough drivers to bring these rigs along."

"You mean leave the food in them? I'm assuming that's so we wouldn't have to try and load it all in a panic, right?" I said around a mouthful of the meat treat.

"Most of the food. We should unload some of it into the barn and house. We could fill the space that's left with camping gear, tools, and whatnot. I mean, as long as we have a good inventory of what's in each van and only use what we need out of each one, they might be helpful. Even if we never leave here again, they'll make good weather and rodent-proof storage units," he stuck his hand into the offered bag for another piece of jerky.

"Rayne was my list person, but if you guys wanna take over for a while, I don't see a problem with it."

"Cool, man. Is it okay if most of this stuff sits in the driveway tonight? We'll move the stuff the critters can get back inside, but we'd like to unload both trucks before we start reloading any of the heavier stuff."

"That's fine. You guys need a hand?" I asked.

"Nah, we unloaded all the stuff we brought back yesterday, and we already know where everything is. It's cool," he shrugged off the question.

Okay. If you don't mind me holding you up just a little longer, can I ask one more question?"

"Anything, man."

"Were both of you in the military?" Chase answered with an immediate shake of his head.

"Nah. That was Kyle's gig," he motioned toward his brother with a thumb. "When he got out, he hooked up with me and helped out with the guided hunts and whatnot."

"Ah, okay," I shifted my gaze from Chase to Kyle. "Any chance you could teach the rest of us what you can? I'll be honest when I tell you this, I felt pretty awkward out there today. Yesterday too."

"You mean like tactics and shit?" Kyle asked.

"Not just that. Weapons handling and communications seem like they are a pretty big deal too. I've just felt like a fish outta water. I can't help but think that if I was a little more knowledgeable and more on the ball, I might have been able to save Rayne a lot of pain and suffering. I really don't want to get caught flatfooted like that again. Know what I mean?"

"Eh, you're selling yourself short, Shane. You did just fine when we were in the hospital today. That place was just a shitshow waiting to happen and you kept it together. As for yesterday, I wasn't there, but from what I've been told, you held it together just like you did today," Kyle offered.

"If I did so good, why is Rayne laid up in there for God knows how long?"

"It happens, bro. Sometimes it's just kismet or some other cosmic horseshit. Once you realized she was in trouble, it was already too late. You didn't abandon her or worse, freeze up. She's laid up in there because you kept it together. If you hadn't, both of you would probably be dead," he paused to pick a sliver of jerky out of his teeth with a fingernail.

"Back to your question though, yeah. I'll teach you what I can whenever I can. We just need some downtime. Hell, I taught this idiot everything he knows," he elbowed his older brother. "Between the two of us, we could probably bring the rest of you up to speed in no time. Angie and Jan both know a little, but I'm sure they'd be down to learn some more."

"Speaking of Angie, would some first aid classes be unreasonable?"

"You'd have to ask her, but I doubt she'd balk at the idea."

"I think I'll do that over dinner tonight," I nodded to myself.

"Mind if I ask you some questions now?" Kyle asked.

"Not at all."

"Tween the way you're talking and all the supplies we've either laid in or are planning on laying in, I assume the plan is to winter here, correct?"

"It seems like the most feasible plan."

"It is. This is a good location. Now even with everything we've hauled in here, you realize that we've only scratched the surface of that big list the girls were going over, right?"

"Yeah. I also realize how many things we need that never even made it on the list," he grinned when I said it. "What? Am I wrong?"

"No, you're not wrong. Even if we brought home every single item on that list, we'd still be in a world of hurt. The problem isn't what we still need. The problem is how do we get it all before the weather turns, and how do we do it in a way that doesn't get anyone killed?"

"I don't....." I started but stopped.

"I think you do," Kyle smiled.

"We need a few more hands and we need a few more vehicles," I said flatly.

"Now you're thinking like a supply chain manager."

"Ya know, Shane, the night we showed up here, you laid down the law. I seem to remember you saying it was your place and your rules," Chase chimed in. "We didn't have a problem with that then and we don't have a problem with it now. That'll never change unless you want it to."

"What do you mean by that?" I asked.

"The way we look at it, the way all of us look at it, is that you're the boss. What you say goes and all of us will do what you ask of us. All we ask in return is that you continue to lead. We can throw suggestions your way, but the final word is yours."

FERAL OUTBREAK

"Shane, we're all good at our jobs. Angie is a hell of a medic. Janice can drive just about anything with wheels. Me and Chase, well, we're kinda all over the place as far as skills go. The thing is, we need a big-picture kinda guy and that's you. You ask the hard questions, and you listen to the answers we give you. You may not always wanna hear the answer, but you listen. I'm pretty sure you actually give a shit about us too. All that considered, we think you'd be good in the lead role, man," Kyle added.

"Even Janice?"

"Yes, even Janice," Chase answered. "Don't get me wrong, she can be headstrong, but I think a lot of that is because she was unsure of your intentions where Rayne was concerned. That's all been put to bed, so you won't have any worries in that department. You got my word on that."

"That was kind of a touchy subject, wasn't it?" I grinned.

"She's that way with all of her friends, man. To one extent or another, that's just the way she is. The good news is that she considers you to be on the inside of that circle now."

We talked for a few more minutes before I left them to the work they had started. It wouldn't be long before dark and they wanted to get as much done as possible before dinner. They had given me a lot to think about and think about it I did. I sat on the porch while absently watching them work. My thoughts couldn't have been farther away though.

The logistical part of my brain was trying to work out some of the details. Things like how many more people would we need for everything we needed to accomplish? How would we feed them and where would we house them? How many were too many? Were there certain skills I should keep an eye out for, or would simple muscle be enough?

As of now, I didn't have a clue how long our food would hold out. I would have a better idea once everything had been inventoried, but now, I just didn't know. What about the fuel situation? The brothers said we could use a couple more vehicles, and they were right. A couple more heavy-duty trucks in the stable could really be useful when making supply runs.

It was warm now, but what would a winter here look like? Admittedly, I didn't know. I'd only ever been here in the summertime. Would we have enough wood to burn? The stove in the kitchen used it and so did the fireplace. What about keeping the RV warm so that everyone had a place to sleep? For now, that was covered, but how would we deal with it if we brought on a few more hands?

The logistical nightmares just seemed to compound one on top of another. More help meant more food. More food meant more trips into civilization. More trips meant more fuel. It was dizzying to try and keep track of. Every single thought led me down another rabbit hole of how to deal with the problem. There were just too many what if's.....

159

Rayne and I had become pretty good at bouncing ideas off of each other, but I didn't have that option at the moment. Were these troubling issues things I could talk to one person about? Was it something that needed group input? After a moment of thought, it was obvious these decisions would need to be made as a group. It was just too much for one or two people to deal with. There were way too many variables and the more people we had looking at the problems only increased our chances of success.

I didn't want to bring it up over dinner tonight. All of us were tired from the day we'd had today. The only proclamation I'd make tonight would be that we would be taking a couple of days to stay home. Tomorrow we could start batting ideas around. These were smart people, and I had no doubt we could figure it all out. Well, some of it anyway.

CHAPTER 34

August 29ᵗʰ, 2023.

As promised, we'd taken two full days to sort of chill out around the house. During that time, Rayne had started to show some signs of improvement. Her voice was still hoarse and scratchy, but she could put more than two words together at a time. Angie had given her a catheter so there was no need to escort her to the bathroom as much. She still needed someone in the room with her at all times, or at least close enough to hear the bell she'd been given to summon help.

The brothers had done a full inventory of everything we'd brought home over the course of the twin trips to Winnemucca. Much to our dismay, there were still so many items left to be crossed off. That was all part of the conversation we were supposed to have after dinner tonight. The other part would be about finding other survivors, whom to make an offer to, and how many people we wanted to bring on board.

I had been thinking about Cody and his family to be sure. The only problem would be his youngest son's medical problems. The sad thought that occurred to me was that it was only a matter of time before he passed away. Diabetes and so many other illnesses that were managed with regular medication would now be death sentences. I guess I sort of had a moment there when the realization hit me that all of us were in a precarious position. A rusty nail, an untreated cut, a slip or fall….. All of them could be deadly now.

Since moving Rayne into the living room where we'd been eating was a bit of an impossibility, all of us gathered in her room to eat. Tonight's dinner of roast, potatoes, and vegetables was prepared by Janice. Fortunately, Rayne was able to eat as long as her food was in very small bites. We ate and joked and then ate some more. One thing that had become rare around here was leftovers. After dinner, we moved the serious conversation into the kitchen so Rayne could get some rest. I would have loved to have had her input, but she was exhausted from eating.

"Cody and his family would be an obvious choice." Kyle started. "He's military trained, she knows her way around medications and Donnie seems like the sort who's got a decent head on his shoulders."

"What about the sick son?" I asked.

"It is what it is. I don't mean to sound harsh about it, but I think bringing them out here would be worth it. The kid's gonna die sooner or later. Would it be better to happen here or there?"

"Kyle's right, Shane. There's nothing we can do about the son, but the other three could be just what we're looking for. I think we should make 'em an offer the next time we go to town," Chase agreed.

"Janice? What do you think?" I looked in her direction.

"I agree with the boys," she said after a sip of beer.

"Angie?" I locked eyes with the paramedic.

"Just going off of what you guys have said, I'd have to agree. If the daughter was a pharmacy tech, I could probably train her to help me with the medical side of things. If Dad was military, he can help in the training. Even if the older brother doesn't have any real skills, he's still a strong back to help with everything else," she offered. I nodded.

"Well, I guess all we can do is make them the offer. They'll either take it or they won't. That leads me to my next question. When do we want to go back?" I asked the whole group. "Do you want one more day to rest up or do you want to go tomorrow and be done with it?" Everyone wanted one more day to relax.

"So, we'll go to town the morning of the 31st. Chase and Janice in Rayne's truck. Kyle, you can ride with me. I still have the master key for the lockboxes at the dealership. We can go pick out a couple more trucks to bring back after we talk to Cody about moving out here. During this trip, we need to do some serious scouting."

"Cody and his family are going to need a place to stay so, we'll need to bring an RV or travel trailer back with us. Even if they decline the offer, we should bring one back anyway. We need to be on the lookout for everything. Firewood, food, fuel, solar gear….. all of it needs to be scouted and marked on the map," I pointed at the rolled-up map on the counter.

"It's painfully obvious that no matter how many vehicles we have, we're not going to be able to bring everything we need in one trip. The more we can scout and mark on Thursday, the better. It'll make the trips more effective in the future. I had to think long and hard about what I'm about to say, but I think it'll benefit all of us in the long run," I paused to make eye contact with everyone.

"Once we've scouted things out on Thursday, we need to plan a return trip to load up what we scouted. For each trip, we need to be scouting for future trips. We also need to think about splitting up once we hit the city limits. The only exception to that would be if we had to go into a high-risk area. Something like another trip to the hospital, for example. We have communications in case anyone gets in trouble, and I think we need to take advantage of that."

"If Cody and his family join us, then we can add their numbers to the existing teams instead of creating new teams. It goes back to the whole safety in numbers thing. Anyway, we can use the map that we got the other day, but we can also use the navigation systems in the trucks. That's one of those resources I'd totally overlooked and forgotten about," my admission earned me a couple of grins.

"The other thing we need to keep in mind are other survivors. If it hadn't been for Kyle's cool head, that encounter could have turned out a lot worse. I guess we need to come up with some rules of engagement for dealing with them. We know they exist, and they are more than likely trying to do the same thing we are. We don't need to get in a pissing match with them. If anything, we need to try and make friends. Kyle, you're the military guy so I need you to be thinking about that," he answered with a nod.

"I know I haven't been really engaged with anyone over the last couple of days, and I apologize for that. I've probably driven most of you nuts with my cryptic questions. To say that I've had a lot on my mind is a terrible understatement. We, as a group, have so much work to do, it seems nearly insurmountable. Nearly. As long as we play it smart and continue to work our asses off, I think we'll be okay. What's more, I think that we can be comfortable here once the weather turns cold." I looked at the faces gathered before me. "We all on the same page regarding what we have to do?"

"I've got one thing I'd like to bring up," this was Kyle.

"Yeah?"

"There's something that has been bothering the hell out of me, and I know you don't know the answer. It's just something all of us need to pay attention to during our next trip," he shifted uncomfortably on his feet. "When we went back to get the moving trucks at the grocery store, Chase said there should have been about a dozen and a half bodies lying about but they were all gone. Now, I don't know about y'all, but that kinda bothers me a bit."

"Yeah, that had me a little freaked out too. What's your take on it?" I looked at Chase when I asked it.

"We talked about it a little," Chase motioned to his brother. "Neither of us really knows what to think about it. The only thing we could come up with is that it's some Good Samaritan taking care of the dead."

"That makes sense," Janice said.

"Yes and no. We didn't do a whole lot of exploring around the hospital, but you'd think there would have been some bodies piled about. We haven't really seen any around town either. All that leads us to think that there are more than one or two people taking care of the dead. We also gotta ask who it might be, why they're doing it, and why haven't they tried to flag us down."

"Another thing, Shane, the population of Winnemucca couldn't have been all that much. Why are we seeing so many ragers? There were 16 or 18 that came after you at the grocery store and we popped another eight or nine at the hospital. That includes the one you mowed down with your truck," Kyle added.

"All things I don't have an answer for," I admitted. "Do you think Cody might know something?"

"He might. I guess we'll just have to ask him when we go back," Kyle said.

August 31st, 2023.

Everything had been going just fine this morning. That is until it wasn't. We'd had breakfast, and the trucks were topped off and checked out. Everything we'd possibly need for the day was loaded up the previous evening. I couldn't have asked for it to have gone smoother. We planned on pulling out of the driveway at 5 am, and we did just that. Everything came to a grinding halt, quite literally, when we came to the intersection at Denio Junction. Fortunately, we weren't going that fast when I jammed the brake pedal.

"That's not a good sign," Kyle said flatly from the passenger seat. He was also looking at the body hanging from the awning of the Denio Junction store. The pair of bodies Rayne and I had left in the parking lot were gone, but this one was on display for the world to see,

"What do you think?" I heard Janice ask in my earbud.

"Stay here. We're gonna check it out," I said into the radio and cranked the wheel of the truck. I checked my mirror as we pulled into the parking lot to make sure she stayed put.

I kept one foot on the brake and the other hovering over the gas pedal as we rolled closer to the gently swinging body. It was a young man, maybe 25. His bound feet were only about six inches off the ground. His hands were bound behind him, and he had a length of rope around his neck that had been fashioned into a noose.

All of his clothes were filthy and so was his exposed skin. Whoever he was, he hadn't been there long enough to begin decomposing or bloating in the late August heat. He hadn't even begun to attract that many flies. As unsettling as all of this was, it was the sign hanging around his neck that sent chills down my spine. In what I could only assume was blood, the warning was loud and clear.

"LOOTERS BEWARE".

CHAPTER 35

"What do you want to do?" Kyle asked.

"We need to cut him down," I said quietly. "Janice, cover us while we get this guy down," as soon as I released the mic button, I put the truck in park and opened the door. Kyle was right behind me.

Kyle wrapped his arms around the man's waist and lifted. It was only a couple of inches, but it took some of the tension off of the rope. I pulled the knife from my vest and sliced cleanly through it in one swipe. After replacing my knife in its sheath, I helped him lower the body to the ground.

"We don't have time to bury him, and I don't really feel like hanging around here. Know what I mean?" I asked. Kyle replied with a shrug and started for his door. For whatever reason, I glanced through the glass doors of the store. What I saw stopped me in my tracks and stole the breath from my lungs. "Kyle...." I hissed.

Inside the store, bodies were stacked like cordwood. There had to be 25 or 30 of them. We hadn't smelled them because the doors had been sealed with duct tape. Kyle joined me at the window, both of us cupping our hands to our eyes to see the dark interior better.

"What the fuck....." I heard him mutter under his breath. All of the bodies were still clothed but you could see the stains of body fluids saturating the cloth. Some of the bodies had bloated to the point that they had popped like overinflated balloons. Others looked like any disturbance at all would cause them to expel their contents onto the floor.

"What the hell are you guys doing?" Janice asked in my ear.

"Just keep your eyes open," I growled and went back to the truck. We'd brought two 5-gallon cans of diesel with us in case the rigs we picked up at the dealership didn't have enough fuel to make it to the gas station. I pulled both of them from the bed and Kyle must have understood what I was going to do. Without so much as a word, he grabbed the second can and removed the spout.

We moved the body we'd cut down onto a wooden bench in front of the windows and then we started dousing the wood siding in diesel fuel. He went one way, and I went the other. We met again on the backside of the building. He handed me his empty fuel can and removed a lighter from his pants pocket. The diesel was much harder to light than gasoline would have been, but he got it going after his third attempt.

The nice thing about the heavier fuel was that it burned slower. We stood back and watched the flames on the outside begin to grow in intensity and before long, the building itself was burning. The flames started by the ground and were soon licking their way up the wooden siding and into the eaves. Sure that it wouldn't go out, we jogged back to the truck. Tossing both empty cans in the bed, we jumped in and pulled away from the gathering inferno. I swung wide and came up on the passenger side of Rayne's truck. Janice rolled down her window and I did the same with mine.

I spent a couple of minutes explaining about the hanging body and everything we saw inside the store turned mortuary. Everyone agreed that it was the best call to just burn the place to the ground. There was nothing to be gained by leaving it standing and none of us had the stomachs to try and make entry.

As much as we wanted to be on our way to Winnemucca, we couldn't leave until the store was fully engulfed. During the 20-minute wait, we discussed why the bodies had been placed there and who might have done it. The other hot topic was over who might have been taking out some vigilante-style justice on a looter.

"Wouldn't we be considered looters?" Janice asked.

"Yeah, probably," I answered.

"You wanna turn around and head home?" Chase asked from behind the wheel of Rayne's truck.

"No. We continue as planned."

When the roof of the store finally caved in on itself, we turned and headed for Winnemucca. The fire we'd started, and the thick black column of smoke faded in the rearview mirror, but the anxiety about what might have been ahead of us only grew with each passing mile. The questions about what happened back there were also growing. Kyle was quiet in the seat next to me. The radio was quiet too. The drone of the tires and the quiet growl of the engine were the only things we could hear.

"Cody, it's Shane. You out there?" I spoke on the radio as we approached the highway underpass. I tried three more times and never got an answer. I looked over at Kyle.

"He could have the radio off trying to conserve battery power," he suggested.

"That's what I'm hoping," I turned at the next intersection. "Let's head on over there anyway."

"Slow down!" Kyle said suddenly. My foot came off the gas.

"What?" I was frantically searching all around us for the possible threat.

"Look," he pointed to a parking lot in front of a chain hardware store. "That parking lot only had three or four cars in it when we were here last. There's what, 50 cars and trucks there now?"

"Town meeting? Do you see any people?" my foot was breathing on the brake pedal ever so slightly.

"No. I don't see anyone," his eyes started scanning everything all at once. "Get us over to Cody's place. I don't like this, not even a little bit," I started to move my foot from the brake to the gas when Chase's voice came from my earbud.

"Shane, we got a bogie running up behind us. He's trying to flag us down."

"Running?" I asked and looked in my side mirror.

"Yeah, running. What do you want to do?"

"Does he look like a rager?"

"Um, no. Looks like he's had the crap kicked out of him though. You wanna try and..... Oh shit! GO, GO, GO!" at the same time I heard Chase yell in my ear, I saw the group of people rushing from one of the side streets. They were waving bats, tire irons, and various garden implements as they converged on the running man. I stabbed my foot down on the throttle as Chase began to close the distance between us.

I was trying to watch the road ahead and the mob behind us. There must have been 20 of them. The ones that weren't involved in beating the man to death in the street were busy watching us leave the area in a hurry.

"Better slow down!" Kyle warned. "Two blocks and take a left."

"Got it," I replied. Instead of gently slowing down, I waited until the last possible second before braking hard and cutting the corner. Chase stayed glued to my ass through the maneuver. I gunned the throttle again. "Keep trying to raise Cody," I told Kyle.

The two-lane residential street was too narrow to try and stay on my side of the road, so I didn't even bother. I just took my half right out of the middle. I heard Kyle call out four more blocks and then another left in between his radio calls to Cody. When I started braking hard for the intersection and impending turn, I heard the faint answer over the radio.

"Help us," the panic-stricken voice of Sarah was barely audible.

"Sarah?" Kyle asked into the mic.

"Hang on!" I said loudly as we took the left-hand turn about 20 miles-per-hour faster than we should have. The tires howled and there was an instant of panic when the understeer had us headed for the curb and sidewalk at an angle. Rather than slow even more, I was hard on the gas causing the rear to slide. It had the desired effect of getting the nose pointed in the right direction again. I looked in my mirror and could see that Chase had slowed quite a bit to make the turn without the theatrics.

"I don't know! There are at least four of them and they're almost through the front door!" I heard Sarah's voice. She sounded terrified. I could also hear loud thudding noises in the background.

"Hang on baby! I'm almost there!" Cody's loud voice broke through. Over the roar of our own engine, I could hear his through the tiny speaker in my ear.

"There!" Kyle pointed to a red Dodge Challenger sliding sideways into the driveway a quarter of a mile ahead of us. "Cody! Wait for us! We're 15 seconds out!" Kyle said into the radio mic. His answer was a pair of clicks.

"You and your brother need to get on the floor in the back bedroom. Get under the bed!" I could see Cody yelling into the radio when he threw open the door of the sports car. He wasn't waiting. At the last possible moment, I stood on the brakes of my truck and slid to a smoky stop behind Cody's car. Kyle was on the ground and running before I got it stopped all the way.

"Chase! Janice! Watch our backs!" I jumped out, grabbed my rifle, and shouted at them all at once. Cody was maybe 20 yards ahead of Kyle. In turn, Kyle was about 20 yards ahead of me. All three of us were sprinting through the kill zone Cody had set up in the narrow driveway.

Without missing a step, Kyle launched himself into the air and ran across the hood of the car blocking the road. He didn't miss a step when he jumped from the other side either. By the time my feet hit the hood, Cody was already firing rounds from his rifle. When I jumped from the hood, I seriously misjudged my speed and height. When my feet hit the ground, my legs folded causing me to tuck and roll. I scrambled to my feet just as Kyle's rifle began to bark.

They were shooting toward the front of the house when a man vaulted the picket fence from the backyard. I don't think he was even aware of my presence. He was trying to run all while watching Cody and Kyle. I lowered my shoulder and plowed into him at a dead run. That was all I had time to do. Anticipating the hit, I was able to stay on my feet, but he flew from his and hit the pavement hard. I heard the breath leave his lungs when we hit, and I heard the hollow thud of his head bouncing off the pavement.

I knew he wouldn't be getting up anytime soon, so I swept the backyard with my rifle. There wasn't anyone else coming my way and the gunfire from the front of the house had ceased. I looked down at the man I bowled over when he groaned. The whites of his eyes had a slight tinge of red. Otherwise, he didn't have any of the telltale signs of a rager. I took a step away from him and leveled the sights of my rifle right between his eyes. As he began to regain his senses, he rubbed the back of his head. His hand came away with a little blood on it.

"You make a move to get up or do anything stupid, and I'll make sure your brains leave that melon you call a head. Got it?" he nodded in understanding.

CHAPTER 36

"House is clear. Four of us coming out to the street," Kyle said ten minutes after he announced he and Cody would be going inside. When they appeared on the street, Cody had his arm wrapped around his daughter and Kyle was carrying a blanket-bound young man of ten or twelve years old. His pasty white complexion was visible even from where I stood. He was still alive, but I couldn't see that as being the case for much longer. As they got closer, Kyle handed the son off to his father. He directed them to go straight to the trucks and not come back. Sure that they understood, he altered course and walked heavily toward me and my prisoner.

"Who are you?" Kyle asked gruffly as he knelt next to the man's head. When he didn't get an immediate answer, he backhanded him with a closed fist hard enough to split his lip. "I ask questions. You answer them. You fail to do that, and I hurt you. Understand?"

"Yes," the man said through tight, bloody lips.

"Who are you?"

"Caleb."

"All right, Caleb. What are you doing here trying to break into that house?" Kyle's voice was low, so low I struggled to hear what he was saying.

"We were sent here."

"Who sent you?"

"Prophet sent us."

"Pardon?"

"The Prophet sent us."

"That's what I thought you said. Why did he send you?"

"To redeem the sick of course," the man said as if he were ordering dinner at a fast-food joint.

"By redeem, you mean kill?"

"In some cases, yes, that unfortunately happens. May I get up?"

"Save yourself the trouble and stay down," Kyle sneered.

"This is no way for civilized men to….." Kyle backhanded him again.

"Nobody accused me of being civilized, dickhead. Now, where can we find your boss?"

"The Prophet is not my boss. He is a prophet sent directly by the Almighty."

"Shane, we got incoming! You got about 10 minutes before they get here. Less time if they decide to start running," Chase's voice crackled in my ear. I clicked my mic twice to acknowledge him. Judging by the change in Kyle's demeanor, he'd heard his brother's transmission.

"Get up!" Kyle ordered as he stood.

"I don't think I will," Caleb answered snidely.

"Have it your way!" I saw the anger on Kyle's face and half expected him to just shoot the man. Instead, he reached down, grabbed a handful of his hair, and started dragging him down the street. His clawing at Kyle's hands didn't seem to bother him either way. Every time he'd try to get his feet under himself, Kyle would jerk him forward again.

When we arrived at the cars blocking the driveway, Kyle slammed Caleb into the passenger door and then dropped the dazed and bleeding man to the ground. He threw the door open and smacked him in the face hard enough for his lower front teeth to pierce his lower lip. The blow severely dazed Caleb. Kyle pulled his knife and cut a long length of the seatbelt from the car.

He roughly flipped Caleb onto his stomach and tied his hands behind his back. He ran the excess length of the seatbelt between Caleb's legs and then shoved him onto his back again. Grabbing the cloth rope, he cinched it tightly between the two front belt loops. It should have been incredibly uncomfortable.

Kyle flipped him onto his stomach again, grabbed his bound wrists, and pulled him to his feet. Rather than lead him between the cars, he shoved him face-first into the hood. That impact caused blood from his nose to join that from his lips.

"You can either do what I tell you, or I can hurt you even more. The choice is yours," Kyle growled in Caleb's ear.

"Wrap it up, Shane! You got maybe two minutes!" instead of Chase, it was Janice calling on the radio.

"Your call," Kyle growled when he didn't get an answer from Caleb. He grabbed him by the hair again and started pulling him toward the trucks. Caleb was having a hard time staying on his feet. Every time he'd stagger, Kyle would give him a hard jerk.

While Kyle dealt with getting our prisoner secured in the bed of the truck, I was watching the angry mob approaching from behind us. They were close enough that some of the rocks they were throwing were hitting the ground and rolling up to where we were parked. Cody was sitting in the passenger seat of my truck with Sarah and the young boy in the back. As soon as I slid behind the wheel, I heard a slap on the back of the cab from Kyle. That was the signal to get moving. I put the truck in gear, and we pulled quickly away from the advancing mob.

"Where's Donnie?" I asked Cody.

170

"I don't know! He and his mom left before sun-up to go find more medication for Riley. I was out looking for them when I heard the call from Sarah," he explained frantically.

"Was today the first time you had ragers at your door?"

"Yeah! I don't know how they found us!"

"What about your neighbors? Did they know you were holed up in your place?"

"It's a small trailer park, man. A few were gone for the summer and I'm pretty sure those that were left got sick and died."

"Shane hit the freeway and get us out of town so we can regroup," Kyle said over the radio.

"East or west?"

"Go east, man. Let's just put a few miles between us and this place."

"Copy that," I looked over at the navigation display and could see that we were running nearly parallel with the freeway. I decided to let several more blocks pass before cutting across.

"Why were you asking about my neighbors?" Cody asked.

"I'm just a little concerned about how the ragers knew you were there. They could have followed you at some point. Or....."

"Or they got Donnie and Kate," he finished my thought.

We hit the freeway and quickly made our exit from the city. With about ten miles behind us, I pulled through the median and got us facing west again. Not worried about blocking traffic, Chase pulled up right next to us. I could see him and Janice eyeing me like they expected some sort of inspirational speech.

"Top the trucks off," was the best I could come up with on such short notice. Cody was already out of the truck and helping Kyle "talk" to our prisoner. Sarah was in the backseat with her brother's head in her lap. She was gently stroking his hair. The kid looked rough when I first saw him, and he looked even worse now. I climbed out of the truck and walked to the back.

"Get him out of the truck," I instructed Kyle when I dropped the tailgate. Once he was standing before me, I sat on the tailgate and just looked at him. He couldn't have been much over 25, maybe 30 on the outside. His hair was greasy, his forehead was covered in pimples, and his fledgling beard was patchy and gross. It was the red tinge around his eyes that threw up flags for me. It wasn't as bad as some of them I'd seen, but it was definitely there.

"Why were you at that house in the trailer park?" I began.

"Prophet sent us," was the scripted answer.

"Yeah, you already told us that. Doesn't answer my question though. Why were you there?"

"We were there to redeem the sick child."

"And?"

"And what?" he seemed confused.

"Did you actually think the kid's family would simply stand by and let you kill him?"

"It was not our intention to harm the child."

"Come again?"

"We saw you, all of you, at the hospital and you were looking for medications. That can only mean someone in your group is ill. The illness always heralds the gift….."

"Whoa, hold on!" I cut him off. "The gift?"

"If the family or anyone else interfered, it only serves to show them for what they are. The gift is only for the strong, for only the strong can survive it."

"You mean the virus?"

"The Prophet tells us that it is a gift from the Almighty. Only the strong can survive receiving it and it makes us even stronger than we were before!" his grin showed me two of his broken front teeth.

"You dumbshit! The kid has diabetes, not the flu!"

"Oh. That's unfortunate," Caleb acted as if he was disappointed.

"You got sick, didn't you? Maybe a week or ten days ago, you got infected, right?" I asked.

"I received the gift and proved myself worthy."

"It sounds to me like this Prophet dude has some really good shit in his stash! Whatever he's smokin', I'd like to get some!" Kyle said as he raised his hand to backhand Caleb again.

"Don't waste your energy, Kyle."

"What?" he looked at me with his hand still raised.

"It might make you feel better, but I doubt he can feel it at all. Am I right, Caleb?"

"Yes, you are correct. I don't feel pain anymore. Praise be to the gift."

"What's this Prophet dude look like and where did he come from?" I changed the subject.

"If you're from around here, you already know. He used to hang out by the freeway offramp, and he held signs warning people of his prophecies."

"You mean that homeless nutjob that lives under the bridge?" Cody asked.

"You only think that because you never paid heed to his warnings!" Caleb retorted.

"You know this guy?" I asked Cody.

"Yeah, I've seen him around. He wears what looks like a gunny sack robe and sandals. Always ringing his damn salvation army bell and tryin to preach to folks about the end of the world and crap. Cops have been tryin to run him off for years, but he always shows up again."

"So, if you saw him, you'd recognize him?"

"Fer sure," Cody replied.

"How did you know there was a sick kid in that particular home? Did you guys follow them home or something?" I switched it up again hoping to keep him off kilter with the random questions.

"Prophet sent us. He knows the truth of all things."

"What do you mean by that? Did he have a vision or some other stupid shit like that?"

"The child's mother and brother revealed his existence."

"Where are they now? The mother and brother, where are they?" I asked the question before Cody could interject.

"They are with Prophet."

"They're still alive?"

"If you consider your weak, meager existence to be living, then yes. They're alive, for now."

"Where's this Prophet dude now?"

"He's at the sanctuary, of course."

"I'm only going to ask you nicely one more time. After that, I'm going to let my friend here start smacking you around again," I nodded in the direction of Kyle. "Where can we find the Prophet? Give me a physical location or I can absolutely guarantee that you'll feel the punishment he can dole out."

Caleb looked smugly at me but didn't answer the question. I nodded at Kyle again. I figured he'd lay hands on the young man immediately, but he didn't. He walked to the side of the truck where his brother was filling the fuel tank. He took the fuel nozzle from the side of the truck and walked back to where we were standing. The hose was barely long enough.

"Can't feel pain? I guess we'll see about that," Kyle said menacingly. He squeezed the nozzle for just a second and splashed diesel on Caleb's legs. Caleb was suddenly looking a little less sure of himself. Kyle started fishing around in his pockets. "Anyone got a light?" he asked all while staring Caleb down.

"There's one on the dash of Rayne's truck," Janice offered. Kyle handed me the nozzle and headed for the cab of the truck. I knew he had a lighter in his pocket, but I also understood that he was just ramping up the anticipation for Caleb.

"You sure you don't feel like answering the question?" I asked.

"No."

"I think he's really gonna smoke your ass."

"You won't do it. Your kind is too weak. You don't have the stomach for it," his tough façade cracked when he saw Kyle coming back with the disposable lighter. When Kyle took the nozzle from me, I saw nothing in Caleb's steely eyes. I knew there was fear in there somewhere, we just hadn't brought it to the surface yet. Kyle squeezed the handle again and doused Caleb's crotch with more fuel.

"Might want to stand back a little," Kyle warned as he tried to light the lighter.

"Last chance, Caleb," I said as I slid off the tailgate.

"You wouldn't....." his voice caught in his throat when the small flame finally appeared from the lighter. Kyle started moving closer to him. "Wait! The clubhouse at the golf course! The Prophet is at the clubhouse!" he nearly shouted with panic. Kyle stopped his advance.

"Is that where the mother and brother are being held?" I asked.

"Yes! Some others too, but not for much longer!"

"What do you mean by that?" Kyle asked before I could.

"When they no longer hold any value to the Prophet, they will be given to the stalkers so they can hunt them."

"Stalkers?" I asked.

"Yes, stalkers. They hunt people like you!" he nearly spat the words.

"I take it you're not one of these stalkers?"

"No, I'm an apostle to the Prophet!"

"How many people like you at the golf course?" Kyle asked.

"Like me?"

"Yeah, like you. People who can still carry on a conversation and take care of themselves. How many are there?"

"Ummm, I'm not really sure."

"Take a guess."

"I can't!"

"I think you can," Kyle splashed more fuel on him and started trying to spark the lighter again.

"No! Stop!" Caleb tried to back away, but Cody shoved him forward again. "I'll tell you whatever you want to know!"

"Then answer the question," Kyle growled.

"There's about 20 of us. It's the stalkers you'll have to worry about! They'll get you before you ever make it to the clubhouse!"

"Just how many stalkers are there?" I asked.

"A couple hundred!"

CHAPTER 37

"Hundreds of them? At the golf course?" I asked rapid fire.

"They're everywhere! What you saw today was only a fraction of our number!"

"The stalkers don't attack people like you or this Prophet guy?" Janice asked from behind him.

"Of course not!" he twisted to look at her. "We've evolved past all of that! We protect each other. It's the new order of things!"

"How many people are being held at the clubhouse?" this was Kyle.

"It's only a guess, but maybe 10 or 15 prisoners."

"How long before they are given to the stalkers?" Kyle followed up.

"Some are released every night. It just depends on if the Prophet has already learned everything from them or not."

With Caleb's last statement, I caught something flash across Cody's face. It was sort of like he'd just put the last piece in a puzzle or something. He was generally looking in Caleb's direction, but his eyes were unfocused. It lasted for maybe 10 seconds when he looked up at me and realized I was watching him. He gently nodded his head toward the front of the truck where we would be out of earshot of Caleb and the others. Without waiting for any form of acknowledgment, he took a step in that direction. I followed him.

"What's up?" I asked in a quiet voice.

"I don't think he's lying," Cody replied when he turned to face me.

"What makes you say that?"

"Every night, usually around midnight, we've heard and seen groups running through the streets around the trailer park. Hell, you can hear 'em all over town. It's been going on for close to a week now. It reminded me of listening to the coyotes when they're on the hunt. Sometimes it would go on for just a few minutes, other times it would go on till the sun came up."

"You think it was these hunts he was talking about?"

"It's the only thing that makes any sense, man. Ya know, today was the first time I've really seen them out in large groups. Usually, it's at night and that's why it pissed me off so badly that Kate and Donnie left so early. They knew it wasn't safe but Riley, he was getting worse, and they didn't think he could wait….. That's why I went ahead and let them go, ya know?" his eyes held the full weight of his remorse over the decision.

"Coyotes….." I whispered to myself.

"What?"

175

"It's what you said. They do the majority of their hunting at night, in packs, right?"

"I suppose, why?"

"They're always around but it's kind of unusual to see one during the middle of the day. They either came across a scent or they're on about something. Seeing a whole pack out during the day is pretty rare. It takes some pretty unusual circumstances to bring out the whole pack, right?"

"Okay?" he questioned.

"Caleb might be telling the truth about the hunts, but now I'm not so sure he's telling the truth about Donnie and Kate," thoughts were flying through my head.

"Why wouldn't he be telling the truth?"

"Maybe there was a hunt going on last night. Say your wife and son stumbled into the middle of it but managed to elude them. Couldn't that account for so many of them being out in broad daylight?"

"That doesn't explain why these assholes showed up at my home," he reasoned.

"Maybe, maybe not. They could have followed us the other day or had people out watching from the shadows. Caleb said they knew someone was sick because you, we, were at the hospital collecting medications. That's part of stalking your prey, right? It could be they saw your son and wife leave the house too. There's a lot of what if's here," I paused and rubbed the stubble on my chin while I thought.

"The other day when my group came into town, we weren't really subtle, and I think we attracted their attention. That had to be why they attacked us at the grocery store. Then we came into the hospital and kicked a hornet's nest with that little stunt," I was talking more to myself. "They had to have followed us, or at least spotted us when we dropped you off at your place."

"The way we hauled ass outta the hospital, there's no way they chased us. They don't drive....." he started.

"They can drive..... shit!" I muttered.

"What?"

"At least some of them can. The day we were attacked at the grocery store, two of them tried blocking the road with cars they were driving," I paused again as I tried to comprehend the thought that had just leaped into the forefront of my mind. "That explains the bodies too....."

"What bodies? You're not making any sense, Shane."

"The bodies that had been moved into the old Denio Junction store. They had to get them there somehow! That also means..... Shit!" I blurted out and ran back to where the rest of the group was.

"What's wrong?" Janice asked seeing the terror on my face. Cody was right behind me asking the same question.

"We need to get back to the cabin!" I shoved Caleb out of my way and slammed the tailgate.

"What happened?" she tried again. As much as I didn't want to, I stopped to explain myself.

"Janice, they can drive cars! Remember?"

"Yeah, so?"

"How do you think they got the bodies out to Denio Junction? They might have followed us back to Cody's place the other day and it's entirely possible they followed us home too!"

"I'm not leaving without the rest of my family!" Cody nearly shouted. I could see the realization quickly dawning on the faces of the people in my group. Caleb was the only one with a stoic, peaceful look.

"YOU!" I grabbed Caleb by his shirt and slammed him against the now-closed tailgate. The action was so swift and unexpected, it expelled the breath from his lungs and caused everyone else to jump. "THEY FOLLOWED US, DIDN'T THEY?" I shouted the question.

"You're too late," he wheezed the answer. I felt the rage boiling up but was powerless to do anything about it. Gripping his shirt even tighter, I flung him hard enough that he went airborne and landed on the dirt shoulder of the highway.

"HOW MANY?" I stomped heavily toward him drawing my Colt from its holster.

"Enough," he spit a mouthful of blood and dirt in my direction. I leveled the .45 and pulled the trigger once. The heavy round impacted the ground next to him.

"How many? I asked again, he was trying to get to his feet, but his still bound hands were hampering his efforts. His immediate lack of an answer only served to fuel my rage. When I was close enough, I clobbered him in the side of the face with the fist holding my pistol. A fine mist of blood and at least one tooth left his mouth before he toppled over backward. I screamed the question again.

"You and your kind can't win. We are the next step in the evolution of man, and we will climb that ladder by crushing you beneath us!" he proclaimed. Blood was pouring from the wound where I'd hit him and judging by the odd angle of his left shoulder, it had been dislocated when he landed on his back.

"You may not feel pain, but I think you can still feel fear!" I pointed my gun right between his eyes.

"Not like you're undoubtedly feeling about now." his grin sent me over the edge. I pulled the trigger and the big semi-automatic bucked once. The back of his head exploded. His blood stained the tan-colored dirt in a deep, dark red. The bad part was the rage had masked any sense of regret at what I'd just done. Before looking back at the group of silent bystanders, I holstered my weapon and took a step backward. When I finally turned, all eyes were on me.

"Chase?" I locked eyes with the man.

"Yeah?"

"Take Cody and Janice, go find his family. Kyle, you're with me!" I stopped and held his gaze. "Locate them! Don't make a move until me and Kyle get back. Got it?"

"Yeah….." he started to answer but was cut off by Janice.

"I'm going with you!" she stated flatly.

"The hell you are!" I moved to block her from moving toward my truck. "Go help Cody find his wife and son. Me and Kyle will secure the cabin."

"Rayne might be in danger, and you want me to stay here?" she tried to sidestep past me. "No way!"

"It wasn't a request, Janice!" my voice was a lot harsher than I'd ever heard it. When she tried to move past me again, Chase grabbed her arm. She tried to shake free of his grip, but he wasn't about to yield, and neither was I.

"What about Sarah and Riley?" Cody asked.

"We'll take them back to the cabin once we're sure it's safe. We got a paramedic there who can look after Riley."

"What about….."

"Go find your family and we'll sort it all out when they're safe! Got it?" I barked and headed for the door of my truck. Kyle was already moving up the other side of the rig.

"Where are we going?" Sarah asked from the backseat. I had the truck in gear before the starter fully disengaged.

"We're going back to my place while the others try to find your brother and mother," I explained as the speedometer rolled past 70 miles per hour.

"What about Riley? He needs his medication."

"There's a paramedic back at my cabin, she might be able to help him. After we locate your mom and brother, we'll see what we can do to find him some more meds," I offered weakly. I didn't have a clue as to what else to say. Kyle craned his neck to look back at the sick boy. When he looked back at me, his eyes told me that trying to save Riley was more than likely a lost cause at this point. I'd had that feeling earlier but never voiced it. I risked a glance over my shoulder and that gut feeling was reinforced by what I saw. The only thing I could do was push the throttle even closer to the firewall.

We had just reached the outskirts of Winnemucca when the onboard navigation told me to take the next exit and turn left. I glanced at the display and could see that the route would take us straight back into the small city. That's not where I wanted to go. I backed off the throttle a hair and started looking for an alternate route to get back on Highway 95 seeing as how there was no direct access from the freeway.

"Where are you trying to go?" Sarah asked from the backseat.

"I need to get back on 95 headed north," I was scrolling through the options frantically.

"Take the next exit but turn right. It's probably quicker anyway."

"You sure?"

"I grew up here! Yes, I'm sure!" her reply was a little terse. I didn't bother with a verbal answer. I just started to apply some brakes because we were closing the distance to the off-ramp at almost 90 miles per hour and it was coming up quickly. I blew through the stop sign, took up the whole oncoming lane, and I was back on the throttle hard.

"Now what?" I asked over my shoulder.

"Right at a mile up the road, take a left. It'll take you over the railroad tracks and dump you out on 95."

CHAPTER 38

August 31st, 2023

Sarah had been spot-on with her directions, and we were able to stay out of Winnemucca proper. The meandering country road took us right to Highway 95 just as she'd promised. When we made the sliding turn north, some of my senses were starting to filter their way through the anger that was seething inside me. Under normal circumstances, it was almost exactly a three-hour drive back to the cabin. These were hardly normal circumstances though.

The big Dodge truck was giving me everything she had. I was holding steady at 118 miles per hour because any faster and she would hit the limiters. She was already pushing redline and running a little hot. I was also 100% positive the tires weren't rated for this kind of sustained speed. At this speed, if one of the oversized tires blew, it would be catastrophic. More than likely deadly. Slowing down could also have deadly consequences for Angie and Rayne too. I was damned if I did and damned if I didn't.

"Y'all need to get your seatbelts on," I told my passengers as I buckled mine. It seemed like a good compromise. "Sarah, can you get your brother buckled in?"

"Yes," her reply was barely audible over the roaring of the engine, the howling tires, and the wind noise bleeding into the passenger cabin. Kyle leaned over and looked at the instrument cluster.

"I know you're in a hurry, bud, but we need to get there in one piece," he said as he sat back and buckled his seatbelt.

"I know," I muttered and backed it down to 110.

I was taking my piece of the road right out of the middle of the two-lane highway. The anger was down to a simmer, but the sense of urgency was still making me want to shove the throttle all the way to the floor. It took everything I had to hold it steady between 110 and 112 miles per hour. Every few seconds I'd scan the gauges for any signs of trouble.

As Denio Junction came into view, I started scuffing off speed at the last possible second so I could negotiate the turn onto Highway 140. I slowed even more when I saw several sets of tire tracks pulling from the dirt lot where the store was still smoldering. They quickly disappeared on the blacktop, but they were headed the same way we were. Kyle saw them too and he had a few more seconds to examine them than I did.

"At least three vehicles. They must have been hiding up toward Denio and waiting for us to leave this morning," he reported. I acknowledged him with a nod and the heavy application of throttle again. With the knowledge that someone was headed toward my cabin and my friends, we were quickly pushing every limit the truck had. I discovered that the maximum speed of the rig was 120 and backed her down to 118 again.

I had to slow to get passed the plane wreckage, but it gave us a chance to confirm three sets of tire tracks on the soft shoulder of the road. Back on the pavement, I was relentlessly taking the rig as fast as allowed. The temperature was climbing but I had no intention of backing down until it crept into the danger zone.

Fortunately, that happened at the same time we reached the turnoff that would put us on the dirt road. I was hoping to find the gate closed and locked, but it wasn't. It looked as if someone had hooked a chain on it and ripped it from the post that it was mounted to.

"Slow down a little, Shane. We've made it this far, let's not shred a tire or anything stupid," Kyle advised. He was making sense, but my brain was having trouble comprehending it. "SLOW DOWN!" he finally shouted.

I lifted my lead foot and slowed us down to about 40 miles per hour on the rough road. It was still about twice as fast as we'd normally drive it, but it seemed to appease Kyle. All bets were off again when we bounced onto the hardpacked BLM road. We fishtailed back and forth several times.

"We can't just go blowing in there, man. You know that right?" he asked.

"Yeah, I know. I was gonna take us to the pond. We can leave Sarah and Riley with the truck. You and I can book it up the trail to the cabin on foot," I answered.

The gate that led to my property was also ripped from its mounts and lying in the middle of the road. As much as I wanted to make that turn, I knew Kyle was right. It was obvious that whatever was happening at the cabin, running into the middle of it would only make matters worse. We needed to be smart about this. I took us to the pond and stashed the truck in the same place as the last time I did this.

"You still have your radio?" Kyle asked Sarah over his shoulder as he checked his weapons.

"Yeah, why?" her voice seemed subdued.

"Shane's going to leave you the keys. If this goes to shit, take the truck, and get back to town," he ordered as he opened his door and got out.

"No. I'm going with you," I heard the door behind me open. Looking into the backseat, I was horrified to see the covered and still form of Riley lying on the seat. She must have seen the look on my face.

"He passed about 20 minutes after we turned onto Highway 95," she said flatly and closed the door. I saw Kyle shaking his head when he opened the back door and retrieved his deer rifle.

"Why didn't you say something?" I asked as I also got out of the truck.

"There was nothing you could do about it, Shane. It's better this way," she slid a Glock from the back of her waistband. I watched her methodically remove the magazine, check it, then reinsert it. She slid the slide back a fraction of an inch to confirm there was a round in the chamber. Her face was eerily devoid of any emotion.

"Son-of-a-bitch," I whispered and retrieved my AK-47. She moved away from the truck and Kyle joined me. He had shouldered his hunting rifle but cradled his AK in his arms. Holding it close to his body with one arm, he reached out and put his hand on my shoulder.

"She's right, man. He wasn't going to make it no matter what we did. She was also right to say it's better this way. It's the ugly truth, and it sucks, but she's right," his voice was low, steely, as he tried to console me.

"I know. I just hope we're not too late on all accounts today," I said as I looked at the trail that would lead us to the cabin.

"Keep your head, dude. Do what I tell you and it'll work itself out." I nodded my response, and he held eye contact for a few seconds. "Let's move!"

Kyle was leading the way with Sarah in the middle. There was only one trail to follow, and he was setting the pace at a brisk jog. The only thing I could think of was that I needed to be sprinting. My mind was running wild with scenarios about what might be happening at the cabin. None of them were good. As we neared the base of the last hill before the cabin came into view, we heard the report of gunfire. Kyle immediately started pumping his legs for all they were worth to get to the cover of the rocks at the top of the hill.

The closer we got to the top, the lower we crouched so that we wouldn't stand out on the ridgeline. Kyle stopped behind a large pair of boulders and pulled his hunting rifle from his shoulder. Sarah and I took up positions next to him. Using the space between the two large rocks, he surveyed the scene 800 yards away through the scope. I tried using the optic on my rifle, but it was nearly useless at this distance.

"I'm counting 10, no….. Make it 11 hostiles. One down on the front porch," he reported. "When you and Rayne snuck up on us, which way did you go?" he never took his eye from the scope.

"We got up in the trees behind the house and waited till full dark."

"This'll be over before dark," he muttered. The loud boom of a shotgun echoed its way up the hillside. "Ten hostiles. One is down on the back porch now. Not dead….." there was another boom. "Scratch that. He's done."

"What's the plan?" I asked.

"Sarah, take my AK and go with Shane. Shane, go the way you and Rayne went and when I see you closing in, I'll try and draw them off or at least distract them a little," he cooly ordered.

"Can you hit 'em from this far away?" Sarah asked before I could.

182

"I'm good to 1200 yards. May not be headshots, but they should be easy for you to deal with. Have you ever shot an AK-47?" the question was for Sarah.

"No," she answered.

"Shane, give her the down and dirty while you guys are on the move. Now, go!" he never did pull his eye from the scope.

It took me all of a minute to show Sarah how to make the rifle work. She didn't have but one magazine, so I didn't bother showing her how to change it. Kyle's rifle had the same optic mine had and I showed her how to turn it on and that was about the extent of the lesson. After that, we ran as fast as we could to where Rayne and I made our approach.

"Angie, Rayne, you got your ears on?" I heard Kyle on the radio. After a few seconds, he repeated the call.

"Is that you Kyle?" Angie finally called back. She sounded out of breath and on the verge of panic.

"Yeah, baby. It's me. I need you to listen closely, okay?" his voice was calm.

"Where are you? We need help!"

"The Calvary is here and almost in a position to help, but I need you to do something for me. Can you do that?"

"Yeah?"

"There are three bad guys hiding behind the red sedan directly in front of the house. I know you can't hit them from your vantage point, but I need you to light that car up with a few rounds when I tell you to. Can you do that?"

"Yeah. Give me a minute."

"Let me know when you're ready. How's Rayne doing?"

"She's covering the back door with the shotgun. I'm ready," came her shaky voice.

"Okay. Does she have a radio too?"

"I'm here," Rayne's scratchy voice came through my earbud.

"Good. Now listen closely ladies. Everyone, listen closely," he began. "They got the numbers, but we've got surprise working for us. Shane, as soon as this kicks off, you and Sarah run your asses down there as fast as you can. I want one of you to go down either side of the house. Once you've reached the western corners, cover the lead car and the tail car. Pop anyone who sticks their damn head out or tries to make a run for it."

"Shane, you got the white car, Sarah takes that little silver pickup. Angie, I need you to pop off a round every couple of seconds into that red car. I don't need you to hit anyone, I just need the noise to cover my shots. Can you do that?"

"Yeah, I can," Angie answered.

"What do you need me to do?" Rayne asked.

"You just sit tight girl and cover that back door. None of our people will be coming in that way."

"Okay."

"Is everyone ready to get this started?" he asked. I looked at Sarah and she gave me a thumbs up.

"Shane and Sarah are ready."

"Rayne is ready.

"Angie is ready."

"On three then. One….. Two….. Three!"

CHAPTER 39

As soon as Angie let loose with her rifle at the front of the house, I heard the distant crack of Kyle's hunting rifle. At the same time, Sarah and I broke from our cover and ran for the back of the house at a full sprint. I hadn't done a 100-yard sprint since I was on the track team in high school, but I felt that my pace was much faster than anything a younger me could have ever pulled off. It took Kyle a couple of shots before his precision shots were timed exactly with Angie's. The closer we got to the cabin, the more the sound of gunfire covered his shots.

"They've figured it out!" I heard Kyle in my earbud. "Shane, Sarah, you're about to have some company coming your way. Angie, you got a herd storming the front porch!" this was the first time I'd heard any hint of excitement in his voice. I saw Sarah come to a sliding stop and she threw herself down on her stomach and elbows. I realized too late what it was she was doing.

She started shooting as soon as the rifle came to level. I knew that I should have done the same thing, but it was already too late. The pair of ragers coming up my side of the house had already spotted me. I stopped my advance and raised my rifle. When the red dot of the optic was center mass of the lead man, I jerked the trigger back.

I don't know what I was expecting. Seeing the pair still coming for me at full speed definitely wasn't it. I had a little time to work with as they were still about 30 yards away. Not much time, but a little. I recentered the reticle and desperately tried to control my breathing. Instead of putting the little red dot on his chest, I was aiming for his belt buckle.

Instead of firing just once, I let three go in rapid succession. All three were solid hits starting at his groin and ending at the base of his throat. I didn't have any time to celebrate because the second man was damn near on top of me. Taking him down didn't require any precision aiming. This time, I pulled the trigger until he went down face-first into the dirt.

Over the ringing in my ears, I heard the ferocious booming of the shotgun from inside the house. In quick succession, I saw Sarah scrambling to her feet, and I saw the back door of the cabin standing wide open. In a split second, I decided I was going inside. I started running again and altered my course for the back steps.

"SHANE! DON'T!" I heard in my earbud. Adrenaline was coursing through my veins at this point along with the desperate need to generously apply my wrath to those who were unwelcome at my cabin. I don't think I could have stopped what I was doing even if I wanted to. My foot had just hit the first step when the shotgun thundered again.

I felt the warmth of the crimson-red blood showering my face. I could taste its coppery flavor in my mouth. The mangled and bloody body of a woman flew out of the doorway causing me to trip over her as she tumbled lifelessly down the stairs. That stumble saved my life. The roar of the shotgun caused the handrail of the stairs to explode in a shower of wood splinters right where I would have been if I hadn't fallen. Instinctively, I rolled to my left to get away from the doorway.

"HOLD YOUR FIRE!" I shouted, scrambling to my feet again.

"Shane?" Rayne called from inside.

"Yeah!" I risked a peek around the doorframe. I saw Rayne sitting on the floor with her back propped up against the doorframe of my room. I also had a clear view of what was happening in the kitchen. There, Angie was locked in a life-or-death battle with two ragers. The bigger of the two had just thrown her like a ragdoll into the living room. The smaller guy had a crowbar and was moving quickly toward where she had landed.

I brought my rifle up and allowed the red dot to settle on the smaller man. Using the lessons I'd learned dropping the two outside, I repeated everything I'd learned. Aim at the waist, lead just a hair, gently squeeze the trigger, and walk the rounds up the body. I fired six times and took six steps that put me even with Rayne. She had curled up in the fetal position with her hands over her ears.

I watched his body jerk with each impact. The sixth round removed the majority of his head along with the look of surprise on his face. I swung the rifle to acquire the bigger man and caught him just standing in the middle of my kitchen. I think he was trying to figure out exactly what was happening and who had interrupted their rampage. His indecision was cut short by a nearly point-blank shot to the back of the head from Sarah who had just come through the front door.

"You got a runner!" I could hear Kyle breathing jarring breaths into my ear. He had to be running toward the cabin from his perch on the hillside. "He's running up the driveway and I haven't got the angle for a shot!"

"Are you hurt?" I took a knee and helped Rayne sit up.

"No, I'm fine."

"Stay here. Kyle is on his way," I stood and moved through the living room heading for the front door. Sarah was helping a battered Angie to her feet. "Secure the house," I ordered. Without waiting for an answer, I ran out onto the deck. First, I looked to my right to see Kyle sprinting across the open ground between his hide and the cabin. Next, I looked to my left and saw the man running away. He was running for all he was worth having already put close to a quarter of a mile between us.

FERAL OUTBREAK

Knowing there was no way I was going to catch him on foot, I leaned back inside and grabbed the keys for the Razor from the peg just inside. Leaping from the deck, I cleared all of the steps. I had to jump over two more bodies as I ran for the barn. Quickly sliding into the seat, I set my rifle on the passenger seat and stuffed the key into the ignition. It roared to life instantly. Dropping it into gear and stabbing the throttle, I bolted through the open barn doors and cranked the wheel hard. Flying past the intruders' vehicles, I ended up running over one of the dead men.

The man I was chasing had disappeared around the slight bend in the driveway where the pinion-juniper trees were. Chewing up the dirt of the driveway, I hurtled headlong around the same bend. I negotiated the turn almost completely sideways but still managed to spot him a couple of hundred yards ahead of me. Straightening the Razor out, I grabbed the AK from the passenger seat.

Resting the foregrip on the steel tube above the dash, I was hanging onto the pistol grip with my right hand and the steering wheel with the left. There was no possible way for me to use the sights, so I just aimed the barrel in his general direction. I was closing on him fast. With the distance between us rapidly diminishing, I squeezed the trigger a couple of times.

One round kicked up dust and dirt about halfway between us and I have no idea where the second went. I adjusted my aim trying to one hand the bouncing weapon. The only effect squeezing the trigger again had was to cause the man to dart from the road into the trees. His sudden course change combined with my speed; I overshot his position. I dropped the AK on the seat again as I stabbed the brake pedal hard.

The hardpacked driveway did nothing to slow me down quickly. The Razor slid sideways in a cloud of its own making. I cranked the steering wheel hard to the left to point the nose in the direction I'd just come from. Still sliding, I jammed my foot on the gas. I knew I was still on the road, or at least close to it. The dense cloud of brown dust was completely obscuring everything.

Accelerating hard, I broke out of the dust cloud only to jerk the wheel and plant both feet on the brake pedal. A rock, no, a boulder that had to weigh over a hundred pounds hit the hood just ahead of the passenger side dash. It shattered the plastic when it bounced into the passenger seat. Its impact was enough to jar the whole vehicle. A second, smaller rock flew into the cabin and struck me in the shoulder.

I released the brakes, floored the throttle, and left the roadway. Another large rock pinged off of the rollbar just above my head. I couldn't tell where the projectile rocks were coming from because I was too damn busy trying to dodge my way through the trees. The first near miss with a low-hanging branch raked the lightbar off of the top of the rollbar. The second tore the molded plastic from the outside of the passenger door.

It felt like I was threading my way between the trees at a hundred miles an hour when it couldn't have been much more than 30 or 40. I was trying to get pointed back toward the rager, but I didn't know exactly where he was. Rather than jumping back into the fray through the dust cloud, I located the road and angled away from the immediate confrontation. I rejoined the driveway about halfway between the dust cloud and the bend in the road. I brought the Razor to a stop so that I could survey the area.

I think that for the first time in recorded history, the air was absolutely still. There was no breeze whatsoever to remove the cloud of dust I'd kicked into the air. From my vantage point, it looked like a dirty beige cloud hanging close to the ground. My eyes were scanning, trying to spot any movement but I wasn't able to pick anything out.

I glanced over at the passenger seat where my AK was. I was thinking that I might be able to use the optic on it to inspect the area ahead of me a little better. The boulder that had landed on it took up the majority of the seat. There was no way I was going to move from where I sat, and I was pretty sure it would be a useless expenditure of energy. The buttstock was visible and so was the end of the barrel. Both were pointed in very different directions.

"What's going on up there, Shane?" Kyle called on the radio.

"I think I lost him," I replied sullenly.

"Shane? You got a copy?" Kyle called again.

"Yeah, I'm here. I think I lost him in the trees."

"Shane? Do you copy?" Rayne's voice came through my earbud.

"What the hell?" I muttered. I plucked the small radio from its pouch on the shoulder strap of my vest. Looking at it, it was obvious it had been damaged by the rock that had hit me. I squeezed the transmit button, but nothing happened. I tried turning it off and then on, but I still wasn't able to transmit anything. I suddenly felt a heavy pit in my stomach when a shadow played across me and the radio. Instantly, I knew I'd screwed the pooch.

The driver's door of the Razor was thrown open and rough, violent hands grabbed me by the shoulder strap of my vest. I was yanked roughly from the seat and thrown to the ground next to the idling side-by-side. With no one to apply the brakes, it slowly started to roll away. I'd dropped the radio long before I hit the ground with a thud. I managed to grab my handgun from its retention holster, but it was just as quickly yanked from my hand. My knife was also stripped from its sheath and tossed away.

I flailed as hard as I could to try and break the man's hold, but it was all to no avail. He couldn't have been any bigger than me, but his grip was like that of a vice. He planted a knee solidly in the middle of my chest with so much force, it felt like I was suffocating. I was waiting to hear my sternum or ribs breaking. With me pinned in place, he trapped my left arm under his free knee and held my right arm to the ground. This was it. This is how I died. Those were the thoughts passing through my mind when my eyes met his.

CHAPTER 40

How was this going to end? Was he going to crush my chest until my ribs broke lacerating my lungs and crushing my heart? Would he just grab my throat and crush my windpipe? Maybe he would just use his free hand to bash my head with a rock. As it was, I was already having a hard time getting any useful air into my constricted lungs. With the panic taking hold, I was just hoping he'd make it fast.

"Stop. Stop fighting me," his voice was hoarse, guttural. He turned his head quickly in the direction of the cabin. "They're coming!"

"What?" I grunted the question. Instead of answering, he grabbed my vest again, stood, and jerked me to my feet. More or less dragging me, he hauled me to the passenger side of the Razor that had rolled to a stop in the ditch about 20 feet away. He threw me against the side of it and yanked what was left of the front passenger door open.

"Get that out of there!" he ordered and shoved me toward the boulder that occupied the seat. There was no way I was going to lift it, so I grabbed the far side of it and rolled it toward me and onto the ground. "That too!" I knew he was talking about the destroyed rifle. It was also tossed to the ground.

"Now what?" I looked in the direction of the cabin hoping help would come around the corner in the nick of time.

"Get in!"

"What? No!"

"You can either get in willingly or I can fold you in half and stuff you in. Move!" judging by the amount of rage seething behind his bloodshot eyes, I figured he could make good on the threat. "I don't want to kill you, but I will," he added with a shove toward the seat.

"Fine," I said under my breath. I honestly didn't know what else to say.

"Buckle up," he slammed the wrecked door. "You do anything but sit there and I'll break your scrawny neck!" I watched him run around to the driver's door and climb in. He floored it causing small rocks and dirt to spray up from the rear tires. There was a whole new cloud of dust to hide behind. I did catch him glancing down at the fuel gauge. He seemed to take some comfort in knowing it was plum full.

"Where are you taking me?" I had to nearly yell over the engine and wind noise. His answer was nothing more than a quick glare. "You know this thing ain't gonna make it more than 50 or 60 miles and you can't outrun my friends. You know that, right?" I tried.

"I don't need to do either of those things," he growled and settled into his seat. Both of his hands were gripping the steering wheel tightly. Every few seconds he would look over his shoulder to see if anyone was catching up to us.

That's when it hit me; he wasn't trying to escape. He was trying to lead any pursuit into a trap. That had to be it, I thought. He was driving hard but he hadn't gotten us up to top speed yet. He was deliberately holding back! The pit that had formed in my stomach earlier was back and bigger than ever. They had executed their plan to perfection, and we'd fallen for it hook, line, and sinker.

The scenario playing out in my mind involved them being able to split up the team that had gone into Winnemucca that morning. They had undoubtedly seen us leaving the city on more than one occasion and it wouldn't have been hard to figure out which way we'd gone at Denio Junction. If there was, all they would have to do is wait and watch for confirmation.

From there, it wasn't hard to find our tracks once we'd hit the dirt roads. They had deliberately waited to begin their attack on the cabin. By all rights, we should have arrived in time to find nothing but the aftermath. We hadn't foiled that attack; we'd played right into it. What was it Caleb had said? It was something about them sending enough people and that there was no way for us to win. There had to be a larger force waiting to deal with those of us at the cabin. There also had to be an equal force waiting for Janice, Chase, and Cody.....

The unadulterated rage I'd felt when Rayne was being choked to death in the back parking lot of the grocery store was back in full force. I had to do something, anything to stop this, but what? I had no weapons and trying to go toe-to-toe with this man wouldn't end well for me. Not that it was going to end well anyway, but that was the surest avenue to a quick defeat. I knew I'd only get one shot at this, so I had to make it count.

I thought about reaching over and jerking the steering wheel in a bid to flip the Razor, but that course of action was just as quickly discounted. My eyes landed on the shifter for the transmission. I could try to get it in reverse and destroy the transmission. That would at least stop us from reaching the ambush point I reasoned. I put that thought on the list of possibilities and continued to search the small cabin for anything else that might work.

Mounted on the "A" piler was a small fire extinguisher. Could I break it free, pull the pin, and discharge it before being stopped? The dry powder inside of it was basically non-toxic but I might be able to blind and disorient him long enough to make a bigger play. Then again, I might be just as blinded and disoriented. Only one way to find out I guess.

I went through the motions in my head while I waited for my opportunity. Jerk the extinguisher free with my left hand. Pull the pin and squeeze the handle with my right. Aim for anywhere near his face while holding my breath and squinting my eyes for as long as I could. In the confusion, clobber him with the extinguisher and jerk the wheel as hard as I could. We'd either wreck, or he'd kill me. It was just that simple.

He twisted in the seat to look over his shoulder again and that's when I sprang into action. It was as if I'd done this a thousand times. The extinguisher came free, and I yanked the pin all in one fluid movement. He was immediately alerted by my sudden movement, but by the time he recognized the danger, I was already squeezing the handle. He flailed through the dense cloud with one arm.

He nearly dislodged the makeshift weapon from my hand with a wild swing of his arm, but I managed to hang onto it. Instead of trying to keep some distance between us, I pushed the discharge nozzle closer to his face. Another wild swing of his arm sent the extinguisher into the backseat. I struck his head with my left forearm and grabbed at the steering wheel. I don't know if it was intentional on his part, but I heard the engine rev from his right foot going all the way to the floor. I tried but couldn't reach the wheel with my right arm because my harness was too tight. Improvising, I slammed my left elbow into his face and then got a good grip on the wheel. There was no hesitation when I twisted it as hard and fast as I could toward me.

The Razor veered to the right, caught the small embankment on the side of the road, and was catapulted into the air. My involuntary response was to suck in a deep breath, open my eyes wide and try to brace for the impact. Doing the math in my head, I knew we were going to land upside down. What I couldn't know was how many times we'd roll over. My last thought before hitting the ground and being slammed against the restraint harness was that maybe this wasn't my best idea ever. This was going to hurt.....

"Shane!" Kyle's voice seemed distant in my jumbled thoughts. I had to ask myself if I'd really heard him. When I felt myself being unbuckled and pulled from the wreck, I knew I had survived the violent rollover. He pulled hard to free me and then put me on the ground. "Shane?" he called again as he pressed two fingers against the side of my neck feeling for a pulse.

"Yeah," I croaked and forced my eyes open. Both were full of dirt and dust grinding against my eyeballs. I rolled to my right side. The taste of dirt, blood, and fire extinguisher chemicals permeated my mouth.

"C'mon man, we gotta move! Can you stand?" he asked with urgency.

"I think so," I spit a mouthful of the foul combination from my mouth and tried to sit up. Everything hurt and my head was pounding.

"Let's go!" he grabbed the shoulder strap of my vest and pulled me to my feet. I wiped the dust from around my eyes in the hopes my vision would clear up a little. My hand came away covered in blood. Instead of making a move toward the little pickup parked on the road, he pushed me against the side of the destroyed Razor. I was about to say something, but through the cloudy vision afforded me, I saw half a dozen men running toward us on the road.

Kyle braced his rifle across the top of the Razor and quickly fired three rounds. The crack of the rifle did absolutely nothing to soothe the pounding in my head, but it made the men scatter into the trees. Shifting the AK to one hand, he tucked himself under one of my arms to support some of my weight and steady me. Before we moved, he unleashed three more rounds to help cover our retreat.

After dropping me in the passenger seat of the little truck, he slammed the door and fired several more rounds in the direction of the attackers. He then moved quickly to the driver's side and slid behind the wheel. Throwing the automatic transmission in reverse, he backed us away from the scene as quickly as the tires could gain traction. In a surprise move, he cranked the wheel causing the front of the truck to swing wildly to the passenger side. Before we could lose too much momentum, he jammed it into drive and fed it the throttle. The maneuver was commonly called a bootlegger's reverse. I'd never performed one myself. It was obvious Kyle had.

When we slid to a stop in front of the house, Sarah and Angie were already coming down the stairs. Rayne gingerly made her way from the front door to the railing. Kyle gave them curt instructions to get me into the house before he sprinted toward their camper. When Angie threw my door open, she started examining the laceration on the right side of my forehead. Her poking and prodding made it immediately clear that I'd smacked my head on something. I watched Rayne working her way down the stairs, her face letting on to how much pain she was in.

"I said get him in the house!" Kyle barked running past the front of the truck. His AK was on one shoulder, and he had a matching rifle on his other shoulder. Each hand held the handle of an ammo can. At his insistence, Angie and Sarah got on either side of me and helped me out of the truck and up the stairs. Since I was managing to climb the stairs mostly on my own, Sarah helped Rayne back into the house. By the time the four of us went through the front door, Kyle was making a second trip to the RV.

CHAPTER 41

"Here," Kyle set another AK on the counter I was leaning against. Angie was busy cleaning the laceration on my forehead. Every time I'd move my head, she'd let a small sigh escape.

"Thanks," I offered Kyle while trying to hold still.

"Are you hurt anywhere else?" Rayne asked from next to me.

"I don't think so. Just banged up pretty good."

"What happened out there?" she asked.

"I don't know. I think we got played pretty hard though."

"What's that supposed to mean?" Kyle asked.

"How long were those guys outside?" I unconsciously turned my head to ask Rayne the question.

"What? Maybe an hour?" she looked at Angie and my head followed. Angie let out a grunt followed by a nod.

"Hold still!" she scolded. "Yeah, they were here for about an hour before they tried to rush the house."

"It was a setup from the beginning. They may have been trying to lure all of us out here but at the very least, they caused us to split up our force."

"You think?" Kyle asked.

"I'm pretty sure. The guy driving the Razor wasn't trying to escape and he straight up said he didn't want to kill me. Trust me, he could have. I mean, why would they just hang out here for an hour before attacking the house? It was also obvious they had an ambush farther up the road from where we crashed."

"Okay, but what would be their endgame?"

"I don't know! C'mon, Kyle. You and I both know that we should have gotten back here well after their attack was over. I gotta ask myself if they were trying to split us up or get all of us in one place for a clean sweep. For all I know, they could be amassing an assault force out there in the trees and it's only a matter of time before they storm the cabin," I saw Rayne and Angie share a worried look out of the corner of my eye.

"I guess one thing is certain though. We know there are more of them out there and there's absolutely no way we can leave the cabin undefended now. We can't break away from here to go help your brother or Janice. It's too risky," I continued.

"No, you're right. Chase and Janice can take care of themselves and if we ain't back before long, they'll know something went sideways on our end. I guess the only thing left to do would be to dig in for a fight."

194

"He said he didn't want to kill you?" Rayne interrupted. Out of habit, I turned my head to look at her.

"Sorry," I grinned at Angie. She shook her head and retrieved a large Band-Aid from her kit on the counter. She peeled it and stuck it on my forehead with enough pressure to make it hurt a little.

"Sorry," she grinned back and started picking up her gear.

"Yeah, that's exactly what he told me. Why?" I rubbed my forehead and looked at Rayne. Angie passed me half a dozen ibuprofen and a bottle of water.

"If he wasn't here to kill you, us, what was he doing here at all?"

"We didn't have a chance to get that far in the conversation," I smirked.

"Maybe it goes back to the conversation we had with Caleb," Kyle offered.

"Who's Caleb?" Rayne asked.

I spent a couple of minutes telling Rayne and Angie about what had transpired when we had gone to Winnemucca. Kyle would throw in the details I might have missed or glossed over. Of course Angie asked about Riley. Sarah took that question before I ever had a chance. Both Rayne and Angie seemed a little horrified that we just left his body covered up on the backseat of my truck. They understood why we did it. I think they were just having some trouble coming to terms with the fact that an eleven-year-old boy was dead.

After that conversation was had, Kyle took Angie and Sarah outside. The girls were going to start bringing weapons, ammo, and other supplies into the house. Kyle was making himself busy closing and securing some of the shutters on the house. The bodies of the dead ragers had already been removed from the house, but there was still a mess to be cleaned up. Rayne was trying to do it, but she was still hurting far too badly. I found the mop and the mop bucket and gave her a hand.

"You're awfully quiet," I remarked while I mopped up blood.

"Sorry, just got a lot on my mind."

"Like?"

"That Caleb guy. The Prophet and the guy who tried to take off with you in the Razor….." she paused to slop some diluted bleach on the tile for me to mop up. "We knew they were capable of hunting, and we knew there were basically two different classes of ragers….. I don't know, this just feels like something else entirely."

"You're feeling that too?"

"Yeah! I keep going back to the part about this being an evolutionary step. That's what Caleb called it, right?"

"That's pretty much what he said," I moved to the sink to wash out the mop. She just fell silent. "Are you buying into that nonsense? It seems like a step backward if you ask me."

"Maybe," she replied absently. Before I could say anything else, she headed into her bedroom. When she returned, she had the CDC binder open and was leafing through the pages.

"Shane?" Kyle called from the front door.

"Yeah?"

"Can I get the keys to the old Ford? I want to load some supplies in the back of it and move it back into the barn."

"On the hook," I pointed at the keys hanging just inside the front door.

"Thanks," he grabbed them and was gone again.

"Were you ever vaccinated?" Rayne asked.

"As a kid?"

"No. Did you ever get the Covid vaccine?"

"No. Why?"

"There are a dozen case studies in here and the one common denominator is the vaccine."

"So?" I went back to mopping the floor when she didn't immediately answer. She flipped through a few more pages, scanning each one intently.

"Here!" she stabbed the page with a finger and then winced from her broken ribs. "Right here it says that those with the highest recovery rate from this new virus were those that were fully vaccinated. It goes on to state that within days of their recovery, they began to show signs of psychosis. The next group, the ones who go totally mad, were the ones who either had the early vaccines or weren't fully vaccinated. There's a third group made up of people like us who were never vaccinated. That's the group that showed the least likelihood of ever getting sick in the first place....."

"We got company!" Angie yelled into the house from the front porch.

I dropped the mop, grabbed my new rifle from the counter, and joined Angie on the porch. Rayne had tossed the notebook on the couch and retrieved her AR-15. Her place was watching the back door from the hallway. Angie pointed one of her long, skinny fingers at the lone man walking up the driveway. Kyle and Sarah slipped past me into the house to take up their positions.

"He's waving," Angie said just before she left to join everyone else in the house. Up until this point, all of the ragers we'd seen looked like what you might expect in the early days of a zombie apocalypse. Dirty and smelly with various stages of destroyed clothing. This guy was something else though.

He was indeed waving at me and once he had my full attention, he raised both hands high into the air. He was wearing black dress shoes, grey slacks, and a white button-down shirt. The tie around his neck was loose and the button behind it was undone. He walked with a mixture of determination and caution.

"That's far enough!" I said loud enough for him to hear. He stopped about 30 yards from the house. "What do you want?"

"I simply bring a message. May I put my hands down?" his voice was loud, and he spoke with authority.

"Keep your hands up and turn around. Let me see your backside."

"I am unarmed," he declared but did a full, slow turn so that I could see he wasn't hiding anything.

"Put your hands down. Fair warning, you do anything perceived as a threat and we'll drop you where you stand."

"As I said, I'm just the messenger. I have no intention of....."

"What's your message?" I interrupted.

"Yes. I am here on behalf of the prophet. He wishes me to tell you that you have proven yourself a worthy adversary. In doing so, he would like to offer a one-time opportunity to walk away from the fight that is sure to unfold should things continue the way they are."

"Really now?"

"Yes. Your continued looting and killing cannot be allowed to continue. This is a one-time amnesty and will never be offered again. Should you decline the offer, we will be forced into taking extreme action. Actions that I assure you, will not end with anything but your death."

"You're standing on my property and making threats? Really? Aren't you and this prophet asshole doing the same thing you accuse us of? Wouldn't I be within my right to demand that you and your pack of animals get the hell out of town?"

"While some of the actions taken in the first few days following our rebirths are very regrettable and unfortunate, we have evolved past that now. Call it growing pains if you will. It is you and people like you who continue to kill us and take the very things we need to survive."

"Growing pains?" I couldn't suppress the dark chuckle, so I didn't bother trying. "Every damn time I try to leave here, your people come after me! I ain't out looking for them but damn straight I'll defend myself! I don't hunt your people, but I hear you all do a little hunting late at night!"

"Sir, we could stand here for the rest of the day debating the moralities of what has transpired. That will accomplish nothing. You are being offered a chance to walk away from here and might I suggest you take it. It's a quarter till three. I'm willing to give you until 4 pm. After that, amnesty is off the table, and you will be dealt with. If I were in your shoes, I'd take the amnesty deal. It's the only deal in which you leave here alive."

"What if I were to offer you a compromise?" I thought I might try a different tactic.

"I'm listening." his reply actually surprised me.

"Might I suggest a parley between us?"

"Go on," he crossed his arms across his chest.

"Here's the thing; you want us to leave but the timeframe you've given us is far too short. We still have people in the city that we'd like to have returned, unharmed. I can only assume you are tired of losing your people and supplies. It only makes sense for you to grant me an audience with the prophet so that we may come to an agreeable outcome."

"The prophet will never agree to this. You've proven yourselves far too violent for such a meeting."

"Under the rules of parley, a temporary armistice will be in effect. I will speak to the prophet, and I will do so unarmed. You will escort me to this meeting, and you will guarantee my safety until I'm returned here, unharmed. In the meantime, all hostilities between my group and your group will cease," I could see that he was at least entertaining the idea.

"C'mon, dude. You'll probably win if you try to rush this house and kill us. I'm pretty sure you'd take us out and I'm not really in the mood for getting killed today. You gotta ask yourself if the price for that victory is one you wanna pay. You'll get us, but how many of yours will be planted right alongside us?" this seemed to push him past the point of just considering the option and he made his decision.

"Parley it is."

CHAPTER 42

"Well, aren't you going to invite me in?" the man in my driveway asked after a few seconds of awkward silence.

"I want to talk to the prophet, not one of his lackeys," I retorted sharply.

"Who do you think you've been talking to?"

"You? You're the prophet?"

"I am. Now that you know who I am, might I learn who you are? Or does this complicate things for you?" his smile was almost gleeful.

"No, it doesn't complicate anything. My name is Shane."

"Well, Shane, I'll ask the question again; aren't you going to invite me in?" I had to admit, his ploy had taken me a little off-guard.

"We can sit on the porch and discuss this. I'll put the warning out there again, just so we're clear. If you do anything perceived as aggressive, all bets are off. Understood?"

"Understood," he nodded and walked to the stairs of the deck. I motioned him up and pointed at one of the chairs by the small table. He sat with his legs crossed and his arms resting on the arms of the wooden chair. I leaned my rifle against the wall next to my chair and sat.

"Can I offer you something to drink?" I offered.

"Scotch on the rocks?" he sounded hopeful.

"Angie?" I called through the window above our heads.

"I heard. Gimme a minute,"

"You're not what I expected," I admitted to the man as soon as I heard ice cubes clattering into a glass inside.

"May I ask, how did you know what to expect?"

"We had a run-in with a guy named Caleb earlier today. From what he said, I was expecting a homeless guy wearing clothes made of burlap sacks," before he could answer, Angie brought out his drink and handed it to him. She passed me a bottle of water.

"Thank you, dear," the prophet said eying her from head to toe. His eyes lingered on her breasts and rear end a lot longer than they should have. He watched her until she disappeared through the screen door.

"You got a name other than the prophet?" I brought him back into the moment.

"The name is avid. David Prophet," he sipped the scotch and locked eyes with me.

"Well, David, why do you want us to leave? We're far enough out that we can stay out of each other's way."

"That may be true, but so far, you haven't. It seems that every single incursion you make into the city leaves more and more of my people dead, and I just can't have that."

"Every attack on my people has been unprovoked," I countered.

"Had you just stayed away, there would have been no attack," he shifted slightly in his chair and took another sip. "I'd say no offense, but I don't care. You and your small band are the outsiders and aggressors here. You say you were simply defending yourself but that would be like a robber killing a homeowner and saying it was self-defense. Do you understand the issues at hand?"

"Maybe I'm in the wrong here, but I'm pretty sure the world has fallen apart on us. Did you expect those of us who survived the plague or whatever the hell this is to just sit back and starve to death? You said something about needing supplies to survive, right? Well, don't you think we need supplies too?"

"Shane, those of us who have been through the rebirth will, without a doubt, outlive you and your kind….."

"You can't know that!"

"Except, I do know that," he pulled up his pantleg to expose his lower calve and two puncture wounds. "Do you know what that is?" he pointed.

"Looks like a snakebite,"

"You'd be correct. A big rattlesnake got me when we were stomping around in the brush this morning. Bugger latched on good too. Do you think you could survive a full venom strike from a rattlesnake without any symptoms?"

"Doesn't mean your immortal."

"I never claimed as much. Shane, we no longer feel pain. All of our inhibitions have been lifted from our shoulders. Our metabolisms have undergone incredible changes and so have our immune systems, and they continue to change. Almost daily in fact. We are an upgraded version of mankind. This winter, you'll need heavy coats to stay warm. Our metabolism can compensate for the cold. I'm watching sweat trickle from your forehead, yet I'm completely comfortable. We can go days without water or food, you cannot," he sipped the scotch again. "We will outlive you through simple attrition, or by force if necessary."

"You can't expect us to just walk away from here, to wander off into the countryside and die. You seem to be forgetting that we have the ability to use a little force of our own….."

"You mean your guns?"

"You may have the numbers. I'll give you that one. Except, your clubs and knives are no match for our guns and ammunition stockpiles."

"Shane," he shook his head slowly. "You assume that since we choose to use more primitive weapons, we cannot use modern weapons. It's simply a matter of choice on our part. Make no mistake, we can do everything you can do. Only we can do it better, faster, and longer," he locked eyes with me as he sipped the scotch again. The ice cubes made the slightest clanking noise in the glass.

"What about the people still in the city?"

"If they choose to stay, my stalkers will hunt them down and eliminate them. Just as you have a choice to make, so do they."

"What's to stop me from just putting a round between your eyes right here and now?" I shifted slightly so that my .45 would be more easily accessible.

"There is absolutely nothing stopping you. In the scheme of things, I'm but one man. You could draw your weapon and shoot me dead. Just know this; before my body hits the deck, you'll have the full fury of my stalkers raining down on this quaint little cabin. I'm not a fool, Shane. I left orders with my men, and they will carry them out with deadly precision," he knocked back the last of the amber liquid in his glass and set it on the table between us. "Any hope you may have of living through this will die as quickly as the report of your weapon across the countryside."

"Besides, do you really want to kill the only man who can maintain control over the stalkers? It might make you feel good for the briefest of moments, I'll give you that. I'd even give you points for taking out a few of my men, but you can't win. You'll feel good until the stalkers overwhelm you and tear your body limb from limb. If you're lucky, you'll die before that happens. If you really want to die right here, today, then go ahead. Shoot me dead and see what happens."

"Fine….." I said just above a whisper. My mind was racing as I tried to come up with a plan to spin this in my favor.

"You'll leave then?"

"Yeah, but we need more time. I also need to get the rest of my people out of the city."

"Anything else?"

"A mother and her adult son went missing early this morning. I'd like them returned. Alive and unharmed," I tried to bargain. "Anyone else that wants to leave the city for that matter. Give me more time and they can leave with us."

"If I didn't know any better I'd think you were trying to form your own army. Maybe try to coordinate a counter-offensive."

"No! I'm trying to get as many people out alive as I can. You gotta know that if you try to go after everyone still living in the city, you'll lose a lot of your people too. It won't be a one-sided fight in your favor. Doing it this way saves a lot of lives. Yours and ours."

"Can I get another drink?" he asked.

"Angie?" I called into the open window again, never taking my eyes from his.

"I heard," came her reply. A second later, she stepped from the house, retrieved his glass, and left.

"Any chance you were a lawyer before your world fell apart?" he asked while he waited for his drink.

"No. Logistics manager."

"Ah. Either way, you drive for a logical and fair bargain, Shane," he paused when Angie returned with his scotch. Again, he allowed his eyes to linger on her shapely body until she was out of sight again. "Anyway, if I should grant you a 12-hour window and your other requests, I want something in return."

"Like what?" I asked suspiciously.

"There's five of you here?"

"Yeah."

"I'm not completely unreasonable, Shane. I'm also not going to allow you to leave here with all of the supplies you've looted," he held his hand up when I started to protest. "You may however take whatever you can load in the truck you left at the pond and the old pickup that is parked in your barn. I'll give you one hour to load up and then you'll be escorted back to Winnemucca. All of you."

"Once there, you will collect your friends and anyone else who wishes to leave the city. Those people will not be allowed to take anything beyond what they can load in their cars and trucks. If you are not out of the city by 3 am tomorrow, well, let's just say that it won't end well for you."

"Where the hell are we supposed to go?" I questioned.

"I don't care as long as it is in a direction away from my city. Another thing: if I ever see any of you again, all of you will be hunted down and eliminated. This is a one-time amnesty. Don't mistake it for anything other than that," his tone was menacing.

"Fine," I grumbled.

"This isn't your fault, Shane. Leader to leader, I understand this may be a hard pill to swallow. You're doing the right thing though. You've realized the fragility of your position and you're trying to give your people a fighting chance to live. You won't get that if you stay here, and I think you're smart enough to know it," he sipped his drink again.

"Sadly, you were passed over when evolution decided to make the next big leap forward. There's no rhyme or reason for it, simply bad luck I should think. I say sadly because I think if you and I were on the same side of things, we might have been friends."

"And there's no room for that now?" I tried.

"No. Unfortunately, there's not. It would only be a matter of time before you decided that our ways are too foreign, too brutal for you. It would only be a matter of time before you attempted to seize control for yourself. Again, not your fault. It's just the way you're wired. It's in your genes, in every fiber of your being," he finished his drink and set the glass on the table. "No, this is the best way for all of you."

"Why?"

"Why what?"

"Why give us the chance to leave? Why sit here on my porch and give me a choice?"

"To you, we may seem ultra-violent, and that wouldn't be far from the truth," he admitted. "My stalkers are capable of incredible violence when needed. To be honest, you're the only one who's offered to sit down with me and have a discussion. I found that refreshing. I understand that you've only done what you perceived you needed to do to survive. At the same time, that's all we've been doing."

"I've heard the reports from my people about the fight at the grocery store and the hospital. You and your ragtag band have done quite well in thwarting our attempts of dealing with you. I find that an admirable trait. Unfortunately for you, you no longer hold that position. I have you cornered and that's a very dangerous position to be in. I'm sure your instincts to lash out and fight are tearing you up inside. I know mine would be," he smiled.

"One gunshot or one yell from me and my people would descend on this place like an F5 tornado. You know that though. My guess is that's why you and I are still talking and not trying to kill each other. Believe it or not, we still have that animal instinct to survive, just like you. I believe that would be why you have accepted this arrangement. I guess you could say you've earned the opportunity to escape because you've earned a little respect from me."

"I don't have to tell you that should you try and double-cross me, all deals are null and void. I think I've made that perfectly clear. I also think you have enough honor to uphold your end of the deal. Find yourself a nice farm or ranch far from us. Settle in and allow the rest of us to move forward."

"What if your people, your kind come to us? You know we'll defend ourselves, right?" I asked.

"Nobody has said you couldn't defend yourselves. I'd expect nothing less. I suspect that in time, you'll have to do just that. I'm giving you a chance at life, not a guarantee."

CHAPTER 43

August 31ˢᵗ, 2023.

"So, where do we go from here?" I asked with resignation.

"I'll give you a few minutes to go inside and talk to your people while I summon mine. It's only fair to warn you though; should even one of your people break the terms of this armistice, retribution will be swift and brutal," he stood from the chair he'd been sitting in. I stood at the same time.

"That goes both ways, Mr. Prophet," I returned his warning with one of my own.

"See to your people while I summon mine," he dismissed me with a wave of his hand and started to turn for the stairs.

"Aren't you forgetting something?"

"What could I be forgetting?" he turned back to face me.

"We shake on it. We shake on it as two men should," I stuck my hand out.

When David Prophet shook my hand and looked me in the eye, I knew what he was planning. Don't ask me how I knew, I just did. Call it a gut feeling. The light red tinge in his eyes and the formidable strength of his handshake were all very unsettling, but there was something more. Something he wasn't saying. It was that absence of information that was triggering all sorts of alarm bells in my mind. I hoped I was wrong, but everything told me that I wasn't. He was right when he said that having a wild animal cornered was dangerous. I'm sure he was thinking he'd done a masterful job of placating me with his seemingly generous offer of amnesty. It took everything I had to keep him thinking that.

After he shook my hand, he turned and walked down the stairs. He only walked 20 or 30 feet up the driveway when he put his pinky fingers in his mouth and let out three earsplitting whistles. He looked at me and smiled. I returned the smile even though it nearly made me sick to do so. I promptly strode through the front door and immediately had Kyle, Angie, Rayne, and Sarah up in my face. They were demanding to know what I was thinking but they were doing it in angry whispers so the man outside couldn't hear them. I held a finger to my lips to shush them.

"I assume all of you heard that?" I whispered.

"This is our home, Shane! You can't just give it up like that!" Rayne was the first to accuse.

"We don't have a lot of time to talk about this, so listen close!" I growled. Sure that I had their attention, I continued. "Kyle, when we start loading supplies, I need you to make sure the Ford is loaded with as many weapons as you can. If you're asked, we need them for self-defense. Angie, I need you to get Rayne ready to do whatever it is we're gonna have to do. Wrap her ribs tight, pump her up with painkillers, whatever you got to do to get her into this fight, and trust me, there's gonna be a fight. Sarah, you're going to have to run back to the pond and get my truck. Remember how to get there?" she answered with a curt nod.

"Good. We're not going to have a lot of time to pull this together and I don't have the time to give you the details. Just do what I tell you and be ready for anything. This is gonna go sideways but we need it to swing in our favor. Follow my lead, okay?" I received nods from the small group. "Look, I bought us some time and hopefully I bought us some better odds. If not, we'll all be dead by this time tomorrow and none of this will matter anyway," I waved my hand around for emphasis. Rayne cleared her throat and nodded slightly toward the front door. She was the only one who had a clear view of Prophet. When I turned, I could see him and two of his men heading for the stairs.

"Are you ready, Shane?" he asked as he stepped up to the open door.

"Yeah. How you wanna do this?" I shared one last look with each of my people before I turned all the way to face him.

"I'm sure you're going to want your people to gather supplies for your journey. One of my men will shadow each of your people. They're not there to help, they're simply there to make sure we keep this all on the up and up. The only exception to that will be for whomever you send to retrieve your truck. I'll send two people in that case."

"Fine," I fished my truck key from my pocket and handed it to Sarah. "Make it quick. We got a lot to do before we leave and we really need that truck," I said when she took the key from me. I heard one of the vehicles, the small pickup truck, start and pull out of the driveway. "Where are they going?" I asked.

"My runners are going back to Winnemucca. They will be passing along word of our armistice," he looked at two more people who were standing at the base of the stairs. "Go with the girl to bring the truck at the pond back. If she becomes hostile, kill her."

"Yes, Prophet," they said in unison. Sarah gave me a worried look.

"Go, Sarah. You'll be fine as long as you don't do anything stupid. We need that truck more than we need any trouble."

"Okay," she said hesitantly before stepping past Prophet and onto the porch. A few seconds later, she and her shadows were jogging toward the pond.

"Let's not waste any more time. Get your people moving, Shane," he ordered.

"Do you want our guns?" I asked.

"No need. Like I told you; break the armistice and all of you die."

"One of my people is injured and I need my medic to tend to her. Is that okay?" I didn't want to press the gun angle any further, so I changed the subject.

"The fewer people you have loading, the fewer supplies you'll have. Not my concern," he moved for the open bottle of scotch on the counter and took a long pull from it. "I still enjoy the taste. It's too bad that's the only thing I get from it anymore," he mused.

"Angie, take care of Rayne, please. When you're done with her, I need the two of you to gather up the most important medical supplies and have them ready to load in my truck when Sarah gets back with it. Kyle, it looks like it'll be me and you loading everything else. We need to start with the Ford in the barn," I got nods from all of them. Rayne and Angie moved for her room turned hospital room. Two of Prophet's men followed them. Kyle and I started past Prophet when he reached out and grabbed my arm.

"Pack light, and remember, this cease-fire is only good if we do this in good faith," he warned.

"Enjoy my booze," I grumbled and continued past him. Kyle and I were followed by two men.

The keys were still in the old truck, so I started it and pulled it just outside of the doors. After shutting it off and climbing out, I noticed a plastic, hard-sided case in the bed that I didn't recognize. I started to reach for it, but Kyle coughed and gave me the slightest shake of his head. He wanted me to leave it alone, so I did.

"We're gonna need fuel for the trucks," he announced moving toward the full yellow diesel cans along the wall. "Gas too," he pointed to the red cans.

"What do you think about a surprise attack?" I whispered when I bent down next to him to grab two gas cans.

"We could get a few but not enough. There are too many of them and they're too spread out. Just bide our time until the opportunity presents itself," he whispered his reply.

As we loaded the plastic five-gallon containers, he kept moving the plastic case in the bed until it was neatly surrounded by gasoline and diesel fuels. I'm not sure what the assignment was, but he clearly understood it. Next, we retrieved a four-by-eight sheet of plywood and laid it over the top of the fuel cans. When we moved the truck in between their RV and the little SUV they'd brought, Sarah and the goons were pulling in with my truck. I directed her to back it up to the stairs of the house.

The entire time we were loading, I was trying to get an accurate count of how many men Prophet had. I was failing at that task because every time I thought I'd accounted for all of them, more would just turn up in random places. My best guess put their number at close to 40 men and women. It was almost as if they were broken up into squads. Each squad leader had a light pink tinge in their eyes while the squad members all had that ghastly red color.

The other thing I noticed was that those with the deep red coloring didn't seem to talk very much, if at all. All of them looked like they were ready and willing to pummel any of us who might cross them. I think they were anxious to do just that by the way they were glaring at us. I'm pretty sure the only thing keeping them from doing so were their supposed squad leaders. Their faces were red, all of them had that protruding vein in their forehead, and some of them were even slightly bug-eyed.

"Their blood pressure has to be through the roof," Angie whispered from beside me at the window of Rayne's room. She was observing the same thing I was.

"You mean like mine right now?" I tried to joke.

"I think it's only a matter of time before the more severely infected drop dead," Rayne said as she came up behind us.

"We can hope," I muttered. "Those bags ready to be loaded in the truck?" I pointed to the pair of medical bags on her bed.

"Yeah, they're good. What are we doing, Shane? Please tell me you've got a plan," she grabbed my arm and whispered in my ear. The stalkers that were supposed to be watching us were standing in the living room.

"Prophet has no intention of following through with this cease-fire. He's just using us to make his work easier."

"Easier? How?"

"By the time we're ready to leave Winnemucca, the majority of survivors will all be gathered in the same place. If I were still in Vegas and putting money on it, I'd say that's when he's going to spring his trap. Fish in a barrel if they decide to arm up and throw some lead," I explained.

"You got a plan?" she repeated the question.

"We beat him to the punch."

"That's it? That's your plan?"

"You got anything better?"

"No," she admitted.

"Angie?" I called quietly. She tore her attention from the stalkers outside. "Kyle put a black case in the back of the truck. Do you know what might be in it?"

"How big was it?" she asked. I held up my hands to demonstrate the approximate size of the case. A grin started to form at the corners of her mouth.

"If it's the one I'm thinking of, it's like 75 pounds of Tannerite," I was about to ask her another question but one of the stalkers came into the room.

I grabbed the medical bags from the bed and hauled them out to my truck. I knew what Tannerite was, and I knew that 75 pounds of it detonating all at once would create one hell of an explosion. Before it was outlawed in Nevada, me and some guys from work had blown up some small containers of it. It was triggered by a gunshot and to be totally honest, I didn't know if there was any other way to make it blow. Seventy-five pounds of it surrounded by 100 gallons of gasoline and diesel..... "Holy shit," I said under my breath. Yeah, Kyle had definitely understood the assignment.

"Time to wrap it up, Shane," Prophet said from the chair on my porch as I dropped the heavy bags in the bed of my truck.

CHAPTER 44

At best, the bucket seats in the old Ford could only accommodate two people. Kyle had been tasked with driving it while one of the stalkers rode shotgun. Two more climbed into the bed and nestled themselves into the gear piled back there. Rayne, Sarah, and Angie occupied the backseats of my truck while Prophet rode shotgun. There were also two more unwelcome passengers in the bed of my truck. While all of us had been busy loading supplies, Sarah had moved her brother's body into the barn and covered it with a sheet and tarp.

The red car that was shot up in my driveway was unusable. The white car had started though, and it was leading us down the driveway at a slow pace. From what I could tell, all of the stalkers who had taken over my property were walking alongside our small convoy. Here again, the squad mentality seemed to be at play. This also gave me a chance to get a decent head count. Twenty-eight in total. That pissed me off a little. The five of us against twenty-eight weren't bad odds and I'd let that opportunity slip by.

Driving slowly next to the stalkers gave me a few minutes to observe them in even more detail. Besides the red faces and bulging forehead veins, I could see the veins in their necks and arms were also standing out noticeably. Many of them looked like they were walking around with their muscles permanently flexed. Even the smaller men and women in the group looked like bodybuilders on a stage.

Those with the most pronounced muscles and veins walked stiffly in long strides. I don't know if it was from trying to move with flexed muscles or not, but it was very noticeable. The ones who most closely resembled normal were what I had called the squad leaders. They showed some of the same signs as the others, just much less pronounced.

As we crept along, my attention was pulled from the stalkers to the wreckage of the Razor. To think I'd basically walked away with nothing more than a gash on my forehead was nothing short of miraculous. I was sure I'd be sore from the violent impacts of the wreck later, but for now, I felt fine. I also learned what had happened to the guy who'd been driving. He'd been partially catapulted out during our first roll. The subsequent rolls had crushed and mangled his body that was still draped over the driver's door.

Another half mile up the road, nestled into a grove of pinion-juniper trees was a school bus and two pick-up trucks. We stopped here long enough for the foot soldiers to load up. One of the trucks pulled out ahead of the white sedan, the bus, and the second truck fell in behind us. All of us were silent, even Prophet, as the convoy made the trek out to the paved road.

"It really is better this way, Shane," Prophet finally spoke when we reached the pavement.

"Better for who? You?" I responded.

"All parties involved, of course. You get the chance to vanish into the vast nothingness that makes up the majority of the state of Nevada, and we can get on with our business."

"What about my cabin? Our supplies?"

"The supplies will be moved back to town so we can make use of them. The cabin and all of the outbuildings will be burned to the ground. That's the only way to make sure someone else doesn't try to move in."

"You sound like you're afraid of something. Maybe a large group of people with some coordination and firepower being able to run you off," Rayne spoke from the seat behind me.

"Of course, that's always a concern, but I don't think it's one I need to trouble myself with," he looked over his shoulder at her.

"Why not?" I asked.

"Once you and the other so-called survivors are gone, there won't be any strongholds left anywhere near us. By removing anywhere for them to hide or gather, we significantly reduce the risk."

"Gone?" this was Rayne again.

"Yes, gone. As in exiled from my sight," he replied quickly. Too quickly.

"So, once you control Winnemucca, then what?" I brought his attention back to me. "Even if you gather up all the supplies, you can only hold out so long before they run out. What are you going to do then?"

"As I told you earlier, we don't consume food at the same rate you do. Ya know, by accepting this amnesty deal, you're saving yourself much more than just being hunted down and killed by my stalkers. If you stayed, that would surely happen, but you're saving yourself from being dined upon by them….." his voice trailed off.

"You EAT people?" Angie blurted out.

"Meat is meat," he craned his neck to look at her and the horror on her face. "The stalkers need to hunt. It's how they're wired. Human, rabbit, dog….. It's all the same to us. Aren't you glad you're leaving before you're invited to dinner?" his grin was pure evil.

"Back to your question though," he returned his attention to me. "It's only a matter of time before we start moving away from the city. We won't be the only ones though. People like you, people who were skipped over in this evolutionary step, your days are numbered. This is worldwide and your kind is already vastly outnumbered."

"Aren't you worried about the military?" I already knew the answer, I just needed him to keep talking in the hopes he'd drop some tidbit of information I could use.

"Not in the least. Here's the thing, Shane; all of you, without exception, are still hung up in your antiquated ways of thinking. You rely on your technology; you're guns and gasoline. Because of that dependency, you've grown soft, and weak. We're here to cleanse the earth of you. You still haven't realized you've been left behind and are facing an extinction-level event. You're dead, you just don't know it yet….."

"What about your stalkers? Aren't they dying already?" Angie interrupted.

"Some, yes," he shrugged his shoulders.

"What happens when they're all dead?"

"Young lady, we are in the beginning phases here. By the time the last true stalker dies, we will have long since laid claim to the throne. They are but a means to an end. Simply a tool in the toolbox if you will. There is nothing that can be done regarding their eventual demise. The only thing those of us who remain can do is to capitalize on their sacrifice."

"That's gotta be the single most short-sighted thing I've ever heard in my life," Rayne chuckled a dark chuckle that held no mirth. Prophet turned to look at her again.

"Got something you wanna say?"

"Have you stopped to listen to your dumb ass ramblings? Your whole endgame is to kill anyone and everyone who can possibly help you lead a remotely normal life! Let's kill all the uninfected, the only people who can still grow things and make other crap work. Let's kill the people who can help keep you alive if you're injured. Jesus, you people are dumber than shit!" she fired off.

"And yet, who lost this battle, and who is being run out of town?" Prophet sneered. I was beginning to wonder if Rayne was pushing his buttons deliberately. "I've heard it all before! I've been trying to warn people for years, but few listened! I've been called every name under the sun, beaten for my beliefs, and persecuted more than you'd ever believe!"

"You're infected with a virus! A virus that has damaged your brain, your reasoning….."

"You call it a virus; I call it a gift from the almighty himself! We are the pale rider known as death! It's all part of the plan for cleansing the earth! We are the chosen! We are the next step in human evolution!" Prophet nearly shouted. Little bits of spittle sprayed from his mouth. He was rapidly becoming unhinged, and I needed to rein him and Rayne in before this came off the rails completely.

"That's enough, Rayne!" I barked over my shoulder.

"You heard the man, little girl! Shut that hole in your face before I come over this seat and shut it for you, permanently!" Prophet growled. His finger was pointed in her direction. I could see Rayne in the rearview mirror and the seething rage behind her eyes had me a little worried.

"Rayne!" I barked again as she started to open her mouth to say something. "That's enough," I softened my tone slightly when she made eye contact with me in the rearview mirror.

"Whatever," she grumbled, sagging back into her seat, and looking out the window.

"You better keep that one in check, Shane. If anybody is going to screw this up for you, it's gonna be her," Prophet turned to face forward again. I didn't dare say what I was thinking so I didn't say anything at all. I knew this whole armistice thing was going to fall apart, I just needed to hold that inevitability off as long as possible. We weren't in a position to retaliate. Not yet anyway.

"Can I ask a question?" I brought Prophet's attention back to me.

"What?"

"How do you keep control of the stalkers? My understanding was that they were mostly stark raving mad."

"Mad? No, they're not mad in the sense you're thinking about. It's more like..... Well....." he looked thoughtful for a moment before continuing. "Have you ever had an intense adrenaline high?"

"In the last couple of weeks, I have."

"Did you feel the rush of power through your body? Did you feel your senses sharpen and your physical strength heighten? Do you remember doing things you never thought you could or would do? Do you remember doing it all on pure, animal instinct?"

"I remember what I felt like after it was all over."

"Exhaustion and mental fog?"

"Yeah," I admitted.

"Imagine if it never stopped. Imagine if the euphoric high of adrenaline-fueled energy never went away. Imagine if it only grew stronger and stronger."

"I could totally understand the allure of it, but how do you keep the stalkers in check?" I repeated the question.

"To be blunt about it, they're like trained guard dogs. They stay with me and respond to me as a dog would. Some understand the simple orders a little better than others, but they all know that I'm the master."

"So, you're telling me that you've domesticated them?"

"It's more of a mutually beneficial relationship."

"Come again?"

"It's like this, Shane; they know I'm not going to hurt them, and I know they aren't going to hurt me. We keep each other safe, and we do what we can to protect each other. Somehow they just know that I'm one of them."

"That's why they will agree to this ceasefire?"

"Basically, yes."

"You tell 'em to sit like good dogs and they will," I heard Rayne mumble from the backseat. Prophet glanced over his shoulder at her but left it at that.

Luckily, the rest of the ride into Winnemucca was made in silence. The only thing Prophet said was to give me directions to follow the rest of the vehicles to the golf course. I did as instructed, but I could feel the tension building inside of me. I wasn't the only one either. A look in the mirror and I could see Rayne's furrowed brow and a little fear in her eyes. Sarah and Angie had the same looks plastered on their faces too.

"You mind if I try and raise my people on the radio?" I asked Prophet.

"Do what you gotta do," he mumbled.

"Rayne? Could you try raising Janice and Chase, please?" I instructed because my radio had never been replaced after the Razor crash.

"Yeah," she answered and began calling them on the radio. She tried unsuccessfully for the five minutes it took us to make it to our destination. We were directed to pull up in front of the clubhouse and park.

"Don't go wandering off, Shane. I need to inform my people of what is happening and if you take it upon yourself to do anything but stay with your vehicles, I cannot guarantee your safety. Understood?"

"We ain't going anywhere."

"Good," he opened the door and slid out of the truck. Without so much as a glance back at us, he and the two men who were riding in the bed walked straight into the clubhouse. The three men from Kyle's truck followed suit, leaving us alone. The four of us also got out of the truck to stretch our legs. Kyle was parked next to us, and he joined us between the two vehicles after a few moments. This was the first moment we'd had alone since the cabin.

"Chase and Janice are fine," he said in a low voice as he leaned against the side of my truck. "Cody is still with them."

"They never answered my radio calls," Rayne said.

"They heard you, Rayne. Had it been me or Shane calling, they would have answered straight away. Because it was you, Chase changed the frequency. It's something I taught him, and I didn't even think to pass that along. Sorry, Shane. My bad. They're on channel 16 now."

"Where are they?"

"Roof of the hospital," he nodded gently in that direction. "Chase has been watching this place through his scope all afternoon. They're dug in and ain't nobody sneakin up behind 'em."

"Have they found Donnie or Mom yet?" Sarah asked hopefully.

"They're in the clubhouse. What's our play, Shane?"

"Gimme a few minutes to put something together. I'm doing my best to make this up on the fly right now. What do you think we should do?"

"I know you know this, but dude ain't gonna let us just walk away from here. It don't matter how much we comply."

"I think he's just using us as bait to round up all the other survivors," I stated. "Pretty sure you can bank on it."

"I also think he's got a weaker hand than he's letting on."

"How so?"

"Why hasn't he just rounded up the survivors on his own? Why did he go along with my suggestion of parley? I don't think he has the manpower he wants us to think he has."

"It's highly likely a lot of his stalkers have dropped dead from massive brain bleeds," Angie interjected.

"So, what are we gonna do about it?" Kyle repeated the question.

CHAPTER 45

August 31st, 2023.

"Let me see your radio," I held my hand out to Rayne. She reached into the backseat, grabbed it, and handed it over. I adjusted the channel and put it to my mouth. "Chase, you out there?"

"Yeah, we got you," his reply was immediate.

"Have you been in your perch long enough to get a count on these guys?"

"There are roughly 50 at your position with another 16 or 18 out and about. Our current position is clear and they ain't slipping up behind us.

"Copy. Any count on friendlies?"

"We're only aware of Kate and Donnie at your location. There could be more, but we haven't seen them yet. There is a small team working on the west side of the highway. They're laying low and moving cautiously. We counted four in that group. Other than that, we ain't seen much in the way of possible friendlies. Heads up, bogies coming out of the clubhouse," he warned.

All of us looked up the sidewalk that led to the glass front doors of the clubhouse. Prophet and four stalkers were escorting Donnie and Kate toward us. The mother-son duo looked a little worse for wear, but they were moving under their own power. Rayne and Angie had to physically block Sarah to keep her from running toward her mother and brother. Her frustration at being restrained washed away as soon as the trio was reunited.

"I'm upholding my end of the bargain, Shane. These two are the only captives we are holding. I brought them out as a sign of good faith," Prophet announced.

"What about gathering up the rest of the survivors?"

"That's up to you. Just remember, the clock is ticking, and it has been for a while now. If I'm not seeing your taillights by 3 am, the deal is void," his demeanor was as dark as his voice.

"Fine. I'll just take my people and go looking," I reached for the door handle of my truck.

"I said nothing about taking your people with you," his words stopped me in my tracks. His stalkers visibly bristled. "You said that you wanted to find the survivors to take with you. You never said anything about looking for them as a group....."

"Now wait a damn minute!"

"A deal is a deal. You either follow through with your end of it, or....." his voice trailed off with a shrug of his shoulders and a glance at the nearest stalker.

"It's kinda hard with you changing the rules!" I growled.

"I've changed nothing. These are details you failed to mention. Details you failed to specify, and I'm in no way inclined to grant you any latitude here. Now, go find the other survivors, then get the hell out of my town. How hard is that?"

"How do you expect me to find them on my own? I need some help, Prophet!"

"Not my problem."

"Bastard," I grumbled and reached for the door handle again.

"Now what are you doing?" Prophet asked as he took a step forward and pushed the door closed again.

"What's it look like I'm doing?" my temper was beginning to get the better of me.

"There was never any mention of using a vehicle to find them. The trucks and your people stay here where we can keep an eye on them," by the grin smeared across his face, he was enjoying this game.

"You son-of-a-bitch!"

"You better get moving, Shane. Time is already working against you," he tapped his watchless wrist for emphasis. The only answer I had was a sharp glare before I turned to face Rayne.

"If I'm not back by 2:30 in the morning, take everyone here and get as far away from here as you can," I held out the keys for her.

"No! We're not leaving you behind!"

"This isn't a request, Rayne! If I ain't back by then, I won't be coming back. You have to get everyone else out of here. You understand?" I took a step closer to her.

"Shane….."

"No. Take the keys and do what I'm asking, please," I took her hand in mine and placed the keys in her open palm. With pursed lips and a stiff nod, she agreed. I released her hand and gently pulled her into a hug. Only when my mouth was close to her ear did I whisper. "Did you bring your frying pan?" she answered with the slightest nod of understanding.

"This is all very valiant and touching, but don't you think you're being just a little overdramatic, Shane?" Prophet asked from behind me. With a heavy sigh, I released Rayne and turned to face him again. While looking at him, I spoke over my shoulder to my team.

"Kyle?"

"Yeah, boss?"

"Make sure Donnie and Kate have weapons and line them out on our plans once we leave here tonight. Once that's done, I want everyone to wait this out in the trucks. There will be no interaction between you and Prophet's people. Understood?"

"That wasn't part of the deal, Shane," Prophet scowled at me in protest.

"You never said it was against the rules of this parley. Since we aren't violating any of the established rules, it's fair play, David," I don't know if it was having the tables turned on him or the use of his first name, but the rage quickly became apparent on his face. "It's this, or we can just climb in our rigs and leave right now. It won't take but five seconds for us to grab the rest of our group."

"What about all the people you said you wanted to save? What about them?" his face grew redder with every word.

"Screw 'em! You just gave us the two we were really concerned about. Hell, the way I see it, maybe we ought to just load up and get gone right now!" I risked taking my eyes off of Prophet long enough to look over at Kyle. He replied with a knowing nod. When I looked back at Prophet, I could see the red around his eyes was beginning to become more pronounced. He was clinching his fists and he started to take a step forward. I heard Kyle say something into his radio, but his voice was so quiet, I couldn't make out the words.

"Let me ask you a question, David," I kept my voice calm and level. The rage was seething just beneath the surface of his now-red face. He stopped advancing though and that's what I really wanted.

"What?"

"Back at my place, you said something about our survival instincts, yours, and ours, being intact. You said that, right?"

"I did and I guess you place less on your survival than I thought," he hissed. Never breaking his steely, red-eyed gaze, I put my radio to my mouth and spoke loud enough for Prophet to hear me.

"Chase, you got a copy?"

"We're here, boss. Whatcha need?"

"You got eyes on this guy standing directly in front of me?"

"You talkin about the geeky lookin tool who looks like he's downed a whole case of energy drinks?"

"Yep, that's the guy."

"Want me to end him?"

"Can you hit him from your position?" I asked already knowing the answer.

"Sure can. I got him locked in at 225 yards for an easy shot. From the time the firing pin hits primer till his head explodes will be about a third of a second. All you gotta do is say when," Chase reported confidently.

"I could be on you faster than he can pull the trigger. I can snap your neck in a heartbeat you arrogant ass!" Prophet said. He was barely containing his anger.

"That brings to mind something else you said. Something about giving your people orders to tear us to shreds if something happened to you. Don't you think I'm smart enough to give my people the same orders? Oh, and there's not one guy out there ready to pull the trigger on you. There's three, and they have enough ammo to tear through your people before you ever figure out how to get to them," it was a partial bluff, but he didn't know any different.

"It looks like we have a standoff," his previously calm demeanor was rapidly returning. You could almost see it wash over him.

"It appears that way," I looked around and could see that we'd drawn a crowd of stalkers. This was gonna be a bloodbath if I didn't do something. "Tell your stalkers to back off or all of us die today."

He didn't answer with words, nor did he start shouting orders. A simple wave of his hand and all of the stalkers began slowly backing away. When the circle around us had expanded to about 150 feet, he waved his hand over his head, and they all stopped retreating.

"Now what?" he asked.

"You never had any intention of allowing us to leave the city, did you?"

"There's no way out now, Shane. All of the roads leading out of the city are blocked."

"We'll see about that. Clear us a path so we can get out of here."

"And if I refuse?" the question wasn't even out of his mouth when my rifle was trained on him. The rest of my group had their weapons up and trained on different targets that surrounded us.

"Then we start shooting and you'll be the first one to die. You gave me a choice when we were sitting on my deck and now I'm giving you one," I eased my finger onto the trigger of the AK. After a moment of contemplation, he pointed to the men and women who were blocking the entrance to the parking lot. Using a gentle sideways motion, he signaled them to move.

"We can all die right here, right now. Or, and I prefer this option, I can allow the stalkers to hunt you down. You've only got another hour of daylight, Shane. The stalkers are masters of the dark. None of you will see another sunrise. You cannot escape."

"Everyone mount up," I ordered over my shoulder. "Anyone moves, drop 'em," I added. Rayne handed me the key to the truck and made her way to the passenger side. "Had you just agreed to live and let live, this could have turned out a whole lot different."

"That was never gonna happen."

"That's what I figured," I held the AK level with one hand and opened the door of my truck with the other.

"Mind if I offer a word of advice, Shane?"

"What?" I slid onto the seat, handed Rayne my rifle, and started the truck.

"Save one bullet."

"Excuse me?" I pulled the door closed.

"Save one bullet for yourself. All of you need to save one bullet for yourselves."

"Why is that?"

"If you are taken alive, you will watch as we eat your compatriots alive. You will watch because we will cut your eyelids from your face. Their screams of agony will carry you to hell on the breeze of their dying breaths," his veins were bulging again, and his eyes were changing to crimson red as I watched.

I took a deep breath and let it out very slowly. His words should have stirred anger and rage from deep within me, but the exact opposite happened. I put the truck in gear but held firmly on the brakes. I nodded at Kyle and Angie who were in the Ford, and they took that as their cue to leave. Prophet glared at them as they pulled past him and headed for the exit.

"Hey, Prophet?" I stuck my left hand out of the open window and motioned him to come closer with one finger. He obliged and stepped up to the door of the truck.

"I will personally eat your heart before it stops beating," he sneered.

"Why don't you eat this!" my right hand, gripping my 1911 tightly, came off of my lap and was only twelve inches from his face when I squeezed the trigger. The right side of his head exploded, and I hammered the throttle pedal to the floor before anyone could react.

CHAPTER 46

August 31ˢᵗ, 2023.

The booming of the handgun and the sudden acceleration caused both Kate and Sarah to let out startled screams. Donnie, who was sitting in the middle backseat didn't make a sound. Rayne was the only one who saw it coming and before my foot was to the firewall, she was bringing her own hand gun up.

One of the stalkers who had come out of the clubhouse with Prophet was standing in the wrong place as we rocketed from the parking spot. He tried to get out of the way but got pulled under the front tire of the truck. It was like hitting a speedbump going just a little too fast. The spinning rear tire bounced over him and spit him out in our wake.

I cranked the wheel hard causing the rearend of the truck to break free and fish tale. The rear quarter panel smashed into a stalker that was rushing toward us and sent him violently cartwheeling through the air. Straightening out when the driveway came into view, I gave her even more throttle. The turbo diesel was screaming, and the rear tires caught traction. All of us were momentarily pushed back into our seats due to the rapid acceleration.

Kyle and Angie had already made it to the street and avoided the ten or twelve stalkers rushing to block the entrance with their own bodies. One of them seemed to be a little more on the ball as she was trying to shove the others out of the way. She'd correctly surmised that I had no intention of slowing down. In fact, we were still accelerating.

I was trying to do the math of what was about to happen in my head when I clipped the first stalker that was too slow to move. Her body made a loud, sickening thud when the massive winch bumper sent her spinning to the pavement. My first problem was all the stalkers still in the way and the probability of doing real damage to the truck was lurking around the back of my mind. The second problem was going to be negotiating the right turn that Kyle and Angie had taken. We were going far too fast for that.

The first problem was beginning to resolve itself. Mostly anyway. I clipped one more stalker with the passenger side of the bumper but instead of going airborne, he went under the tires. The only one left in my way was the one who was trying to get the others out of my path. The last I saw of her was when she slammed into the center of the bumper. Her head, with its mop of brown hair impacted the leading edge of the hood with enough force to dislodge her brains from their protective casing.

Blood and brains mixed with bone and hair splattered against the windshield with a grotesque slapping noise. I didn't have time to deal with that problem as the turn was approaching incredibly fast. At the last possible moment, I jammed on the brakes hard enough to cause the anti-lock system to engage. Knowing we couldn't make the turn to follow Kyle, I opted for the wider left turn. As we swung through the turn, the body of the woman who'd hit the bumper was dislodged and thrown free, tumbling until it hit the concrete curb.

"Kyle! We had to go left. We're not behind you!" Rayne was yelling into the radio.

"Okay! We're headed south on Haskell. Where do you want to meet up?" Angie asked through the speaker. Kyle must have had his hands full with the driving. Rayne looked at me for an answer. I didn't immediately have one seeing as how my hands were full at the moment also.

I made the mistake of trying to clear the front window with the windshield wipers. The combination of the wipers and wiper fluid left the window streaked with a thick bloody mess. The whole time I was trying to keep from running into parked cars and figure out where I should turn. As the next major intersection came into view, I started applying some brakes to make the turn. Before Rayne could respond, Chase's voice came over the radio.

"We got a problem, Shane!"

"What now?" Rayne asked calmly.

"Remember them cars that were in the parking lot when we came into town the other day?"

"Yeah?"

"Well, there's a whole passel of 'em moving out in a hurry! They're loaded with people and there's a whole bunch more on foot!"

"Shit," I muttered under my breath as I steered us through the turn.

"Copy that! We're headed south on...... We're headed south on Minor Street," she announced when she caught a passing glimpse of the street signs.

"We see you but not for long. We're giving up this position and moving to the truck. It's time to go! As soon as we've got wheels, we'll be headed south too!"

"Tell everybody that we'll meet up at the grocery store on the south end of town," I instructed. Rayne did as I asked and got affirmative replies from everyone.

Two blocks into our southward trek, a black four-door sedan came screaming into the intersection just ahead of us. The driver had come in too hot and with a considerable amount of understeer, tried to put himself between the intersection and us. Rather than slow down, I swerved to avoid a head-on collision and got past him. I glanced down the side street he'd come off of and could see several more vehicles racing toward us.

"They're following us!" Donnie shouted from the backseat. I checked the rearview mirror. The black sedan had spun all the way around and was now coming up behind us. Donnie switched seats with his mom. He rolled the window down and climbed up to rest the upper part of his torso in the window sill. Kate passed him his rifle and held onto his legs to keep him from falling to his death.

I was doing my best to keep the truck straight knowing that any sudden movement could topple Donnie from his perch. He was rapidly popping off rounds at the black sedan that had been joined by a white panel van. Both vehicles were swerving erratically in an effort to avoid the gunfire. Rayne brought her rifle up, pointing it out the window as we rapidly closed on the next four-way intersection.

My eyes were darting between both side mirrors and the road ahead of us. This was a nice long straightaway, but there were a lot of intersections. The black sedan had sustained enough damage to drop out of the chase and was replaced by a little Honda type of car that was gaining ground fast. Donnie had just swapped a fresh magazine into his rifle and leaned back out the window when we tore through the next intersection. I saw the small car coming into that same intersection too late.

I started to yell for everyone to brace themselves, but the deafening sound of the impact cut my words short. The little coupe clipped the quarter panel and rear bumper of the much bigger truck. The nature of the 90-degree impact instantly sent the heavy truck into an uncontrollable spin. With the impact being on Donnie's side of the truck, he was thrown all the way out of the window.

We'd spun around a full 180-degrees when I saw his crumpled body lying on the asphalt. I also saw the panel van swerve intentionally to run him over. I was still fighting for control as we came all the way back around to face the direction we'd originally been travelling. The truck was still running, and we were rolling along at maybe five miles per hour. I was just about to hit the gas again when I heard Sarah scream her brother's name.

Before I could warn her, she threw the back door open on my side of the truck and launched herself into the street. She was still screaming for her brother when the panel van took her and the open door out at almost the same time. She was crushed violently between the front of the van and the door. So violently that her warm blood sprayed the side of my face and arm as the truck was shoved several feet to the right.

The shrill scream of horror that emanated from Kate was like nothing I'd ever heard in my life. Before I could get my foot on the brakes and stop the truck from rolling, Kate threw herself out of the gaping hole where the door used to be. The van was still rolling alongside of us, and I saw the sliding side door open. Stalkers began pouring through the opening.

Kate was just standing there in slack-jawed terror as she stared at her daughters mutilated body. The stalkers were on her in a heartbeat with bats, pipes, and axes. I started to push the throttle pedal to the floor, and much to my surprise, the engine responded instantly. I paused for the briefest of moments because I was torn between fleeing or staying and trying to help Kate. The decision was made for me when one of them started coming into the cab through destroyed door on the rear driver's side. Rayne was already facing that direction and she grabbed my 1911 off the seat and fired three rounds into the man's face.

"GO, GO, GO!" Rayne screamed as two more started moving toward the truck. I put more pressure on the pedal, and we quickly moved away from the scene of the carnage.

"Son-of-a....." I was cut short when we were hit hard from behind. The only thing I could see in the rearview mirror was the red and blue light bar on top of the car that had hit us. My foot was still planted firmly on the throttle and the car backed off enough for me to see that it was a police cruiser. When he came at us again, it was obvious that he was trying to get in a position to spin us out. The only thing I could do was to keep swerving in front of him. The third solid hit nearly did just that. I had to let off the gas to regain control.

"Shane!" Rayne yelled from the passenger seat. She was pointing at a county dump truck that would hit the next intersection at the same time we did if I didn't do something. I could see the cop car gaining on us and I started to have a really bad idea. Instead of trying to accelerate away from the hit, I stuffed the brakes hard. The cop car caught the corner of the bumper and spun us a little more than 180 degrees. We were now facing the direction we'd just come from.

"Hang on!" I shouted at Rayne. I pointed the nose of the truck for the barbed wire fence that separated the parking lot of a school from the two-lane street.

"Ya think!" Rayne answered. She was also fastening her seatbelt.

Flooring the throttle again, we tore through the fence and jumped the curb with three-foot-tall shrubs on the other side of it. The parking lot was mostly empty but we both spotted the dump truck and the cop car coming into the southern end of the lot. We cut back to the east and across the backside of the school. There was a six-foot-tall chain link fence around the school's back boundary. Rayne spotted the closed double gates that led to the street behind the school.

I steered toward them hoping the heavy-duty bumper and the mass of the truck would be enough to get us through cleanly. We didn't need to be dragging a couple hundred feet of fence behind us. I took a second to look over my shoulder at the pursuing cop car and dump truck. We had close to a 300-yard lead on them.

"You see anybody else chasing us?" I asked Rayne.

"No! Just these two assholes behind us," she said after a second of looking around.

"This is bullshit! Gimme my rifle!" I demanded and planted both feet on the brake pedal. The truck slid sideways to a stop with my open window facing the rapidly approaching vehicles.

CHAPTER 47

August 31st, 2023.

Using the window frame as support, I sighted in the windshield of the cop car and triggered off a dozen rounds. Through the optic on the rifle, I could see the glass shattering and spiderwebbing. Finally, the car swerved and crashed into the back of the elementary school. I shifted my aim for the windshield of the dump truck and emptied the magazine.

The big rig never tried to evade the gunfire. It belched black smoke from the exhaust stacks and sped up! As it got closer, I could see that the inside of the windshield was coated in blood and the driver's arm was dangling out of the open window on the side. Dark red streaks of blood dripped from the lifeless fingers leaving erratic lines down the outside of the door.

I knew the truck wasn't going to hit us, so I took an extra few seconds to change out the mag of my rifle before handing it back to Rayne. Both of us watched the truck pass behind us as it barreled directly through the double gate I was originally worried about. The heavy rig smashed through the chain link gates like they were made from matchsticks. It bounced across the two-lane road before it crashed into the front of a two-story house.

Before the dust even thought about settling, I spun the truck around and steered us through the gaping hole in the fence. Turning us back to the south, Rayne began calling out directions. For now, we didn't have anyone behind us, and all of the side streets were coming up clear too. Even if it were just for the moment, things were starting to look slightly better. Even if the severely damaged rear door fell off the truck when we made the next right turn. I was surprised it had hung on this long.

"Uh, Rayne?" I said when the truck suddenly began to bog down. I immediately checked the gauges with my eyes settling on the fuel gauge.

"What?"

"We're about to run out of fuel."

"What?" she asked again. This time she leaned over to look at the gauge. "Shit," she muttered.

"Yeah. That seems appropriate."

"We're only a block and a half from the grocery store. Think we can make it?"

"I guess we'll find out," I pulled my eyes from the accusing gauge and warning light to check the mirrors for any signs of pursuit. I pushed the pedal all the way to the floor in the hopes of making it to our destination.

The big engine was coughing and chugging as it pulled every usable ounce of diesel fuel from the tank. We'd just made the turn into the parking lot when it finally choked out. The only thing I could do now was try and get us as close to the front of the store as possible. Drawing closer and slowing considerably, I aimed the nose of the truck for the ground to ceiling glass windows next to the store entrance. We came up just short of smashing through them, stopped by the curb of the sidewalk.

"Let's go!" I barked. Rayne bailed out but my door was completely jammed shut. The damage from the impact to the rear door had wedged my door closed. Not wanting to waste any more time with it, I climbed over the center console and out Rayne's door. I found her struggling to pull one of the heavy first aid kits from the bed. She was wincing from the pain of broken ribs and torn cartilage.

I took the strap from her and hoisted it out. Dropping it on the ground, I grabbed an ammo can that was full of rounds for my rifle. I set it next to the medical bag. Rayne helped me clip my AK-47 to the sling that was still around my neck and shoulder. She then grabbed the radio off the dash and stuck it in the pouch on my left shoulder. Next, she handed me my .45. It was secured in its holster.

"Anybody got their ears on?" I cocked my head closer to the radio when I made the call.

"Kinda busy, bud!" Chase answered.

"We're at the rendezvous spot. You guys still headed this way?"

"Yeah, man. We're working on....." his transmission was interrupted by gunfire.

"Kyle, Angie? You guys out there?" I tried.

"We're getting blocked at every....." the pop of a pistol could be clearly heard. "We'll get there but these assholes will probably be right behind us!" tension was heavy in his voice.

"Copy all. Rayne and I are headed inside. Will advise further," the only replies I got were double clicks. I hefted the strap of the medical bag onto my left shoulder and picked up the heavy ammo can. I had one free hand to hold the AK with. While I was doing that, Rayne had gotten her AR-15 clipped into its sling. Out of the corner of my eye, I could see that just about everything was causing her some degree of pain.

"Which way?" she asked.

"Inside! It'll be full dark soon, and we don't want to be outside when that happens," I pointed toward the open doors with the barrel of my rifle.

"What about the others?"

"As soon as we find a defendable spot, we'll let them know where we are."

"Okay," she switched on her flashlight and led the way into the dark store.

Upon entering, we were enveloped in the inky darkness. The only sources of light were being emitted by our weapon mounted flashlights. The only sound reaching our ears was the creaking of our soles on the floor. We moved slowly and with utmost caution. Every few seconds, one of us would turn a full 360 degrees to make sure no one was trying to sneak up behind us.

"All the way to the back. I'm thinking we can find some access to the roof back there," I whispered.

"Right," she acknowledged.

At first, the store smelled like day-old gym socks left in the hamper for a week and wet cardboard. The further we advanced, the worse it became. We were passing by all of the rotting meat, fruit, vegetables, and a pair of severely bloated bodies. There was a third one, but it had already exploded its innards all over the floor in a black pool that was writhing with maggots and flies.

Rayne wisely picked up the pace and pushed us through a pair of doors that were marked for employees only. The smell was slightly better back here. We worked our way to the back wall, and I found the loading dock doors where we'd backed the moving trucks in. Sweeping my flashlight along the wall and high ceiling, I found what I was looking for, sort of. I'd been hoping for stairs but found a wall-mounted ladder that led to the roof access. It was probably a forty, maybe fifty-foot climb to the roof access hatch.

"There," I motioned for the base of the ladder. "You gonna be able to climb that?"

"Do I have a choice?" she tried a small smile as she looked up to the hatch above us.

"Go, I'll bring up the rear," I set the bag and the ammo can down. It was obvious I was going to have to do something about the super awkward steel can of ammunition. I was going to need both hands free for the ascent. Rayne slung her rifle to her back and started up the ladder.

There wasn't enough room in the bag for the ammo can. That just wasn't going to happen no matter how hard I pushed and shoved. I discovered that the shoulder strap was detachable though. I unclipped one end of it, ran it through the handle of the can and then reattached it. It wasn't pretty by any stretch of the imagination, but it was functional.

The ammo can was able to lay on its side on top of the bag, but it did add considerable weight to the strap. If it tore through the stitching or the buckle broke, all of it would go crashing to the floor. With no options left, I hoisted the whole thing up. The main strap hung opposite my rifle sling. The two making an X across my back. Looking up, I could see Rayne about the halfway point, so I started up behind her. Our next hurdle came when she reached the top of the ladder.

"Shane, it's locked," I could hear pain and desperation in her voice. I was only eight or ten rungs below her at this point and panting from the exertion of climbing with the extra weight.

"You sure?"

"I'm staring at the fucking padlock!" she retorted. I climbed another four rungs and locked my left arm around one of the rungs. I looked up but couldn't see much with her blocking my view.

"What is the padlock attached to? Is it something you could shoot through?"

"Yeah. Let me back down a step or two," she did and then used one hand to raise her AR. She fired twice and then let the rifle hang again. She moved to the top and pushed the steel hatch open. Thirty seconds later, we were standing on the roof in the warm evening breeze. I gladly dropped the extra weight of the bag and ammo can. Not wasting any time, I pulled the radio from its pouch and put it to my lips.

"Kyle, Chase! We're on the roof. In the southeast corner of the building, you'll find the access ladder.

"We copy, Shane!" Janice answered. "We're comin in hot with a whole bunch of hurt right behind us! Any chance you guys could distract them long enough for us to get inside?"

"We'll do what we can! Which direction are you coming from?"

"Comin from the....." her transmission was filled with gunfire. Rayne and I both heard it from the speaker and through the air. She pointed to the front of the building. Leaving the bag and ammo can where I dropped them, I broke into a sprint while Rayne jogged behind me.

The breeze continued to carry the sounds of a fight rapidly closing the distance between us. I took a knee behind the three-foot tall cinder block wall that separated the roof from a really nasty fall to the concrete and asphalt below. Through the reticle of my rifle optics, I watched Rayne's big truck lock up the brakes and slide sideways in the street. The maneuver got them pointed at the entrance of the parking lot and the exhaust billowed black smoke as they were hard on the throttle again.

Not five seconds after they appeared, six more cars raced into the parking lot behind them. I fingered the safety lever off, slipped my finger onto the trigger, and began to shoot at the leading cars. Rayne's AR began popping from her position next to me. Between the two of us, we completely destroyed the hood and windshield of the lead car. The occupants didn't escape our wrath either.

The car veered hard to the right clipping the front of the car next to it. The impact caused the driver to lose enough control that they collided with a concrete light pole base. The first car continued on until it smashed through a shopping cart corral and into the parked car on the other side of it. I took my eyes off the sights just long enough to see Chase, Janice, and Cody vanish around the corner of the building. Rayne had already picked another target and unleashed her rifle.

Our assault was having the desired effect of slowing the stalkers down considerably. They were beginning to abandon their cars in favor of hiding behind other parked cars. This tactic was making them much harder for us to pick off. We managed to wound a couple of them, but that was about it.

"Don't shoot us! We're coming up the ladder!" Chase's voice came through the speaker on my radio. I answered him with a double click and went back to trying to pick out targets on the ground below us. About a minute later, I heard the roof hatch open. I looked just to make sure it wasn't some uninvited guests. Janice was the first on the roof followed a moment later by Chase. I was a little surprised when he slammed the hatch closed again.

"Where's Cody?" I asked as soon as he and Janice joined us at the wall.

"He ain't comin," Chase answered flatly. He checked the magazine in his AK, reseated the mag, and joined me in searching for targets.

"What?"

"They got him when we were tryin to get out of the hospital. Crazy bastard stayed behind to draw them off of us," Janice said as she too joined us on the wall. She paused long enough to look around as if she was looking for someone. "Where's your....."

"They ain't comin," I cut her off and returned my attention to the parking lot.

CHAPTER 48

August 31ˢᵗ, 2023.

"Anybody heard from Kyle and Angie recently?" Janice asked as she peered through the optics of her rifle. It was dark enough now that it was hard to pick out any of the stalkers on the ground.

"No," was my curt reply. I'd just picked out a shoulder sticking out by the rear bumper of a car. I gently applied pressure to the trigger until the rifle barked. There was an almost instant howl.

"Hey, Kyle. You still out there, bro?" Chase spoke into his radio. He gave it a few seconds before he tried again. "Kyle, Angie, you guys out there?"

"It looks like there's a small group falling back," Rayne announced from her end of the line.

"I see 'em," Chase set his AK down and picked up his hunting rifle. "Looks like eight of 'em falling back to the street," he continued to watch them through the high-powered optic.

"More of 'em over there doing the same thing," Janice remarked.

"Where?" Chase asked.

"North end of the parking lot," she pointed.

"You think they're giving up?" I asked. I was trying to make out the shadowy figures.

"Doubt it. They're probably realizing that a head-on attack just ain't workin. If'n it was me I'd be doin the same thing so I could try to sneak fighters past us when it's full dark. If they can make it inside the store, there ain't nothin we can do about it."

"Right. We can't see them or shoot at them," I muttered.

"That ladder we came up, is it the only roof access?" he asked.

"I don't know to be honest. We didn't have any time to scout the rooftop once we got up here."

"We need to do that. Janice, take Rayne and go have a look-see. Make sure you check over the sides for any access points too," he pulled his eye from the scope and closed both of them momentarily. Janice shot a glance toward Rayne and both of them backed away from the short wall. It didn't take them long to disappear into the rapidly encroaching darkness.

After watching until I couldn't see the girls anymore, I glanced over at Chase. He stoically settled in behind the optic of his AK again. The hunting rifle was leaning against the wall well within his reach. I also took to looking through the sights of my rifle. As much as I tried not to, I couldn't help but think about the losses we'd sustained today. We'd come back to town to rescue Donnie and Kate,

230

but we'd lost the whole family of four in a matter of minutes. Maybe if I'd taken a different course in my dealings with David Prophet, things might've turned out differently.

"Chase?" I spoke quietly.

"Yeah?"

"I'm sorry, man."

"Sorry? Sorry for what?" he questioned.

"I screwed the pooch on this whole thing. I'm the reason Cody and his family are dead. I'm the reason we're stuck on this roof. I should've just….."

"Just what? Played along with that Prophet guy a little longer?" he interrupted. By the sound of his voice, I could tell he was looking directly at me. "This was gonna happen one way or the other, Shane. If you didn't blow half that fuckers head off when you did, I was gonna do it when you were in the clear."

"But….."

"No! You stow that shit right now and get your head back in the game. I don't know if any of us are going to live to see the sunrise, and I'm fine with that! This ain't my first rodeo, man. If I'm a dead man walking, I'm doing it on my terms and I'm gonna take as many of them with me as I can! You need to get right in your head and come to terms with that!"

"You don't think we're gonna get out of this?"

"I don't know if any of us are gonna make it, no," he expelled a long, heavy sigh. "What I DO know is that if they want me that bad, it's gonna cost them a fortune in blood. I'll stack bodies like cordwood until I run out of ammo and then I'll kill 'em with my bare hands if I have to. When they finally take me down, they are gonna have to swim through the blood of those that tried and died."

"I can't say that I planned on dying today," I said after a moment of thought.

"Dude, none of us had that in our playbook for today. You just gotta fight like a pissed-off badger and make 'em work for it!" he was about to add to that when we both heard a weak call on the radio.

"Chase….. you copy?" it was Kyle calling but something was definitely wrong. The transmission was strong, but his voice sounded weak.

"I'm here. What's up?" Chase answered.

"I need….. I need you to….. do something for me," Kyle's breathing was heavy and labored.

"What? Where are you?"

"Listen….. Angie….. she's dead….."

"Where are you? I'll come to you!"

"No! No….. bringing them to you….."

"Say again?"

"Between the wheel wells…… black box….. shoot it when they….. when they come for me."

"What's he talking about?" Chase directed the question at me.

"The case full of Tannerite. He loaded it in the truck before we left the house," I blurted out what I knew.

"Shit," he mumbled before he squeezed the transmit button again. "Where are you, bro? We'll come to get you!"

"No time….. I'm dead….. just shoot….. shoot the box! You….. you'll know when….." his transmission abruptly cut off with the sound of him coughing.

"Kyle!" Chase barked into the radio but there was no answer.

"Chase! We can see headlights coming down the main road from the north end of the building. They're moving slow and it sounds like he's leading a riot down the street!" Janice said from the other end of the building. He answered her with a pair of clicks instead of words.

It took another ten or fifteen seconds for he and I to make out the ruckus coming toward us. About the same time we heard it, the stalkers in the parking lot must've picked up on it too. Most of them broke from their hiding places and sprinted toward the truck coming down the road. Kyle now had a hoard behind him and in front of him.

There was only one working headlight on the old Ford as it came into view. It illuminated twenty or thirty raging men and women racing to confront him. The battered truck lurched forward and plowed headlong into the group. Many jumped out of the way as their self-preservation instincts kicked in. Some leaped onto the moving vehicle and yet others were pulled under its mass.

When the truck swerved abruptly into the parking lot, four or five were thrown from the hood and bed. That's when we spotted the group that had been following him on foot. Several shots rang out from the cab, the muzzle flash muted by the stalkers swarming onto the hood and cab. There were no more course changes and Kyle piloted the truck toward the front of the store. A grim-faced Chase had switched back to his hunting rifle to make this shot.

"See you on the other side….." Kyle's voice broke into the tension on the roof. Half a second later, the truck began to lurch to a stop. The shape of the big Ford vanished as it was overrun by a mass of stalkers. There were so many that it looked like ants swarming the carcass of their kill.

"Until then," Chase whispered under his breath. "Janice, Rayne?" he called on the radio.

"Yeah," Janice answered with no delay.

"Light 'em up. Target the center of the bed. You too, Shane," he said and then pulled the trigger of the rifle.

At his command, Janice, Rayne, and I all opened fire. All of us were pulling the triggers as fast as we could and burning through the magazines in our rifles. Chase was the only one holding back, waiting for the perfect shot. It only took a fraction of a second for me to realize that he was waiting until he had a clear shot at the explosives in the bed of the truck.

I had just run my magazine empty when I heard Chase take his shot. We had killed or wounded a bunch of the stalkers in the bed of the truck, many of the others were now taking cover behind it and the cars closest to it. Only a few were still trying to pull Kyle's lifeless form through the driver's side window opening.

I was expecting a short, sharp explosion. What followed the round fired by Chase would have been epic had it not been for Kyle's death. Seventy-five pounds of pre-mixed Tannerite surrounded by close to fifty gallons of gasoline and diesel looked like something straight out of a Hollywood movie.

The shockwave and fireball vaporized the entire truck. Parts of it exploded in every direction mowing down anyone within the blast radius like shrapnel from a grenade. The fireball that followed spread both vertically and horizontally. Anyone or anything within fifty feet of ground zero was set ablaze. The yellow, orange, and red ball of flame rolled several hundred feet into the air and bathed everything in its glow for a few seconds.

The blast wave that hit us forced us to take cover behind the short brick wall. The heat was fairly intense, but it was the singing of shrapnel past us that had me concerned. There was only about six feet separating me and Chase and something flew right between us. After dropping behind the wall, we could hear it pinging against the wall and stuff began to rain down on the roof.

CHAPTER 49

August 31ˢᵗ, 2023.

As soon as things stopped pinging off of the wall, Chase and I were both up and surveying the absolute carnage in the parking lot. The area was lit by the flickering glow of three burning cars and the burning wreckage of the truck. Dead stalkers littered the area along with savagely ripped-apart bodies of other stalkers. Many of the bodies and body parts were burning.

Chase was the first one to have his AK pointed at the few that were writhing on the ground. Their bodies were too damaged to allow them to run away and he was picking them off in the eerie light provided by the fires. After swapping magazines on my rifle, I joined him. Moments later I could hear Janice and Rayne's weapons join the cacophony. This was short-lived but by the time we were done, I was changing magazines again and nothing was moving on the ground.

"What do we do now?" Rayne asked when she and Janice rejoined us.

"What did you find for roof access?" Chase asked.

"There's another hatch coming up from the inside and one exterior ladder at the other end of the building. We couldn't get the hatch open, so it must be locked from the inside," she reported.

"Okay. We need to get the hell out of here before they get a chance to regroup," Chase looked at all of us when he spoke.

"You want us to go down there in the dark?" Janice questioned.

"We don't have a choice, Jan! If they get a chance to get their shit together, we don't stand a chance! We gotta move before they figure out what happened," he argued.

"But….."

"He's right, Janice! Hell, they could burn this building to the ground and us along with it. They could just wait us out and let us die from exposure. This wasn't a good spot but it's what we had at the moment. We need to move, now," I picked up my empty magazines and started toward the medical bag and ammo can we'd left by the access hatch. I heard her let out a mad huff but wasn't in the mood to stand there and argue with her. Rayne quickly joined up with me and we walked in silence to our supplies.

I had her hold her gun light on the can while I opened it and refilled my magazines. Each one was tucked back into its pouch as it was filled to capacity. I didn't bother to ask her if she needed ammo. I knew she did, but her AR was the wrong caliber for what we had available. Next, I opened the medical bag and retrieved the four bottles of water Angie had packed into it. I handed the first one to Rayne and she gulped down half of it before coming up for air.

"Thanks," she finally said.

"Want another one?" I offered her the one I was planning on drinking.

"No," she shook her head. She grimaced at the gesture and rubbed her chest with her free hand. I reached back into the bag and grabbed the bottle of Aspirin. She snatched it from my hand when I offered it to her. "Is it that obvious?"

"The pain, how bad is it?"

"It's bad."

"Can you make it down the ladder?"

"I think so," she swallowed the painkillers and hungrily drank the rest of her water.

"I guess the real question is, can you make it down and to your truck?"

"As long as we don't have to run anywhere, I should be able to. All this running around is killing me!"

"What if we have to run?" I asked.

"Then I might as well just stay here."

"That's not gonna happen!"

"Shane..... everything that's happened today has just been too much. All of the jostling and jolting around..... it's been too much. I can't do it anymore....." her voice trailed off.

"Okay, c'mon," I said after about a minute of silence. Grabbing the three remaining bottles and the ammo can, we walked back to where Chase and Janice were quietly talking.

"We got a plan yet?" this was Janice asking.

"Yeah," I passed out the water and set the ammo can down. Both of them drank from the bottles and then proceeded to reload their empty magazines. "When you guys are ready, we can go back down the ladder and get in Rayne's truck. From there, we can get the hell outta here."

"No good, man," Chase said.

"What? What do mean?" I asked.

"There's a hole the size of my foot in the radiator and intercooler. Probably won't even start again. We're gonna be on foot till we find something else."

"Shit," I grumbled.

"I'll stay behind," Rayne said to the surprise of everyone but me. All of us looked at her. "The only thing I'll do is slow you down. I can't run. Hell, I can hardly breathe from the pain. I can cover you as you....."

"No!" I held up my hand to stop her from saying anything else.

"Shane, it's the only thing that makes sense," she tried.

"I said no, and that's final. Chase, Janice, as soon as you're ready, I want both of you to make a break for it. If you find a set of wheels or help or whatever, come back for us. Rayne and I will cover you the best we can so you can make your escape."

"Shane…." Rayne started but stopped.

"You sure about that, Shane?" Janice asked.

"Yeah, I'm sure. Now hurry up and get outta here," I sat with my back to the wall and drank about a quarter of the bottled water. I hadn't realized how thirsty I was until now.

"We'll leave you the ammo. You can hold them off for a while with the six or seven hundred rounds in there. Have Rayne reload your mags as they run dry. We'll leave the medical bag behind too. It'll slow us down," Chase finished loading the last of his magazines at the same time Janice did.

"You got a minute, Shane?" Janice asked as she stood.

"Yeah?"

"C'mon," she motioned me away from the others. We only went about thirty feet away before she stopped and leaned close to me.

"What's this about?" I asked.

"I admire what you're doing, I really do. If you hadn't volunteered to stay behind, I would have. That said, I need you to make me a promise," her voice was quiet.

"What?"

"Don't let them take her. Don't let her suffer anymore!"

"Excuse me?"

"If you get overrun up here and you're down to your last bullet….. Don't let her suffer. She doesn't deserve that. Do you understand what I'm trying to say?"

"Yeah, I understand. Perfectly. I need you to do something for me too."

"Huh?" she asked slightly confused.

"I don't know what your plans are, Janice. I, for one, plan on living, and yes, that means Rayne too. That means both of us are relying on you and Chase to find us a ride and come back for us. I need you to quit worrying about her and worry about your own ass. Got it?" she answered with a curt nod. "I need you to trust me just a little bit with our girl. Think you can do that?"

"Yeah," she sighed.

"Do what you have to do, Janice. Do your fucking job so I don't have to put a bullet in her head," I growled. My anger was getting the better of me.

"Fine!" she growled back. "I'm telling you right now that if you come out of this and she doesn't….."

"Enough with the goddamn threats! You're wasting time!" I barked loud enough that Rayne and Chase both turned to look in our direction. I took in a quick breath to regain some of my composure before I started again in a quieter tone. "Get your shit and get the fuck outta here before none of us make it off this roof, Janice!"

I don't know if she was embarrassed by my outburst, and to be honest, I didn't really care at that point. It did shut her up and, after staring at me for a moment, she did a smart about-face. The only thing she said to Rayne was that they'd be back. Then she and Chase made their way to the roof access and disappeared down the ladder.

"I'm sorry," Rayne said barely above a whisper. Both of us were looking over the wall at the fires burning in the parking lot.

"What are you sorry for?"

"This….. You're stuck here because of me. You should have let Janice stay….."

"What? Why?"

"We're the ones who've earned this fate. Not you. You don't deserve this," her voice was soft, resigned.

"Shane, we're in the clear and over the fence behind the building," Chase interrupted on the radio.

"Copy that," I replied.

"It's eerie as hell down here. Ain't nothin moving but us. You guys just sit tight and with any luck. We'll be back soon," I answered him with a double click. Rayne and I hadn't spotted any movement from our rooftop position either. I turned, placed my back against the wall and sat on my butt. Rayne did the same.

"So, you think you deserve to be here?" I asked quietly after a long silence.

"Yeah," she whispered. She laid her rifle down next to her and cupped her face in her hands. She was quietly crying. Rather than say anything, I scooted close enough to put an arm around her shoulders. We stayed that way for close to half an hour before her soft shudders subsided. When she wiped her eyes and sat up straight, I withdrew my arm.

"That night Janice and I walked down to the pond to get the trucks; she told me you were her ride-or-die chick and she's yours. There's a lot more to that than just a slogan, isn't there?" I asked.

"We've been through it if that's what you're asking."

"Why didn't you just call the cops?"

"Huh?" she glanced over at me.

"The night you killed Rick; why didn't you just call the cops?"

"When he showed up or after I killed him?"

"Either."

"He'd have made bail right away and then he'd have been back. Except instead of being drunk, he'd have been pissed. That's why I didn't call when he first started beating on the door," she explained.

"You didn't call because you were afraid of his wrath?"

"Yeah. I kept trying to tell him to just go sleep it off but that only made things worse. Janice wanted to call but I wouldn't let her."

"She was there?"

"We were planning a girl's weekend. You know, get our nails done, go to the spa. Maybe go up to Tahoe. That never happened."

"Which one of you opened the door and let him in the house?"

"He kicked it in." she tried.

"Didn't the cops come by and question you later? I mean, you're the ex-wife. Weren't you suspect number one in his disappearance?"

"Yeah, but what's that got to do with anything?"

"How'd you hide the broken front door?" I asked. She just started at me. "Rayne, I don't care if you offed that son-of-a-bitch. I really don't. In fact, I'm pretty sure he had it comin," I paused to let that soak in before I continued.

"I think you opened the door that night because you were looking for a fight. All of it had come to a head, but this time, you had Janice with you for back-up. You'd been fighting for your life the entire time you were married, and he came around looking for trouble. You'd had enough and it was time to end it. Wasn't it?"

"So what if I did?"

"Just proves one thing to me."

"What's that? I'm a murderous bitch?" she scoffed.

"No. It proves to me that your will to fight and survive is a lot stronger than you think. Right now, it seems like you're ready to give, ready to die on this rooftop. Except, I don't think you know how to quit. I don't think you have it in you," I said evenly.

"Things ain't lookin real good right now, Shane."

"I don't know about you, but if I'm dying up here, I'm gonna do it on my feet with every last ounce I have to give. If you wanna go out whimpering in the corner, that's on you. Yeah, it ain't lookin good, but we're holding our own right now. I hope you're with me on this. Whatever ending might present itself; I hope you're with me all the way."

She seemed to quietly contemplate that for a few moments in silence. While I waited for her answer, we heard several distant gunshots ring out from the north side of town. It was too far away to have been Janice or Chase and they had moved off to the west. I didn't bother to look over the wall to see if I could see anything. I just stayed by Rayne's side.

"Guess I'm a pretty lucky gal," she finally spoke.

"How's that?"

"Most people only have that one friend. It appears I have two," she let a slight smile work at the corners of her mouth, and she took one of my hands in hers. "We're still breathing, so I guess we gotta keep fighting."

CHAPTER 50

September 1st, 2023.

We sat there, leaning against the wall in complete silence. Every now and then, sporadic gunfire would reach our ears. Sometimes a racing car engine could be heard that was usually accompanied by squealing tires. The sound of several motorcycles also rumbled through the air a couple times. This went on until well after midnight. Rayne had stretched out with her head in my lap to try and relieve some of her pain. It didn't take but a few moments for her to fall into a light sleep. Meanwhile, my back was aching, and my ass had gone numb from sitting in the uncomfortable position for so long.

"Chase, Janice, you out there?" I spoke quietly into the radio so as not to disturb Rayne. The volume was way down, and I'd stuck the earbud on my ear. I made the call three times but gotten no reply. That didn't surprise me. The range on these little radios was fairly limited. I kept reassuring myself that was the issue and not something more nefarious.

"No answer?" Rayne asked. Her eyes were still closed.

"No."

"What time is it?"

"I dunno. It's gotta be two or three. It sounded like there was a lot of activity up around the hospital about an hour ago, but things have quieted way down since then.

"You think Chase and Janice are okay?"

"They're probably out of range. I haven't heard anything from the direction they….."

"Who was that trying to make radio contact a few seconds ago?" the voice emanating from the earbud cut me short.

"My name is Shane. Who am I talking to?" I answered. Rayne sat up with a groan and a confused look on her face.

"Who are you talking to?" she asked with her head cocked to one side. I held my finger up and unplugged the earbud so she could hear too.

"Copy, Shane. Are you sick?"

"No. Beat up but healthy. Who is this?"

"You can call me Buck. Where are you and how many with you?"

"Before I give you anything, Buck, are you infected? Nothing personal, I just need to know."

"That's a negative on being sick and trust me, I get it. If you're in trouble, we might be in a position to lend a hand," the man on the other end of the airwaves offered.

239

"What do you think?" I asked Rayne.

"He said WE. How many is WE?"

"How many of you are there, Buck?" I asked into the microphone.

"There's nine of us. All healthy. We're at the National Guard Armory if you can make it to us. It's surrounded by tall fences and barbed wire. I just need to know if you're coming so nobody accidently gets shot."

"Well?" I looked at Rayne when I asked it.

"How far is it?"

"Ya got me. If I ask, I'll have to give away our position," I reminded her.

"Ask," she nodded slightly.

"Okay, I'm gonna put it out there so you better be the real thing. We're on the roof of the Value Mart at the south end of town. We're pretty much stuck here."

"Copy. We can send a rescue party, but it may take us a few to cobble something together. How many are we extracting?"

"There's two of us, one has been roughed up pretty bad. Broken ribs and whatnot. Two more left a few hours ago to try and find transportation. We haven't heard from them since."

"Copy that. Is the injured party in need of urgent medical attention?"

"Nothing urgent but I'm sure she could use something a little stronger than Aspirin right now."

"Gotcha. We're not all that far from you but if you could hang on for another 45 minutes, help will be there. My guys will be keeping an eye out for your other party too. Has there been any enemy activity in your area recently?"

"No. Not for a few hours. I think we took the fight out of them just after sunset," I answered.

"Was that your pyrotechnic show earlier?"

"Yeah, that was us."

"Copy. Just hang tight and we'll be there. If your situation changes, gimme a call back. Will be monitoring this channel. Buck, out."

"You think they're military?" Rayne asked.

"Couldn't tell ya, but they sound pretty serious. Probably a bunch of locals who got it together and found a safe place to hold up. I guess we'll find out before too long."

"I guess if they ain't afraid to be out here in the dark, they must know what they're doing. Right?"

"Let's hope so."

We decided to keep trying to raise Chase or Janice on the radio while we awaited rescue. It was about the only thing we could do that wasn't sitting on our butts. Rayne wanted to get up and move around so we walked the length of the roof calling out on the radio every minute or so. We walked the whole perimeter, ending up back where we started, never making radio contact with our missing people. I was forced to stop transmitting because the low battery indicator was flashing on the little screen.

Before resuming my position with my back against the wall, I decided to look over it first. At first, I saw nothing. All the fires that were burning earlier had burned themselves out and there was very little ambient light to see by. It was the slightest crunching noise that caused me to look straight down. My eyes settled first on the dark outline of my wrecked truck. I could swear I saw something move in the even darker shadow of the rig.

Rayne must have heard it too because she'd joined me looking into the abyss below us. She put the barrel of her rifle over the edge and toggled the bright white light. Below us, in the spotlight it created, two men stared up at us shielding their eyes. Neither of us had the chance to call out to them before they scurried into the store through the shattered glass front.

I flipped on my light and played it across the parking lot. I cursed loudly to myself when the tight beam caught over a dozen stalkers between cover. Just as I fingered the safety off and opened fire, they spread out and broke into a sprint straight for the building. I winged one or two of them in the rapid firing that followed. Think Rayne might have gotten a couple more.

"Buck! Shane! We've got a whole herd of stalkers closing in on us! They're inside the building!" I nearly shouted into the radio mic.

"I copy, bud. We're still trying to get there! ETA is maybe 15 minutes," he responded immediately.

Rayne was in the middle of reloading her AR and I was scanning the parking lot when both of us heard the metal roof access hatch slam open. My light landed on it first, but nobody was there. A second later, we heard loud banging coming from the second hatch at the other end of the building. After the fourth bang, it also crashed open. The sudden flurry of activity and noise was followed by an unnerving silence.

"Rayne?" I asked quietly.

"Yeah?"

"Where were the outside access points?"

"One on each corner at the far end of the building," she answered.

Both of us shown our lights in that direction. As I played my beam along the far wall, I realized I hadn't turned on the electronic sights that were on the top of my rifle. I looked and felt for the button. I'd just found it when Rayne let a round fly from her weapon. I was about to see what she was shooting at when I heard a clattering noise from the closest hatch. My light landed on two people. The man was already running straight for us, and the woman was just planting her feet on the roof.

I centered the red reticle in the middle of the man's chest and squeezed the trigger. I was expecting the recoil and had properly braced for it. All three rounds flew true. He was dead before he landed face first. The woman who was behind him had been hit by both a bullet and blood spray. Behind her, I could see another man clawing his way onto the roof. It took half a dozen rounds to put the woman down and by the time I was done with her, three more had already made it onto the roof.

"Reloading!" Rayne exclaimed. She'd been dealing with the stalkers coming onto the roof at the far end of the building. Just as my rifle ran out of ammo, Rayne got her's back into the fight. I'd gotten two of the three who had come through the closest hatch, but more were already on the roof.

Rayne quickly engaged the closest one and then switched back to shooting at the farther ones as soon I was shooting again. There were so many of them we were being overwhelmed. For each one we put down, four more would appear on the roof. Each one we killed or severely wounded made it a little closer than the last stalker did. It was only a matter of time before we ran out of ammo and there was no way we could stand toe-to-toe. Duking it out with bare hands just wasn't an option.

"Back-up!" I told Rayne. Both of us began stepping backward toward the corner of the building.

"Reloading! Last mag!" she declared.

"Hurry up, Buck! We're moving to the southeast corner of the roof and running low on ammo!" this time, I did shout into the mic. "There's too many of them!"

"Stay cool, man. We're almost there! Thirty seconds out!" he reassured me.

Rayne and I backed into the three-foot high brick wall that marked the exterior wall of the Value Mart. There was nowhere left to run. The stalkers were pouring from the roof access points and charging straight at us. Each one getting closer than the last under the fire from our rifles. Rayne emptied the last five rounds from her magazine into a rather large stalker as he launched himself through the air. She ducked out of his flight path and his wide-open arms. She had the wherewithal to help him clear the wall. When she faced the onslaught again, her Springfield was in her hand and barking rapidly.

As I was seating another mag into the magwell of the AK, she grabbed my Colt from its holster and covered me. Once I was back in the fight, I covered her while she reloaded her Springfield. The task was made more difficult by the fact that she was having to use the Colt to fend off stalkers that got close. When it went to slide lock, she shoved it back in my holster and two-handed the small frame of the Springfield.

I dropped to one knee and continued to hit targets as soon as the lighted reticle passed across them. I was holding the heavy rifle up with one hand on the pistol grip while I fished another magazine from the pouch on the front of my vest. The sudden and horrible realization came to me that the one in the gun and the one in my hand were all I had left.

A stalker had gotten close to the wall and was coming at us from a near ninety-degree angle. I didn't see him until he was nearly on me and even then, I'd only caught him in my peripheral vision. This rage contorted face was being illuminated by the muzzle flashes from our weapons. I brought my rifle to bare on him and pulled the trigger. Nothing happened. The AK was empty, and I didn't have the time to change mags.

As he lunged for me, I lunged up and into his midsection. The barrel of my rifle caught him in the gut, and I used his momentum and mine to divert him over the wall. He grabbed the foregrip of the AK with both hands and nearly drug me over the side too. The webbing and buckles that held the rifle to my vest held tight. The only reason I didn't follow him to my death was that he lost his grip on the exposed portion of the barrel. It was so hot that his hands sizzled likes steaks on a BBQ grill.

I turned just in time to see a woman wielding an axe like a crazed Viking. Rayne shot her once in the chest before her handgun was empty again. The stalker / Viking raised the axe high above her head and her eyes were locked on me. I raised my rifle to try and either block or deflect the blow that was surely coming. Just as she started her downswing, her head vanished into a mist and her banshee-like scream choked out.

I involuntarily jerked from the close proximity of the muzzle blast that originated from behind me. I felt the heat and the concussion at the same time. The deafening blast was disorienting. Every instinct I had was to throw myself down and that's exactly what I did. As I was freefalling, I saw Rayne throwing herself in the opposite direction. Both of us were reflexively trying to get out of the way of whoever was shooting.

CHAPTER 51

September 1st, 2023.

Flashlight beams and muzzle flashes bathed the area in a ghastly, yellow, and white light. The noise assaulting my eardrums was unlike anything I'd ever experienced. Each flash and resulting pressure wave was felt all the way to my core. I was scrambling to get closer to the wall when a hand grabbed my upper arm. I tried to jerk away but the grip of the man was unrelenting. I made eye contact with a man about my age. His eyes were both hard and comforting all at the same time. While I couldn't hear what he was saying, I understood that he was trying to get me up.

There was a second man pulling Rayne to her feet and pushing her closer to the wall. She was resisting and flailing wildly. Three more men had moved past us and were actively engaging the rushing stalkers. It dawned on me that this was our rescue party. Instead of continuing to resist, I got to my feet and helped the second man with Rayne. She was still fighting the hands that were grabbing at her. I ended up kneeling in front of her and pulling her face close to mine with both hands.

"Rayne! It's me, Shane!" I could see the terror in her eyes in the flashlight beam that had settled on us. "C'mon, babe! We gotta go! Our ride is here!"

"Shane?" recognition was edging its way into her eyes. Again, I couldn't really hear what she was saying, but I understood the movements of her lips and the understanding flooding across her face.

"Yeah! C'mon, we gotta go!" I yelled. It stood to reason that if I was having a hard time hearing, so was she. She allowed me to grab her arm and pull her to her feet. When I turned, I came face-to-face with the man who'd been trying to get me to move. He was ushering us toward the wall. That's when I saw the ladder that barely extended above the cinder blocks.

When I looked over the wall, I could see the foot of the ladder was actually cupped into the bucket of a massive front-end loader. That bucket was raised as high as it would go. On the ground, surrounding the loader, were three more men giving cover fire to the rescue operation. I helped Rayne over the ledge and made sure she had a good grip on the aluminum ladder. As soon as she started her descent, I joined her.

I was looking down to keep an eye on her progress and then I'd look up toward the top of the ladder and the man who was holding it. The ladder was trying to bounce and shift under our weight, but he was keeping it steady. Once Rayne and I were off the ladder and safely in the bucket, two of our rescuers started down. Instead of going rung by rung, they gripped the rails with their gloved hands, placed their feet on the same rails and slid all the way down.

Another man came over the side of the building and repeated the rapid descent into the bucket. A fourth man started down the ladder and I could see the fifth waiting for his turn. When the fifth man climbed onto the ladder, he didn't immediately descend. Instead, he threw three objects over the wall in rapid succession and then started sliding down the ladder. When he was at about the halfway point, there were three explosions from the roof. As soon as he joined us in the bucket, the loader backed away from the wall rapidly. The bucket was lowering and tilting back to keep from spilling all of us onto the ground.

The bucket came to rest a few yards from a massive, six-wheel drive military vehicle and we were urgently ushered toward the back. Rayne didn't have it in her to make the climb. The pain and exhaustion were finally winning the internal battle she was fighting. She didn't even have it in her to resist me scooping her up and hoisting her into the waiting hands of the two people in the back of the truck.

After she was loaded, a hand reached down to help me up. In the lights of the loader, I could see it was Janice. She looked like she had gone a round or two with the world heavyweight boxing champion. Her left arm was tied up in a makeshift sling, but her right hand was still extend. I took it and scurried into the back of the truck. That's when I realized my hearing was beginning to make a comeback. I also realized that the amount of gunfire had slacked off. Instead of a constant barrage, it was just the occasional popping from inside the Value Mart.I looked at the second figure that helped me get Rayne in the back of the rig and it wasn't Chase. It was a young woman.

"Where's Chase?" I questioned Janice as I sat between her and Rayne. Rayne leaned close to me and rested her head on my shoulder.

"He, Cody, and a half dozen others are out ruining things for the stalkers."

"What?"

"Yeah, Cody made it out of the hospital and linked up with the group we'd spotted before everything went to shit. Me and Chase got backed into a walk-in cooler in a corner store. We were fighting them off until we ran out of ammo, and they rushed us. That's when Cody and the Calvary showed up. Now they're out headhunting!"

"Did you tell him about his family? Why aren't we moving yet?"

"We're mopping these assholes up. That's why we ain't movin yet," a vaguely familiar voice said from the tailgate of the truck. "You Shane?"

"Yeah. Buck?"

"The one and only," he grinned and stuffed a fat cigar between his lips and teeth. He took a few puffs with a lighter held to the end. When the cherry glowed a bright red, he spoke again. "Ya wanna know something?"

"What?" I asked.

"Tween you guys and them biker boys downtown, y'all gave us a golden opportunity this evening," he took another heavy draw on the cigar.

"How's that?"

"Way I hear it told, you're the one who popped that Prophet guy and got the ball rollin'. Is that the truth of it?"

"Yeah. I shot him."

"Don't get me wrong, Mr. Shane. We been holding our own and poppin 'em when we could, but we never could get a shot at the head honcho. When you evacuated what was left of his brains from his skull, you came in clutch and hit the homerun all of us were waiting for!"

"What do you mean?" I asked. Rayne shifted and stretched out on the wooden bench seat. Her head was resting in my lap.

"That the young lady that needed a Doc?" he pointed at Rayne with the glowing end of his cigar.

"Yes," I replied. He leaned around the side of the truck and whistled for someone. A couple seconds later, a young man appeared. He had a red medical bag like the ones we'd solen from the ambulances hanging from his shoulder.

"Hey, Doc. Young lady there needs you to take a look at her," Doc hopped into the back of the truck and knelt next to her head. He had a penlight tucked into his ballcap above his right ear. Buck continued. "You kicked the shit outta that hornet's nest and got most of 'em out in the daylight. Ya kinda had us scrambling to take advantage of that twist of fortune."

"They were plenty worked up and they were lookin for a fight. Guess my intel guy was right when he said we needed to take out Prophet. He said they'd lose their shit, and boy did they! Y'all set 'em back on their heels with that explosion though! Damn near sent 'em back into hiding. Ya hurt 'em some sort of bad with that one!"

"Trust me, Buck. That wasn't the plan and it cost us a couple of our own," I looked down at Rayne and she was looking back at me. Doc was starting an I.V. in her arm. She was pale from pain and exhaustion.

"I heard that. Your girl, Jan there told us about that. Just sayin, it was a hell of a clutch play by your people. Damn admirable! Anyway, we were just gonna come bail you two out, but we've got 'em swayin from all the hits tonight, so we decided to stay and capitalize on our advantage. The biker boys linked up with a couple other small groups and they're out doin the same thing. Thanks to you, we got 'em on the ropes tonight!"

"Buck?" Doc asked from his place next to Rayne.

"Yeah, son. Whatcha need?"

"Can you cut us loose? I'd like to get my patient back to the armory. She needs a little more than I got in my bag."

246

"Is ten minutes gonna make a difference?" Buck asked.

"Just that much longer she's going to be uncomfortable," the young man admitted.

"I hate to be this way, son, but I'm gonna hold ya here for a spell longer. I don't want to send this rig back without an escort. The ranchers said they should be linking up with us in about ten minutes. They can spare the escort to get you guys back in one piece. That cool?"

"Yeah, cool," Doc replied then began taking another set of vitals on Rayne.

"It sounds like there are quite a few survivors," I stated.

"Most of us come from outside of the city proper, but yeah. There's a bunch of us."

"Are you guys' military?"

"Nah, well, there's a few. Doc there was a Navy Corpsman. He was home on leave. We got a few that have been retired for a bit too. Most of us are just folk though. What about you?"

"No. I was just a boring corporate dude before this shit started," I glanced at Janice when I said it. She smiled and shook her head slightly. I got a grin from Buck too.

Shortly after that, Buck excused himself to go take care of other things. Janice took me back to the question I'd asked her about telling Cody about his family. She said that when Chase told him, it was like the man instantly turned to steel right before her eyes. She said it was the absolute worst thing she'd ever seen in her life.

Our conversation ended when the ranchers showed up. There were six big 4x4 trucks that looked like they were older than me. Men jumped from the beds and climbed out of the cabs when they came to a stop. There were cowboy hats mixed with baseball hats and bandannas. All of them were bristling with weapons and ready for a fight. Buck instructed them to help his men in clearing out the Value Mart. Two of the trucks with four men in each escorted us back to the National Guard Armory.

The sun was just beginning to make itself known on the eastern horizon when the three of us were shown to an office that had been turned into a small infirmary. I'd carried Rayne inside and placed her on the gurney. Doc asked Rayne a few more medical questions and left the room. He returned a moment later with two syringes. Both were administered through her I.V., and she was made comfortable. She was out like the proverbial light.

"She gonna be okay?" I asked Doc before he could leave the room again.

"Yeah. She needs rest and fluids. Here in a few hours, I'll re-wrap her ribs but that's about the extent of what I can do. You two need to get some rest and fluids too. How's that sling treating you, Janice?"

"It's good," she replied.

"Okay. If you get any numbness or lose the use of your fingers or wrist, let me know right away. Dislocations can be tricky sometimes. You need anything?" he looked expectantly at me.

"Whisky and a cheeseburger?" I quipped.

"I'll see what I can rustle up," he grinned and left Janice and I alone with the sleeping Rayne.

"Janice?" I said after a few minutes of staring at the ceiling from one of the gurneys.

"Yeah?"

"You asked me a question a while back and I told you that I didn't know how to answer it. Remember that?"

"You got an answer now?"

"Yeah. Yeah I do."

"So, do you?"

"Yes, Janice. I can say with one hundred percent certainty, I love Rayne."

"You're not saying that just because you almost died on that rooftop? Being in that kinda situation can make a person say things they really don't mean."

"No, I'm not. I'm saying it because she's got so much fight in her. I'm saying it because I don't really know what I'd do without her now. She's taught me a lot about myself..... The problem is the other thing I told you. Do you remember what that was?"

"The part about not pushing a relationship on her?" she asked.

"I wasn't going to do that then, and I won't do that now. I told you that ball was in her court. I meant what I said. If she chooses the friend zone for me, then so be it."

"Are you asking me to put in a good word for you?"

"No, I'm not. In fact, I'd urge you to never mention this conversation to her."

"Why tell me then?"

"Trust, Janice. You and I will never see eye-to-eye on anything without it. You know all of her secrets and you've kept them. I'm telling you my secrets and I trust you will treat them with the same care you've given hers.

"Hmmm..... You've kinda put me in a hell of a position, Shane."

"How's that?"

"You just told me you love the same woman I've loved for years. For her, it's always been a sisterly love. For me, it goes so much deeper than that. I guess we've all got secrets now, don't we?"

CHAPTER 52

September 3rd, 2023.

"I know I've said it several times already, but I can't thank you enough for saving our butts, Buck," I told him as we sat at a picnic table just outside the doors leading into the Armory offices. Lunch today was the same as it was yesterday, an MRE (Meal Ready to Eat) package.

"Nothin' to it, bud," he dismissed my ongoing gratitude with a wave of his hand and the stogie he was smoking. "I done told ya already; it was you guys who set the whole thing in motion the other night. Ya gave us the momentum we needed."

"Well, I still feel like I owe you and your guys. If ya hadn't shown up when you did, we'd have been finished. Probably would have lost Chase and Janice too," I shoved a spoonful of the beef goulash into my mouth.

"I mean, if y'all wanna stay here with us, you're more than welcome and we could always use the fighters."

"Ya wanna know something, Buck?" I grinned.

"I know, I know!" he held up his hand. "Ya came up here with your lady for some vacation, not the apocalypse! Ya got the two-fer-one deal, bud!"

"Yeah, and I've had enough of the end of the world and not enough vacation!" I laughed. "Seriously though; we appreciate the invitation, but Rayne and I are ready to go back to the cabin. Look at the bright side though, you get Janice and Chase out of the deal."

"Well, I'm thinkin we break even on the deal then. When did y'all wanna head home?"

"Probably give Rayne one more day to relax. That and I gotta procure some new transportation. All the vehicles we had got wrecked."

"I'm going out on a patrol at four, wanna tag along? There's plenty of rigs to choose from out there."

"Sure, I'll tag along. How's things lookin out there?"

"Pretty damn good, man! We're still coming across pockets of stalkers but they're getting fewer and farther between. Truth is, we'll probably be cleaning them out for a while to come. Since we been going building to building, we're coming across quite a few folks who just locked themselves in their basements and stayed outta sight. They're joining up with our different groups and helpin us out."

"Thinking back to the first time we came into town; I remember thinking we were the only folks left alive. I'll tell ya, that was downright unsettling!"

249

"I think all of us were thinking the same thing! It got mighty lonely 'round here for a spell," he admitted after a long pull from the cigar.

"Have you heard anything from anywhere outside of Winnemucca?"

"Yeah, not much good though. Most of it's been second or third-hand information. HAM operators passing along what they know or heard. Not really sure what's the truth or fiction anymore. It's for sure that the big cities are total no-go zones though. Ain't nothin' there but trouble for anyone who tries to go there."

"I sorta figured that would be the case. Guess it's a good thing we don't have any plans on going anywhere," I grinned and shoveled more of the goulash down my throat.

"Some of the small towns are holding their own and gaining ground. It's just gonna be an ongoing thing though. I guess this is our new normal....."

September 4th, 2023.

During the patrol with Buck and his men the previous day, I was able to recover some of the gear from the wrecked trucks at the Value Mart. I was also escorted to the roof to recover our empty magazines and other gear that had been left behind. The amount of stalker bodies that had been stacked in the parking lot was unfathomable. Buck told me that Rayne and I had accounted for seventy-five percent of them. The plan with the pile of corpses was to have a massive pyre once they were all accounted for. Many still had some sort of identification, so their names were recorded in a registry of the dead.

The search for a truck turned up a beautifully restored, 1977 GMC K20 4x4. It was just a standard cab but that was all Rayne and I needed. I figured that down the road, parts for the 454 engine would be easier to scavenge. We were able to recover one of the fuel transfer tanks and a transfer pump, so they were all loaded in the truck bright and early this morning. With everything loaded and fueled, Rayne and I were ready to leave by noon.

There were tearful goodbyes and hugs between Rayne and Janice. Chase was content with handshakes. Buck insisted that we be escorted a few miles out of town. Rayne and I were happy to accept the offer. We settled in for the drive home and didn't speak much until after we made the turn-off onto Highway 140 at Denio Junction. I think part of that was the lingering effects of her pain medications. By the time we passed the site of the plane crash, she was perking up quite a bit. Every little bump in the road was causing her discomfort, but she took it all in stride.

"The other night, on the rooftop, did you mean what you said?" she asked as she watched the debris of the plane diminish from view in the side mirror. Both windows were down and we were enjoying the early afternoon breeze through the cab.

"The part about you being stronger than you think or the part of you having a killer survival instinct?" I glanced over at her. Both of us had gotten a shower at the armory but she looked especially radiant. Her honey-brown eyes were soft and easy to look at. Her hair was pulled up into a ponytail that exposed the ugly bruises around her neck. The black, blue, and yellowing bruises didn't detract from her natural beauty in the slightest.

"That's not what I'm talking about....." her gaze was unwavering.

"I'm not following."

"Shane..... Do you remember what you called me when I was having a meltdown because I thought we were dead?"

"Babe," the word escaped my lips before my brain could stop it. "Listen..... I..... I was....." I stammered. She reached across the bench seat and put her hand on my thigh.

"Between that and what you told Janice..... Did you mean it?"

"She told you?" I was instantly turning red and flustered.

"No, she didn't. I wasn't asleep yet when you two started talking. I've always known about her feelings. They're pretty obvious to anyone looking. I wasn't sure where your head was at though."

"Listen, Rayne....."

"It's okay. I'll tell you what I told you before. I'm not saying yes, but I'm not saying no either. Let's just see what the tide brings in, shall we?" as she finished her sentence, she scooted over to sit in the middle of the seat.....

THE END.....

Maybe.....

FROM THE AUTHOR:

For those that know me and my books, you've figured out that this new series is a pretty big departure from The Ranch series. Like the Legacy Series, the characters we got to know in this book have also been living rent-free in my mind for years. Their story has been begging to be told, and I finally found the time to do just that. Hopefully, I did it well. As always though, I'll let you be the judge of that.

A lot has changed since I penned the first book in the Legacy Series, but my passion for delivering a good read has not. We're just breaking into the Feral world and there's still a lot of story to be told. Together, we can continue to flesh out the world of Shane, Rayne and so many others you haven't met yet.

As always, there are a lot of people I need to thank! Let me start with my Beta Reader team. Joshua, Kim, Jessica, Gary, Chris, George, and Melanie. You guys are the rock stars! Sometimes I'd dump ten chapters on you in a week, and other times it'd take me five weeks to get five chapters together. You hung in there and I really appreciate that! I also gotta give a huge shoutout to the one Beta Reader who gets the final draft all at once. Peggy, I don't know how you do what you do, but THANK YOU!

My guy over at Creative Texts, Dan. I'm not sure when you sleep seeing as how you always return my emails so quickly. Even the ones I send late at night! You've taken this whole writing thing to a level I never dreamed possible and you're always surprising me. You take care of all the things I never wanted to deal with, and you do it so well! Thank you, my friend!

Last, but certainly not least, my wife. You're always there when I need help with motivation. You're understanding when I just zone out of a conversation because I'm working a plot point out in my head. You're there when I need to bounce an idea around and you give excellent, insightful feedback. Thank you, Denise! I love ya Smallz!

The last thing I need to get out there is for you, the readers. This isn't just for me, but it's for all the authors whose books you read or listen to. Please take a few moments to leave some stars or write a review. You're feedback only helps us grow as authors and helps us to hone our craft!

To my readers: I appreciate each and every one of you! THANK YOU! Don't be shy! If you want to hit me up on social media, please do so! Contrary to popular belief, I don't bite!

Sean Liscom

ABOUT THE PUBLISHER

Creative Texts is a boutique independent publishing house devoted to high quality content that readers enjoy. We publish best-selling authors such as Jerry D. Young, N.C. Reed, Sean Liscom, Jared McVay, Laurence Dahners, and many more. Our audiobook performers are among the best in the business including Hollywood legends like Barry Corbin and top talent like Christopher Lane, Alyssa Bresnaham, Erin Moon and Graham Hallstead.

Whether its post-apocalyptic or dystopian fiction, biography, history, true crime science fiction, thrillers, or even classic westerns, our goal is to produce highly rated customer preferred content. If there is anything we can do to enhance your reader experience, please contact us directly at info@creativetexts.com. As always, we do appreciate your reviews on your book seller's website.

Finally, if you would like to find more great books like this one, please search for us by name in your favorite search engine or on your bookseller's website to see books by all Creative Texts authors. Thank you for reading!

Made in United States
Troutdale, OR
06/11/2023

10554259R10149